PRAISE FOR *GIRLS' NIGHT OUT*

"*Girls' Night Out* is a heart-stopper of a thriller, rippling with suspense from its opening pages. But it's also much more: Liz Fenton and Lisa Steinke plumb the intricacies of female friendship with skill and depth and heart. It's a deeply satisfying read, and one you won't want to miss."

—Megan Abbott, national bestselling author of *You Will Know Me*

"It's trouble in paradise for three best friends struggling to make amends in the latest thriller from the dynamic writing duo of Liz Fenton and Lisa Steinke. *Girls' Night Out* is a chilling page-turner full of secrets and hostility that will leave readers shocked again and again . . . and again. I loved it."

—Mary Kubica, *New York Times* bestselling author of *The Good Girl* and *Every Last Lie*

"A wild ride into a high-powered girls' trip to Mexico. Suspense at its best. Liz and Lisa have taken their writing partnership to a new level!"

—Kaira Rouda, *USA Today* bestselling author of *Best Day Ever*

"This suspenseful novel is full of twists and turns and makes clever use of chronology. It will make you think twice about going on a girls' night out!"

—Jane Corry, bestselling author of *My Husband's Wife* and *Blood Sisters*

"In *Girls' Night Out*, Liz Fenton and Lisa Steinke guide readers on a suspenseful international tour of friendship at its best and worst. As enviable fun takes a turn through suspicion toward pure fear, you'll find out just how wrong a trip to paradise can go."

—Jessica Strawser, author of *Almost Missed You* and *Not That I Could Tell*

PRAISE FOR *THE GOOD WIDOW*

A *PUBLISHERS WEEKLY* BEST SUMMER BOOKS 2017 SELECTION, MYSTERY/THRILLER

"Fenton and Steinke deliver a complicated tale of love, loss, intrigue, and disaster . . . This drama keeps the pages turning with shocking twists until the bitter end. A great read; recommended for admirers of Jennifer Weiner and Rainbow Rowell."

—*Library Journal*

"Fans of Joy Fielding will appreciate the story's fast pacing and sympathetic main character . . . [a] solid psychological thriller . . ."

—*Publishers Weekly*

"Fenton and Steinke's talent for domestic drama comes through . . . For readers who enjoy suspense writers like Nicci French."

—*Booklist*

"A fantastic thriller that will keep you on your toes."

—PopSugar

"Accomplished authors Liz Fenton and Lisa Steinke make their suspense debut with great skill and assurance in this enthralling novel of marital secrets and lies, grief and revelation. *The Good Widow* led me along a winding, treacherous road and made a sharp, startling turn that I didn't see coming. Unputdownable!"

—A. J. Banner, #1 Amazon bestselling author of *The Good Neighbor* and *The Twilight Wife*

"Liz Fenton's and Lisa Steinke's *The Good Widow* begins by asking what you would do if your spouse died in a place he wasn't supposed to be in with a woman he wasn't supposed to be with. What follows is a gut-wrenching thriller, sometimes heartbreaking, sometimes darkly funny, but always a page-turner. And as you read it late into the night you'll look over at the person in bed next to you and wonder how well you really know him. A wild, skillfully written ride!"

—David Bell, author of *Since She Went Away*

"An irresistible and twisty page-turner, *The Good Widow* should come with a delicious warning: this is not the story you think it is."

—Deb Caletti, author of *He's Gone*

"*The Good Widow* is both heartrending and suspenseful, deftly navigating Jacks's mourning and the loss of her less-than-perfect marriage. The writing is sharp and evocative, the Hawaiian setting is spectacular, and the ending was a wonderful, twisty surprise. A quintessential summer beach read!"

—Kate Moretti, *New York Times* bestselling author of *The Vanishing Year*

"*The Good Widow* is a fresh take on your worst nightmare—your husband dies, and he isn't where, or with whom, he said he was. I ripped through these pages to see where Fenton and Steinke would take me, which ended up being somewhere unexpected in the best kind of way. You will not be sorry you read this!"

—Catherine McKenzie, bestselling author of *Fractured* and *Hidden*

THE
TWO
LILA
BENNETTS

ALSO BY
LIZ FENTON & LISA STEINKE:

Girls' Night Out

The Good Widow

The Year We Turned Forty

The Status of All Things

Your Perfect Life

THE
TWO
LILA
BENNETTS

LIZ FENTON & LISA STEINKE

LAKE UNION
PUBLISHING

Text copyright © 2019 by Liz Fenton and Lisa Steinke

Published by Lake Union Publishing, Seattle

www.apub.com

Amazon, the Amazon logo, and Lake Union Publishing are trademarks of Amazon.com, Inc., or its affiliates.

ISBN-13: 9781542093712
ISBN-10: 1542093716

Cover design by Faceout Studio, Lindy Martin

Printed in the United States of America

To Riley, who sparked the idea for this book

Thy fate is the common fate of all; Into each life
some rain must fall.
—Henry Wadsworth Longfellow

PROLOGUE

Wake up! Wake the hell up!

The sound of my own voice shakes me out of my deep slumber, and my stomach lurches. I've lost track of time.

I'd been doing so well, counting the minutes. Second by second. Focusing on the rhythm of the numbers rather than the tightness of the bonds around my wrists and ankles, the way darkness bleeds into blackness behind my blindfold, my hair haphazardly trapped underneath, my bangs tickling my forehead like a feather every thirteen seconds or so.

I attempt to assess how long I was asleep. The pain in my ass, which has been pressed against the rock-hard floor, has magnified, but only slightly. The crick in my neck feels about the same as it did before I lost myself to my exhaustion. I release a quick breath. I was probably out for only a few minutes—at least that's what I hope. I need to keep track of how long I've been in here—it's the only thing keeping me sane, reminding me I'm still alive. I resume my count, this time out loud, my voice quietly echoing off the walls that I may never see.

But in between the numbers, the counting, in that space where seconds turn to minutes, my life haunts me. Because you don't end up blindfolded and restrained if you've made the best choices. My mind begins to drift, not back to sleep, but to every fork in the road that brought me here.

CHAPTER ONE

MONDAY

"On the count of murder in the first degree, we find the defendant, Jeremiah Taylor, not guilty," a slender woman says softly. I know her only as juror number eight—but she looks like a Gwendolyn to me, and based on her age, I imagine her to be someone's grandmother, baking heart-shaped sugar cookies when she's not reading a verdict in a murder trial. Her silver hair is pulled into a bun, her reading glasses hanging from a chain around her neck. She fidgets with them as she waits for the judge to respond, and I wonder if she doesn't agree, if she voted to convict initially and was eventually swayed by another juror—number ten, most likely, his strong chin and confident stature probably giving him power in the jury room. I caught him watching me while the first officer on the scene testified. Juror ten stared right into my eyes. I held his gaze for a long moment before turning back and pulling out the jury sheet, making a small mark near his number. At that point, I calculated ten voting not guilty.

I can picture the bottle of red I'll open tonight—ironically called the Prisoner. It's waiting for me in the wine fridge. The plump red blend from Napa is a postcourt case-win ritual. The first glass will give me a subtle buzz. The second will settle me. And if I allow myself glass number three—actually, scratch that, *when* I allow myself glass number three, because who am I kidding, it's two fifteen, and I'm already thinking about it—I'll get all warm and fuzzy inside and probably break into some Scotchmallows from See's Candies. Around glass four I'll be sure to text someone something regrettable that will likely involve some dumb emoji no one uses anymore, like the dancing woman in the red dress, which is highly underrated, if you ask me. She's in a red dress! She's dancing! So many different ways that one can be interpreted. But most important, as I reach the bottom of the bottle, I'll forget how it feels to be Lila Bennett at this moment.

Despite my better judgment, I look for Stephanie in the courtroom. She's wiping tears from her dark-green eyes and hugging her mother. She looks up, maybe sensing me, and locks her stare onto mine. We remain there for what feels like a minute. Me, expressionless. Her, scowling. It's because she hates me. And I don't blame her. I would probably hate me too. In her mind I helped her dead sister's husband get away with murder.

And it's possible I did. But it's not my job to know the truth; it's my duty to give my clients the defense they are legally entitled to. In my mind I see my husband rolling his dark-brown eyes, his thick brows raised in mockery. Because Ethan knows that's not necessarily how I really feel. That's my dinner party shtick. But behind closed doors, in my weaker, Prisoner-inspired moments, I have confessed that oftentimes my gut knows the difference. But Ethan says there's no way I could know if they are lying. That I have to believe them if I represent them. Oh, how I love that he doesn't judge me. That he can look away from my flaws when I need him to, much in the same way I do for my clients.

Stephanie grabs her mother's hand, and they storm out of the courtroom. At the same moment, Jeremiah grabs me and hugs me hard, picking me up off the floor in the process. He whispers "Thank you" in my ear before he is escorted out of the courtroom.

Call me Jerry, Jer, shit, call me anything as long as you get me off, he said when we first met: him out on bail, having fired his first attorney because he was an idiot—his words, not mine—cruising into my office in downtown Los Angeles as if he were picking me up for lunch instead of attempting to hire me to defend him for murder. He doesn't look like someone who could kill, but my clientele often doesn't. They are distinguished, rich, powerful, their slick suits and expensive ties or couture dresses and Louboutins distractions from the anger dancing in their pupils—if you look close enough to see it. Jeremiah's lips part slightly as he pushes his blond hair away from his eyes before shaking my hand vigorously. I wonder if he is like many of the others—a sociopath who charmed his way through life all while hiding his cruel, unstable, and often dangerous side from the outside world.

I make my way out of the courtroom and into the hallway, my assistant, Chase, squeezing my arm, his silent way of saying, *You did it again*. I can't help but think of Jeremiah's wife. I should call her by her name—*Vivian*—although it's often easier when I don't. When I imagine the victims simply as the deceased. Because, dammit, the bad guys never get murdered. It's always good people—like Vivian—who were in the wrong place at the wrong time. Or in her case, the right place at the wrong time. She'd come home early from her yoga class and stumbled upon an intruder. The prosecution argued that Jeremiah killed her in cold blood, then staged the scene to look like it had been a burglary in progress. In the end, because of a lack of evidence—no murder weapon and no eyewitnesses—they couldn't convict. I won. But as I push the doors open to exit the building and squint into the glaring afternoon sun, that little voice inside me whispers, *Did you really win, Lila?*

I slide my sunglasses on, blow my bangs out of my eyes, and vow to get a haircut this week, my hair an inch too long, covering my shoulder blades and probably making me appear more like a collegiate than a professional. And I already look younger than my thirty-eight years, am still carded regularly. Often given a once-over when a client first sees me in person. Their expression is always the same—*Aren't you a little young to be representing me?* But my track record speaks for itself. I've won far more cases than I've lost. I have a reputation for being a ballbuster in the courtroom. My clients almost always walk away as free men or women, their burdens lifted off their shoulders, transferred slightly onto mine.

"You!"

I swivel my head in the direction of Stephanie's voice. I take a deep breath and brace myself. She's storming toward me, her ankles wobbling slightly in her heels. But still, she doesn't slow. In fact, she increases her momentum as if she plans to run me down.

Chase tries to pull me away, but I stop him. "No, it's okay. I'm going to let her say whatever she has to say." He gives me a concerned look, but I shake my head. "I've got this."

But whether I really do or not remains to be seen. My heart is pounding. I hate confrontation. And I know how that sounds—a defense attorney who doesn't like conflict? I can hear all the bad jokes now. In the courtroom I feel protected, like the law is my shield. But now, as Stephanie points her finger at me, her nostrils flaring, I feel much smaller than my five-foot-seven frame.

"How are you going to live with yourself? You *know* he did it. You *know* he killed her." Stephanie's voice is shaking slightly. Her eyes are swollen, and she's biting her lower lip as if to keep from crying. I almost reach out to touch her arm, to console her, but I know that would be ludicrous. "What? Nothing to say? You had plenty to spew in there." She points to the courthouse. "Character witnesses testifying to what a *good* guy Jeremiah is—how he donates to charities, volunteers his time." She laughs, a high-pitched, clipped sound. "It's all an act. Don't you get it? He's a monster, a murderer!" she screams. "And my sister is never coming back."

I do get it, I want to say. *I do understand that he probably hides who he really is. But if he murdered your sister, he didn't make any mistakes in the process.* He crossed every *t*, he dotted every *i*. She was killed in her own home, so his fingerprints were everywhere—because he lived there. Not because he killed her. The fact that he was arrested and charged still shocks me, as the DA didn't have anything more than circumstantial evidence at best. But Jeremiah didn't have an alibi that could be corroborated—he said he'd left a meeting at 6:45 p.m. that multiple people from his staff confirmed had happened. But he couldn't prove what time he'd arrived home. He said it was after eight o'clock. That he'd stopped to watch the sunset, as he'd been known to do before continuing to his house. This means he wasn't at home at the time of the murder. But no one saw him watching the sun disappear into the Pacific Ocean, and no one had seen him pull into his driveway at the time he claimed. There was also the domestic dispute three months before her death when Vivian had called the police. The DA had ballooned it into a much bigger story than it was. But it still wasn't enough to get him convicted. Even juror number eight probably knew it.

"I'm sorry for your loss," I finally say and immediately regret it. Ethan will have a field day with this when I tell him—*You said what to her?*

"You're sorry for my loss? That's the best you can do?" Stephanie scoffs as if reading my mind, and the tears she's been trying to hold back finally escape.

"Yes, I am," I repeat. Because it's true. Vivian was young—only thirty-three. No kids, but according to her sister she had wanted them. I pause and consider my next words. "He was entitled to a defense."

"*You* didn't have to take the case. *You* didn't have to be the one to defend him."

She was right. I could have said no. But as I'd listened to him paint a picture of Vivian, a loving wife, but one who struggled with depression, he had no idea I understood that scenario better than anyone could have known. He claimed she'd taken Lexapro and Zoloft and had an affinity for Vicodin. A marriage that wasn't perfect but that was solid. He said he had spent his life trying to make her happy. He told me he wouldn't have hurt a hair on her head. And he'd explained away the domestic dispute. Said she had been loaded. And later, when I'd looked at the police report, it was true that she'd been acting drugged. Jeremiah had been completely sober. He cried as he talked about finding her bludgeoned to death. And there were things missing—valuable things. It could have been a break-in. I decided to take the case because maybe this was an innocent man. Maybe he didn't do it. There was enough doubt for me to say yes. And if I'm being completely honest, the money swayed me too. I knew a case like this would be several months of work. Jeremiah runs a hedge fund and would pay for any legal necessities to make sure he wasn't convicted.

"I'm sorry, but I have to go." I turn to look for my Uber that will take me back to the office—only a couple of miles away—when I feel her hand on my arm. I pull away from her grip and turn to face her. I decide to swallow the comment I want to make, *Get your hands off me*, and let her take one more dig. Then I really am leaving.

"Karma's a bitch, and I have no doubt you'll get yours."

Stephanie's eyes are steely, and I feel a chill. I try to shake it off, pull my shoulder blades down my back, and walk away with as much dignity as I can muster. It's not the first time I've been threatened, and I'm sure it won't be the last. As we make our way toward the waiting Uber, Chase is reeling off the messages I've received while in court as if I weren't just basically told I was going to hell. A high-profile lawyer has been arrested for manslaughter, and he wants to meet with me. On to the next case, it seems. But as we're rounding the corner, I feel the urge to look back. Stephanie hasn't moved. She's still glaring at me with her arms folded across her chest.

The cold spike shoots through me again, and this time I have a harder time shaking it away.

My phone rings, breaking the moment. I exhale when I see Ethan's name on the screen. "I'm going to take this," I say to Chase, who nods and taps his phone, indicating he'll call the Uber for us.

"Congrats," Ethan says when I answer.

I'm trying to decide how to respond when he adds, "I know this was a tough one for you."

"It was," I agree as we pass a homeless man with a red scarf, rooting around in a trash bin. I pause and take in the shopping cart that most likely holds his every possession, and it shifts my perspective, albeit momentarily. There are people with much bigger problems than me.

A black Lexus pulls up to the curb, and Chase motions for us to get in.

"You okay?" Ethan asks, his voice warm and soothing, and I find myself leaning into the phone, wanting to be closer.

"Yes," I say reflexively. I always do that. Say I'm fine when I'm not. Ethan once joked that if I'd had a limb chopped off and you asked me how I was, I'd answer that I was okay. Would he know this was one of those times? When I wasn't fine at all?

"That's good," he says, and I exhale. "You got a second? I need to talk to you about something."

I straighten my back against the seat, unable to recall the last time Ethan called me in the middle of the day to tell me something. I rub the base of my neck with my free hand.

"What is it?" I ask as the Uber pulls up to a stoplight. I can see the tip of my office building peeking out several blocks up, the sun reflecting off the windows.

"I did something. Something big!"

"What?" I ask, and sit up straighter in my seat. Chase glances at me, and I mouth, *Ethan*.

"You know those community work spaces where you can rent a cubicle? Remember, I showed you one on my friend's Instagram page?"

I nod even though he can't see me.

"I rented one. I'm getting out of this house, out of my joggers." He laughs nervously. "And I'm finally going to write that second goddamn book that I know I have in me."

My body tingles at the news. I hear my husband's voice for the first time in a long while. The man I married. The novelist. With motivation. Confidence. And I realize how much I've missed him. The man I fell in love with. Stephanie's accusations blare in my mind again, and I push them away. Ethan calling me to tell me this right after I won a case I don't feel good about, right after the victim's sister screamed at me and said so many of the things I was already thinking, feels like a sign. I need to redirect. I need to give my marriage the attention it so desperately needs and my husband the love he deserves.

"Lila?"

"Sorry," I say, realizing I drifted off. "I'm so happy for you, Ethan. This is the best news."

"I feel really good about it," he says, and I can hear the smile in his voice. "And I'm sorry I've been so down for so long. I know I've also pulled you down with me."

"It's okay," I tell him. Because I've made worse mistakes. The only difference? He doesn't know about mine.

"There she is—the woman of the hour!" my boss, Sam, a managing partner at the firm, says when I walk into the conference room a few minutes later. He hands me a glass of champagne and toasts me, looking around at a small group of my coworkers who have gathered. "To another victory!"

I take a long sip as my colleagues mutter their congratulations, and I grab a slice of the red velvet cake that had been cut and set on small plates next to the plastic champagne glasses. After everyone has filed out of the room, I sit down and close my eyes.

"There you are—Sam said I'd find you in here." Sam's wife and my best friend, Carrie, bustles into the room.

"Hey," I say, smiling, taking in her white-blonde hair, which is swept into a loose ponytail, her makeup-free face that always shines as if it's been freshly washed. "What are you doing here?"

She heaves a two-inch-thick manila folder out of her tote bag. "Sam left this at home and called me, freaking out. I guess he needs it for a meeting later today."

"Has he heard of this thing called the cloud?" I laugh. Sam pushed back on storing files digitally; he said the weight of the paper in his hands helped him think.

"Tell me about it." Carrie rolls her sky-blue eyes as she sits in the chair next to me. I envy her choice of a mint-green apron dress. She's always wearing bright clothing—skirts or rompers—a near-perfect reflection of her personality and warm disposition. Meanwhile, if I take a risk and wear something other than black—a perfect reflection of my own disposition— like olive green, Chase taps the back of his hand to my forehead to check my temperature. And my dark hair and blunt bangs accentuate this even more. Carrie catches me looking her over and smooths the green cotton. "You like? I went on a bit of an Anthropologie binge." She blushes slightly. "Sam says I need to watch my spending." She shakes her head.

"It looks great on you." Sam had mentioned the same thing to me on more than one occasion, but I always defended Carrie. I wish I had the desire to buy myself things just because. I strained to remember the last clothing purchase I'd made—a pair of charcoal-gray pants.

"Sam told me the sister of your client's wife really handed your ass to you after the verdict today, so I wanted to check on you. You okay?" She eyes me curiously. "I know you. You keep it all bottled up in here." She points a finger toward my chest.

"I'm fine," I say unconvincingly and catch her knowing look. The truth is, I feel rattled, like a piece of me has come loose, but I can't bring myself to say it. Maybe it's because Stephanie's accusations still ring in my ears. Or because I don't want to admit that cases like that make me question if I'm still cut out for this career. "Just part of the job." I purse my lips. "Right?" I add, because she understands from a peripheral point of view that Sam's work comes home with him whether he believes it does or not.

"I suppose, but it doesn't mean you can't talk about it," she says and waits, but I don't bite. She tries again. "She was surprised by the verdict, I'm assuming?"

I nod, remembering the fire in her dark-green eyes, the way her fists balled at her sides. "But the state had no evidence. They were rolling the dice taking this to trial."

"Especially against you," Carrie says with a small smile.

I tilt my head in thought. "But still, I understand her shock. Her sister was her best friend, and now she's gone. It's natural she's looking for someone to blame." I think about the broken look in Stephanie's eyes earlier. That part never got easier—getting a not-guilty verdict for my clients left the victim's family at square one, with no answers.

"True. I can't imagine. Being her." She looks down at her french manicure. "Are you *sure* you're okay? You seemed unsettled."

"What are you talking about?" I protest weakly.

"You're usually fist-pumping after winning a case. But despite your mediocre attempt at masking it, I can see you're upset. If I didn't know better, I'd think you wished you lost."

I move my chair closer to Carrie, closing the small gap between us more. "I don't feel good about this one," I confess quietly and instantly feel relief, wondering what would happen if I talked about all the cases that left me feeling this way. How much lighter would my steps be?

"Why not?" Carrie asks.

"I can't put my finger on it. Even though it was a slam dunk, it doesn't feel like a victory."

"Is there anything you can do about it?"

"Wine." I laugh. "I can drink lots of wine."

"I'm being serious."

"I'm not joking!"

Carrie folds her arms over her chest. "I swear you are going to implode if you don't start opening up to *someone*."

"I need to move on with my life. To the next case. What's done is done." I push away the thought that the next case will leave me feeling as empty as this one.

"You sound like Sam," she admonishes. "But I know that's your campaign trail speech. You care more than you want to admit."

"Maybe I do." I glance around the room, still empty save for two clerks who've come in to snag a piece of cake. "Don't tell anyone. That can get you in big trouble around here."

She purses her glossy lips. "Your secret is safe with me."

"And hey, thank you," I add.

"For what?"

"Everyone else is patting me on the back, assuming I'm thrilled," I say, thinking she's had this skill since the night I met her at our company holiday party four years ago. Seconds before, I'd been chewed out by a senior partner over a loss I'd had in court. He'd had one too many bourbons, the alcohol thick on his breath as he cornered me and told me how much money I'd cost the firm after the family pulled their company from our client roster. I'd looked around for Ethan but had lost track of him in the crowded room. Once the partner finally finished humiliating me and stormed off, Carrie came rushing over, asking me if I was okay, telling me she'd witnessed the last few moments. As I always do, I said I was fine. But I choked slightly on the words as I said them— my embarrassment and indignation sitting in a tight knot at the base of my throat. She ignored my platitude and grabbed my elbow, leading me to a deserted corner of the rooftop balcony that was partially hidden by the bar, where she pulled a cigarette and lighter from her purse. "I keep this for emergencies only," she said. "I'm Carrie, Sam's wife, by the way."

"I'm Lila."

"I know. Sam pointed you out earlier. Said you're a rising star at the firm." She cupped her hand and awkwardly lit the cigarette, then held it out to me.

"Oh, I don't smoke," I said, shaking my head.

Carrie stared at me and took a deep drag, tilting her head to blow the smoke away from me a second later. "Neither do I," she said with a smile.

She held it out to me again, and this time I grabbed it from her dainty fingers and took a small puff, grateful for the first time in my life that someone had been able to see right through me.

"You're pretty transparent to me—and it isn't always pretty!" Carrie jokes now. She squeezes my arm gently. She knows this is hard. That I'm not fine. She looks like she wants to say something else when a few partners walk into the room. We exchange greetings as they pour themselves some champagne.

"You're glowing, by the way. Did you work out?" I ask after they leave, wanting to change the subject.

Carrie pauses before answering. "Yes. Probably the Blast Zone class I went to this morning. We were running at an eight percent incline on the treadmill. My heart rate was through the roof!" She laughs at herself. "I've got to get you in there—there's one over on Figueroa. Did you know that?"

I shake my head. Maybe I should try it? I'd refused when she attempted to push me into Pilates, even when she sent me videos of her hot spin instructor with the caption, *Come ride this!* And now that this trial is over, I will have a break between cases. Maybe I'll try this Blast Zone thing. Or walk up my stairs more. Or drink less wine.

"It was a high-impact day today. I swear. I almost didn't make it through the floor work at the end." She pauses again, as if she's going to change the subject, but then blurts, "I got thirty boom points!"

I frown at her. Something seems a little off with Carrie.

She waves her hand. "After you go, you'll get the lingo. Anyway, the short answer is yes, I worked out. But enough about me. Your day was much more important."

"Is everything okay?" I ask, leaning forward.

"Well . . ." Carrie's eyes widen, and she half smiles like she's ready to spill a secret. "I wasn't going to say anything yet because it's still early, but I've been dying to tell you . . ."

"About what?" I ask. But instinctively, I already know the answer.

"I think I might be"—she looks down at her flat stomach—"you know."

"Pregnant?" I whisper.

She nods, and her cheeks seem to glow brighter. "I mean if three tests don't prove it, I don't know what does!"

I feel like the wind has been knocked out of me, my stomach twisting so tightly I have to exhale hard.

"Are you okay?" Carrie leans in.

"Yes. Sorry. It's such a shock!" I say, because it is. And that part of me, that voice that scolds me when I'm making bad choices, chimes in, telling me this is a sign. First Ethan calls, reminding me of the man I fell in love with, and now Carrie tells me she's having a baby.

"I know. It is for me too!" Carrie smiles.

Ethan and I don't have kids and have agreed we probably won't. *Never say never*, Ethan always says. I can't recall exactly when he started saying that, but when he does, I can feel that tightening in my chest. Because though I nod, deep down my vote is never. Not because I don't like kids—I do. I mean, I'm not the first to goo-goo and gaga over a baby, but my niece, Ethan's sister's daughter, seems to like me just fine. She was the one who broke the news that the emoji of the woman dancing in the red dress had become obsolete without my permission. But as much as I enjoy hanging out with her for the afternoon or holding the occasional toddler, I've never pictured myself with children. I'm not exactly sure when I started feeling that way.

My mom thinks it ties back to my dad's death when I was twelve. And maybe she's right. His accident rammed me hard in the gut, and I felt like I couldn't catch my breath for years. Sometimes I still can't. I often think of him taking me for walks outside, me perched high up on his shoulders, him telling me to duck when we were coming toward hanging branches on the trees; watching Chargers games with him, his face bright as he explained the nuances of the game; him sitting on my bed and fluffing my pillows each night, right up until the night before he died. It's true that when he passed away, a piece of me went with him. But is that why I don't want kids? I would need a lot of therapy to get to that conclusion.

"Congratulations," I force myself to say and hug her.

"Wow, a hug from Lila." Carrie laughs into my shoulder. "This is big news!"

"I know; I looked out the window and saw a pig flying." I laugh as I pull back from her and try to ignore the ache in my heart.

The door to the conference room opens, and Chase walks through. I'm grateful for his interruption.

"I came to get a piece of that." He points at the sheet cake on the table. "You know how I feel about thick white frosting full of high-fructose corn syrup." He licks his lips and theatrically cuts himself a piece. Carrie and I laugh. "And this arrived. It looks fancy!" He hands me an envelope as he leaves the room.

I stare at the calligraphy of the return name and address and tear it open. A friend from law school is getting married.

"What is it?" Carrie asks.

"A wedding invitation," I say flatly.

"I love weddings." Carrie claps her hands. She glances at the invite. "And it's at Shutters on the Beach! If Ethan doesn't want to go, I'll be your plus-one!"

"Don't get too excited. I'm not going."

"Why not?" Carrie frowns.

"It's Tiffany, an old friend from law school. I'd like to go, but I can't."

"Because of Janelle?"

I nod, my throat tight. After all these years, hearing her name still pinches a nerve.

"Maybe it's time to face her." Carrie tucks a strand of hair behind her ear. "The only way to achieve redemption is to face the things you've done," she says softly as her husband, Sam, walks by. He slows slightly, taking us in through the glass wall of the conference room, but keeps going before Carrie notices.

CHAPTER TWO

MONDAY

"I see that." Chase points to the bottle of champagne I'd smuggled from the celebration peeking out from under my fitted black blazer.

"You see nothing!" I say playfully as I breeze past his sleek glass desk and through the doorway of my expansive office, the floor-to-ceiling windows rewarding my return with a birds-eye view of the Staples Center and LA Live. I used to sit on my desk at dusk and watch the Lakers fans gather for that night's game, bemused by their undying loyalty for what used to be the best team in the country but had become average at best, the glory days of Kobe, Shaq, and Phil Jackson feeling like a lifetime ago.

I'd said as much to Sam once, when we'd stayed at the office late to prep for a deposition.

He'd cocked his head. "It's the hope that keeps them coming back. Everyone needs to believe in something, Bennett." He liked to call me by my last name, as if we were starring in some bad court procedural drama on CBS. It bothered me that I'd come to almost like it.

"Wouldn't they be better off believing in the Golden State Warriors right now?" I'd cracked. This was before the Lakers signed LeBron. Before the entire city erupted in the great hope that the glory days were returning, something Sam still rubs in my face.

"Where is your loyalty?" he'd kidded.

Even back then I understood this was a loaded question. Still, I'd look up and catch him watching me in partner meetings. He'd smile. I'd smile. He'd go out of his way to make sure I was put on cases that would make me look good. He could be harsh, yes, but also encouraging. He took a personal interest in my career. For my part, I initially chose to ignore what it might imply, instead telling myself that he was looking out for me because he saw my true potential and wanted to help me rise quickly. And the truth is, that's surely been part of it. But in the midst of that goodwill, I could still feel the spark against the flint of our alliance, one that would eventually ignite. But that day I wasn't ready to give an inch, so I'd let his question about loyalty sit in the air between us as the sea of people in Black Mamba jerseys filed into the arena.

Now, as I stare at the red neon Staples Center sign, that night with Sam feels like forever ago. Back when I'd still had a chance to make different choices. I take a long swig directly from the champagne bottle (they'd sprung for Veuve, a very good sign for me) and hear a faint knock on the door. Before I have a chance to answer, Chase pokes his head in. "Your six o'clock is here. Do you want me to put that away for you?"

My eyes dart to the half-empty bottle of champagne in my hand. "He's early."

"Not that early—it's five fifty-two," he says, walking in, grabbing the neck of the bottle and opening the minifridge, settling it in between the Smartwater and Izzes. He pulls a file from under his arm and sets it on my desk. "Do you need to review this?"

I shake my head. I already know from Sam that Steve Greenwood wants to destroy his wife of ten years, and the stay-at-home mother of his two children, by making sure she doesn't get a penny of his trust fund money supposedly protected by his ironclad prenup. Not that that's how Sam said it. He knew better than to use the word *destroy*.

But he did imply it was contentious. And that Greenwood had millions. Oh, and that apparently he'd insisted on me.

"But I specialize in *criminal* law," I'd said.

"Apparently after frequently seeing your name in the news representing high-profile cases, he believes you're the best. What kind of law you routinely practice is lost on him. He wants a star. And Greenwood gets what he wants."

"We'll see about that," I deadpanned, then requested to have David Croft present in the meeting. Croft is the smarmy, albeit brilliant shark who heads up our family law department.

"Bennett," Sam said, giving me a look. "Divorce and murder really aren't that different. Just pretend he killed her, and everyone wins."

I'd flipped him off and walked away.

"Greenwood can wait his eight minutes," I say to Chase and nod toward the fridge, flipping open the file and skimming the first page. He calls her a bored housewife. They have a nanny, but she doesn't work. She's a bad mom. He wants full custody. Claims she's a boozehound. I slam the file shut. "Please call David and let him know we're ready, and then offer Mr. Greenwood an Izze. I bet he's a sparkling grapefruit kind of guy," I say, already suspecting he's not. He'll probably scoff, wondering where his two fingers of Johnny Walker Blue are. The same scotch his allegedly alcoholic wife is probably expected to bring him when he gets home at night. The idea of Chase handing him sparkling water gives me tremendous pleasure. It's the little things.

Chase grabs a pink can from the fridge and heads toward the door. "Oh, and your mom called. Twice. She said you need to answer your cell phone."

She must have seen the verdict on the five o'clock news. "Will you let her know I'm swamped and that I'll call her later?" I say, knowing I won't. She's going to want to discuss the murder trial in detail, and I can think of nothing I'd rather do less right now than defend why I defended Jeremiah. My mom's been peppering our conversations with little jabs since I took the case. *Ignore her*, Ethan says when I recount her digs. *She doesn't get it.* And it's true—she doesn't. It's easy to judge me from her two-bedroom condo in Redondo Beach. Easy to make assumptions as she sips her skinny vanilla latte with her other retired teacher friends. *What do I tell people? That my daughter is helping a murderer go free?*

Yes, Mom. Tell them that.

I open the fridge and take one last swig of the Veuve, popping three breath mints into my mouth after. I pick up the phone and tell Chase I'm ready to help this douche formulate a game plan to make sure the woman who put up with him for ten years will be robbed of everything to which she is entitled.

Chase replies evenly that he'll send him in. I know I'll get a lecture later—about how I can't do that to him when he's sitting across from the client. Then he'll ask me why I take the cases if I can't stand the people I'm choosing to represent. And I'll tell him I'm a partner now, and I need a certain number of billable hours. Then he'll roll his eyes and start filing or scheduling something the way he does when he knows he's in an argument he can't win. Because, of course, I've got all my reasons ready when anyone says that, including my mom.

An hour and four Izzes later—all drunk by me and David—we usher Steve Greenwood to the lobby, the champagne from earlier still swirling in my gut. In addition to being the questionable human being I predicted he would be, he's also ruined my buzz. Tragic. David tells him we'll be in touch with his wife's attorney, a guy named Mark with a small firm from Culver City whom I know from past experience won't stand a chance against us. I wince slightly, wishing she hadn't made it so easy for him. I decide that maybe she's so disgusted by Greenwood that her main priority is to escape, and that narrative makes me feel a little better.

Maybe that's what I'll tell my mom when she asks. Although she's proud of how I got here—working my ass off to get an academic scholarship to Loyola Marymount undergrad and student loans for law school—I think she'd be happier if I was fighting what she calls the *good fight*—taking on slumlords, maybe a few human-rights cases. And sure, there's a part of me that would love that too, but I fought my way to get to the top of this heap. My dad was killed when he was hit head-on by a teenage drunk driver. The girl spent a year in juvenile hall. And that was that. From that point on, my mom struggled. Struggled to make the rent. Struggled to be both a mother and a father to me. Struggled to put her shattered heart back together. I decided long ago that once I made it on my own, neither of us were ever going to struggle again.

During my first year of law school, my mom told me that before my father died he was a philanderer. I have no idea why. Maybe it was the third bottle of rosé we'd opened. Maybe she needed to release it so I'd understand the sacrifices she had made. What she had given up for me. Maybe she wanted to push him off the pedestal I'd placed him on since his premature death. Something shifted in me the night she shattered the picture-perfect image of my father. A fire that had been smoldering inside me was ignited. I distinctly remember transferring that burning anger toward my career path and deciding to practice criminal law. Maybe it was because I finally understood the juxtaposition of good people doing bad things and why it was still important that they get a fair defense. And sometimes that meant I had to defend people exactly like that teenager who killed my dad. But in *this* life, defending the Jeremiahs and Steve Greenwoods ensured we wouldn't struggle financially.

My dad was a wonderful, attentive father but betrayed my mother in the worst way. My mom loved me so fiercely but was also capable of selfishly tarnishing the image I'd held of my dad to offload some of her own pain.

And it was then that the two voices inside me made themselves heard for the first time.

Lila, you are nothing like your mother and father.

Lila, you are just like your mother and father.

It's dark by the time I head to the elevator, the lobby now deserted. I had told Ethan I'd be home by seven o'clock, and a glance at my phone tells me it's pushing seven thirty. If I haul ass, I can be running through our front door in forty minutes. He said he was going to order Chinese earlier when I texted that I'd won the case, and I was already dreaming of the way the Mongolian beef would melt in my mouth, how the perfectly cooked brown rice would stick to each piece. I hadn't eaten since the sesame bagel Chase had shoved at me on the way to court that morning.

The elevator finally arrives, and I push the close door button several times impatiently, then count down the floors before it sways slightly as it brings itself to a stop on the parking level. I step out and look left to see my Range Rover tucked into the back corner, one of the few cars left. The hairs on my arms shoot up, and I look around.

Someone is here.

I freeze and clutch my phone, letting out a yelp as a car door opens. I swivel to see Sam stepping out of his black Tesla.

"Oh my God! Are you trying to give me a heart attack?"

He smiles. "Sorry. I was getting ready to leave and saw you come out. Want to go grab a drink? To celebrate?"

"Didn't we do that earlier?" I say coyly.

"Not properly," he counters. He walks around and opens the passenger door of his sleek sedan. "Come on. They're holding a table for me at Bestia. Let me buy you a proper cocktail."

"No, sorry, I can't," I say quickly. "I need to get home and wash that meeting with Greenwood off me. That guy, don't get me started."

"Maybe it's not as clear-cut as you think, Bennett. Greenwood might be sleazy, but there are still two sides to every story."

"True," I say, but I'm not referring only to Greenwood, and Sam knows it.

As if it's a sign from the universe, I get a text from Ethan.

Mongolian beef here. Also got you the cream cheese wontons you love that you pretend not to like. Have pics of the new office space I want to show you too. ETA?

I hold up my phone. "Ethan is expecting me." And the truth is, I want to go home to him. I want to dip my chopsticks into the same container while we watch bad TV and talk about his day. His renewed vigor for writing. Our conversation earlier reminded me of who we used to be. Of who we could be again.

"That's never stopped you before," he challenges, then softens when he sees my face fall. "You've had a big day. Let's end it right," he adds, his words filled with a million meanings.

I look at my car, parked a few feet away, then back to Sam, picturing Carrie's face, bright and shiny, as she revealed she might be pregnant. I feel the pressure of my two worlds—the one where my dutiful husband waits patiently with cheap wooden chopsticks and low-sodium soy sauce. And the one right here, with my boss, powerful and expectant. Both of them knowing me and not knowing me all at the same time, in completely different ways. Almost as if I'm two different people. Tonight I feel the chasm become visceral, like my life could split in two—the choices laid at my feet leading me on completely different paths.

CHAPTER THREE

MONDAY
CAPTURED

"Come on, one little drink," Sam presses, his eyes full of promise. "Bestia is our place, or have you forgotten?" He grins earnestly.

That smile. Sometimes I hate the way it possesses me. The way the image of his grinning face flashes through my mind at the most inopportune times—as I'm lying in bed with Ethan while CNN drones on in the background, the same five stories running on a loop. As I'm about to nail a closing argument in court. When I'm having lunch with Carrie. Each time, I shove the thought of his even white teeth, the cleft in his chin that becomes more pronounced when his lips are curled upward, out of my head. But the truth is, there are days I'd still love to lose myself in his lopsided grin, one side lifting a little bit more to the right than to the left. I feel some pride knowing there is softness underneath his intimidating veneer. As if he lets me know him in a way no one else does.

"I'll tell you what, we can make it a shot if you're in a hurry," he adds, running his hand over his chin, as he does when he's strategizing.

And this *is* strategic. He knows I like a good shot. Especially purple ones. So efficient. The sharp edges of anxiety are blurred in those moments. Wanting to blunt the questions swirling inside me, I feel my lips start to form the word *okay*.

But Ethan. Chinese food. Sweatpants instead of my pencil skirt and heels that have been pinching my pinky toes for hours. My husband home waiting, excited to tell me about what the rest of his life might look like. And Carrie. What she said. The way it made my insides curl up into a tight ball. All reasons not to go. To say goodbye to him and all the complicated feelings that came with this relationship that started six months ago one evening when my defenses were down.

He smiles again. Damn it.

The bad girl inside me is cheering. The other voice, the one that is so damn good, is telling me this is a very bad idea. Not to go. But she's overly cautious. What's one drink?

I pull out my phone and send Ethan a quick text. So sorry! The partners are insisting I have dinner to celebrate the big win. Can't say no. Will be home as soon as I can.

One lie and a truth. At least that's what I tell myself. That I'm honest more often than I'm not.

No, you aren't, the voice says.

"One beer. And no shots!" I insist, reasoning that driving there myself and sipping a pale ale will ensure I'll keep my wits about me. Because this is how it starts—one drink leads to one more, which takes us to places I don't want to think about going right now. Because what we're doing is wrong.

Sam holds his hands up in surrender. "Okay. But can we order a couple of apps too? What about the pâté and those mussels you love? Oh, and maybe the burrata pizza? I'm starving."

"Fine." I relent, not at all surprised that the second I agreed, he changed the terms. I walk over and climb into my car, ignoring the twist in my stomach as the ignition turns over, and I follow Sam out of the garage, staring at his taillights until my eyes become blurry.

~

"To big wins." Sam holds up his Chef's Old Fashioned, his favorite drink off the cocktail menu. I clink my Citra Pale Ale against his glass and look past Sam, his back to the entrance. We're at a table in the rear corner of the bustling restaurant, but I still worry about being seen by someone we know. Having to lie. Again.

"It didn't feel as good as I thought it would," I confess, feeling a jab in my gut for telling him so quickly how I feel after making Carrie pull it out of me. But I'm desperate for someone to understand how I'm feeling about this case. Sometimes Ethan plays that role for me, the objective sounding board I need after a long day. But tonight I want someone who already knows the case intimately to tell me it was all okay. That the jury was right.

That's how you're justifying it to yourself, anyway, the voice reminds me.

"Really?" Sam replies, raising his eyebrows. And I'm not surprised. My relationship with Sam doesn't have room for my soft spots, but there's a part of me that wants it to—at least right now. Our strength was the magnet that drew us together, our weaknesses and fears typically saved for whispered conversations with our spouses. "Your career is going to skyrocket now. The name partners are particularly impressed with the way you handled your closing argument—you humanized him. Tied back his community service. All the character witnesses who think he's an honest man. You worked around his lack of an ironclad alibi. You highlighted the missing murder weapon. You reminded the jury of the meaning of probable doubt. We have big plans for you."

I swallow my uncertainty about the verdict and my desire for Sam to make me feel better and focus on his words. The three name partners, the ones who founded the firm thirty years prior, are notoriously hard to please. When they want to send you places, you go, whether it's to pack up your desk because you failed to bill enough hours or on the fast track to high-profile cases and huge bonuses. I take a drink of my beer and let the words sink in. If Sam is telling the truth (and he's always sworn he saves his lies for Carrie, which pleases me in a way that I'm not proud of), then it means something. That creepy partner who always finds a reason to brush my ass when he passes me in the break room? Worth it. The time I'd had to pull an all-nighter to comb through the cell phone records of our client's wife only to discover she used a burner phone for all of her *important calls*? Fine. I'd do it again. The hopelessness that tries to cling to me every time I visit a client in prison? Shake it off. My high-profile win today has changed my trajectory from a Ford Fusion to a rocket ship.

"That's nice to hear," I say evenly, watching a couple outside sharing a plate of pasta. Are they married to each other? Or are they like Sam and me—faking it in public, pretending to be something we're not, all while our real spouses are waiting for us at home? I finish my beer, hear myself ordering another. So much for controlling my wits.

"So, what doesn't feel good about the win?" Sam is careful not to ask me whether I'm questioning Jeremiah's innocence. He knows better.

I wave my hand. "Nothing. The victim's sister was really upset after the verdict. It got to me. That's all."

Sam slides his hand under the table to rub my knee, moving his way upward. "It's really sexy how much you still care."

The comment stings, and I move my leg away. "And what, you don't?" I snap as the server delivers the pâté and mussels, pretending she didn't hear my comment. "Whether Jeremiah is guilty or innocent, she still lost her sister." I stick my fork into the bowl and stab a meaty mussel, chewing slowly as I watch Sam swirl the liquid left in his drink, considering his answer.

"You have to be like a surgeon—keep your professional distance from these cases. Otherwise you'll begin to second-guess everything."

"Like I'm doing right now." *Like I want you to let me do. Just once, can we break through that barrier? Be, dare I say, vulnerable?*

"Exactly." He sets down his glass and locks eyes with me. "I can't afford to care that much, and if you want to get where I think you want to go in your career, you can't either, or you won't survive. I thought you knew that."

"I thought I did," I say quietly.

Sam continues as if he didn't hear me. "Carrie woke up in the worst mood this morning—freaking out that I have to travel to New York next week. Told me I was a selfish bastard and then ignored me the rest of the morning. And then was so pissed she had to bring me a file. Like her Blast Zone class is more important than my appeal?" He shakes his head. "She has no clue the pressure we're under. She thinks it's a bad day when they run out of organic red kale at the farmers market."

"That's not fair. Maybe she wants more time with you," I suggest, thinking the outburst sounds out of character for Carrie. Probably pregnancy hormones taking over.

"No, thanks. Now I can't wait to go to New York." He leans in. "I feel like you could use a change of scenery. Why don't you come? I can probably say I need more help and get you added as second chair on this case. We could make a long weekend out of it. I feel like I haven't seen you much since the Taylor trial started."

"I've been swamped," I say, then stare at my napkin because I don't want him to see the truth in my eyes. That I've been trying to pull away from him recently, avoiding him in the office when I can, taking a different route to the conference room so as to not cross paths.

"I know. I miss you. Is that so bad?" He rubs my leg under the table again.

I'm surprised to hear him articulate that he's missing me. We typically hold sentiments like that close to the vest. We don't fantasize about what it would be like to leave our spouses and run off together and get a shitty condo in Venice *just as long as we are together*. The most romantic thing we've ever done is drink a bottle of Dom in bed at a conference in DC. And we never, ever utter the *L* word. But of course we care about each other. I wouldn't have taken on so much risk for meaningless sex. I revere Sam in a way that I never have with Ethan. Sometimes I lie awake at night and try to put my finger on why. With Sam I'm a savior, slaying dragons and saving the innocent. With Ethan I often feel like a failure, unable to drag him out of the slump he's slid into.

So, yes. There are feelings. But Sam and I have convinced ourselves that we're above talking about them. That that somehow makes us less culpable.

But Carrie's confession has broken me open, shaken me in the most unexpected way. It reminds me that Sam belongs to someone else. That there are consequences, even if we don't care to acknowledge them. Stephanie prophesied earlier that karma was coming for me. Is this my penance? To watch Sam start a family with my best friend?

"Sam—" I break eye contact and glance at the entrance of the restaurant to regain my composure. A tall woman in a black jacket catches my eye. Dark hair. Shoulders hunched so slightly you almost don't notice. Piercing forest-green eyes that are staring at me, unflinching.

I draw in a sharp breath.

"What?" Sam asks, following my stare.

I point. "Stephanie! She's here. She must have followed me!"

Sam squints at me. "Who is Stephanie? And why is she stalking you?" Then he sits up. "Is she hot? Because I have a fantasy about this exact scenario."

I swat at him quickly and look back to the front.

The woman begins to walk toward the large glass doors leading into the restaurant. My stomach slides into my feet. What will she say to me? Will she make another scene? Slap me? Or worse?

But when she walks inside, shrugs her black leather jacket off, and saunters confidently over to the bar, where she hugs a stout man in an expensive gray suit, I realize it's not her. I hold my hand to my chest and feel my heartbeat downshift.

I turn back to Sam, who is looking at me curiously. "What was that all about?"

"Nothing. I thought I saw someone I knew." I watch as the woman orders her drink and leans toward her companion. "I was wrong."

"You didn't seem too excited to see her, whoever she was."

"It was an old client," I lie, not wanting to appear weak. Not wanting Sam to know I thought it was the sister of the woman—*Vivian*—Jeremiah was accused of murdering. How that woman has worked her way inside my head. Not wanting him to see how badly my interaction with Carrie has rattled me.

I carefully spoon some pâté onto a piece of perfectly grilled bread but find that I've lost my appetite. Each glance at Sam reminds me of Carrie—and the baby. I know I have no right to be angry—this is what I signed up for, isn't it? He belongs to someone else, as do I. The thing is, I'm not upset Carrie is pregnant. In this really weird way that I compartmentalize things, there has always been a part of me that has been happy for my friend, the same part that knows she'll be a great mother. I think what has shaken me is what this pregnancy means for Sam and me.

"I can't go to New York with you," I blurt. The thought spills out before I can stop it, and that affirms every small doubt, every shard of guilt, every jab to my conscience I've tried so hard to ignore.

"Fine. There's a conference in Chicago next month, then."

I feel a lump form in my throat. "I won't be going to that either." My voice is shrill, and there's an anger deep inside my belly that I haven't been able to shake. And I know exactly why.

Carrie. The pregnancy.

Sam frowns. "Lila—"

"We've got to end this," I say abruptly, and Sam nearly chokes on the brown liquid in his highball glass.

"Bennett," he starts. "What the hell is going on with you today?"

"I mean it, Sam. I'm done," I say and see a flicker of something in his eyes before he recovers. Surprise? Sadness? Anger? I understand—I also feel a mix of those emotions. I've always known we had an expiration date—that one of us would eventually stop this train before it derailed. Today is that day. And the person coming to her senses is me. Something about my uneasiness with the verdict and Ethan's phone call and renewed enthusiasm, combined with Carrie's pregnancy, has shocked me into facing the truth I've been hiding from myself all along: I'm gambling not only with my life but with the people I love most. And that has to stop. Now.

"Is this about the case? You've been acting weird since the verdict."

"No," I say. "This is about you and me, going nowhere. There's no future for us."

Sam runs his fingers through his thick hair. "I didn't think that was what you wanted."

"I don't," I say, although the truth is I don't know what I want. Who I want. All I know is I'm done fucking my pregnant best friend's husband. And ready to go back to mine. Everything else I can figure out later.

Sam searches my face. "You're serious about this, aren't you?"

"I am," I say, nodding. "I'm sorry."

"So am I," he says under his breath.

I grab my purse off the seat. "I should go." I glance at my watch. If I hurry I can still get home before Ethan falls asleep, before the Mongolian beef has gone cold, before Julianna Margulies beats the odds and wins another impossible case. I feel light as air as I begin to stand up. It is time to go.

"Wait." Sam grabs my wrist. "Stay. Have one more drink. I don't want to go home. Not yet." His eyes meet mine, and I look away, not wanting to see his feelings for me reflected in them.

I pull my arm back, and his grasp slackens. "If I don't go right now, I never will," I say and stand up, hurrying around the tables, picking up my pace as I push through the door and down the stairs, away from Sam and the parts of our lives we've shared for the past six months, and onto the dark industrial street lined with warehouses.

Good job, says the little voice inside me. But I don't feel resolved. I feel unsure as I walk briskly to my car.

I attempt to ignore the tingle at the back of my neck making me feel as if someone is following me. I swing my head up and swivel around, only to breathe easier when a couple heading toward the restaurant nod at me as they pass. Still a bit spooked, I pick up my pace to a light jog and glance back toward Bestia, toward Sam, who is most likely still at the table, sipping his second old-fashioned slowly. There's a part of me that already misses him, but that voice inside me is correct. I made the right decision. The *only* decision.

I unlock the door and climb in quickly. I sit in silence staring at my dashboard, not bothering to turn on the engine. My phone buzzes. Sam? But no, it's Ethan. And when I see his name on the screen, calm washes over me. I'm going home to the right man.

On my way, I type. Had a quick drink and need to stop for gas, I add, to buy myself a little more time to process what's happened with Sam before I have to arrive home. This is a lie, of course, but it's my last lie. It has to be. This thing with Sam is over, and I'm going to make my marriage work. The way I vowed to do when we held hands on the beach in Malibu six years ago.

A fluorescent streetlight above goes out, and darkness falls across the nose of the Range Rover. My heart starts to beat faster, and I peer into the rearview mirror and then the side mirrors. I turn and look over my shoulder. I let out the breath I was holding. Why am I so jumpy? There's nobody there. Only a minivan and a Toyota Prius on either side of my parking space.

Suddenly, out of the corner of my eye, I'm sure I see a shadow pass by the back of my car. I reach over and double-check that my doors are locked, letting out a sigh of relief when I realize they are.

A large hand closes over my mouth from the back seat as I reach to start the ignition.

I try to scream, but the sound is trapped deep within me. I catch a glimpse of a ski mask in the rearview mirror and panic, shoving my elbow back fiercely, but the person quickly wraps his other arm around my neck, and I freeze with fear.

I feel a cloth over my mouth, and everything blurs. I fight to keep my eyes open, but I can't. I'm being pulled away—it feels like it did when I had knee surgery years ago. When the anesthesiologist put the mask over my mouth and asked me to count.

And just like that: three, two, one, everything goes black.

I'm floating through a dark space. My mind and body disconnected. My limbs feel light. My head heavy. My eyes are sealed shut, and I try to force them open, but sleep is like a long arm, pulling me back. I want to succumb, but I know I can't. I need to break free of this black hole. To fight hard against the exhaustion. I must wake up. I hear the raspy sound of my own breath. I feel the irregular rhythm of my heartbeat. Quick, slow. Quick, quick, slow. The blurry edges of fear are starting to crystalize—my memory returning.

And then there it is, like a sharp slap across the face. The sting of the recollection burning.

I was taken.

Finally, I make my eyes open. But everything is still so dark. My eyes are covered with something. I try to reach up to take it off, but my hands are bound by what feels like metal cuffs. And my ankles are also restrained by something that's cutting into my skin. My feet are bare against a cold surface.

Panic zigzags through me.

A scream lunges from my mouth. I jerk my arms back and forth, trying to get out of the cuffs, the metal cutting into my wrists. I wince from the pain, but I keep trying.

Eventually I give up, because I'm stuck. I'm still screaming. My throat is burning, and after what feels like an eternity, I have to stop. I work hard for minutes to get to my feet. But as soon as I'm upright, I lose my balance and fall. I land on my side, my cheek hitting the floor. The pain that radiates through my jaw is excruciating, but I can't do anything except feel it. I lie here realizing I'm trapped. I have no idea where I am. Or who has me. I've been taken from my car and brought to a second location. And I've handled enough murder trials to know what that means.

I'm going to die here.

CHAPTER FOUR

MONDAY
FREE

"What's it going to take for me to convince you to go out with me?" Sam's eyes dance, and he shoves his hands deep inside his pockets. When did he change out of his custom-tailored charcoal-gray suit and into dark jeans and a crisp white T-shirt—his signature after-work outfit? I don't think I've ever seen him wear anything else after hours. "One little drink." He pinches his pointer finger and thumb in the air. Before I can respond, he says, "I'll tell you what, we can make it a shot."

I smooth my wrinkled pencil skirt, noticing a small stain on my white button-down, and sigh. I feel rumpled and exhausted, not at all like going out. But it's hard to resist him as I take in his dark mop of hair and study how his moss-green eyes light up against his olive skin, the way his five-o'clock shadow enhances the sharp lines of his jaw. I love his jawline. I've traced my finger around it more times than I can count, always trying to memorize the shape.

I start to walk toward him—thinking that yes, one quick drink is what I need—but then I picture Carrie again. The way she glowed from the inside out, as if her pregnancy were literally lighting her up. The twinkle that sparkled in her eye as she confided she was having a baby. And no one knows but me, her *very bestest friend*, as she likes to call me.

The same slutbag who's been sleeping with her husband.

Sam doesn't know yet—he hasn't yet been changed by the news, by the choices he'll have to make. But *I* know. I get that this growing life inside her changes everything. It's already been six months. We're in so deep now, it's almost impossible to think anything can pull us out of this rabbit hole. But this baby, this tiny seed, will. I can feel it. And surprisingly—or maybe not surprisingly—I also feel relief. To finally be done. To stop betraying my best friend. My husband. Whatever the reason I became entangled in *this*, whether it was boredom or selfishness or maybe even true love, I haven't been able to find the strength to end it on my own.

Ethan texts again. I had a great writing day! And I found The Good Wife on Hulu. Up for a binge session?

Ethan sounded happy on the phone earlier. I know happy is a broad word. What does it mean, anyway, to be happy? Prior to his call, he has been in a good place for a while. And when I say a while, I mean one week. A record for him. If his willingness to watch *The Good Wife* doesn't prove it, I don't know what does.

I look up at Sam, who rolls his eyes.

"That him again?"

"He has a name."

"That *E-than* again?" He drags out the two syllables as if my husband is the one who has done something wrong. As if it's Ethan who's been having an affair for over 180 days.

I think of the tiny notebook in my purse and pull my bag a little closer to my body. In the pale-blue spiral pad I've kept a log of my betrayal. It started the first night Sam and I kissed. We were working late and discussing his current case: the owner of a billion-dollar private equity firm who was being accused of embezzling his clients' money.

One minute Sam was showing me a portion of the transcript of his client's deposition, and the next he was pressing his mouth to mine.

I still play back that moment sometimes, the way I tilted my head back as I giggled, how he gently grabbed my neck and pushed away a strand of my hair that had circled my face. He held me there for one beat as if to say, *Last chance to exit what's about to happen, Bennett.*

But I didn't stop him. Instead I took his chin in my hand and pulled him closer until our lips met again. We stayed like that for a long time. Me leaning over his desk, the edge spiking me in the stomach, his breath hot as his mouth found so many parts of me, our hearts racing the way they do when it's new. But when I got home and washed my face, looking over at Ethan's sink, his toothbrush resting next to it, I felt it. The guilt. And I told myself I couldn't let it happen again.

But then it did, the very next night. And so I started keeping the tally marks. Because I would stop after a week. Which became three. Which turned into six months. And here we are. Me, tired of telling myself you can do bad things but still be a good person. The tallies a reminder of what I've done, what I'm doing. Somehow giving me the illusion I'm in control.

I often ask myself why I let him kiss me that first night. Why I let it become a regular thing. That evening in Sam's office when we went from being coworkers to something more, Ethan's mood had been at an all-time low for as long as I could remember. I remember feeling as if we were lost in the middle of a desert, with no escape for miles. He hadn't written a word in months. He could barely get out of bed. He'd lost sight of one of the things I'd been most attracted to—his ambition. Before he became the best-selling author who sat on Oprah's couch and discussed his novel as I cried with pride in the green room, I'd already been drawn to his intense drive. When he stopped caring enough to try to write, to even get out of bed long enough to say goodbye to me in the morning, to look up from the TV when I got home at night, it felt like a betrayal. A rejection. Was that fair of me to feel that way? I don't know. And Sam, who pulsated with ambition and looked at me as if I were the only one in the room, had been like a magnet, pulling me toward him and away from my husband. Am I choosing an easy scapegoat—my husband's depression—to justify my affair? Maybe. But at the time it felt like an antidote to what had ailed me.

"Not tonight, Sam," I finally say. *And probably not ever again*, I want to add but somehow can't. I picture Carrie's bouncy ponytail as she popped into the conference room, her sparkling eyes, the ignorance of my betrayal painted across her face in the form of a sincere smile as we talked about my day in court. As she tried to make *me* feel better.

Sam gives me a look as if he can't believe I'm saying no.

Have I ever turned him down before? I can't remember a time.

"I need to go home . . ." I look down, suddenly overcome with emotion. Am I going to cry? God, it feels like I'm going to lose it. I bite down on my lower lip hard. I need to say the rest. "To my husband. I need to go home to *E-than*. And you . . . you should go home to your wife."

"What is this, Bennett? What are you saying?"

"You know what I'm saying." I lock eyes with him for what feels like minutes. This isn't how I saw myself ending it. In my mind when I told him it was over—because I had always planned to stop our relationship—we would have one final night together. And the next morning I would make my last tally, and then I'd rip up every page in the notebook and dispose of it in some dumpster. But of course, life isn't that simple. I almost laugh out loud at my stupidity.

"Do I?" He steps closer and tips my face to his, kissing me. He's so close I can smell a hint of shampoo—is that sandalwood? And then I notice that his hair is slightly wet. He must have showered in his private bathroom. Did he plan this—wait for me so he could convince me to go out?

I recoil at his overconfidence—his ego—that of course when he intercepted me in the parking garage I would go with him, choose him over my husband. Yet again. "There are cameras." I pull away from him quickly. "We've been lucky until now that we've been able to keep it quiet. Let's stop while we're ahead."

"Since when do you quit anything when you are winning?"

"Are we really winning, Sam?" I ask, but he doesn't answer. We both know my question is rhetorical. "I'm serious, Sam. It's over." I say the words quickly and reach down, squeezing his arm before backing away. "I have to go."

"Lila," he calls after me.

The only sound is the clicking of my heels on the concrete. I don't turn around, but I can feel his eyes boring into my back. I unlock the car and throw my purse on the passenger seat. Slamming the door behind me, I can see him in my rearview mirror watching me, his face twisted with emotion. Sadness? Anger? Confusion? I can't read it. Finally he gets in his car, and after what feels like forever, his headlights come on, and I watch as he drives out of the parking garage. I take out my notebook and make my final tally. I draw a line across four marks that are already there, making five. Six months and five days.

I start the car and look over my shoulder before pulling out. I see a figure pass behind my back window. I turn to see who it is, but no one is there. I take a deep breath and try to focus, still rattled from my conversation with Sam.

As I drive toward home, to my *other* life, I realize that I'm choosing it for the first time in as long as I can remember.

CHAPTER FIVE

Monday
Captured

I wake with a start, my cheek still pressed against the cold floor. Did I pass out? I hear footsteps that grow louder and then what sounds like a key in a lock. A creaking sound cuts sharply through the air, a door closes, and the steps grow closer. Still on my side, my face throbbing, I slide my body away from the sound until I hit something hard—a wall.

"Going somewhere?"

I scream, and the sound of my voice echoes.

A man's voice. Deep. Assured. The tone bordering on jovial. As if he's recently drunk a cup or two of coffee. Maybe he got a run in. He's ready to face the day.

The man laughs. It's a deep sound that radiates hard from his chest.

My insides go cold. Is this it? The moment I'm going to die? Despite the freezing temperature, I start to sweat.

His steps are closer, and he's so near that I can smell him—a combination of cologne and coffee. I was right: He's caffeinated and ready to . . . to what? To maim? Torture? Kill? I shudder at the thought.

Beads of sweat trickle down the back of my neck. Is it still Monday? How long have I been here—wherever *here* is?

"I'm going to remove this," he says, and I feel him at the back of my head trying to pull the blindfold free. He tugs at it hard as I flinch, terrified at what he'll do next. He grunts and rearranges his body until finally he yanks the blindfold off.

I blink several times, the dim light a shock to my pupils.

I look at his hands first, expecting him to have a gun or a knife, but he doesn't appear to have any kind of weapon—at least not that I can see. A ski mask covers his face, his dark eyes and full lips peeking out from small holes. He's muscular, wearing a tight black long-sleeve T-shirt and gray joggers, and about five feet ten—it's hard to tell with him standing and me sitting. New Balance sneakers on his feet.

I quickly take in my surroundings—brick walls, concrete floor. Small—maybe ten by twelve, the size of my living room. Exposed pipe runs across the high ceiling—a single fluorescent light bulb hanging from it. There are no windows. The only way in or out is a large steel door.

"I'm Q," the man says gruffly. "No need to tell me your name." He smiles, which looks terrifying through the ski mask. "You are Lila Rose Bennett. Attorney—mostly criminal defense, but you've dabbled in other areas. Five feet seven, one hundred and twenty-seven pounds. You used to be an avid runner—a couple of half marathons before the ski accident and then the surgery."

I take in a sharp breath. This was no accident. Not a carjacking gone bad. Q had come for *me*.

"You live in Santa Monica with your husband, older than you by eight years—Ethan, a novelist. Well, can we still call him that? His first and *only* book debuted on the *New York Times* bestseller list, but that was six years ago. Is a novelist still a novelist if he only writes one? What's that saying about the tree in the woods?" He makes that same deep cackle, and my skin crawls with fear.

I play back his coarse voice in my head. Is it familiar? Is he a defendant I'd represented or—I think of Stephanie—a family member upset about one I'd freed? Could he be a witness I cross-examined too harshly? I stare at his broad shoulders, his average height and weight, contemplating whether I've seen his body before. I'm not sure I have. As far as I know, this man could be anybody.

"Is this a hostage situation?" I ask, staring at his mask, the black woven cotton tight against his face, praying the fact he's wearing it means he's not going to kill me. But I can't bring myself to ask him.

Not knowing who he is—not understanding his connection to me—makes my heart pound hard and fast. I force my face to remain neutral, but I know I'm trembling. "Have you been hired by someone?" I ask when he doesn't respond to my hostage question, trying to keep my voice balanced. The cuffs are cutting into my wrists, the blood in my legs not flowing well because of the bindings around my ankles. My feet seem to have fallen asleep. I shift, trying to alleviate some pressure.

Q crouches down in front of me, and I can see that his eyes are not nearly as dark as they looked when he was standing. But they are unique—split pea soup–green with flecks of gold—different enough that I would expect to have a spark of recognition had I seen them before. But there is nothing—no memory of exchanging a glance on the sidewalk, being stared at by them in court, or seeing them in passing as one of us stepped off an elevator and the other on.

His close proximity makes me shake harder. I bite firmly on my lip and try to control my tremors. Is this where he reaches over and chokes me? I tense, desperately wondering how I can defend myself while bound. The answer is: I can't. Fear from this realization dizzies me—rushing through me from my toes to the top of my head and back down again.

"I thought you'd never ask what is going on here, Lila. Let me give you all of your answers, and then we can both be on our way." He stares at me for a while, and I try to regulate my breathing, but it's impossible; I'm sucking in short gasps, releasing even less. "Not." He doubles over with laughter. "I'll be doing the question asking, the talking, everything.

You . . . well, you can hang out. Make yourself comfortable." His eyes rest on my bound bare feet. I wonder where my shoes are. My purse. My cell phone. My car. Has he gotten rid of them? Does he plan to do the same with me?

I suck in another shallow breath and stare at him hard. All the information he has on me. Has he been stalking me? His demeanor reads almost as if he's proud of his accomplishment—of holding me captive.

"I'm about as far from comfortable as someone could be." I hold my wrists up. I shift my legs, and my feet start to tingle again. "Please," I plead. Not sure what I'm pleading for. The desperation has set in so quickly. The feeling of being trapped, of the walls closing in. Not being able to breathe. I would have thought I was stronger than this. But it's as if he's stripped away all the armor I'm normally encased in.

"Oh, you're uncomfortable? Well, why didn't you say so? I'll be right back with a Casper bed and some silk sheets. While I'm at it, a glass of wine? You like red, don't you? The Prisoner is a favorite, isn't it? Although you'll settle for Meiomi in a pinch."

His last comments bring bile to the back of my throat. I imagine him watching me through my living room window as I bring my glass to my lips, savoring the bold berry flavor, totally unsuspecting I'm being stalked.

Could he be connected to the family of Jeremiah's wife? To Stephanie? Did she hire him to kidnap me? I remember being outside the courthouse, turning and looking over my shoulder before I got into the Uber. There was something about her stare that gave me chills. And she told me karma would take care of me. Was this what she had in mind? Did she get impatient that the universe wouldn't deliver justice quickly, so she took matters into her own hands?

He waits a beat. "Nothing to say? Wondering how I know all of these intimate details about you?"

"Is this about Jeremiah Taylor?" I ask, watching for signs he recognizes the name, but if he does, he gives nothing away.

"For an attorney, you're not very smart, are you? Didn't I say *I'll* be asking the questions?"

I freeze. Nod. "You did, sorry," I say, my voice shaking in response to his sharp and biting tone. My gut tells me it could lead to something far worse if I push him.

"That's better. You'll get the hang of this, I promise." He sits down and crosses his legs.

Crisscross applesauce. I hear a voice in my head. It's my mom's. Her voice was always airy, although she was usually exhausted. She'd say it when she wanted me to sit in front of the TV so she could rest her eyes before her night shift. My chest tightens at the thought of her. Will I see her again?

I think of the front room in my house; its thick rug and bookshelves lined with our favorite novels immediately make me conjure Ethan's face—frowning, his eyes squinting at his phone. I keep telling him he needs reading glasses, but he refuses. He's probably trying to figure out where I am—so many times I've been stuck at work. Or told him I was on my way out the door, only to leave two hours later. So he might not be looking for me yet. Or if he is, where is he searching? Who is he calling? Sam? That thought I can't digest. I can picture the Styrofoam container of Mongolian beef on the coffee table where we usually eat. It's been opened, Ethan's chopsticks stuck haphazardly in the middle—he'd have one bite, okay two—because the poor guy was hungry. Didn't realize I'd never make it home after lying about getting gas. Shit. He's going to search gas stations—aimlessly—taking him nowhere near me. Thanks to my lie. He can't track my phone because I wouldn't agree to have one of those apps he wanted me to get for safety after Franklin. I told him it drained my battery. But really, I didn't want him obsessing over my every move from our living room couch. I go back to taking in the room I'm currently in.

"Wow. This floor is hard as a rock," Q says, his voice still unfamiliar to my ears.

I move my legs slightly, wincing as the zip ties cut into my ankles. The waistband of my pencil skirt is cutting into my stomach, my white button-down mimicking a straitjacket.

"Let me go over the ground rules," he says.

If there are ground rules, maybe I'll be here for a little while.

"This is your new home," he continues, waving his left hand back and forth like a Realtor might.

I notice his nails are trimmed and clean. His hands smooth. He doesn't wear a wedding ring. The details I was taught to take in about a client. The little signs—possible tells. You never know what will be a significant factor. Serial killers can get their nails done and manual laborers can deliver babies. There isn't always a rhyme or reason to it.

"As you can see, it's about one hundred seventy-five square feet," he continues. "There is absolutely no light. But it's a fine concrete square— the exposed brick on the walls gives it a nice touch, don't you think? Imagine all the ways you could decorate." He grins. "Oh, and there's room service! You'll get the finest tap water and only the best mush. We will take you on two bathroom breaks per day. Any other needs, you'll have to handle in here." He points to a bucket in the corner.

We. He said *we* will take you on two bathroom breaks per day. Is there more than him? Was that a slip? Or does he see himself as multiple people?

He's still talking. "As for who I am, why you're here, that is all for later. For now, you wait."

Later. So there will be a later.

"Wait for what?" I feel it again. The tightening in my chest. Like my skin is being pulled inward. I push a breath out, just to make sure I still can.

He presses his pointer finger to his pursed lips and watches me for a long beat. I begin to wonder whether I'll want there to be a later.

When he finally speaks, my body goes numb. "You'll see."

CHAPTER SIX

MONDAY
FREE

I drive home slowly, lost in thought. My phone buzzes, and my stomach flips.

Sam?

I glance at the screen exposed from the inside of my bag. It's not him. Of course it's not. He'd never call me now, not after our exchange in the parking garage. Because we have a deal. When one of us is not at work, we never call or text. Too risky, even for us. And besides a few sloppy drunken moments over the past six months, we've both honored it.

I exhale, not sure whether I want it to be him or not. Do I need him to fight me on the breakup? Show me he wants me? That although we promised not to fall in love, he has anyway because I'm so amazing? That's so damn high school of me. We're both *married*. What did I think? He'd show up at my house wearing a trench coat holding a boom box overhead?

I debate not answering, but it's my mother. I swear she had an emotional tracker implanted in me when I was born. Every time something goes wrong, she seems to know. And she doesn't text. She calls. She says it's because my voice always gives me away, and she's probably right.

I answer. "Hi, Mom."

"What's wrong?" I can picture her sitting in her reading chair in her living room, looking out her window, the ocean in the distant background. A half-read copy of the most recent Reese Witherspoon recommendation balancing on the arm of the chair. Her peppermint tea long ago gone cold. "You don't sound good."

"I only said, 'Hi, Mom,'" I refute weakly. She already knows. No sense in lying. I really need to stop that in general.

"Tell me what's going on."

"Nothing. Or at least nothing I can talk about."

"You can tell me anything."

I roll my eyes. "Not about *this*."

"Is it something legal? Attorney-client privilege?"

"Not exactly," I say vaguely, wondering whether I should take the fifth. Really, this woman missed her calling as a prosecutor. She is relentless.

"Then tell me. I can help," she presses.

Because of what she went through with my dad, I know my mom would *not* understand what I'm feeling right now about Sam. Not one bit. But I suddenly understand there's something I need to clarify after all this time.

"Why did you tell me about Dad cheating on you?" I say as I slow down for a red light. "What purpose did you think it would serve?"

"What?"

"Mom . . ." I say, because I know she heard me.

"Is this what you're upset about?"

"Yes," I say, telling myself this is somewhat truthful. Not an outright lie. Because I do need to understand her motivation. Maybe it can shed some light on my own.

"Oh, honey, I'm sorry. I knew the moment I said it that it wasn't right."

"Then why didn't you say so?" A tear rolls down my cheek, and I wipe it away hastily as the light turns green.

"I never should have told you. I'm so very sorry. I got drunk, and it was the anniversary of his death, and it came out. I promise it wasn't any more calculated than that." She starts to sob. "Lila?"

I don't answer. Instead, I suck in a long breath and let it out slowly. I do this again and again.

"Lila?" My mom says my name again, and her voice cracks.

"It's okay, Mom," I say. Because what else can I do? She's sorry she said it. I believe her. I'm certainly sorry she did it. But most of all, I'm sorry my dad gave her something to tell me. It's like a bad game of dominoes. The choices he made forced them down, one by one. I think of Sam. Of my own poor choices. Have I cut bait in time? Before the dominoes were tipped? Can I step back into my own life without consequences? Only time will tell.

"But it was your dad. He was your hero, and I ruined that. It's one of my biggest regrets."

I swallow hard at her confession. I can see Dad in one of his polo shirts, watching from the sideline as I dribbled the ball through my opponents on the soccer field, erupting in cheers when I took the left-footed shot we'd worked on for weeks in the backyard to score the winning goal. And then I envision him in bed with a woman whose face I can't see. I recoil almost as if the image is an actual picture in front of me.

"What's done is done," I say. And I'm not sure if I'm talking about my dad or my own affair with Sam.

"Can you forgive me?"

"I already have," I say.

But you won't be able to forget, the voice says.

"Are you sure? I feel like you're letting me off the hook too easily. Do we need to talk about this more? I can set up a time with my therapist for us."

"No, I'm fine," I assure her. "I think I needed to understand why."

"But why did you ask me about it today, of all days?"

"I'm trying to figure out why I do some of the things I do, and in order to do that, I think I needed to understand why you did what you did."

"I was selfish. Petty. That was why." She pauses. "The thing is, Lila, in that moment, I didn't want to be your mom with ideals who took the high road. I wanted to be your friend who confided something terrible that happened. Something that changed who I was. But that wasn't fair."

I choke back the tears that rise in my throat and think of my own regrets. "You're only human."

She sighs. "At some point we all seem to fail, don't we?"

I think of Ethan, Carrie, the ways I've failed them. "We sure do."

"I love you," she says. "You know that, right?"

"I know. I love you too."

"So can we talk about this case?" my mom says. "Is that the catalyst for all this self-introspection?"

"It's a lot of things," I mutter. "Not only that."

"You aren't happy? But you won." I know she's sitting up in her chair now, her reading glasses on top of her head, trying to figure me out. If I'm unhappy I won, maybe I'll stop defending *them*. "Does this mean . . . ? Are you rethinking? All my friends in my Pilates class think he's guilty."

"You already told me that. And no, Mom, I'm not rethinking. I'm *overthinking*. The victim's sister was upset after court. She confronted me."

"Are you worried for your safety?"

"Maybe."

"Wouldn't be the first time." She attempts a joke.

I've received hate mail, hate email, threats, even had a stalker once, like Mom was referring to. Franklin would come to all my trials. Sit in on them like he cared about the case, but he would look only at me. And I got that tingling feeling up my neck that would make me turn, and then we'd lock eyes, and he'd nod his approval. I suppose he took that as a sign, because he started bringing me flowers. Cards. He wrote that he was in love with me. Then he showed up in person one night. I got a restraining order, and he went away. It was almost too easy.

"You need sleep," she says when I don't respond.

"Right," I say as I pass the exit for La Cienega Boulevard.

"You sure there's nothing else going on?" Mom asks.

I wish I could tell her. I haven't confided in anyone. And it would feel good to get it out. But I can't. There's no one I can talk to. And maybe I deserve that—that I can't tell Carrie, my best friend. It's doubtful she would want to hear about my breakup with her husband.

"I've got to go, Mom. I'm pulling up to the house," I say instead of answering her. Although I'm still lying, because I'm miles from home. I hold my breath and hope she takes me at face value. I should really get a shirt made: **No More Lying**.

"Okay, well, I'm here if you need me," she says, her voice unsure. She's not ready to let this go. She wants to fix whatever is wrong. It's both her greatest strength and biggest weakness.

And she can't fix this.

I start to say goodbye, but she interrupts me.

"Wait, before you go. Dinner tomorrow night? It's the last Tuesday of the month. You and Ethan still coming down here?"

"Yes," I say, wondering about time. Lately it seems to drag, almost as if I'm living days two times over, yet those Tuesdays come so frequently. Guilt shoots through me because a part of me doesn't feel like going. Wants to blow it off because of everything that's going on.

Worried she'll want to dissect this conversation more. But I won't cancel. I never do. My mom needs this. And I probably do too.

"Bring some good wine. I think we deserve it!" she says, and laughs awkwardly.

"Will do. Love you."

"Love you too."

"Bye," we chime.

Still a good twenty minutes from my house, I reach over to the passenger seat and run my finger over the notebook where I made the final tally mark. Wondering what exactly it means. Yes, it signifies that Sam and I are over. But it also represents an opportunity to start fresh. To make sure those dominoes don't fall. To give my marriage the attention it deserves. But how? How do I go home to my husband and wipe away the sadness I feel over losing my boyfriend? Sure, Ethan will be happy to sit in bed with me and binge-eat a pint of Halo Top Mint Chip ice cream, but only one of us will know the real reason why.

"I can do this," I say to myself when I pull up to our house and click the garage door open. It creaks as it fights its way up. I park and open the door to the house, part of me hoping Ethan fell asleep on the couch so I can let my conflicting feelings simmer a little longer, but it's unlikely. Maybe it's better if he didn't—if I'm forced to draw my attention to him. To see him and hear him and plug back into the life we share.

I put my key in the lock and push the door open. I suppose my fresh start needs to begin right now.

CHAPTER SEVEN

MONDAY
CAPTURED

If my count is accurate, Q has been gone for roughly 143 minutes.

There is a dim light bulb screwed into a socket in the ceiling. It flickers from time to time, and I wonder when it will go out. When it does, I'll be left in total darkness. My breathing quickens at the thought, and I try to steady myself. Q could walk in and shoot me in the head or slit my throat, and I'd never see it coming. My limbs are still trembling, partly from the coldness of the room and also from the fear that has grabbed me and refuses to let go. Every time I try to focus on hope, escape, a future, the panic that I won't survive this wins out.

I can't shake Q's unsettling demeanor. His taunting. The way he looked at me through the slits in his ski mask. What does he know that I don't? What have I done that is so bad I've ended up here? I stare at the cuffs around my wrists until they become blurry. My chest feels like a clamp is tightening around it. I try to inhale a deep breath, but I can't. I slide backward until I'm flush against the wall and farthest from the door where Q will enter. What will happen to me when he returns? Who has me here? Who wants me *like this*? Bound, freezing, scared out of my mind in a semi-lit concrete room? I think of Stephanie's last words to me again. And not only her words, but the way in which she said them. How her eyes had gone cold, as if the life had been sucked out of her body. How the way she looked at me sent shock waves of worry through my chest. Had she already planned this—if Jeremiah were to go free, if her sister's death was not avenged, she would make a call for Q to intercept me outside Bestia? Does she have the capacity to be who she thinks Jeremiah is—a murderer?

Her sister is dead, and no one is in prison. Seems like a strong motive. Seems like that could stir up a lot of fucked-up feelings. I've been chloroformed, kidnapped, and held the Prisoner. Someone who would do that, that's a person who's really pissed off—and they want to see their own justice served, no matter the consequences. Stephanie fits the profile.

Q scares the fuck out of me, but he could be an amateur. Maybe he didn't think this through the way he should have. And if he was hired by Stephanie, there's a chance she also doesn't have the smarts to truly pull this off. She's too emotional. Maybe she made mistakes. She was sloppy. She left a clue that will lead the police to this godforsaken place. And I will be free, like Jeremiah. I wonder where he is tonight—probably smoking a cigar, eating a steak, patting himself on the back. Was he ever really worried? Or was he confident all along that I would secure his freedom? It's hard not to play back every interaction with him, every doubt or tickle in the back of my mind. Was Stephanie right? Did I help her sister's killer go free? Did my desire to win blind me to the truth? Is that why I'm here now? I squeeze my eyes shut and will myself to think.

Because *if*—and it's a big if, I know—*if* I survive, it will only be because I'm smarter than Q. I'm smarter than whoever hired him.

$$\sim$$

It was storming the day I first met Jeremiah. I remember because I was late as hell, cutting in and out of the traffic on the 110 Freeway, muttering under my breath as the clock ticked closer and closer to nine o'clock. I'd left Ethan tucked snugly under the covers, snoring as the rain pelted the large window in our bedroom that overlooked Santa Monica Boulevard. As usual, I'd tiptoed out of our bedroom holding my shoes in one hand and my cell phone in the other, telling myself that I was being kind by letting him sleep but secretly knowing I'd been avoiding dealing with what we'd become.

Once at work I'd jogged from the elevator, breathing hard, and didn't see Jeremiah rounding the corner near my office. I'd collided with him hard, sending my bag and all the files inside flying. I cringed. He bent over and began to collect them, handing them back to me in a neat pile.

"You must be Lila," he said, his steel-blue eyes shining, which I thought odd for a man being accused of murder. But from the research I'd done leading up to this meeting, I knew that he didn't give much away. That the smile he flashed me was standard, no matter the circumstances. In fact, it was one of the reasons he had become a prime suspect—the police were bothered that he hadn't ugly cried when he told them how he'd found Vivian facedown in their living room, clubbed in the back of the head with a large object that the forensics team could only speculate about because it had never been found. The house had been turned upside down, and all the electronics and her jewelry were missing, but whoever killed Vivian didn't leave a single fingerprint or shoe marking or some good ol' DNA. Unless it had been Jeremiah, whose fingerprints were, of course, everywhere. Because it was his house.

The DA also didn't like how Jeremiah had seemed too calm when he called 911, the prosecution putting the emergency dispatcher on the stand so it could be on record that she had been more distressed than Jeremiah that night.

As I led him into my office that day, making a motion to Chase to hold my calls, I was evaluating him, as I do with all my new clients. Dirty-blond hair that fell below his eyebrows that he kept brushing out of the blue eyes I'd noticed earlier. The slim-fitting expensive suit of a guy who gets them custom made. The confident way he strode in and took a seat in the mahogany leather chair across from my desk. Assuming where he'd sit, where I'd sit, even though there was a couch and two chairs as well.

"So you fired your other attorney?" I said after I sat down. I'd been following the case closely and had been surprised Jeremiah had hired him in the first place. I knew the lawyer well—arrogant and incompetent, a lovely combination.

"He's an idiot," Jeremiah said. "He was going to get me sent to prison for the rest of my life!"

I leaned toward him. "Do you deserve that?"

He looked surprised I asked the question. "Are you asking me if I did it?"

"No. That's the one question I won't be asking."

"Ms. Bennett. I did not kill my wife," he said, his eyes locked on mine, unmoving.

I held his gaze, studying his face for a tell, any tic that might reveal the truth within his soul. But there was nothing there. His eyes were blank, like a whiteboard that's been wiped clean.

"Tell me what happened," I asked.

"You know what happened," he said, pointing at the files on my desk. "I have no doubt you know more about the case than I do at this point."

He was right. I probably did. But I wanted to hear it from him. I told him as much.

He balked slightly but started from the beginning. At first he seemed rehearsed, but I noticed his eyes flicker and his shoulders tense as he described discovering Vivian when he'd arrived home from work, the world standing still as he realized he was too late—she was already dead, the blunt trauma to the back of her head killing her almost instantly, according to the autopsy report. A crime of passion, the prosecutor had argued in court. A quick way for an intruder to silence her, I'd rebutted.

"Tell me how you were feeling when you made that 911 call," I asked next.

He shook his head and looked down. "I was in shock. To be honest, I barely remember it."

"Never say that—'to be honest.' That's what dishonest people say," I said abruptly.

"Oh, okay. But I'm not. Being dishonest," he said.

I brushed over his proclamation. People made them all the time, and really it meant nothing. "We're going to need to move quickly. File a motion for new counsel, and see if we can get the trial date moved back so we can be prepared."

"Does that mean you'll take the case?" he asked, a hopeful lilt to his voice. I'd recently gotten a very prominent surgeon acquitted who'd been accused of murdering his business partner. My stock had been rising, and I was now at the point where I could pick and choose my cases, for the most part. There had already been an insane amount of press around this case, Jeremiah and Vivian's seemingly perfect life picked apart by the vultures to keep the story alive, something that both appealed to and dissuaded me. If I took this case, I had to win. There was no other choice.

∼

The door creaks open, and Q fills the doorway, tearing me from the memory, his presence making my blood pressure spike and dissolving any other thoughts except survival.

"Hey, Princess," he says gruffly as he sets two bags on the floor. "Hope you aren't gluten intolerant." He chuckles at his joke as he pulls a burger from a grease-stained bag. My stomach rumbles. He hears the sound and looks over. "Oh, you think you're getting this? No, no, no.

This baby is mine." He licks his lips, his face still covered by the mask, but I can still see the amusement in his eyes. "This is for you." He pulls a baguette from another bag and rips off a small section. He sets it on the dirty floor, and I look away.

How long has it been since I've eaten? There were some grapes during the champagne toast at the office. And I scooped up a handful of mint M&M's from the dish on Chase's desk before I headed to the parking garage to go home. How many hours have I been here? I have no idea how long I slept. I only know how many minutes it's been since I woke. Probably three hundred—or five-ish hours. I'd estimate I've been here close to ten, maybe twelve. But it's a guess, because there are no windows, no clocks, absolutely no sense of time other than the one I've created by counting: one one thousand, two one thousand, three one thousand.

"Does the bread mean you're going to take these off?" I ask, my eyes darting to the cuffs locked around my throbbing wrists. "So I can actually eat?"

"Either that or I feed you." He cocks his head. "But then again, we hardly know each other. Seems a bit intimate, wouldn't you say?"

It's that look again—the way he surveys me. His eyes unblinking through the holes in his mask. His stare makes my heart beat faster. My mouth gets drier.

"What's wrong?" He crouches down in front of me. "Don't like my joke?" He touches my chin with his finger, and I flinch. He keeps his finger there, and my pulse races faster. "You're scared."

I shake my head. Feeling small. Weak.

"Don't lie to me, Lila." He touches my chest over my hammering heart. It takes every ounce of my control to not move away from him. "Your heartbeat is giving you away. It's going a mile a minute."

I don't answer. I breathe slowly. In and out. In and out.

"Fear is good," he says when I don't respond. "It will keep you on your toes." He looks at my bound feet. "Well, you know what I mean."

I clench my jaw and inhale sharply through my nose. I cannot let him get to me. But as we lock eyes, it's clear we both know it's too late for that. I'm at his mercy whether I like it or not.

"Before we eat, we're going to hit the bathroom. Unless you don't need to go?" He smirks.

I flinch, wondering if when he says *we*, he means he's going to watch. Or worse. I've been so fearful for my life, rape hadn't crossed my mind. But it does now so forcefully, crashes over me like a tidal wave. My hands begin to shake hard against the cuffs that bind them. Would I fight it like a rabid animal, scratching and clawing my way free? Or would I sit still, choosing my life over my dignity? Q crouches down again and removes a knife from his back pocket. I look away from the sharp blade.

"If you fight me after I take these off, it will be the last time I do . . . and the last time you do," he says, his voice dropping an octave. He cuts the ties on my ankles, and they start tingling, the blood circulating again. He pulls me up by the wrists, and I wince as the handcuffs cut into my skin.

He shuffles me toward the door, then stops abruptly and looks at me. He leans in, and I feel his mouth on my ear. "Don't worry, you aren't my type. Too skinny," he adds.

He leads me down a dark hallway and to a closed door that must be the bathroom. "I'm going to remove these cuffs now, because I don't get paid enough to wipe your ass." He pulls out his knife again. "But I promise you, if you try something, you will regret it, Lila. Do you understand?"

I nod, too terrified to speak.

"Good girl," he says and unlocks the cuffs.

This is my chance. I could kick him in the balls and run. But where? What if there isn't a way out of here? And then what?

He removes them, and tears of relief well in my eyes as circulation begins to return in my fingers. I look down at my wrists; they are raw and red. I rub them, realizing I'm not going anywhere. Not yet. It would be stupid to blow my only chance at getting away.

"You have two minutes." He gives me a small push toward the door.

I open it and close it behind me. The room is dark, save for a dim bulb similar to the one in my room. My eyes adjust, and I take in my surroundings. A dirty toilet in the right corner, a roll of toilet paper on the floor beside it. A filthy sink with exposed rusted pipes underneath it. No window. No way out.

My legs still shake slightly as I make my way over and pull my skirt up, my thighs burning as I squat. I'm trembling as I try to pee, the reality of where I am—in this filthy bathroom, God knows where—smacking me in the face. I'm crying suddenly, wanting my mom so desperately I can't breathe. Thinking, of all things, of an article she quoted from BuzzFeed about cell phones being as full of germs as toilet seats. I was barely listening, scanning a brief on my desk while she chattered on. Why hadn't I paid more attention to her when she called? I wonder if she's already trying to track me down. She calls almost every day—and when she doesn't reach me, she hunts. Something that normally irritates me but makes me hopeful now.

I pray she'll stalk the detective in charge of my case, and if the cop tries in vain to stonewall her, she'll push harder. Most detectives despise me, as I often get acquitted the people they arrest. But my mom will get them to succumb to her persistence. She has that personality—convinces you to do what she wants even if you think it's an insane idea. She once talked me into buying a pale-pink romper at H&M—a store I'd never set foot in before. There's a picture of me modeling it for her in the dressing room, my skin glowing under the fluorescent lights. I've still yet to wear it out, but every time I see it in my closet, it makes me smile. So maybe, just maybe, she'll be able to make the detectives believe that I'm the type of woman who deserves to be found alive. The thought hits me hard, and the tears fall again.

A bang. I jump. I grab the wall to steady myself.

"You done?" Q's voice barrels through the door. "I was nice, gave you an extra minute."

"Yes," I call out, reaching for the toilet paper, wiping quickly and pulling up my skirt.

Suddenly something Q said earlier hits me as the door swings open. *I don't get paid enough to wipe your ass.*

So he's not working alone. He *was* hired by someone.

"Let's go," he says, still holding the knife in his right hand, grabbing my arm with the other. We walk slowly and silently down the hall, me counting the steps back to my prison, my mind working in overdrive to figure out who hired Q.

CHAPTER EIGHT

Monday
Free

"I'm home!" I say when I walk through the door. I'm met with silence. I toss my keys in the dish on the table. "Ethan?" I slip off my shoes, studying myself in the mirror on the wall. I look tired. A little sad. I pinch my cheeks, run my fingers through my hair, and walk around the corner to look for Ethan.

"Hey," Ethan says, pausing the TV but not rising from the couch. He looks over, his expression hard to read. "Started without you." He points the remote toward the frozen image of Julianna Margulies's face.

I glance at my watch. It's after eight.

"Sorry I'm late. Had a little trouble getting out of there," I say, trying to lighten the mood in the room.

He puts his hand up. "Not tonight, okay?"

My chest tightens. I've ruined it. His one-week streak. Why did I linger in the garage with Sam? Especially since I had already been running late to get home to Ethan? I study my husband, obviously fresh out of the shower. His sandy-blond hair is still wet, making it look darker than it is. He's wearing faded jeans and a pale-gray T-shirt, wet in some places from where he didn't dry his torso. The Mongolian beef and wontons sit untouched on the coffee table. Two glasses. An unopened bottle of wine. He sat here. He waited.

I walk closer to him. "I'm sorry. Let me make it up to you."

Ethan sighs, his eyes flinty.

I reach for him, and he moves away. "I know you're sorry. You must tell me weekly. But why isn't it important for you to be *here*?"

He's not asking me where I really was, yet he is. His eyes are searching mine. Was it really that hard to get out of the office? Or did I choose work (and ultimately Sam) over him *again*?

Or maybe that's my guilt talking.

"It is important. No more late nights. I promise. It was a big win today. Things should calm down now."

His shoulders relax slightly, and I breathe. "You shouldn't make promises you can't keep."

I move toward him again, and this time he doesn't step back. I wrap my arms around his waist, lean my cheek on his shoulder. "I won't," I whisper. And I hope I'm telling the truth. That the little voice inside me that I hear chanting, *Oh yes you will*, is wrong.

"Subject change?" Ethan says abruptly. But I'm used to how he pivots. Tense one moment, seemingly fine the next.

"Please," I say.

"I wrote three thousand words today."

"That's great." I try to remember the last time he wrote any words. I can't. Usually he sits, laptop open, fingers poised, but nothing.

"I was feeling it, you know? I went for a run on the beach and had all these ideas. I came home and wrote nonstop for hours."

"When can I read it?" I ask, sinking into the sofa and opening the bottle of wine that I now see is the Prisoner. I guess I'm getting my celebration tonight after all.

"Soon—I'm not that far in. But this is different from the others I've abandoned. This manuscript feels special. I think this will be it. A worthy follow-up. Finally!" He leans in. "I think this one will shock everyone, coming from me. A little more controversial than my last."

"Your agent must be happy."

"I haven't mentioned it yet—don't want the pressure to finish any faster than I want to."

"I get it," I say, although I don't. I wish he would put himself under a deadline, but he won't. If his agent knew, he'd push him. And it's not about the money—sales from his debut, which hit the *New York Times* bestseller list and stayed there for twenty-two weeks, are still solid all these years later. It's about the fact that I want him to be *that* Ethan. The one who wrote like it was his job, not like it was a hobby. That Ethan was driven, determined. And after his huge success right out of the gates, I thought he would be motivated to do it all over again. But he said he was worried about a sophomore slump. That he couldn't supersede his success, let alone match it. He got into his own head. He became depressed.

But tonight he seems to have bounced back from my tardiness and moved on to his day. So I'll take this Ethan and hope he sticks around. Because he's exactly the Ethan I need right now—focused on himself and not me.

"I'll be right back," Ethan says. "Going to grab a bottle of water. Want one?"

"Sure." I take a long drink of my wine and curl my feet underneath me. I'm happy for the few moments of silence. The lights are dim in the room, so the front is illuminated by a lamppost. I stare out, a few cars passing by on Montana, the street that runs in front of our house. I take a deep breath and start to sink deeper into the sofa when I see a woman on the other side of the road.

It's Stephanie.

I set my wine down and slowly walk to the window. Not entirely trusting myself, I peer out at the woman. Long dark hair. Medium height, medium build. Wearing something entirely different than she had been at court. But still, it looks a lot like her. And she's staring this way. I pull the window open and call out to her, "Stephanie!"

A car pulls up, and the woman gets inside. I watch as it pulls away, not sure whether it was her.

"Who were you calling to?" Ethan asks, handing me a bottle of water.

"Stephanie," I say, embarrassed. I feel my cheeks flush. Am I losing my mind?

"Who?"

"The sister of Jeremiah's wife."

Ethan blinks several times. "And she's at our home why?"

"I don't know. But I think she followed me. If it was even her."

He grabs my hand gently and squeezes it. "So was it her or wasn't it?" he asks, not unkindly. I can see the concern in his eyes. He's always been protective—wanting me to call him on my way home from work, needing me to lock the doors whenever I'm home alone, insisting I sleep with a Maglite by my bed in case someone were to break in.

"I don't know. But I feel like it was." I glance toward the window again.

"Then we should call the police." Ethan lets go of my hand and walks toward the coffee table where his cell phone is resting.

I half laugh. "And tell them what? A woman matching the description of the sister of a murder victim my client was accused of killing was standing on a public sidewalk on the other side of the street from my house? For all I know, she lives in Santa Monica."

"Well, I don't like knowing sisters of murder victims who were married to your clients are showing up anywhere near where we live. It reminds me of Franklin."

"He never came to our house."

"He showed up at your office. That's not much better," Ethan says.

"I know, but it was that one time. The restraining order scared him off after that. I think I'm probably just being paranoid. Let's have our wine and relax."

Ethan looks at me hard.

"What?" I ask, but I already know. The pendulum has swung again.

He shakes his head. "You're *finally* home, and now disgruntled people are showing up at our house? How am I supposed to believe you have any control over how much your job affects us? And it was *not* only that one time. Need I remind you of how long this has been going on, since your first case? How your client's wife wrote you letters for months about how her boys were destroyed by the guilty verdict? And then after he was killed in prison, more letters . . ."

I rub my temples, not wanting to think of that case. Of those letters. "They eventually stopped."

"Oh, I'm sorry, am I irritating you?"

"Ethan," I start, taking him in. The dark circles under his eyes. His rumpled hair. "I was young—like you said, it was my first case when I was new to the firm . . ." But I can still hear the guilty verdict being announced and recall the defeated look in Ed's eyes as he'd stared at me. The way the prosecutor had smirked in my direction. Then the subsequent life-in-prison sentence. I had been sure we'd prevail. But that was the thing—you could never predict what was in the jurors' hearts. To which side they would tumble.

"Please." Ethan rolls his eyes, reminding me of an annoyed teenager. My focus on my career has always been a point of contention.

I walk over and thread my arm through his. "I hear you, and I'm sorry my job has had such an impact. I'm also sorry I didn't take Franklin's stalking more seriously. That I let my work get in the way of our lives. I think I'm exhausted and imagining things. It wasn't her."

"I'm sorry too—I shouldn't have brought up that case. I know how hard it was on you."

"It's all right. You were upset."

He puts his arms around me, and I lean into him, inhaling his scent.

"You're sure you didn't see her outside? That I shouldn't call the police?"

I'm not sure at all. But I tell my last lie of the day (I swear!) and say that I am.

CHAPTER NINE

TUESDAY
CAPTURED

I don't know how long I've been watching the spider on the wall. It crawls, then stops, then inches up a little more, then freezes. This is the spider's entire existence: searching for a way out of this concrete cell, just like me. Only this eight-legged creature actually has a chance. He can crawl through a crevice. He can spin his sticky web high enough to find the best escape route, while my only way out is to use my mind.

Q left 319 minutes ago with no promise of return. He let me eat my bread and take two gulps of water from a bottle he held to my lips, then announced that he had things to do. *What?* I wondered. *Pick up his dry cleaning? Go to the gym? Call his mom?*

He still hasn't taken off his ski mask. And best I can tell from the condition of his hands—smooth, no bulging veins, no age spots—he could be anywhere between twenty and thirty-five years old. His nails are clean and manicured. To me this means he's not someone who works with his hands. He cares about his appearance. It's not much. But at this point, my small observations are all I have to go on.

When I met Ethan, the first thing he said to me was that he felt like I was sizing him up. That my eyes seemed to pierce right through his chest, and he'd felt it physically somehow and had to take an extra breath. He'd said it exactly like that too—that was the author in him, always brushing words onto a beautiful canvas. At the time it struck me as interesting and different, and I was in desperate need of both in my life.

We'd been set up on a blind date by someone I worked with. We'd agreed to meet at a Starbucks in Venice Beach, both of us admitting later that a coffee was all either of us had in us, our dating lives both riddled with one disaster after the next. We were both weary.

"I am sizing you up," I answered, studying his intense brown eyes, his sandy-blond hair, suddenly feeling self-conscious in my jeans and plain white tank top. I glanced at my toes—I should have gotten a pedicure.

"And?" He cocked his head and adjusted his glasses, which I loved immediately—not hipster but not boring. Something perfectly in between.

"You eat healthy and take care of yourself, but exercise is not your friend."

He started to say something, and I kept going. "I don't mean it like you're out of shape. I mean I'm not going to find you on Muscle Beach anytime soon—and that's a good thing."

"Okay, go on."

"You're smart with money—in fact, maybe a bit frugal. Maybe your friends make fun of how cheap you are?"

"Wow—harsh." He grinned. "But true—how did you know?"

"The frayed laces on your shoes—the faded jeans that you *didn't* buy that way."

"Patrick could have told you all this." He paused, referencing the man who had set us up. "But he didn't, did he?"

"Nope." I crossed my arms over my chest.

"You're good. Real good."

"I have to be—it's my job."

"To size up blind dates?"

I let out a short laugh. "No, to make quick but accurate assessments of others. By the end of this date, I'll be able to tell you a lot more."

"So we're staying? Going to order coffee and everything?"

"Yes."

"If you can tell me my drink, I'll buy you dinner."

"What if I don't want to have dinner with you?" I retorted, feeling a rush of blood to my face. Because I'd already decided I very much wanted to have dinner with him.

"I already know you do," he said, now seemingly reading *me*. "You're blushing."

"I'm hot . . ." I fanned my face and looked away.

"Uh-huh." He gave me that look he still gives me, the one that both pisses me off and makes me happy, depending on the scenario.

"Your order is a tall Blonde with raw sugar," I said, wanting to turn the focus back on him.

"Oh, come on. I'm not *that* frugal!" he quipped, but a microexpression passed across his face. He *was* probably that frugal.

I went on, feeling bolder. "In fact, my suggestion we meet at Starbucks probably made you roll your eyes. You strike me as more of a local coffee shop kind of guy. Or maybe a diner? But not an ironic one. A real one. Where you're sitting at the breakfast bar sandwiched between two eighty-five-year-old men enjoying your four-ninety-nine special with bottomless coffee as you write." My prerequisite Facebook stalking had informed me he was a writer. Freelance mostly, as he worked on his novel.

"Guilty as charged." He smiled. "And that is my drink, but no sugar. Trying to stay healthy, as you mentioned earlier."

"Aha!" I held up my finger.

"And that's why they pay you the big bucks." He walked toward the counter to order our drinks.

~

Is Ethan looking for me now? I have no idea how long I've been gone, but I know it's long enough that Ethan *should* be worried. I know if he didn't come home, I'd be out of my mind with concern. Calling everyone we know, police stations, hospitals. In my line of work, I deal with terrible things happening to people every day. I would automatically assume the worst. It's what I do. But Ethan? Would he immediately do those things or assume I hit some bad traffic on the way home? My phone died? I've done it to him before—told him my battery died so I could steal a couple of hours with Sam in a hotel room. Or texted that I was crashing at Carrie's after too much wine. I've lied one time too many, and now could be my penance for those indiscretions. Or what if Q took my phone and texted him something that made him think all is okay? A shiver runs through my body. What if he has no idea I'm in danger? The thought shakes me hard.

Is Sam looking? It's been at least twelve hours but likely a lot more, so my not showing up for work would have alerted him that there could be a problem. I haven't missed a day, save for vacation, in over two years.

Chase will be trying to reach me. Wondering where I am. Of all the men in my life, I seem to count on him the most. He has the best grasp on my life—my schedule, my habits, the intricacies of my every day. In reality, he's my best hope to ring the alarm that something's really wrong. I try not to realize how sad that is. That although I have an intimate relationship with not one but *two* men, it is my assistant who I know will miss me right away.

I hear the now familiar sound of the door being unlocked. Slowly it slides open, and Q walks in. He shuts it behind him and locks it again, this time from the inside. It's a combination lock, and he blocks it so I can't see. Smart, I think. If I were to somehow take him over, knock him out, I couldn't escape because I don't know the combination.

The first thing I notice is that he's changed his clothes. He's wearing black joggers and a quarter-zip long-sleeve Adidas shirt. Different running shoes this time: Nike. A black Apple Watch is now strapped to his wrist. A backpack is slung over one shoulder. He sets it down by the wall and looks at me. He hasn't pulled the mask all the way down, and I can see a bit of dark hair sticking out from the back.

"Hello, Lila Bennett," he says in a mock southern accent, his eyes glowing through the slits in the mask.

My body involuntarily shakes in response. There's something different about Q since the last time he was here.

"Not going to say hi?" He crouches down in front of me. "I can tighten these if I have to," he says as he touches the bindings around my ankles, and I flinch. I can't imagine them any tighter.

"Hi," I manage.

"That's better," he says, then presses his lips together. He looks me up and down, his eyes resting on the bottom of my skirt. I can't cross my legs because of the bindings around my ankles. I wonder what he can see. I look away from him, not wanting to know.

"You look uncomfortable," he says.

No shit, Sherlock.

But I just nod, not wanting to upend whatever nervous energy is going on right now.

"Well, it's time to get comfortable." He pauses and gives me a long look that makes me shudder. When I think I can't take him staring at me for one more second, his grimace turns into a lazy smile. "Darn, I should've brought popcorn. Because I've got something you're going to want to see." He pulls an iPad from his backpack and taps the screen several times. Then he studies me as if he's trying to gauge how I'm going to react.

My heart starts to bang. What's on that iPad? His green eyes are boring into mine with such an intensity I finally have to look away. I take a deep breath to steady myself.

"Are you ready, Lila?" he asks, a sneer forming on his lips as he lowers himself to the floor and sits cross-legged in front of me, the iPad perched on his lap.

I squeeze my eyes shut before opening them again in an attempt to build strength for whatever it is he has in store for me.

CHAPTER TEN

TUESDAY
FREE

As I often do, I wake exactly two minutes before the buzzing of my alarm. It has always amazed me how our minds know things like that, like the way I can almost hear Chase open the door to my office before he actually does or how my skin crawls slightly sometimes when I meet a client, causing me to doubt his innocence before he utters one word.

My wrists ache, and I rub them softly. Did I sleep on them wrong? I search for evidence of the pain—redness, a scratch, wrinkled skin—but they are pale and clear. Odd.

Ethan breathes in and out deeply next to me, curled up in a ball with a pillow over his head. In the past he wouldn't be rising for at least another two hours, not until eight at the earliest. But now that he has his rented writing space, I wonder if he'll wake sooner, if those three thousand words will snowball into three thousand more, and then he'll finally be freed from the prison of his own mind. But a big part of me worries that he'll get stuck again and revert back to his black hole. I know I shouldn't think that way—but this isn't the first time he's had a renewed passion for his writing. Although it is the only time he's found a space other than home to write.

I've never understood the whole writer's block thing. I've often told Ethan that writing a book isn't all that different from arguing a case in court. We are both telling stories.

But I can't afford to freeze up—it could literally mean life or death for my clients. I can't understand how someone could willingly walk away from the pinnacle of his career, to go from an accomplished best-selling author being interviewed by Oprah-fucking-Winfrey to the guy currently twisted into the fetal position in his faded striped boxers.

Hold on, Lila, I admonish myself. *Aren't you supposed to be turning over a new leaf with your husband? Believing that he's really ready to get his career off the ground?* I deliberately avoid the mirror as I pull off my tank top and pajama bottoms and step into the shower, letting the scalding water cascade over my concerns about Ethan's ability to pull himself out of the deep hole he's been in for so long, about my ability to truly put my marriage first. It's easy to say, hard to do. I've had my relationship with Sam playing in the background in every interaction and conversation with Ethan for the past six months, numbing me. Do I know how to jump back in? Do I have the capability of putting aside the resentment that's built inside me like the pressure in that damn Instant Pot Carrie is always going on and on about? Can we move past the way Ethan's moods swing from ecstatic and talkative to brooding silence and then back to neutral?

I guess I'm about to find out.

I'm leaning over the counter delicately applying my mascara when Ethan walks into the bathroom, rubbing his eyes.

"I'm so sorry. Was I too loud?" I've perfected the art of tiptoeing in the morning. I told myself it was because I was being kind, but I've often wondered if part of me was avoiding Ethan by sneaking out before he woke. Not wanting to deal with whatever direction his mood was swinging.

"No, not at all," he says as he squirts toothpaste on his toothbrush. "I'm anxious to get to my work space and back to my manuscript."

"Oh, that's great," I say, trying to conceal my surprise. The last time Ethan was up at six o'clock was when the battery in our smoke detector started chirping, his pillow not enough to drown out the sound.

There you go again, Lila. Being a bitch. Give him a chance to show you he's capable of change.

He finishes brushing his teeth, wipes his mouth, and comes up behind me, pulling my hips to his and placing his lips on my neck. I feel him getting hard. "Got a few minutes to spare?" he whispers.

This also surprises me, because I can't remember the last time we had sex. Wait . . . yes, I can. It was three months ago. We walked to Umami Burger and sat at the counter and shared a truffle burger, onion rings, and several IPAs. We stumbled home, Ethan grasping my arm with one hand and my ass in the other. I was intoxicated, yes, but I was also drunk on his good mood—he'd been dark and dreary for the six weeks prior, some days not getting off the couch. But that night he was the Ethan I adored. He was confident and funny, and oh so in love with me, leaning in close to tell a story like we were the only two people in the place, running his hand over my knee and then slightly farther up my thigh, almost as an invitation for later. Once home, we'd pushed through the front door, not bothering to close it all the way, Ethan holding me up with ease as we moved in sync for what felt like the first time in a long while. After, we lay on the cold hardwood floor intertwined with each other. "We should do this more often," he said, and we both laughed, me silently hoping it was a sign that the old Ethan would finally return to me.

Now I find myself wanting to say no. I need to get to work. Need to find out how my breakup with Sam is going to play out. I need to be strategic. Make sure it doesn't spiral into something bad. Make sure his ego stays intact. But this Ethan, the one poking me with his erection, is a rare thing, like an endangered animal that is only spotted in the wild every so often. If you move wrong, you could scare it away. And the truth is, I wouldn't mind if this Ethan stuck around. Catching a glimpse of him makes me contemplate that we might not be as far off from happy as I'd thought.

I turn and kiss him hard, his mouth tasting like toothpaste. "I always have time for you," I say and lead him back into the bedroom.

I strategically strut into the partners' meeting four minutes late, forcing myself not to glance at the seat at the head of the table, which I'm quite sure is occupied by Sam. I've been hiding in my office since I snuck in around eight o'clock, Chase sitting guard at his desk. I left Ethan smiling and pouring his favorite Colombian coffee into his travel mug, his laptop in his messenger bag next to the door. He said he was right behind me, wanted to get to his new desk by seven thirty. I found myself smiling too as I opened the garage and pulled out onto the busy street. Maybe this is a new beginning for us. For me.

I take my seat next to Adam, another junior partner. As always, his jet-black hair is parted on the side and stuck against his head with what I've always assumed must be some Krazy Glue–like man gel. He's also wearing what I refer to as his uniform, a pair of khakis so stiff they could walk to court without him, a blue blazer, a white shirt, and one of his many bow ties. "It's where I show my personality," he said when I'd once made fun of his Santa Claus–patterned tie.

"You'll offend people who don't celebrate Christmas," I pointed out.

"Stop thinking like a lawyer, Lila. It's what always gets you into trouble." He laughed.

That was ten years ago, and since then we'd developed a rivalry—not always a healthy one—both of us fighting to bill the most hours, to get the best cases, to get anointed partner first. For the record, I had bested him on all three counts, a stat I enjoy rubbing in his face via text often. I reach over and grab a handful of grapes from the plate in front of him.

"Hey!" he hisses. "You'd better have washed your hands."

I lick my fingers in response. "Like this?"

"God, you are so disgusting, Lila." He pushes the bowl toward me. "You can have them. Congrats on the case, by the way."

"Thanks," I say with my mouth full.

"Let's get started," Sam says stiffly and clears his throat. Adam and I shuffle our files and sit up straight in response. "What's on the docket for today?"

Several partners weigh in on current cases. Sam peppers questions here and there but mostly listens and takes a few notes.

"We're moving forward with the Steve Greenwood divorce case," David Croft pipes up a few minutes later. He nods toward me. "Lila has insisted on taking the lead, so I'll oversee. Keep an eye on it here and there."

I snap my head up. That's not what we agreed upon at all. After Steve left, I told David I really didn't feel comfortable as first chair, and we came to the consensus that I would take the meetings with Greenwood and stay up to date to satisfy him but that David would be doing the heavy lifting.

Sam nods his head at me. "Sounds good. Keep me posted on this one."

A sound escapes my throat.

"Lila? You have something to add?" Sam asks, a hint of a smirk dancing on his lips.

I start to protest but notice a quick glance pass between David and Sam. Did Sam convince him to change the lineup, hoping I'd throw a fit in front of the other partners? Or worse, does Sam want me to sabotage my career by botching the divorce of one of our wealthiest clients? His eyes betrayed nothing last night. But now his actions unveil what's behind them: anger.

"Just that I'm really excited to take the case and to get some new experience. Thanks for trusting me with it," I blurt, catching Sam's eye, who winks at me in response before dismissing everyone.

Shit.

I stand up in a daze. Adam touches my arm. "What did you do to piss off Sam?"

"Nothing!" I reply. "Why do you think that?"

"The wink," he says simply. We've both worked here a long time. We know what that wink means. Sam wants to destroy me. "You'd better kill it on that case," Adam adds. "Otherwise . . ."

"I know," I interject. "I'll be toast."

"Speaking of cases, I need to ask you a favor."

"Okay," I say uneasily. Adam never asks me for a favor unless he has an agenda.

"I know that face," he says, flashing me an attempt at a smile, but it looks more like a cross between a smirk and a frown. "But I promise you this request is well meaning."

"Uh-huh," I say as I pick up my folder off the conference room table.

"I've recently been assigned a case, and I need some help on it. I immediately thought of you," Adam says.

I search his face for evidence he is lying, but he actually seems sincere. "Okay, I'm listening."

"It's a drunk driv—"

"Nope," I cut him off and start toward the door.

"Lila, wait . . ."

"Listen, Adam, you could never know this, but I have my reasons for not so much as consulting on a case that involves alcohol and a car and a person."

"But I do know about your past. That's why I asked you," Adam says. "We could use your insight."

"You what? How?" I can feel my cheeks getting hot.

"I'm sorry. I didn't know it would make you so upset."

"What do you know? Tell me." I step toward him.

Adam inches backward. "Listen, I've obviously touched a nerve here. I was told you had a personal experience. Your dad . . ."

"A nerve? You think my dead dad is a nerve?" I can feel the veins in my neck protruding.

Adam holds up his hands, his palms facing me. "Sam mentioned . . ."

That bastard. How dare he! the bad girl voice shouts.

I told you he'd use your secrets against you, the good girl voice says.

I storm out of the conference room before I can hear the rest of Adam's sentence.

～

I allow myself a few hours to calm down before heading to Sam's office. I know he has a thirty-minute break between clients because I forced Chase to barter a Green Nutty Buddy smoothie and Bianco Verde pizza from the Whole Foods down the street with Kylie, Sam's leggy assistant, in return for his schedule. "Is he in?" I ask innocently, and Kylie nods as if she had no idea I'd be showing up.

"Go on in," she says.

"Knock, knock," I say as I enter his office, with its beautiful dark hardwood floors and strong leather chairs. A signed Alex Rodriguez baseball sits on the third shelf of a large oak bookcase—Sam is a huge Yankees fan, having lived in New York City as a child. A sterling silver frame on his desk showcases his love for Carrie. My friend. She's wearing a coral strapless dress that shows off her chiseled arms and heart-shaped face. He's dashing in a charcoal-gray slim-fitting suit and skinny black tie. They're at a wedding of one of our colleagues, midlaugh at a joke I had told. I know this because I was behind the camera, trying to get Sam to smile, knowing it bothered Carrie when he didn't. Later, Sam and I snuck out to the dark alley behind the hotel, and he pulled up my black silk dress and slipped inside me, biting my neck so hard I was terrified it would leave a mark. We were being sloppy, possibly brazen, and in that moment I didn't care, part of me wondering what it would be like to destroy the seemingly perfect life I'd built from scratch. But my tryst with Sam was like an addiction. There was a high associated with taking this risk, like a gambler in Vegas. The question circling as you double down: "Am I going to lose everything right now?" But later that night the guilt seeped in as we sped home in our Uber, Ethan's arm draped over my knee effortlessly. He pulled me into him and took a deep breath, the enormity of my bad decisions hitting me, making me wonder, as I had more than once, what it would take for me to stop gambling with his loyalty.

"Yes?" Sam looks up from the brief he was working on, his dark eyes cold.

I shut the door behind me and lean against it. "Come on, Sam. Don't be like this."

"Like what?" he asks. "Aren't you the one who ended things?"

"I did what was best for both of us. For our careers. For our families." I emphasize that last part. Has Carrie told him she's pregnant? She texted me first thing this morning with a picture of her flat belly and the caption, Can't wait to fill this thing up! with a baby face and bottle emoji next to it.

"You did what was best for you, Lila. Which is pretty much par for the course."

I take a step toward him. "What does that mean? Is that why you told Adam about my dad?"

Sam looks up, his eyes soft. "No, I told him about that last week. I honestly thought . . ."

I turn away from him so he can't see the tears brimming in my eyes. I didn't realize how much rage I'm still holding inside me about what happened.

"Lila, I thought with your past, you'd be able to lend Adam the help he needed in defending our driver. Give us some perspective on what it's like to be on the other side of . . ."

I swivel around, my face reddening again. "You what?" I blurt and realize my voice is louder than it should be. I glance at the door.

"Don't worry about Kylie—she gets paid not to listen," Sam says plainly, and I'm not sure what he's referring to. Us having sex in this office?

"You actually want me to help Adam prepare against the state? To give him expertise on what it feels like to lose someone to a drunk driver?"

"This is *work*, Benn—"

"Don't call me that. Not anymore." I realize I sound like I'm pouting. I look at Sam, who seems pleased. He knows I'm still emotional about the breakup. I'm losing ground.

"If he needs your perspective on this case, you *will* give it to him. You need to leave your personal shit out of this."

"But you want me to get personal, to tell him what it feels like," I say quietly.

"Jesus, Lila. Wasn't this like two decades ago? I'm looking for your perspective. Grow up," he says, and it stings.

I stare at this heartless person as if I'm seeing him for the first time. I knew he wasn't my emotional sounding board—not by any stretch of the imagination—but I didn't see him as callous. But maybe it's because I only told him briefly what happened when he asked whether both of my parents were still alive, and I kept my emotion out of it. Would he have told Adam if he thought I was as affected by it as I am? I guess I'll never know.

When my mom told me my dad was dead, I sobbed into her lap. I heard her saying it was a teenager who'd had too much to drink. "She was sixteen . . ." My mom's voice trailed off.

"That's only three years older than me," I said.

"I know, honey, I know."

I looked up at her then, barely able to see her through my tears. "Is she dead too?" I asked.

"No, she has a broken arm, but other than that, she's okay."

"She should be dead too," I screamed.

"Lila, she's a child."

"She took my dad. She took my dad," I sputtered and ran into my bedroom and slammed the door, crying for what felt like hours into my floral bedspread.

"And Greenwood. That case you will also work on," Sam says, pulling me back.

"I'm not going to know what the hell I'm doing!"

"You'll have David," he says evenly.

"Bullshit. I saw the look that passed between you two. He's going to hang me out to dry, isn't he?"

Sam shrugs and smiles, and I fight the urge to slap him.

"Don't you care that I might bungle the case of one of our most important clients? What that might mean for the firm?"

"It's a tough case that could go either way, even with an expert attorney at the helm. The firm will bounce back. You, on the other hand . . ." He trails off. "It might not be good."

I blink hard. I've always known Sam could be a bastard. I've watched him take out plenty of his enemies, whether they were on opposing counsel or in his way here at the firm. But I've always been under the solid umbrella of his protection. I suppose that, along with our relationship, is over. I ponder telling him about Carrie. The pregnancy. So he can understand why it needed to end. Help him come to his senses. Yes, I'd be betraying her, but what's one more notch on the belt? I open my mouth to share her secret, to explain my sudden change of heart, but I stop short. Carrie trusted me with her husband. With her secret. I failed with the first, but I still have a chance to redeem myself with the latter. I have no idea why she hasn't yet confided in Sam, but she must have her reasons. And I can't screw her over to save myself. Not this time. I'll have to try another way.

I walk over to where he sits, my eyes pleading. "Sam. Did we really mean so little to each other? For you to do this?"

Sam takes me in, his eyes scanning mine. "Bennett, that's what you don't get. I'm doing this *because* it meant something."

And it's then that I get it. I hurt him.

And now he's going to make sure he hurts me right back.

CHAPTER ELEVEN

Tuesday
Captured

It takes me a second to comprehend what I'm seeing.

Men and women in blue uniforms are standing behind Chief Reynolds, his tall frame towering over the podium, the LAPD emblem proudly displayed in front. I recognize the black-and-white-speckled concrete and large glass doors as the entrance to the downtown Los Angeles police station, not far from my office. Somber faces. Microphones. Camera crews. My heart lifts as I recognize that they must be gathered for *me*. They are looking for *me*. Which means they may actually find me.

I gasp as Ethan comes into view, standing back to the right, his full lips in a straight line, his eyes bloodshot and swollen. I ache for him, my body feeling a physical withdrawal, my chest throbbing for every penance, each misstep, every last betrayal hitting me like a strong wave crushing the sand. How silly I've been to think I could have both a man like Ethan, who loves me in the gentlest way, shielding me from pain, and Sam, who drew me in with the power he wielded, possessing me. You have to choose, you know. The power or the peacefulness. You can't have both—at least not for the long term. I understand that now as I watch my husband's shoulders shake as he tries to stay strong. As I take in the crowd waiting to hear what Chief Reynolds has to say, I'm slammed in the heart by my wrongdoings, sitting here bound in this cold and dirty room, trapped by this animal named Q and worse, by my own thoughts.

Chief Reynolds runs a hand through his thick salt-and-pepper hair and begins to speak. "Lila Bennett, a well-known criminal defense attorney, was last seen by her assistant leaving her office right here in downtown LA at approximately six thirty Monday evening. She did not show up at home or at work the next day, missing several appearances in court, which is very out of character, according to those who work with her."

That's true. I don't think I've missed a court appearance or an appointment in years, once throwing up in a trash can before an important deposition when I had the stomach flu. When I didn't arrive this morning, Chase was probably fine at first. I can see him texting me, then calling, then finally starting to worry when after an hour or two I still didn't respond. I was always reachable via my cell. I remember when I interviewed him four years ago, his slicked-back thick blond hair and expensive black suit unable to hide the fact that he couldn't have been older than twenty-three. But he swore that day that if I hired him, he'd make my life easier. There was something about the way he said it, like he knew he had the job. How he looked me in the eye and held my gaze. His tight grip on my hand as he shook it before he thanked me for my time. I concentrate and try to recall my calendar from Tuesday in my mind. Who did I fail to show up for? But I can't—the lack of food, sleep, and water have depleted my memory.

An outline of a thought sweeps through my bleary mind like a shooting star. I blink hard and try to grasp it, because I know it's important. I push a long breath out, and it comes to me: Chase wasn't the last person to see me—Sam was. Why don't the authorities know that? Have they not interviewed Sam? Or worse, when he spoke to the police, did he omit that we'd been at Bestia? There are CCTV cameras everywhere—they could figure out we were there together even if he didn't. Couldn't they? Did they look at the security cameras in the parking garage of the office? If so, they'd see that Sam and I talked before both leaving at the same time. Is he so intent on protecting himself, worried our affair will get out, that he'd withhold pertinent information that could help the investigators find me? Do I mean that little to him?

I look at Q, who is fixated on the iPad. Who is he? Why does he have me locked in this room? The questions are on repeat in my mind. I want to scream at him, *Are you getting off on the fact my disappearance is on the news?*

"Have you checked the cameras in the parking garage?" a reporter in the crowd asks. *Thank you.*

The chief rubs his temple. "They were disabled. The last footage we have is from hours before she was last seen."

My heart sinks.

Q smirks. "What can I say? I'm camera shy. And I didn't think you'd want everyone to see you left the garage with your boyfriend. So really, I was doing you a favor."

"By our count, she has been missing a little less than twenty-four hours," the chief continues. "Her car, purse, and phone are all missing."

"Where are they?" I turn and ask Q.

"You really are a stickler for details, aren't you?" Q rolls his eyes. "I took a nice little drive after I dropped you here. Parked the car on some random street up near the Burbank airport. Street sweeping is on Friday, so they'll probably find it then."

"You parked it near the airport—"

"To make them question whether you took off on your own? Of course," he interjects.

"The purse and phone?" I ask.

"Incinerator. Man, you should have seen how stubborn that Louis Vuitton leather was! Took forever to melt!" He scratches his chin. "No wonder it's so pricey. It's practically indestructible!"

I cringe at the thought of two very important pieces of evidence to help find me going up in flames. I pray they find the Range Rover quickly and that Q left some DNA in there.

"Why are you already holding a press conference if it's been less than a day? She's an adult. What's to say she didn't take off, decided she needed some space from her life? Are you really going to use taxpayer money on this?"

A flicker of annoyance flashes in the chief's eyes, but he clears his throat and begins to answer. "I cannot comment on the decisions we make about an ongoing investigation. But what I will tell you is her family and coworkers are very worried about her and suspect foul play. So we are considering all options."

"A lot of people suspect foul play when their loved ones go missing and don't get a press conference hosted by the chief of police himself," the reporter clips.

The chief ignores the accusation, and I'm grateful. Because I didn't get bored with my life and take off. There *was* foul play involved, and I'm in serious danger. Q smiles, clearly finding amusement in the reporter's words, pursing his lips as if he'd say the same thing if he could. The police must know more than they are letting on about my case, because it's early to be having a press conference. For the police to have already spoken to my coworkers and family. But it's not about special treatment. The chief and I are far from best friends. I've often heard through the grapevine he's not a huge fan of mine, as we work on opposite sides of the courtroom, me often getting off the very people he'd like to see behind bars. So, to the reporter's point, why is he holding a press conference? Perhaps it's because I'm a high-profile attorney and possibly considered a minor celebrity because I'm often interviewed on the local news? Or perhaps the timing of Jeremiah's high-profile acquittal made me more newsworthy.

The camera pans out, and I spy Detective Sully standing next to my mom. Only I might notice, but I can see the watchful look in his eyes, the way he's standing, holding his shoulders back. He's being protective of her—and me. Sully had been my ally in the department for years—he had helped my mom with an unruly neighbor a few years back, and they've been friendly ever since. As I see them standing tall just off to the side of the podium, I realize that those two may be the reason for the premature press conference. Sully calling in favors and my mom's persistence may have tipped the scales the right way. The thought gives me a small sliver of hope.

"If you have any information about the whereabouts of Lila Bennett, please call this number . . ." the chief says, and the camera pans to a blown-up photo of me with a 1-800 number under it. I let out an involuntary chuckle, causing Q to whip his head in my direction. He pauses the video.

"You think this is funny?" he growls, his eyes growing a deeper shade of green, his fists clenching. "Because if you're having fun, if you think you're on a fucking vacation, we can make this much more uncomfortable."

We. There's that word again. He hasn't admitted to working with someone, but I highly doubt he's in this alone. Simply because I'm now sure, after all our interactions, that I don't know him. I can't see his full face, but I've studied his demeanor, his voice, the things he's said. I would bet that he's nothing more than a mouthpiece.

He hovers over me, and I start to tremble. He could be insane for all I know. The type of guy who could snap me in two in a heartbeat, then go to dinner with his friends. What if he loses his patience with me? Is he authorized to kill? To torture? My voice shakes when I speak. "I'm sorry I laughed. It's the picture they used," I say, nodding toward the screen, which is frozen on my face, my wide, toothy smile and sparkling eyes a huge contrast to what I must look like now. Actually, if I'm being honest, a huge contrast to what I look like most days. It's the photo of me in the pink romper in the dressing room at H&M. The one my mom begged me to try on. Tears spring from my eyes before I can push them back. God, what I wouldn't give to have my mom burst in here and tell me how tired I look and ask if I've been eating dairy again because I look *a little bloated*. I'd do anything to hear a lecture on how milk isn't good for my digestion and that the gut is the brain of the body. I've always told Ethan how much I hate clichés, refusing to use them in my opening or closing arguments, but right now they're all I can think of—how you don't know what you've got until it's gone, how absence makes the heart grow fonder.

Turns out, most of them are true.

Q is still gaping at me, waiting for what, I don't know. So I keep talking, choking on the words through my sobs. "It's . . . that of course my mom picked that picture . . ." The silence in the room is starting to suffocate me as I watch Q watching me. Why won't he say something? Why is he looking down at me, his eyes squinting through the slits in his mask? I start to cry harder now, unable to wipe the tears from my eyes with my bound hands, instead shaking my head and sending my arms plummeting to the floor, the cuffs making small marks on the concrete. I cringe from the pain that sears through my wrists. "I miss her. I lost my dad when I was young, and I'm all she has."

"I know all about your dad," Q says, his tone sharp, bordering on scathing.

I jerk my head up at him. Something about the way he says this sounds different from when he brought up the other people in my life he has so much information about.

"How can you possibly be angry at me for my dad being dead?" I ask, something inside me giving me the courage to challenge him.

"Oh, I'm not upset with you about that," he says, letting his statement float there between us like a balloon that's about to fly away if one of us doesn't grab it.

I do. I can't help myself. "Oh?" I question, deliberately making my reaction as neutral as possible.

"I know your dad lost his life to a teenage drunk driver who got off with barely a slap on the wrist."

"True," I say simply and try to disregard the sharp jab to my heart. "You could have googled that. Big deal."

"And maybe I did," he says, then moves his head side to side, his neck cracking in the process. "But what I don't get, Lila, what is so very odd to me, is why you didn't become a prosecutor, taking on the drunks and the thieves and the murderers who get away with so many bad things. Why you chose to represent the accused. The ones who may or may not have been guilty. It's odd to me, your choice. Maybe your dad didn't mean anything to you? Money mattered more? Prestige?" He stares at me in a way that causes me to turn my head. "Am I right?" I hear him say.

I press my lips together as hard as I can and close my eyes, suppressing a scream. My first year of law school, when I wasn't yet sure what type of law I was going to practice, my mom came to my apartment in Marina Del Rey to catch up. We hadn't seen each other in a few weeks, as I'd been slammed with papers. She brought two bottles of rosé and takeout from my favorite deli. She suggested we stay in for the night and chat and watch *Sex and the City*—it was a Sunday night, when groups of girls gathered around their TVs watching HBO. In hindsight, I should have known she had an agenda. Showing up with two bottles of wine on what would have been my dad's fifty-sixth birthday. Another date that had somehow escaped me until she pointed it out. It was that evening she told me about his many affairs. We were into the second bottle of wine and watching the season finale—the one where Carrie first meets Aleksandr Petrovsky, or "the Russian," as we'd come to know him. Then she blurted it, or at least it seemed like it had popped out. Maybe the Russian's reputation for sleeping around gave my mom her opening.

It felt like someone was sitting on my chest, pressing all the air out of my lungs. I could barely breathe, let alone respond. My mom took my silence as an opportunity to keep talking. And over the next several minutes, as I heard about fling after fling—this one emotional, that one physical—the image of the man I had idolized during the twelve years I knew him and in the ten years since his death was forever tarnished. I could not polish him up again. My mom had started crying at some point, but I was numb. Feeling as if everything I knew had been a lie. Worried she was going to reveal something about herself that would also ruin my image of her. I chose criminal defense shortly thereafter, deciding you never really knew anyone.

"You're not right, Q. Not by a mile, but you could never understand."

Q opens his mouth, then closes it. His eyes harden, and I wonder, *When he leaves me here, who is waiting for him at home? Who are his friends? Who is his family? Does he have a wife or girlfriend who is oblivious to this side of him? A mother or father who thinks the world of him? Or is he all alone, his dark side having pushed everyone away?*

Before I can ask him, he taps the iPad, and the video begins to play once more.

"There is a reward, and the family spokesperson is going to give more details."

The camera pans over to Ethan, so close that I can see the lines etched on his forehead. He hasn't slept.

I flinch slightly. Again, my actions are hurting him. Guilt mixes with fear and anxiety, and I close my eyes for a moment to retain whatever composure I have left.

My mom has moved and is now standing next to Ethan, his dark-blue shirt freshly ironed, tucked into his favorite pair of gray pants, the belt I gave him for his birthday last year wrapped around his waist.

Seeing him hits me hard. My heartbeat speeding up as I take him in—dressed for the cameras, dressed for me? Wishing desperately I could read his mind—know what he is thinking as he leans into my mom. She has her arm around him, almost as if she's propping him up. And I realize, as I take in her peach sweater and navy-blue pants, that I have forgiven her for telling me. Maybe it wasn't the best choice, but it was the one she felt she needed to make. I can certainly relate to making bad choices. I bite my lip to keep from bursting into tears again and decide that having the people you love most being so close, yet so far away, is the worst kind of torture. I'd much prefer some waterboarding right now. My chest bursts open, and I force myself to steady my breathing. There'll be time to fall apart later, when Q leaves—if he leaves. I'll cry until there are no tears left, if I can.

I wait for my mom to step forward to the mic, but to my surprise it's Carrie who walks up, clutching a stack of flyers. I'm not sure where she's come from, as the camera didn't show her before. But it's a relief to see her face. She's wearing the mint-green top I bought for her birthday last February, and I feel a stab of hope. Is she sending me a message by selecting it for this event? Is this her silent way of telling me not to give up? The camera zooms in, and I'm not surprised that her eyes are clear and bright. I've always said, whether it's chairing the local chapter of Mothers Against Gun Violence or simply fighting for the best table at Nobu, when the shit hits the fan (can't stop with the clichés now), I want Carrie on my team. People, sometimes even Sam, often mistake her shiny personality as a weakness. I asked him why he'd ever cheat on her—she caters to his every need: his laundry is handled and folded, fine-tuned organic meals are on the table when he walks in the door, she makes delightful conversation with his colleagues. *Because she's weak, Bennett. Not like you. You're strong,* he said. It was then I realized he might not know either of us as well as he thought he did. Because I'd always understood I was the weak one. The one who was sleeping with her best friend's husband. The one who was attracted to him for the very reason he thought he was attracted to me—because he was strong. He didn't let me be vulnerable and weak like Ethan did. With Sam, I felt bulletproof even though I sometimes felt like I could be pierced by the lightest of feathers. And I had realized long ago that underneath Carrie's perfect veneer lay a Teflon coating. She didn't need Sam to be strong.

I see it now as she speaks. It was smart for my family to choose her. Ethan is clearly a mess. And my mom is clearly his comfort. "We are offering a two-hundred-and-fifty-thousand-dollar reward for Lila Bennett's safe return or for any information that leads to finding her," Carrie says, holding up the flyer with my picture and the word *reward* in bold. "Please," she pleads. "We want her home safe." She looks directly into the camera. "Lila, if you are watching this, we are doing everything we can to bring you back home. Please hang on. We're coming for you."

She chokes on the last part, a tear escaping from her eye, and I force myself not to cry with her, the knowledge that I will probably never see any of them again hitting me hard. Because the other thing they say about someone who's been missing for more than twenty-four hours, which I'm sure has passed by now, is that they're usually not found. And the other reason I know I'm screwed? There was nothing said about a ransom demand. There's a chance that's because the police don't want to reveal this to the public. But something about the look on Q's face tells me there was no mention of it because no one wants to exchange me for money.

Which means I must be here to suffer. To die.

CHAPTER TWELVE

TUESDAY
FREE

So many different thoughts and emotions are swimming inside my head when I burst out of Sam's office and slam the door that I plow right into Carrie. "Oh my God, I'm so sorry," I say, then find myself peering at her stomach, as if knocking into her has done something to the baby.

"It's okay, I'm fine," Carrie says, following my gaze. She reaches down and picks up her bag, which fell to the floor in our collision.

I glance back at Sam's door, but it's still closed. He must not have heard the commotion or is pretending he didn't. Either way, I'm relieved he hasn't come out.

"You looked upset when you charged out of there . . ." she says.

Her statement or question—I'm not sure which—hangs in the air longer than I want it to. But I'm frazzled, finding it hard to grasp any words that will explain why I clearly *was* upset. If I tell her he's making my life hell at work, I won't be able to tell her why. But if I don't give her a reason, it's going to look worse. She might wonder, *Why was my best friend so emotional when she came out of my husband's office?* Or at least that's what I would think. But Carrie . . . Carrie is different. She has a loyalty to Sam, to me, that seems to wash away any cynicism.

"It's about a case," I finally say, knowing it's weak. That she should be able to see right through it.

"Attorney-client privilege. Believe me, I get it." She tucks a strand of her hair behind her ear.

"I wish I could tell you, Care," I say, meaning it. I would do anything to be able to heave this rock of guilt off my chest. But the only person who would feel better after would be me. And that would be selfish. Despite what my track record would indicate, I do love Carrie; I do appreciate her as a friend.

I think of the time I had bronchitis last year. I had a trial starting in a few days, so I couldn't stay home. So she brought home to me. Chicken noodle soup, water, homeopathic oils, a humidifier. I stare at her full pink lips, her big blue eyes, and I wonder what kind of person I must be to be able to betray someone I love. Who loves me. Who has been nothing but a good friend to me.

The Monday after we met at the holiday party, Carrie called me. I was surprised but also excited to hear from her. She wanted to take me out for lunch and make sure I was okay after what happened with the senior partner. But I remember hesitating, being afraid that I couldn't be the friend she was hoping for. As we'd sat out on the rooftop and finished off that cigarette, she'd mentioned she'd found it hard to make friends after she and Sam moved to the Palisades a few years before. They'd relocated from New York, and she said she felt like she was in high school all over again. I knew she was taking me for a test drive—would we connect while sober, while away from her husband's and my workplace? And it turns out we did. We talked nonstop for two hours, waving our hands in the air as we told our very best stories. I'd called the office to cancel my afternoon appointment. As we'd hugged goodbye at the end of our meal, I vowed that I would be loyal. That I wouldn't betray her the way I had Janelle. This friendship would be different. And it was, for the first three and a half years. And then Sam kissed me.

As I think about the two people in my life I've screwed over without much deliberation, the resonating guilt is a slow build. I might be a terrible person.

"I know, I get it. I shouldn't have asked. But I worry about you," Carrie says, interrupting my thoughts.

"Thanks," I say, noticing a huge scuff on the toe of my red pump. I make a mental note to have Chase order another pair. It's out of his job description, but he insists on doing it. He tells me he's proud of how his fashion influence has changed me. Because of him, I've agreed to wear heels that are colorful. But I still refuse to stray from what he calls my bland suit palette of black and gray. *That's our next hurdle*, he always says.

"What are you doing here?" I ask Carrie. "Not that I'm complaining. But two days in a row? We might need to put you on the payroll."

Carrie hesitates for a moment, and I see something pass across her face. Like she's not sure she wants to tell me. Finally, she leans in. "I was a real bitch to Sam yesterday, so I brought him cheese rolls from Porto's as a sorry."

I have never seen Sam eat a cheese roll in my life.

"I also wanted to check on you," she adds quickly. Her phone buzzes, and she looks at it, then drops it in her purse.

"Need to get that?" I ask.

"Nope," she says.

"So why are you wanting to check on me?" I ask, my heart beating faster.

"I texted you a couple times, and I called," Carrie says as a colleague passes by us in the hall. We move into the break room, which is adjacent.

"You *called*?" I say, leaning against the wall and eyeing the Keurig. Caffeine is exactly what I need right now.

"Yeah, I did." She breaks into a grin. "People still do that."

"Did you leave a voice mail?" I smile back and walk over to the machine and make a cup of coffee.

"I'm not *that* old school." She laughs.

"Want one?" I ask. "There is decaf—and tea."

She shakes her head but opens the fridge and grabs a bottle of Fiji. "This is all I need. I swear I'm so much thirstier. Have you ever heard that?" She drops her voice. "Pregnancy makes you thirsty?"

"I have no idea, but I'm sure it does!" I say, then take a long drink of my coffee. "So what was up? Why did you call?"

"I've missed hanging out. Wanted to make plans. Are you free tonight?"

I shake my head. "Dinner with Ethan and my mom."

"Ah, the last Tuesday of the month! How is Alexis?"

"The usual. Wants me to quit my job. Work as a lawyer for a non-profit. Or maybe become a prosecutor. Get the bad guys instead of save them."

Carrie gives me a look.

"What?" I ask. But I know what she's going to say.

"She's not totally wrong, you know."

"Not you too," I say playfully. "You're married to a criminal defense attorney!"

"I know. Why do you think I agree with your mom? She means well, is all I'm saying. If she'd seen you so upset over a case like I did, it would only concern her more."

"I get it. I do," I say, thinking about my meeting with Steve Greenwood tomorrow. My gut has been knotted about this case—only tightening more after my conversation with Sam. I need to read over Greenwood's file again—hopefully I'll find something that makes me feel better about representing him. That helps me see his side. "But I have responsibilities."

"Your mom doesn't need you to take care of her. She has a pension. Her place is paid off. She'll be fine."

I shake my head. "It's not only about money. It's hard to explain . . ." I think about my dad. About all the recent doubts I've been having about this job.

She takes a small sip of water. "It's the drive. You can't stop until you're at the very top. Until you've knocked everyone else off." Her words are slightly harsh, but her expression stays neutral. "Sorry," she says when I don't respond immediately. "I see the same thing with Sam. With everyone who works here."

I know she's right, at least partially. But it's always uncomfortable when she aligns me with Sam. "I hear you, but I don't know how to change at this point," I say, more to myself than to her.

"What time are you guys having dinner?" she asks, changing the subject.

I shrug. "Depends on when I get out of here. Then I have to go home and get Ethan."

"Isn't it easier for you to meet there?" she asks. "Because of traffic," she adds, checking something on her phone.

"I was going to take the 10 straight out to Santa Monica, grab Ethan, and then take PCH down. But I could take the 110 to the 105 to the 405, I guess, and meet him there. But without the carpool lane . . ."

"This is such an LA conversation to be having." Carrie pretends to stick her finger down her throat. "Can you grab a drink before you go home?"

"I wish. But you and I both know what will happen. One will lead to two, and I won't make it to my mom's. Then she'd kill me. How about tomorrow night?"

"Perfect," she says, then types something into her phone again. "I have to go," she says, tossing her empty water bottle into the recycle bin. "Blast Zone class. You have to come try one with me—like I said, the first time is free."

"You are really into this," I say.

"Well, my coach is also really good." She smiles, then catches my look. "I don't mean it like *that*."

"It's okay, a little flirting never hurt anyone." There were so many moments with Sam before we crossed the line. Running into him in the law library, joking about carrying books the size of me. Banter in the break room. Coming to my office with things he would normally task to his assistant.

"Oh, I would *never*," she says seriously. "But he does have the most interesting eyes. Hard not to stare." She blushes slightly. "Anyway, I should go. If you don't get there early, you can't start on the treadmill."

"Wait—weren't you on your way to see Sam? The cheese roll peace offering?" I ask.

"I'll drop it to his assistant and talk to him later. If you're upset about the case, I'm sure he is too, and it might not go well. I'll text you about a time and place for tomorrow."

"Okay, thanks—I'm looking forward to it," I say, although I'm relieved she's leaving. I watch her walk out of the kitchen, and then I slump into a chair, sipping my coffee, thinking about all the things that are weighing me down. I notice a small spider making his way up the wall by a trash can that's in dire need of being emptied. A strange sensation passes through me that feels similar to déjà vu. Like I've been here before. I can't seem to look away until he crawls through an opening in the baseboard and disappears.

My phone buzzes with a text from Chase.

Greenwood is here

What? Our meeting is tomorrow.

He says he needs to see you now. That David told him it would be fine.

I grit my teeth and fight the urge to storm into David's office and tell him exactly what I think of this.

I'll be right there. I let out a long breath as I stare at the screen, watching as Chase's response comes in. I'm smart. There has to be a way out of this.

Chase sends the red-faced Muppet devil emoji, and I send back an LOL. It's a perfect representation of Greenwood.

Chase is going to ask why in the world they've made me the lead on this case. Especially when it's obvious I don't want it. And I'm going to have to lie—again. So much for my vow to stop. And as much as I'd love to confide in Chase, it's better if he doesn't know.

When I reach my office, Greenwood is pacing in front of Chase's desk. Chase rolls his eyes, and I suppress a smile when Greenwood almost catches him.

"About time, Bennett," Greenwood says, tapping his gaudy gold watch. I bite my lower lip, thinking of Sam—that was his nickname for me. Only when it slips off Steve Greenwood's tongue, it sounds like fingernails on a chalkboard. I take him in—his almost entirely gray thick hair is in need of a cut, too long around his ears, skirting his forehead, with bushy eyebrows to match. His cheeks are ruddy and full. His beady eyes almost get lost in his face. I'm not quite sure where his chin ends and his neck begins. He's wearing an expensive black blazer, and underneath is a white button-down that hugs his gut and is tucked into faded jeans. He's finished the terrible look off with a pair of scuffed cowboy boots.

"Hello," I say, ignoring his remark. "Come on in." I walk into my office, and he follows. "I thought our meeting was tomorrow?" I ask as I sit in my chair.

"It is, but I've moved it up." He smiles, exposing a top row of yellowish teeth. I've seen pictures of his wife; she's attractive. A petite brunette who looks like she could rival Carrie at that Blast Zone place she joined. What drew her to him? I recall from the file that they've been married a decade and have twin five-year-old boys. He's originally from Texas, his family's wealth tied to oil. About ten years ago he and the family moved out here and bought a string of car dealerships, leaving his brother to run the company in Texas.

"So I heard."

"Well, it seems like good timing. You don't appear to have much going on." He motions toward my desk—the only items on it my laptop, a picture of Ethan and me, and a container full of pens. I think of the million replies I could fly at him, but I bite my tongue. I can't fight back. And clearly he knows it.

"Listen, I'll get right to the point." Greenwood leans forward. "Every day I'm still married to this woman, she has access to my money, which she is spending like the world is about to end." His face turns redder than it already is. "Also, since our last meeting, I've discovered she's been fucking around with some guy in her book club for at least a year. *Book club.* A dude sitting around with a bunch of chicks. I can only imagine what he's like. Not to mention she's been a terrible mother to the boys. She doesn't make them a proper meal. She doesn't go to the grocery store. My sons have been eating fucking Froot Loops for dinner. She doesn't drive them or pick them up from any of their activities. She tells them to *Uber.* And I'm pretty sure it's because she's drunk. The neighbors have told me she's tipsy when the kids come home from school at three o'clock. I do not think they should be living with her. So I want primary custody. When can we get in front of a judge?" He slaps his hand on my desk, and I jerk my head back, startled by his aggression.

My armpits dampen with sweat. There's something about him, the way he's ranting, his nostrils flaring, that makes my stomach lurch.

"You're going to have to be quicker than this in court," he adds before I can respond.

I take a deep breath, grasping the last bit of patience I have left. "Listen, I was prepared to meet with you *tomorrow*, and *tomorrow* I will be ready to answer all of your questions, and we'll put together a solid plan for the preliminary hearing on *Friday*. I appreciate the additional information you have brought me, and I will consider it."

"Consider it?" he huffs, shooting up out of his chair. I glance behind him and notice Chase watching us. He nods toward the door, wondering if he should come in. I shake my head quickly.

"What I mean by that is I will factor it into my plan for your case. I need to talk with your wife's—"

"Ex-wife." He balls his hands into fists at his side.

"I need to talk with her attorney. See what she's asking for. What her side is. If we can settle out of court."

"We're not settling. She doesn't have a side. My side is the truth. She's a money-grubbing bitch. Plain and simple. I want the boys. I want the house. And I don't want to pay her a fucking dime. Can you handle that? Or do I need to call Sam?"

My head is suddenly throbbing. We're just getting started, and Greenwood already seems much more demanding than my other criminal defense clients, which is saying a lot. Those people are literally fighting for their freedom. This guy wants to be free of the woman he married. I rub the back of my neck. I'm stuck with this man. I can't quit—Sam and David have made that impossible. I can't admit I've handled only a handful of divorce cases early in my career, because Greenwood expects me to be like the lawyers in those goddamned TV shows who handle corporate litigation one day and a murder case the next. And yes, there are real lawyers, jacks of all trades, who do that kind of thing. And if I were getting the help David had initially promised, I'd probably be fine. If this was a client who would be reasonable and willing to compromise and settle, I would be able to skate a little bit. But Steve Greenwood wants a fight. And I have to give him a good one, or my reputation will be forever tainted. And that will mean Sam wins. That, I cannot allow to happen.

"I need you to let me do my job, Mr. Greenwood."

He scoffs. "Fine. But I'm still coming back tomorrow, and you'd better bring your A game." He flies out of my office without saying another word, and I slide back into my chair and put my head in my hands.

"You okay?" Chase asks.

I look up at him, study his hazel eyes framed by perfectly arched eyebrows. He couldn't be more opposite of the maniac who left my office moments ago. I want to tell him that no, I'm not okay. Not by a long shot. But of course I can't do that. My heart burns as I think about how alone I really am. "He's an ass. God, I could never be a divorce attorney," I say.

"Then why represent him?"

"I'm not just representing him; I'm now the lead on the case. Sam is insisting upon it," I say and look down, not wanting to meet Chase's eyes. I've always wondered if he suspected our affair. How could he not? Chase notices if I forget to apply my green tea eye cream the night before, frowning at the tiny creases the next morning as I soar in for my first meeting. There's no way he hasn't noticed the stolen looks, the electricity that passes between me and Sam when we're in the same room.

"Why? What about David?"

"I don't know—maybe his plate is too full. Sam told me it needed to be me, and it wasn't up for discussion."

"I guess we're going to need to read up on divorce law in California." He smiles.

"We sure are." I laugh.

"Fuck that devil Muppet."

"Yeah, fuck him. What would I do without you?"

"You would wear boring-ass shoes," he deadpans.

"These are scuffed pretty bad, actually." I show him.

He shakes his head. "Girl, what am I going to do with you?"

"Order me another pair?"

"Done," he says and makes a note on his phone.

"Thank you. So devil Muppet is coming back tomorrow, and we need to be ready. I'd like to have our investigator follow his wife. I need to know if the things he is accusing her of are true."

"I'm on it. Do you need anything else right now?"

"A shot of tequila?" I smile wanly and glance toward the cabinet where we keep a secret stash for these sorts of occasions.

Chase shakes his head. "After work?"

"I can't. Dinner with my mom and Ethan." I glance at my phone. "Shit! How is it already five o'clock? I have to go."

"Really? Because we have so much work to do to prepare for tomorrow."

"I know, but I can't cancel on my mom—again." I think about the last time I was supposed to have dinner with her. I called an hour before I meant to arrive, and she was not happy. Especially when I told her I was stuck at work. "I'll come in super early tomorrow."

"What time? I'll meet you here."

"You don't have to do that," I say.

He gives me a look. "I'm coming, and I'll have coffee. Six a.m.?"

I nod, grateful.

"Now go see Mama. You're lucky to have her. I have a private investigator to brief."

"You're the best."

"I know. That's why you pay me the big bucks."

It's true. We do. Before Sam turned on me, I begged him to help me get Chase a huge raise, making him the highest-paid assistant at the firm. *Someone has to fund those tailor-made suits*, I told Chase.

As I walk to the elevator bank, I'm stabbed with guilt. I shouldn't leave Chase at work. I should go back into my office and make sure I'm ready for my meeting with Greenwood tomorrow. If I'm not prepared, it will only make the situation worse. But how do I explain that to my mom—who already wants me to quit? Who already texted me to confirm I'll be in her kitchen in the adorable townhome I'd bought her, the down payment coming from my first year's bonus, by 7:30 p.m. on the nose? I pause by the elevator, debating.

My phone buzzes.

Can't wait to see you!

God, my mother has radar.

Before I can respond, she sends three pink heart emojis, and my heart sinks. She is an expert at emoji guilt.

Can't wait, I type, then press the elevator button. When the doors part, I'm relieved to find it empty. When I reach the parking level, I step out into the garage, which is mostly dark. Several of the lights are out, and the one that is working is flickering. It is so quiet, I can hear myself breathing. There are still a lot of cars, as it's only five o'clock—early for the workaholic crowd in this building. But I can't shake the feeling that I'm not alone. I glance around, but all the cars appear dark, no one inside any of them as far as I can tell. I walk quickly to mine and open it, locking the doors behind me. I start the car and grip the steering wheel. Nervous energy balls in my stomach. I check the monitor on my backup camera, then glance over my shoulder, reversing quickly. As I head out of the garage, another car's headlights go on in the row behind where I was parked. In a car I'm sure had been empty. I glance in my rearview mirror, but I can't see the driver because of the low lighting. The car pulls out but seems to keep its distance as I wait for the security arm to rise. Am I being followed?

I gun it and take a quick right, not wanting to find out.

CHAPTER THIRTEEN

TUESDAY
CAPTURED

Rage burns hot inside me as I stare at the iPad. Q has stopped the video on a shot of Ethan hugging my mom, his head buried in the shoulder of her peach sweater. Carrie squeezing his hand. Reporters swarming the three of them. I imagine my anger as a swirling ball of fire that is making its way up my body, soon to ignite and explode with the words I want so desperately to scream: *Why, why are you showing me this video? Why do you have me here? Are you going to kill me?*

But I know I need to control myself. To restrain myself from spewing the venomous things that are poised to launch from my mouth. I force myself to look at this masked man who is taunting me with my husband, my mother, my best friend. How can any human do this to another? Although I have seen worse in my line of work. And because of this, what I've come to know about the depths of a sociopath's soul, I'm terrified of what Q may be capable of. Still, controlling my emotions seems impossible.

The minutes have felt like hours. The hours like days. The police chief said I've been missing under twenty-four hours, but it feels like years. Not to mention I don't know when the press conference happened. It's impossible to keep time, no matter how hard I try. Did it happen days ago? Part of me wishes Q would get it over with already. Put me out of this misery. This despair. The unknowing is almost worse than my fears of what's coming.

But as I'm opening my mouth, the fabric of his mask expands to accommodate his grin. He reaches into the inside pocket of his black Adidas track jacket and slowly pulls his arm back out, deliberately taking his time. It's obvious he wants the drama, the show. He wants me to feel scared. Unsure. But again, why? Who is he, and how is he connected to me?

Finally he jerks his hand out like a magician pulling back the cloth. He's holding a gun.

My anger freezes as quickly as it formed, and I'm hollow with fright. It's amazing how fast that can happen—your emotions swinging from one extreme to the other.

I'm numb now as I stare at the sleek black weapon that Q is stroking like a puppy.

So this is it. My answer.

"Are you going to kill me? Is that why you have me here?"

Q laughs, but it comes out clipped, like he wasn't expecting it, confusing me more. Each time I think I have him pegged, he changes direction. "Shut the fuck up."

"Y-you have a gun," I stammer, hating the shakiness in my voice. How vulnerable I am.

He watches me for a moment, sees my fear, smiles again. This was the goal. But again, why? If he's going to murder me, why not just do it?

Which means maybe he's not going to end my life. Maybe there's another plan. He might not be holding me for ransom but for something else. That introspection punches the fear back into my gut, understanding that there are things much worse than death.

"Wow, nothing gets by you, observant one. No wonder you're such a successful attorney." He bends down in front of me and strokes my bare leg with the gun, teasing the bottom of my skirt with the barrel. The weapon is lighter than I would have thought—but the heaviness of what it represents is still there, my leg tensing from its touch. My eyes sting with tears.

Maybe he *is* going to murder me. I think of the people I've hurt. The other mistakes I made, long before my affair with Sam. The wrongs I won't have time to right. He moves the gun to my chin.

"Please," I mutter.

"Please kill you?" He jabs the barrel against my neck. "Because there's no doubt you deserve it."

"No . . . no, please don't." My lips shudder, and a tear rolls from my eye. If he pulls that trigger right now, oh my God. Will it be quick, like a light bulb that pops and goes dark? Or will the pain shoot through me like a lightning bolt? Will I watch myself bleed out as I desperately pray to a God I've ignored for years to save me? Will he hear my pleas? I'd never put that much thought into what the afterlife might look like, but now the options race through my mind. I can hear my heart drumming in my ears. I can feel the blood pumping through me, like my body is reminded how very alive it is right before . . .

He jams it in harder, and I try to scream, but my throat is closed. I can't speak. I can't beg for my life. I squeeze my eyes shut, and he squeezes the trigger.

There is a click.

Q's laughter is loud. Obnoxious. He's doubled over. "You should have seen your face. Did you shit your pants? I bet you shit your pants."

My heart is still ramming, my body not understanding what my mind does: The gun is not loaded. Or if it is, the bullet was not in that round. He could be playing Russian roulette with my life. The tears are falling now, hard and fast. I don't care what Q thinks of this. He wanted to make me feel weak, helpless. He has succeeded.

"So now that I have your attention, I'll tell you why I have this beauty here." He pets the pistol again. "Consider it a reminder of how powerless you are. Of how you've used your own power in the past to ruin people." He glares at me.

As if I needed another reminder.

He puts the gun in the front waistband of his track pants. "How was it to see your family? Your best friend?" His words are sharp, tinged with anger.

I barely hear his question, the sound of the gun clicking still ringing in my ears. I'm still alive. But for how long?

"I asked you a question," he says, putting his hand over the gun in his pants. A sign of what he could have done. Of what he could still do.

I stare at his mask, wondering again who is behind it. Who would kidnap me, restrain me, play Russian roulette with my head? I swallow hard, trying to decide how to answer him, what combination of words won't set him off, won't make him reach for his weapon again. "Yes, it was hard," I finally say, then debate my next sentence. If he's a cold-blooded killer it could be enough to make him pull the trigger. But if he's got a heart, a conscience, maybe he'll show me something that will help me figure out who he is. "I'm sure you can understand that despite the things I've done wrong, I'm still human. I miss my family and am scared I might never see them again." I pause. "Don't you have people you love?" I hold my breath.

He turns away from me, and I can see his shoulders tense. He makes fists with his hands.

It feels like all the air has been sucked out of the room. I said the wrong thing.

In two strides he's right in front of me, inches from my face.

"Don't you dare ask me something like that again. Do you understand me?" he yells.

I nod my head.

His eyes dart upward for a split second, and I follow his gaze. That's when I notice it. How have I not seen it before? A tiny camera in the top right corner of the room. A pit forms in my stomach. Someone is watching me. But who?

Franklin comes to mind first. I think of him in his short-sleeve white button-down tucked into his perfectly pressed, pleated khaki pants. The way he sat erect on the court benches, watching. Often smiling if he'd catch my eye. He had a little notepad that I later realized must be what he was writing his letters to me in. I'd always considered him a harmless stalker, if such a category exists. He thought he was in love with me; I got a restraining order; he went away. Or so I thought. But—and I never told anyone this—the night they dragged him away after he showed up at my office that night . . . there was something about that look—like he was sending me a message. *This isn't over.* What if he hired Q to take me and hold me hostage? It seems far-fetched—the police said he had no criminal record, not so much as a speeding ticket. But isn't that always how it is? There is no record until there is?

Q takes a step backward. "You're right."

"That you have your own family?" I ask, a tiny spark of hope shooting through me that maybe I've gotten through to him.

Q smirks. "No, Lila. You're correct that you aren't going to see yours again."

I see it then. He's telling the truth. I'm not going to make it out of here alive.

I think of Ethan tucking a stray hair behind my ear as I read my vows, the wind from the ocean kicking up, my hair flying everywhere during the ceremony. Then a piece of sand lodged in my eye. Both of us laughing. I picture my mom the day I graduated from law school, the pride on her face. The relief I felt that I could finally take care of her financially. I remember Carrie on that night we met at the cocktail party for the firm. I had no idea when she offered me a cigarette how important she would become to me . . . and how I would betray her in the very worst way. I get that it might be hard to understand—how you can love someone yet still choose to hurt them. How you can be loyal to them in so many ways except the most important one. All I can say is that I've compartmentalized it for the last six months—the pull to Sam and my love for Carrie. My commitment to Ethan. I put them each into these little boxes and shut them tightly so I don't have to think about any of them too much. Until now. Now it's all I think about as I sit here with my back pressed against the cold concrete wall, contemplating how terribly I'll be paying for my sins when I die.

My lip quivers as I imagine Ethan at my funeral. Contemplating the wife he thought he knew. My secrets surely coming to light after my death. He'll be equal parts mourning me and hating me as I'm laid to rest. Having to live with the fact he may not have known me at all.

And Sam. Will he attend my service? Will he still come if Ethan and Carrie find out about us? I picture him the last time I saw him as I stormed out of Bestia after ending things. Why didn't he tell the police we went to dinner? What reason does he have for keeping it from them, unless . . .

I glance up at the blinking red light again. Could *he* be the one staring at me from behind the camera? Did he hire Q? His only motive would be that he's afraid I'll tell Carrie about us. But he knows I would never do that—I have as much, if not more, to lose. He could also be upset I broke up with him. I shake my head. But he didn't know that was coming. And my abduction was clearly planned for some time. I glance at my wrists, rubbed raw from the cuffs. This feels creepy. Personal. Like I'm in the center of someone's mind-fuck. But whose mind-fuck is it?

And next time, will there be a bullet in the chamber?

CHAPTER FOURTEEN

TUESDAY
FREE

I'm so lost in thought that I let out a small shriek when my car door
jostles, my heartbeat only slowing when I realize it's Ethan. He smiles
and nods slightly toward the door. I fumble for the unlock button,
flustered. "Sorry," I say as he settles into the tan leather interior. "I'm a
little jumpy tonight."

"Why?" he asks, frowning. "Did something happen?"

I pause before answering. No, nothing has actually happened, so
why does it feel like something has? Almost as if there's a muffled alarm
ringing deep down in my psyche. I can't explain it—maybe it's the
breakup with Sam and the ensuing fallout that has me on edge. Or
it could be Greenwood and that sixth sense I get about my clients,
warning me that something is off about him. Whatever is going on, it's
causing a rumble within me, shooting off sharp blades of anxiety. "No,"
I say to Ethan. "It's probably stress. They've given me a divorce case at
work, and it's going to be messy."

Ethan cocks his head. "Divorce? Why?"

"He's a big client, and he asked for me. Guess he's a fan."

"That makes no sense. Is that divorce lawyer going to help you—the short, aggressive one with the bad sweater vest that I met at the holiday party last year? What's his name?"

Ethan hated coming to those parties with me. He thought the attorneys I worked with were patronizing. That they treated him like a kept husband. Last year it had been held at the Ritz-Carlton, and he'd grabbed a bottle of good scotch and hunkered down at a corner table and gotten shit-faced with Chase. "David," I answer. "And no, not really."

"Why the hell not?" Ethan demands as the light turns green.

I accelerate and choose my words carefully. "They think I can handle it on my own."

Ethan is exasperated. "What does Sam think of all this? He always seems to look out for you. Can't he help get you out of it?"

I play back Ethan's words for any hidden meaning, any latent sarcasm. But there's none I can detect. I've always painted Sam as something of a savior for me at work, looking out for my career. And it's true—he has. But now I'm experiencing the other side of Sam—the one who goes through three assistants a year, the Sam who will smile at you one minute and then cut your throat out in the next. There's a reason he rose to managing partner so quickly—he likes to win, no matter the cost. I think I romanticized the soft side he'd always held for me, long before we became involved. There's a part of me that feels like I know him in a way others don't, that Carrie doesn't. That there's a kind heart underneath the ambition.

I was so wrong.

"There's nothing he can do," I say evenly, careful to keep the emotion and the lie out of my voice. Because the truth is, I am deeply hurt by the way Sam has turned on me. I am surprised by my own naivete—thinking I could walk away from a man like him without any consequences. He helped build me up, which I thought would protect me. I thought that no matter what, he valued my equity. But it turns out it made it easier for him to tear me down, exposing my weaknesses one by one until there was nothing left. "Don't worry; I'm sure I'll figure it out."

Ethan seems to sense I don't want to discuss it anymore and changes the subject. "I wrote another chapter today," he says, and I can hear the smile in his voice, the cabin of the SUV too dark to see. "The work space is so inspiring. There's another novelist writing her first book. There's a screenwriter. So many creative minds."

"That's great!" I exclaim. "So when are you going to tell me what your book's about?" Ethan has always liked to hold his writing close to the vest. He says it's a writerly thing. I secretly think it's because he is terrified of being critiqued. The mere idea of negative feedback seems to paralyze him. He had to stop reading the reviews of his first one, each critical word like a shard to his insecure heart.

But to my surprise, he answers me now. "It's about a complicated marriage," he says, and my pulse quickens.

Is his book about us? Our marriage is complicated, for sure, but I've often mused that I'm the only one between us who realizes that. Ethan is often too caught up in his own challenges to comprehend how much of the time I'm merely phoning it in. Or so I thought. But was I wrong? Is he more insightful, more aware than I give him credit for?

"Don't worry," he says, moving his hand to my knee, as if he can read my mind. "It's not about us. I don't want to say too much, but it's the story of a woman cheating on her husband and the fallout after he discovers the affair. He goes off the rails a little bit. Does some crazy shit."

I slam on the brakes to avoid running a red light. "Sorry," I mutter under my breath as I collect my thoughts. *Does he know?* No. People write books about cheating spouses all the time. *Calm down, Lila.* "That sounds really interesting!" I say with what I hope sounds like enthusiasm and not the horror I'm actually feeling. "I'm happy you're writing again." That part's true.

But I wish he weren't writing about some cheating whore and pray it isn't because he recently realized he's married to one.

~

I manage to calm down before we pull off the 405 Freeway at Artesia and head into Redondo Beach, forcing myself to enjoy a story Ethan tells about a woman he encountered earlier at the local coffee place near his new writing space. (I was right the day I met him—he hates Starbucks! "Corporate greed at its worst," he always says when he finds the discarded white-and-green cups in my car.) His voice is pitched high as he imitates the way she yelled at the barista for putting 2 percent rather than nonfat milk in her vanilla latte.

"How can you tell the difference?" I ask.

"You can't, that's the point! Sometimes people just want others to be as miserable as they are," he says, and it makes me think of Steve Greenwood. There is something miserable about him too, and I hope the investigator is able to figure out whether his wife is part of the problem or if he's like the woman at Starbucks, pissed off and wanting to take everyone he can down with him.

I park in the closest spot I can find—almost two blocks down from my mom's townhouse—tucking the Range Rover in between two large vans. Ethan grabs my hand as we walk to her place, and I find myself leaning into his fingers, the warmth of his grip making me feel safe for the first time all day.

My mom hugs me when we walk through the door and then draws back, giving me a long look as she squeezes my shoulders. "You okay?" she asks, and I can feel Ethan's eyes on me.

"I'm great, Mom. A little bit tired."

"You're always tired," she says, disapproval dripping from her voice. "You need to rest. Take some time off! I worry I set a bad example for you growing up."

I laugh. "How do you figure that?"

"I worked nonstop after your father died. Never took a second to myself." She peers at me. "Didn't spend as much time with you as I should have."

It's true. After my dad passed, my mom became the superhero of our family, working summers as a server at one of those tourist traps near the Hermosa Beach pier. Tutoring struggling students most nights during the school year in our cramped living room at the shabby wood table we found at a yard sale. And I worked my ass off too—babysitting and then joining her when I turned sixteen as a hostess at the same restaurant, hating every minute in that tacky Hawaiian dress they forced me to wear. I understood that we had a responsibility to each other. But I could probably count on one hand the times she and I went shopping or out to lunch.

I hug her again. "You did your very best. And I'm grateful. It's because of you that I'm where I am today."

"That's what I worry about sometimes," she mutters, but I choose to ignore the comment and disentangle from her and walk into the kitchen, inhaling the scent of garlic and basil. "It smells wonderful. Pasta?"

"Sausage and peppers, with penne. Your favorite," she adds proudly.

"Garlic bread?" I ask, but I already know the answer.

"Of course!" She smiles, and I'm hit by her love for me. The way she craves my happiness as much as her own. She's always told me that it comes with being a parent—the willingness to trade your own happiness for your child's. But I've often feared that, with the exception of her, I don't have that in me—that I'm incapable of being that selfless.

"And Ethan, how are you?" she asks as she hands him a stack of plates and nods toward the distressed round table behind him.

"He's writing again," I interject.

Ethan smiles shyly. "It's true. I am."

My mom's face explodes in joy. "Well, that's wonderful! How long has it been—"

"Mom," I warn.

"No, it's okay," Ethan says, waving me off. "Alexis, it *has* been forever, hasn't it? What can I say? The inspiration finally struck me."

I inhale sharply. Was I that inspiration? Does he know everything, and this is his way of torturing me? No, this is Ethan. He would never do that.

"I'm happy for you, Ethan. If you need a beta reader . . ."

Ethan smiles politely as he fills the water pitcher with ice. "I'll let you know."

"Honey, we're about ready to eat. Where's the wine?" my mom asks.

"Oh, shoot. I left it in the car," Ethan says, glancing down at his full hands, then back at me. "Can you grab it, Lila?"

"Sure." I scoop up my keys from the counter. "I'll be right back."

I head down the steps to the sidewalk, jogging lightly in my three-inch heels through the semidarkness, the air chilly from the beach breeze, goosebumps popping up on my bare arms.

I reach my car and open the back door carefully so I don't bang it against a truck parked a little too snugly next to me, the van that was there before now gone. Reaching over and cursing as the wine bottle rolls to the floor, I lean in more, my back leg lifting off the ground, and set the bottle back on the seat so I can regain my balance.

It takes me a second to process that someone is behind me.

Before I can react, I'm being pulled by my hair and then by my chest, my screams hushed as another hand moves to my mouth. My heart pounds, and I slam my heel hard on my assailant's foot, causing him to groan and lose his grip slightly, but it's enough for me to grab the bottle of wine, swinging it hard, making contact with his head as it shatters.

"Help!" I scream. "Somebody help!" I shriek again as the masked man reels backward, stumbling slightly and using his arm to balance himself on the truck. Every muscle in my body tells me to run—to take flight! But instead I reach for the ski mask. I grab the fabric and start to pull it up, but before I can, he grabs my wrist and twists it, making me writhe in pain.

"You should have run when you had the chance," he says, his voice breathless, and then he raises his fist to my temple, and I crumple to the ground before everything falls away.

~

I hear my name, softly at first. Then louder. I force my eyes open, wincing from the ache in my head, and find myself surrounded by a group of people, including my mom and Ethan, sirens wailing in the background, getting louder each second.

"Oh, thank God!" my mom cries out.

"What happened?" I whisper, but as I ask the question the last few minutes return to my memory with a sickening thud. The wine. The man with the mask. His fist.

"You were attacked," Ethan said, his face pale.

"I heard you screaming and came running out with my dog and a baseball bat." A slight woman in her thirties steps forward, gripping the leash of a thick blue-nosed pit bull. "He ran away when he saw me and Rex."

I let that sink in. What would have happened if this woman hadn't heard me? If she didn't keep a bat and a guard dog handy in this seemingly safe neighborhood? *You should have run when you had the chance*, he warned. The fear I felt in that moment hits me hard and fast. "Thank you," I say to her and Rex and gulp back the sob in my throat.

"I'm glad you're okay," she says.

The ambulance pulls up a moment later. A police cruiser arrives, and two officers emerge and disperse the crowd. The officers wait patiently as the EMTs attend to the lump on the left side of my head. They want me to come to the hospital to make sure I don't have a concussion, but I refuse as my mother protests loudly. "I'm okay," I try to say with confidence, but I can't stop shaking. Can't stop thinking of where I'd be right now if that woman hadn't heard me.

One of the EMTs shrugs and gives my mom and Ethan a list of symptoms to look for. He's seen it all before. My life was just changed forever, but this was only another call for him.

We head back with the officers into my mom's townhome, the smell of dinner now making me feel sick. My mom mutters about how safe she always thought Redondo Beach was. That maybe she should move.

"Can we open a window?" I ask, and Ethan immediately does. We all settle at the kitchen table—my mom, Ethan, and the two police officers, all of us ignoring the flowered china and overflowing basket of garlic bread. It's almost as if my attack stopped time.

My mom picks up the bread basket and offers it to the policemen, who both politely decline. Then they ask me to walk through what happened, and I do, trying to not look at my mom out of the corner of my eye. To not see the horror in her face as I describe how he pulled me from the car, to not comprehend the anger in her eyes when I admit how I chose to pull his mask rather than run for my life.

"Why not run?" one of the police officers, the younger one, asks. His name is Detective Franco, and he sports a head of thick black hair and a strong right dimple.

"I'm not sure." I pause, remembering the moment I could have fled. When my adrenaline was pumping so hard I could feel it charging through me. But my mind had a different plan—to try to pull off the mask, to find out who it was. It was almost as if I were being told to do it. To find out who was going to capture me. "It was instinctual, I guess. I needed to know who it was." I glance at my mom finally. Her lips form a tight line. "I'm sorry. I wasn't thinking."

"Can you give us a description?" Franco asks.

"A male. He seemed average height, but it was dark. I have no idea how tall he was. He was sturdy, though, strong, definitely works out.

Oh, and he was wearing track pants and Adidas tennis shoes," I say, thankful that my job has taught me to memorize descriptive details.

"What color?"

I think for a moment. "The pants were dark. The shoes were red with white stripes."

"Eye color? Ethnicity?"

I shake my head. "He was wearing a ski mask, so I'm not sure. His face was shadowed. I think he was Caucasian."

"You said you didn't have your purse with you, right?" the older officer, Detective Johnson, asks.

"Right," I concur.

"It doesn't sound like a mugging or a carjacking, based on what you've told us. Do you think his intent was to take you? Hurt you . . . or . . ."

"Rape me?" I add.

Ethan swivels his head my way, giving me a horrified look.

"It could have been any of those things. Or maybe he wanted to kill me?" I say, surprised by how detached I feel. As if I am simply speculating about the details of a case I'm working on.

"Did it feel personal?" Franco asks.

I give him a half shrug. "I'm not sure." *You should have run while you had the chance.* "But there was something about how he told me I should have run. Like he had plans for me. Bad ones."

"I bet it was Franklin!" Ethan says, his voice filled with anger.

"Who is Franklin?" Johnson asks.

I put my hand over Ethan's. "Franklin is someone who used to stalk me. But he hasn't been in contact since he showed up at my office, and I got a restraining order a few months ago. And this man, he seemed larger."

"It's been a while; maybe he's started lifting," Ethan says flippantly. No one responds.

I fill them in on the details of Franklin's stalking, and when I'm finished, Franco asks me his last name and writes it in his notebook. "We'll check him out."

"Is there anything else?" Johnson asks, not unkindly.

I remember the car that seemed to follow me out of the parking garage at work. Was the driver tailing me or simply leaving at the same time? There's no way to know, and if I bring it up now, I'll seem paranoid. Stephanie also comes to mind. The way I could have sworn I saw her outside my house the other night. But whether she followed me or not, she made it very clear she's pissed off at me. That the man she thinks killed her sister is free, and in her mind I'm responsible.

She could have hired this man to attack me, but I'm not sure she would. Or maybe I don't want to believe that could be true. Plus, do I really want to anger her more by having the police show up at her doorstep, asking questions? Hasn't she been through enough?

The room is silent for several minutes, everyone waiting for me to answer. "No," I finally say. This is a lie, of course. There could be so many people from the course of my career, beginning from my very first trial. The one that still haunts me—the two adolescent boys sitting on each side of their mom in court, the sobs from the younger one when the verdict was read. The older boy simply stared straight ahead as if he hadn't heard. I lost that case. Unexpectedly—when the jury had begun its deliberations, we'd all thought a nonguilty verdict was in the bag. Until it wasn't. Until the kids watched their father get taken away in cuffs, never to return.

"Okay, I think we have everything we need." Franco stands, and Johnson follows suit. We walk them to the door, all of us silent as we watch them get in their car, turn off their flashing lights, and drive away.

An hour later Ethan and I head home, despite my mother's protests that we stay the night with her. She argued her case as we ate the cold sausage and peppers without any joy, finally conceding when I told her

I have an early morning at work and that sleeping in the old, sunken double bed in her guest room wasn't going to cut it. She promised to deadbolt the lock on the door and call me in the morning. My instinct is that the attack was only meant for me and that my mom is safe, but how can I know that for sure?

I lean my head against the window as we speed down the freeway, away from what almost happened to me. My near miss.

"I'm sorry I brought Franklin up. That was juvenile. But I'm worried about you," Ethan says, and I nod. "You going to be okay?" he asks after a long period of silence. I appreciate the question, although we both know the answer.

"I don't know," I say and pick up my phone from the center console. I shoot off a quick text to Chase, letting him know I might be a little later than six tomorrow morning and asking him to call the investigator and have him check in on Franklin. I don't think it's him, but Ethan could be right: maybe he gained some muscle. Or maybe my skills at describing my attacker aren't as good as I think they are.

My heart stops for the second time tonight when I check my inbox. It's an email from Janelle. I haven't heard from her since we graduated from law school. And the truth is, I was hoping I'd never hear from her ever again. I wonder if it's the wedding invitation from our old college friend Tiffany that has her thinking of me. I'm hoping that's all it is.

There's no text in the body of the email. Just in the subject line.

Back in town and want to see you. I'll be in touch.

CHAPTER FIFTEEN

Tuesday
Captured

"I'm surprised they're looking for you," Q says after a few minutes of silence between us.

"I'm not," I say defiantly. "And they're going to find me." I look up at him, searching for a sign that I can reason with him, but the mask covering his expressions makes it impossible. Which gives me an idea. "If you let me go now, I'll never be able to identify you. I haven't seen your face. You still have a chance."

"*You're* trying to scare *me*?" Q asks, his voice dancing.

"No, I'm being realistic. If they're holding a press conference less than twenty-four hours after I went missing, that means they have solid suspicions already."

Q squats, his large thighs bulging against his black track pants. "Or maybe it's because you have a quasifamous husband, and they don't give two shits about you. You know as well as I do that no one at that precinct gives a shit about finding you after all the killers you've set free."

"They're professionals—they won't hold what I do against me," I assert. But deep down, I know he's right. And I also realize that even though Ethan hasn't written a book since his runaway bestseller, he's a big enough name to garner this kind of attention. All it would have taken is someone in the chief of police's office pointing this out or—I'm suddenly struck with a thought. My mom. That's something I could see her doing. Calling in and reminding them that my husband has Oprah's phone number. (Which is true; he really does.)

It's true that the LAPD detectives hold a fair amount of resentment when it comes to me, making my job more difficult whenever possible. Detective Sully is the only one at the precinct who still seems to tolerate me, and that's because we both started our careers at the same time. I met him in the cafeteria at police headquarters, grabbing a coffee before I attempted to track down the cop I needed to interview. Sully was recently out of the academy, and I asked him where I could find the officer I needed to speak with. And I'm not sure why, in fact I've never asked him, but he suggested I sit down because he wanted to give me some information on this cop. Turns out he was not a very nice guy, and Sully wanted to warn me. He was worried I was so green he'd eat me alive.

"What are you smiling at?"

"Nothing," I say and wipe it from my face.

"Anyway it doesn't matter. Because they can have all the press conferences they want. They aren't going to find you. I can guarantee they don't have a single lead," Q says, tipping his chin upward.

"How do you know they didn't follow you here?" I ask.

Q laughs. "Don't you think they'd have broken the door down by now? Considering you're a big-time author's wife," he jabs.

"How did you know you'd get me that night? What if I hadn't gone to the restaurant with Sam?"

"I was pretty damn sure you'd go somewhere other than home." Q smirks. "But if you hadn't, if you'd actually shown some loyalty to your fucking husband, I planned to nab you at your mom's, where you have dinner on the last Tuesday of every month."

"How do you know that?" I ask, my pulse quickening. The visual of Q following me, watching me as I naively lived my life, gives me chills. How long was he tracking me? Is anyone else in my life in danger?

"Are you really asking me that question? I know everything about you, Lila Bennett." He scowls before heaving me up and half dragging me down the bleak hallway to the bathroom.

I break down at the truth in his words as I give up on squatting and sit in vain on the toilet seat, my body so dehydrated that there is only a small trickle. I struggle for breath as I cry, trying to push out all of my pain before Q bangs on the door and tells me to hurry the fuck up. But to my surprise, there is only silence as I fall to the filthy ground and sob a full five minutes until I'm exhausted. Defeated. It's then that I hear two soft knocks on the door before it's shoved open.

"Get up," Q says harshly. "I'm tired of hearing you cry. It's fucking annoying." I hesitate, and he grabs me around the waist and pulls me up like a rag doll, his breath hot on my ear. "I thought you were a fighter. Is this it? You giving up?" he asks pointedly. "Because that's boring."

I say nothing. Does he want me to fight so he has the justification to hurt me in response? I still haven't seen his face, have no idea if he has a weak chin or a large forehead. I don't know if the lines around his eyes crinkle when he laughs or if his eyebrows fold when he is thinking. All I know of him are his green eyes, flecked with gold, that stare back at me now with . . . curiosity? Hate? It is impossible to know.

Q leaves without any promises of when he'll return. I despise the fact that part of me hopes he'll come back soon. It's like choosing between two evils—the torture of Q's head games or the masochism of my own mind.

∼

With him gone, I tuck my head into my shoulder and let my eyes close, feeling my mind drift off before my body eventually follows, collapsing into the exhaustion. I lie there, somewhere between the sharp edges of complete unconsciousness and acute awareness, and dream.

Franklin is there. He doesn't say anything, rather he watches me as I walk down what seems to be a never-ending corridor. I search frantically for the door, any escape from his prying eyes. But there is none.

I shake myself awake with a start and instinctively look up at the camera I noticed earlier. "Franklin?" I squeak, my throat dry. "Are you there?"

The blinking light stares back at me, revealing nothing.

Franklin had been sending me letters and following me for quite a while before I noticed him in court, which I think annoyed him. Maybe it was because he was so unassuming, light-brown hair cut short and small brown eyes, his nondescript face blending into the rest of the world. Or maybe I was so self-involved I didn't notice. He wasn't the first weirdo to send me a creepy email or letter. Either way, it wasn't until he slipped past security and into my office late one night that he really grabbed my attention, made me realize he could be more than harmless.

It was a Tuesday evening, and I'd sent Chase home. Not because I was such a caring boss but because I wanted him gone when Sam stopped by later. Things were new between us, and we'd been texting about meeting up all day, my breathing growing shallow as he outlined the things he was planning on doing to me and the places in the office we were going to do them. I was trying to concentrate on the brief I was working on, but my mind would drift every few seconds to how his lips would feel on mine, the way my stomach would flutter slightly when he walked in, the anticipation of what was about to happen almost better than the actual act. I'd grown addicted to that—the prospect of what was to come. It was as if nothing else mattered—this brief, the trial that was starting the next morning. Ethan. Carrie. They all fell away somewhere between Sam's texts and his arrival.

When the shadow first appeared in my doorway, I'd smiled, thinking Sam had gotten away a bit earlier than he thought. "Hey," I started to say, but the words got stuck in my throat as I realized the man in my office wasn't Sam. He was thin and pale and holding a bouquet of red roses.

"Can I help you find someone?" I asked, glancing at my phone, which sat out of reach on the edge of my desk. Something about him seemed off. It may have been the intense way his dark eyes were boring into mine or the empty smile he wore on his face. I slowly moved my hand toward the phone. Just in case.

"These," he said, taking a step forward. My hand inched closer to the phone. "They are for you, Lila."

"I'm sorry, do we know each other?" I said as I tried to place his face. Former client? He looked too old to have been a classmate. Too young to be one of Ethan's friends.

He looked hurt at my question. "I've been sending you letters. Haven't you read them?" His voice rose slightly at this part.

Oh, okay. This must be Franklin. He'd been sending me handwritten letters for three months. Nothing too threatening. More like a very serious crush. I'd handed them over to the firm's security department, and they'd said to keep an eye out but that he was probably harmless. Sam and I had joked that I'd finally made it, because I had my very own stalker.

But there in my office it felt a little less harmless. My hand grasped the phone, and I began to slowly pull it off so I could dial the building security. I calculated. They were located several floors down and would take precious minutes to get here. Was I better off calling Sam, who was down the hall? But it was possible he wouldn't pick up. And I was worried I was only going to get one chance. The good news was that Franklin was a slight man, and if he didn't have a weapon, I was pretty sure I could take him.

"Oh, I'm sorry," I said with a forced smile. "I did get those. Franklin, right?"

His face registered relief, and he relaxed slightly. "Yes."

"Can you do me a favor?" I asked, pointing to a corner of my office. Away from me. "Can you set those beautiful flowers over there? That way I can see them as I work."

"Sure," he said and turned away from me as he set them down carefully. I quickly dialed security and gave them the code we'd been instructed to in an emergency. "Code red," I whispered and set the phone down quietly.

Poor Franklin. He'd been still hard at work fluffing those flowers when two large men barged in moments later and tackled him. I'd calculated wrong—they'd made it to my office in less than one minute. I guessed they patrolled each floor after hours. I hated myself for wondering in that moment if they'd ever heard me and Sam behind our closed doors.

Franklin screamed, "I love you, Lila!" as they'd dragged him away in handcuffs, Sam walking up as they exited my office.

He looked from Franklin to me. "What'd I miss?" he said, calm and collected, a small smile playing on his lips. The sight of him made my shaking hands steady.

"Nothing much," I'd said, nodding him in and then shutting and locking the door behind me, deciding I'd worry about Franklin and a restraining order in the morning.

Now, alone in my cell, the camera watching to make sure I pay my penance, I wonder once more if Franklin is on the other side. Is he watching from his bedroom, getting off as Q defeats me? As he breaks my spirit? I become obsessed with the thought, that night in my office running through my head. The way he must have felt. What does he need to hear? That I love him too? That we can run off together? That I promise I'll never leave?

No, I think. *He wants more than that.*

"Franklin," I call out. "Franklin, if you're listening, I'm sorry. I'm so, so sorry," I shout over and over until my voice fades away.

CHAPTER SIXTEEN

WEDNESDAY
FREE

"Oh my God—look at you. Are you okay?" Chase bum-rushes me when I walk into the office, pulling my tote off my shoulder, guiding me to my chair. "Sit, sit."

I texted him a short version of what happened last night when I got home. He wanted to talk, but I begged off, simply too exhausted. Especially because I'd already talked to Carrie, who wanted me to walk her through every detail of the story. Part of me has been trying to convince myself that I imagined the car that was following me out of the parking garage last night, that the attack on me *was* random. That Stephanie isn't pissed at me over what happened. That Ethan's book isn't about me. That my entire life hasn't come to a fork in the road, asking me to deal with my choices. But that's how it feels—like all my wrongs are coming back to haunt me. I think of Janelle's email last night. The timing of it after so long.

You should have run when you had the chance.

I hear my attacker's words again. His voice. It felt personal.

A shock jolts up my arm, and I rub it. I'm suddenly hit with a feeling like I've said that same thing before. But when?

Chase pulls a bottle of Fiji from the fridge, screws off the lid, and hands it to me. I take a generous sip. "You are so *not* okay. Did you get a good look at the guy? Anything seem familiar?"

"No. It was too dark. But he was strong and wearing track pants and Adidas shoes. I got really, really lucky."

"You sure did. It sounds like he's stuck in some kind of 1990s fashion time warp," he adds. "Nobody needs that." He laughs, and I smile wanly. "Sorry. Bad joke. But that's a serious bruise on your arm . . . and the one by your eye. You should have stayed home."

"No," I say flatly. "I needed to come in. We have the Greenwood meeting—"

"Screw that devil Muppet!" He puts his hands on his slim hips, and I laugh.

"I wish I could tell him off, but I can't."

"He's such a jerk."

"I know, but he's one of the firm's top clients. Customer's always right, blah, blah."

"It's the part of the job I do *not* like." Chase rolls his eyes.

"That's the only one, huh?"

"You know what I mean."

"Will you trust me on this one, okay? There are no other options."

Chase walks over and closes the door. "When are you going to start trusting *me*?"

"What?" I ask reflexively, but I know exactly what he means. At least I think I do.

"I'm not an idiot. I know what's going on."

"What do you mean?" I try to sound convincing, but my voice is too high when I say it.

Chase simply gives me a look.

"Fine, what do you know?" I say, thinking of something Sam told me once when he was explaining how he approaches meetings with opposing counsel—never show your cards first. I shake the thought away. I don't want to be thinking of him right now.

"I know about Sam."

I guess the not-thinking-about-Sam option is out.

I nod, silently telling him to continue.

He lowers his voice. "I know about you two. The affair."

"Okay," I say, surprised by how the pressure in my chest lessens the moment I hear him say it.

"And I'm figuring that you've ended things, and now he's retaliating."

"The lesson here is don't ever have an affair with your superior. Although I'd be much nicer if you dumped me," I deadpan.

Chase doesn't respond to my joke, his eyes narrowing. "You could totally sue. This is classic sexual harassment."

"I'm not interested in suing. I'd like the whole thing to go away. Because Ethan cannot find out. Carrie cannot find out."

Chase gives me a sad smile.

"I know. I'm a whore," I say, surprised by how quickly my eyes fill with tears. How I have to inhale sharply to stop myself from crying.

"You're not a whore, Lila. A little slutty maybe." He winks at me. "But not a whore." He reaches in and gives me a hug, and I squeeze him back, hard, not wanting to let go.

"Thank you for not judging me," I say in a small voice.

"We all make mistakes, right?"

I pull back from his embrace. "How did you know?"

"Girl, how could I *not* know? You'd have to be blind."

"Oh God, really?" I shoot up in my chair. "Is it like the worst-kept secret around here? Does everyone—"

"No, no," he cuts me off. "But as your assistant, it was super obvious. You had patterns. I started to pick up on them. You'd say you were one place, but I realized you were at another. You'd slip and say something that didn't add up. That type of thing."

If Chase picked up on my lies, my patterns, as he calls them, then how could Ethan not? Which could mean that Ethan does know. Hence his sudden interest in getting an office space, his burst of an idea for his novel about a wife having an affair. Panic rises from my gut, but I force it back down.

Deep breaths. Ethan doesn't know. It's all a coincidence. You can still fix this.

"Do you want to talk?"

It feels freeing to tell him everything. He nods occasionally and smiles as I share an anecdote about once almost getting caught by Andrew, the night janitor. When I finish, my chest aches a little less, the burden of the lie I've been carrying slightly lifted.

"What now?" he asks when I'm done.

"I work and keep my head down and hope this all blows over."

"You know Sam better than anyone—do you really think that will happen?"

I think of the way he treated me in his office yesterday. "Probably not. But you know me—it's going to take more than that to break me." I smile.

"You're the toughest bitch I know. That's for sure." He points at me. "And you have the bruised-up face to prove it!"

"Damn straight." I gently touch the tender patch of skin. "We should get to work. Sorry I left you here working last night. See what karma did to me?" I half joke.

"As if you believe in karma anyway," Chase says.

I pause. I've never really thought too much about karma. "Do you?"

"I probably shouldn't, in this job. But I do. Always have."

"So you think there is some universal force that rights things?"

"Maybe," he says. "But what do I know? I also believe that JonBenet Ramsey lived and grew up to be Katy Perry."

I laugh. "Oh. Come on. You're the most levelheaded millennial I know."

He shrugs in response.

"So, any leads on the Greenwood case? Has Joe gotten back to us with his findings after following Greenwood's wife?" I ask hopefully.

"When I read through Greenwood's file, there was an affidavit from his wife that he'd been physical with her. That she'd filed a police report. But there was no report included. I called his wife's counsel, who said he looked into it, and no such report existed."

"Interesting." It leads me to believe that Greenwood likely did something to get rid of it. Or his wife dropped the charges and didn't realize it meant the report would be expunged. I make a mental note to call Detective Sully to look into it.

"Right? I thought so too." Chase nods at my laptop where he sticks my messages. "And a woman named Janelle called."

My face must change, because Chase frowns at me. "Not a friend?" he asks.

I can feel my cheeks flush. "Nope," I say honestly. "Well, she was once. A story for another time, but one I will tell you. I promise. No more secrets."

Chase smiles. "I need to go down to the mailroom. We have some packages," he says, obviously giving me space to make my call.

"Thanks."

He walks out and closes the door behind him. I pick up the Post-it with Janelle's name and number written on it, wondering what she wants. I question again if she's simply calling because she's also invited to the wedding and wants to clear the air.

Don't call her. You need to protect yourself! bad Lila whispers in my ear.

It's time to face your demons, good Lila murmurs.

Good Lila is right. My hand shakes when I reach for the phone and punch in her number. My heart is in a full pound by the time I push the last digit. I haven't talked to her since I got the internship and she didn't. Does she somehow know what happened? Has she found out what I did?

Just when I think I'm going to get voice mail, she answers. "Hello?"

"Hi . . ." My voice sounds hoarse, and I clear it. "Hi, Janelle, it's Lila. Lila Bennett."

"Lila, hello. Thanks for returning my call."

I search her voice for a trace of irritation, but I'm not sure it's there. "Of course. It's been a long time," I say.

"I know. Since graduation," she says.

"Gosh, that's been what? Thirteen years?"

"Fourteen this June," she says simply, and we fall into an uncomfortable silence. Has she been keeping track? Keeping score? The last I heard of Janelle, she was a prosecutor up in Sacramento. Another friend from law school ran into her and told me.

"So, how are you?" I ask.

"Good. Married, two kids. I'm a prosecutor."

"Up in Sac, right?"

"Oh no . . . well, yes, that's where I was. But now I'm going to be here in LA. I transferred last month. That's why I'm calling. Well, I wasn't sure I should, but I got Tiffany's wedding invitation, and I took it as a sign to reach out."

So that's all this is. But why doesn't that thought make me feel better?

"Oh, wow, that's . . ." I try to think of a word to throw in. "Great," I finally say, but my mouth has gone dry. Without Janelle in my life, I can often convince myself nothing happened so many years ago. That I got this job fair and square . . . or at least earned the right to have it by now.

"I've read up on you—you're quite the star down here," she says. Again, not a trace of anger. At least not one that I can sense.

"Well, I don't know about that. Just doing my job."

"I thought we might have lunch—catch up. Especially if you plan to attend the wedding." She half laughs. "Anyway, not only that, but if I'm in LA, I'm assuming we're going to be crossing paths a lot."

I forgot how deep her voice is. Strong, we always joked. She'd joke that she was going to scare juries into submission. She never showed much interest in being a prosecutor, and I swallow hard and hope my actions didn't influence her choices.

"Right. Yes, okay. Let's do that," I say. We hang up, and I sigh. I don't want to have lunch with her. I can think of nothing I want to do less. Because if I'm right, if she really does want to get together without any ulterior motive, she must not know, which will make seeing her worse. The guilt slowly tearing me apart. Of course, there is a chance she knows. That she's chosen now to confront me. Possibly wanting to clear the air now that we'll be in the same city?

I glance at the Post-it with her number and toss it in the trash can and pray she doesn't follow up to make plans with me. My office line rings, startling me. The caller's number is blocked, and I debate whether to let it go to voice mail, but it could be the private investigator, Joe Dennis. And if it is, that's a call I need to answer. I wait another ring, hoping Chase will sail in and save the day. But he doesn't. "Hello," I finally say.

"Lila, it's Joe."

"Hey, Joe. I was hoping it was you. How's it going?"

"You know, same ol' same ol', following rich stay-at-home moms around. A regular day." I can hear him inhale his cigarette. For as long as I've known our private investigator, he's been a chain smoker. At my urging, he once quit for a day after I ordered him the patch on Amazon.

"And?"

"Well, if Greenwood's wife has this book club boyfriend, she is an expert at hiding him. Got him locked up in the dungeon or something. In fact, I couldn't find truth in any of Greenwood's claims. If I didn't know better, I'd think she was the most routine—dare I say boring—stay-at-home mom on the planet. I followed her around all day, nothing."

"So she's not an alcoholic? Day drinking?"

"From what I could see, the only liquids she's consuming during the day—or night—are coffee and herbal tea. I went through her trash. Not one bottle of anything in there."

"And the kids?"

"Seem happy. She picked them up from school. Took them to and from activities. They all had dinner together. After they went to bed, she watched TV. Lights out by ten. I never saw a nanny either."

"Hmm."

"Look, Lila. It's only been a day, and of course I'll stay on her, but the woman doesn't seem to have a vice so far. And my gut tells me we won't find one."

"Thanks, Joe. Let's talk again tomorrow."

"Right. Chase told me you wanted an update on Franklin."

"Yes, please."

"I'm on it."

After we hang up, I lean back in my chair and stare at the ceiling. Is it possible Greenwood made it all up? That his wife really is that clean? Or did she sense she's being followed or watched and change her routine? My gut tells me it's the former. Joe's the best of the best.

Greenwood is proving to be the bad guy in this scenario. I pick up the phone to call Detective Sully. I need him to find that police report on Greenwood. Or at least help me figure out why it no longer exists.

CHAPTER SEVENTEEN

WEDNESDAY
CAPTURED

I wake to the sound of my own screams—my throat raw, my lungs collapsing under the weight of the intensity of my cries. I'd been dreaming I'd escaped and was running down the street, barefoot, errant pebbles and debris getting stuck in my feet, chest heaving as I gasped for breath, but I pressed on anyway, my pencil skirt ripping as I broke into a full sprint. But then I turned, and Q was there, reaching for me, pulling me back. Finally free from the nightmare, I shoot upright in my concrete prison, and pain rockets through my ankles and up my legs. I look down—the bindings have worn the skin down, and it's red and blistered. My eyes water, and I wince until finally the radiating jolts of anguish subside.

I have no idea how long I was passed out, but I'm groggy, the corners of my eyes caked with sleep, my mouth dry, indicating it's probably been many hours, perhaps overnight? I've been trying to keep track—still counting the minutes—but it's become almost impossible. Q keeps me on irregular patterns, never coming and going in any way that makes sense, changing outfits frequently, but I know from the video it's been at least twenty-four hours, and Q more or less confirmed that when I challenged him about the police's efforts. I would guess, at this point, I've been here closer to thirty-six or forty-eight. I use the wall to get myself upright, careful not to pinch my wrists or bother my ankles, and lean against it, my eyes adjusting again to the semidarkness. I glance up at the blinking light. "I have to pee," I say. "Badly," I add, grimacing. "Anyone? Anyone?" Then I can't help myself. "Bueller?"

I close my eyes and count. By the time I've reached eighteen hundred, no one has come. I eye the bucket and blanch, but it's my only option because I cannot hold it another minute longer. I shuffle over to it, turn my back to the camera, hike up my skirt, and do my best to squat. It's not pretty, but it's fairly successful—and I exhale when I'm finished. As I'm pulling up my panties and pulling down my skirt, I hear the lock.

"Well, if it isn't Ms. Sleepyhead. Nice Ferris Bueller reference, by the way."

"Were you watching?" I nod toward the bucket.

"No way," he says, scrunching his nose as if he's smelled rotten fish.

Holding me hostage, putting a gun to my head, those things aren't beneath him. But watching me urinate—that's where he draws the line?

"I already told you, you're not my type. Plus, I don't have a fetish— at least not that kind."

"Then why didn't you come when I asked to use the bathroom?"

"This isn't the Four Seasons! I'm not your fucking concierge. I don't work for you!"

"Obviously," I mutter.

We sit in silence for a few moments. What could be the purpose for taking me? Is this a sick and twisted game, or is there an actual plan? "So what's on the agenda today? Torture? Maiming?" I ask flatly. "Murder?" I add, a little bit quieter.

"You want to find out?" Q thrusts his shoulders back, which makes his chest puff out.

"I don't know. Depends. What's it going to be, Russian roulette, or do you have another adventure in mind?" I say, then press my lips together and wait. I know I'm pushing, but I have to see what I can get out of him. He didn't kill me yesterday, so maybe today's not the day my life ends either.

He steps closer, leaving mere inches between us. "Look, you really need to realize your place here. Watch it." His eye flicks up toward the camera so fast I almost miss it.

"Or what?" I ask, noticing his forearms are tensing, his shoulders lifting up toward his ears. But it's been two, maybe three days, and I'm still trapped in this room, eating scraps of bread, tablespoons of water, pissing in a bucket. I need answers. What have I got to lose by asking for them?

Your life, Lila.

Q starts pacing. I glance up at the camera again. Who's watching me? Why did my outburst cause him to look up? Is it his boss who's behind that camera? The person who's really calling the shots?

"Or I could put a bullet in your leg and let you sit with the pain," he blurts, jolting me out of my thoughts. "No, actually, I think the knife might be more effective." He pulls the blade out of its sheath and flashes it. "Carve a little drawing in your thigh so you never forget about me and our time together. *Q plus L forever*, with a little heart around it maybe?"

Seeing the sharp edge of the weapon, imagining him slowly penetrating my flesh, the blood spilling out, sends a rush of fear through me. I start to shake.

"What happened, Lila? You were acting so tough before . . ." He walks around somewhat aimlessly for a moment, then plants his feet in place and jumps toward me. "Boo."

I clench my jaw to keep from reacting.

He walks toward me and puts the knife against my neck. I freeze with fear.

"Or we could end it real quick. This here is your carotid artery. One slice and you'll bleed out. Well, your blood will spurt all over the place. You'll die in minutes. You hear me?"

I'm trembling now, so much so that I'm afraid I'll cut my neck on the blade of the knife, which Q still has pressed firmly against my throat.

"I asked you a question," he yells. "Because I need to know that you understand you are not the one in control here. *I am.*"

I flinch, and the blade moves slightly. "Yes. Yes. I hear you," I say, the fight I had in me earlier vanishing like a puff of smoke.

He pulls the knife back and gives it a kiss before sliding it into the sheath. "Good."

I'm still shaking and try to stop the tremors, but they only seem to be getting worse. My teeth begin to chatter, so I thrust my mouth open. I try to breathe, but I can't seem to catch my breath. I feel tingling in my hands and up my arms and through my legs; then my hands go numb.

Am I having a panic attack?

I focus hard on my breathing. In and out. In and out.

"You don't look too good," Q says, cocking his head at me.

I try to say the words I'm thinking. *I'm not okay. Help.* But of course he's not going to help me. I concentrate my gaze on a spot on the floor and breathe until the feeling starts to come back into my hands. Until my heartbeat slows.

Q pulls his backpack off and unzips it. He thrusts a bottle of water toward me. "Here."

I hold it awkwardly between my bound hands and guzzle half of it down so quickly that I start to choke a bit, then cough several times. "Thanks."

He nods at me, taking the bottle away, but stays silent, as if he's considering his next move. A moment later he grabs his backpack and heads for the door, slamming it. I hear the lock click, and I curl up on the floor again and start to whimper, wondering when—or if—this will ever make sense. I start counting again. I've lost track, so I start over.

One, two, three, four . . .

~

"Get up." Time has passed. I have no idea how much. Q is standing over me. "I said, *Get. Up.*"

"Okay," I say slowly, trying to move, but my leg is cramped from where I must have fallen asleep on it.

Q has changed again—this time he's wearing a red track suit and white Adidas tennis shoes with black stripes. How long has he been gone?

I finally get myself to a seated position, and he grabs me under my armpits and drags me over to the wall. He leans me up against it.

"I want to talk to you about Janelle Anderson."

"What?" I ask, my eyelids heavy. My mouth is drier than it's ever been. I feel like I'm in a haze. Not quite awake, but not asleep either. Almost as if—

"I said, *Janelle Anderson.*"

"Did you drug me?" *Have you been drugging me?*

Q nods as if I've asked him if the sky is blue. "You were getting too riled up, so I gave you something. You think I was really that concerned about your little anxiety attack or whatever it was?" He laughs. "Come on now."

"How long was I out?"

"Nice try. I know you want to figure out what day it is, how long you've been here. But I promise you that won't be possible. So you might as well save your energy."

For what?

He sits down, leaning his back against the adjacent wall. I notice a new bucket has replaced the old one. Which means he came in while

I was knocked out. But why? Why not make me live with the stench? Maybe he simply didn't want to smell it when he entered the room. He sees me notice the bucket but doesn't say anything about it. I wonder if he did that on his own, unbeknownst to his boss. If there is a boss. Maybe the camera is part of the game.

"Anyway, it's time to discuss your old buddy Janelle. Remember her?"

"Who?"

"I thought you might play dumb. Want me to refresh your memory?"

No, I really don't want to think about her. Or more specifically, why you know *about her.*

He pulls out his phone and starts reading. "Law school friends. Roommates for a while. Then there was that class you had together— Ethical Issues in Criminal Practice—so ironic the name of the class, don't you think?" He looks at me but doesn't wait for me to answer. "It was in *that* class that you all competed for the internship that would lead to the job. At Douglas, Shirby, and Jones. Recognize that name?"

I don't respond. But yes, I recognize it. It's where I work now. Where I've always worked.

I visualize Janelle. Her long red hair, pale skin, and eyes the color of dark chocolate. It was the first day of our second year, and she walked into our administrative law class twenty minutes late. The teacher scolded her, and her cheeks darkened to a color that matched her hair. She quickly slipped into the seat next to mine and smiled at me through her watery eyes. I smiled back, moved by her ability to be kind in such a humiliating moment. After class, I offered to share the notes from the portion of the lecture she'd missed, and over coffee that afternoon I decided I liked her a lot. She had a sweet voice and kind eyes. I hadn't connected with anyone my first year and worried I might go through my entire law school experience without making a real friend. I had always considered myself independent, with a few close friends here and there, but I hadn't had time for parties and boys and all the other things that made friendships tick. I had been focused on getting into college and then law school.

But Janelle was different. Focused like me. I could see it in her like a reflection. Unlike so many of our classmates, she didn't need to show you how smart she was. There was a quiet confidence about her that I grew to envy as we became closer. How was she so sure of who she was? Sometimes when I looked back at our friendship, I wondered if I'd hoped the best things about her would eventually transfer to me as well.

Clearly, that hasn't happened.

"But the thing is, Janelle didn't get that internship, did she?" Q's voice cuts through my thoughts.

I shake my head lightly, my eyes fixated on my lap.

"I see I've helped jog your memory."

My mind is still foggy, and I blink several times, trying to think. "How—"

"How do I know about Janelle?"

I nod.

"Let's just say that I have a very reliable source."

I look up at the camera.

He smirks. "You want to know who's watching, don't you?"

I nod again.

"Maybe it's all the people you've wronged, Lila. Although . . . we'd have to rent an auditorium for that, wouldn't we?" He shakes his head. *We.*

I know he's working for—with—someone. The question is who?

"Does Janelle know why she didn't get the internship?"

I don't know. I hope she doesn't.

I've lived in denial for a long time about what happened with Janelle. What *I did* to Janelle.

But as Q stares at me now, it's obvious he knows the truth. And I know as I think back on that night in 2006, I'm going to have to see it as it really happened. Not as I have chosen to remember it all these years.

The visual makes my stomach recoil—Professor Callahan's steel bed frame, his sleet-gray comforter rumpled at the foot, his black thick-rimmed eyeglasses on the bedside table. He said he was going to take a shower, and the second the water turned on, I yanked my jeans up over my hips, pulled my sweatshirt over my head, and forced my feet into my boots. I wanted to be anywhere but there. I cracked the bathroom door, the steam hitting me in the face. I looked away, not wanting to see him naked again. "I have to go—early test tomorrow," I lied, not wanting him to resent me for running out. "Okay," he called back, oblivious.

On my way out of his condo, I glanced toward his study and saw the piece of paper on his desk. It was a referral letter written for Janelle—but I already knew that. I'd seen it when I'd first arrived and asked to use the bathroom, then ducked into his office while he poured the wine.

It's why I slept with him.

Survival of the fittest, I told myself at the time. When I walked back into his kitchen, downed my glass of wine, and asked him where the bedroom was, he raised his eyebrows, but it was clear it was what he wanted. Why else would he have invited me to his apartment that night? Not to look at the rare book collection, as he'd claimed and I'd pretended to believe. Sure, I had been attracted to him—I hadn't missed how his chiseled chest barreled out from his fitted button-downs and his ice-blue eyes danced behind his wire-rimmed glasses as he lectured. And I had flirted shamelessly too. Yet I still felt a hesitation as I walked through his faded green apartment door, the dirty linoleum floor and cluttered counters making me feel uneasy. But when curiosity got the better of me and I saw Janelle's name in the letter on his cheap plywood desk, the way Callahan had showered her with accolades, I felt a sudden renewal of interest. A desire for him to pick me. To write those things about me. To succeed, at any cost.

Nausea overcame me as I rushed out of his condo and to my car. I told myself if he called my name in class the next day, our mediocre roll in the hay would be worth it. And if he didn't, well, then I supposed I would have learned my lesson.

The next day I managed to avoid both the professor and Janelle, sneaking into the lecture hall right before class began and slipping into the back row, typically where the students who don't want to get called on plant themselves. I sank down in my seat and tried to disappear, the double shame of my indiscretion and the fear of discovering that I did, in fact, get the internship making my limbs feel heavy. Because of that, I almost didn't notice when Professor Callahan called my name. In fact, he had to say it a second time, his voice booming over the applause. "Lila," he bellowed from the podium. "Stand up and take a bow! You've earned it!"

I stumbled slightly as I launched myself upright, the realization sinking in that my plan had worked as intended. That only yesterday, before I slipped under his sleet-gray comforter, the internship had been Janelle's. Before the slightly drunken striptease I'd performed that led to the semienjoyable sex in his bare-walled two-bedroom apartment. Now it was mine. I finally let my eyes find Janelle, and she smiled, but it didn't quite reach the corners of her eyes. It was as if we both knew that I was a fraud.

"So, I'll ask you again, does Janelle know what you did?" Q is focused on me, waiting for the answer he already knows.

I shrug, my cheeks warming in embarrassment. But deep down in the darkest parts of my gut, I've always wondered if she put two and two together. My guilt drove me away from her slowly at first and then all at once when I stepped foot in the lobby of the law firm I'd sold a part of my soul to work at. I told myself it was because of the long hours I had to put in that I didn't return her calls, her offers to meet for a quick coffee, to catch up. She wanted to see how the internship was going. The one I had stolen from her. Then she took a job up north, and I was incredibly relieved. As I soared at the law firm, I reasoned that although I came here unfairly, I earned my place. Maybe I was the best choice all along, my intervention with Professor Callahan a tiny nudge in what should have been the right direction.

Denial, my friend once more.

"You don't know if your ex-friend is aware that you literally screwed her out of a job?"

"How do *you* know?"

"Ah, ah, ah." Q holds up his finger like a teacher giving a warning. "I already told you I'm not going to answer that. And you keep forgetting I ask the questions, remember? You were near the top of your class at Loyola, but you're a terrible student here."

I sigh, exhausted by Q and his emotional mind-fucking.

Q takes his backpack off and removes a sheet of paper and a pen. Then he pulls out one of those lap desks and sets it on my thighs.

I rack my brains to figure out who knows about this. Professor Callahan, obviously. But he would never tell anyone. He had a reputation for sleeping with students, one that he didn't ever want confirmed. Who else? Ethan. I'd confessed it on our fourth date, almost as a test, needing to know if he could love someone who was capable of that. He'd brushed it off, as people do when they are falling in love and willing to accept almost anything.

Does Sam know? It's possible that he put it together. They were colleagues. Maybe Callahan told him in the way of locker-room talk. Have I mentioned it to Carrie? There were a lot of drunken nights over the course of our friendship—ones where we confessed things to each other. Of course I did most of the conscience cleansing, Carrie's mistakes hardly rising to the level of mine. I can't recall having told her, but it's a possibility. And it's also a likelihood that if I did tell her, then she told Sam. I often confide things to Ethan that friends told me, expecting him to keep the secret. And as far as I know, he always has. Has Sam failed to keep mine? Is he the reason Q took me captive? But then why would Carrie care about that enough to have me kidnapped? Unless she also found out about Sam . . .

"So as you can see"—Q starts talking again, snapping me to attention—"I've got some supplies here. You're probably wondering why I have them." He waves the pen and paper in front of me. "They are for you."

Me? Oh, you shouldn't have.

"I'm going to need you to write a letter." He pauses, tapping the pen against the lap desk. "To Janelle."

He waits for me to react, but I don't. Not outwardly anyway. Inwardly I'm cringing.

"Confessing what you did."

"No," I hear myself say.

"What?" Q's voice is sharp.

"I said no." I look up at him, and our eyes meet. My heart is thumping as I hold his gaze.

Q inches closer to me, and I frantically push myself backward but hit the wall after only a few inches. There's nowhere to go.

Q lurches forward and is face-to-face with me in mere seconds. "You know you can't get away from me," he says so quietly it's almost as if his words are part of his breath.

A cold chill shoots through me as I see him reach inside his jacket. He pulls out a knife. I see the blade first. It's sharp and thick. It looks like my mom's chef's knife, the one she uses to chop the onions finely, the crisp blade cutting through the layers so efficiently her eyes don't sting. He puts it to my neck, and I start to shake. It's cold and hard against my skin. "Remember the artery I mentioned? I can slice it right now. You want to die? How much is your goddamned pride worth, Lila?" His breath is hot against my cheek. He doesn't move the knife.

I stay as still as I possibly can, because if I move, I'm sure the blade will slide through my skin. My heart is beating so hard it feels like it's going to explode. I see my mom's face. The one person who has always loved me unconditionally despite my many flaws. The one who will be the most devastated if my life is cut short.

"I don't want to die," I say quietly, my chin quivering.

He jerks the knife away from my neck, and I gasp for a breath. He swirls it in the air, and then I feel it slicing through the skin of my arm. It happens so quickly, I almost wonder if it really did. I look down, and blood starts gushing from the laceration. I scream out in pain. The wound is burning.

"You ready to write now?" Q asks.

I nod, crying. The cut stings so badly I have to bite my lip to keep from screaming again. My distress is acute as I realize this is a man who is willing to inflict great pain to get what he wants.

This is not a game, and I'm not in control.

He slides the knife into his sheath and pulls out the gun. He unlocks my cuffs, keeping the pistol trained on me as he hands me the pen and paper. "Get writing, Princess."

I nod again, tears flowing from the corners of my eyes. Blood flowing from the gash in my arm.

Dear Janelle, I write with shaky hands.

CHAPTER EIGHTEEN

WEDNESDAY
FREE

I force a smile as Steve Greenwood makes himself comfortable in the deep cushions of the couch in my office.

He's fifteen minutes late, his gaze lingering on my bruised face for a few beats before he asks if I got into a bar fight. Before I have time to explain that I was attacked by a masked man, he quips, "I sure hope you won."

Charming.

"Let's get started," I say through clenched teeth, ignoring his joke and launching into a recap of the private investigator's report, breaking the news that he's found nothing so far to corroborate Greenwood's allegations.

"Impossible!" Greenwood says, pounding his meaty hand on my desk.

"Can you please not hit my furniture?" I ask.

He throws up his arms as if shocked by my response. "Sorry," he says, clearly not sorry at all.

"He's going to stay on her," I offer. "If there's something to be found, he will find it. But we are in a time crunch since you switched counsel so close to the preliminary hearing. We are doing the best we can."

I open the file and start asking Greenwood a few questions that came to mind as I reviewed the case earlier this morning. We also discuss his expectations for distribution of assets and custody.

"Zero alimony. That's nonnegotiable," he commands. I nod but say nothing, so he takes this as a sign to continue. "I want the house, the cars. Full custody. She can see them after she goes through rehab."

"Anything else?" I ask.

"That should do it," he responds, my sarcasm lost on him. "She cheated on me, and you know what that means? She gets nothing!"

I release a slow breath and refrain from asking him if he is aware of the divorce laws in California. This is a no-fault state. If I could get my hands on footage of her riding her book club boyfriend, it would make no difference except to shame her, I suppose. But the drinking, that's a different story. If we can prove that she's reckless with the children as a result of her alcohol consumption, it could affect custody and the ensuing child support and possibly alimony. But the children would have to be involved. They'd have to talk to a guardian ad litem, answering questions about what she was doing. *If* she was doing it. They are only kindergarteners, far too young to be put in the middle of something like this. But when I mention this to Greenwood, he doesn't skip a beat.

"It's not a problem," he says. His conviction and willingness to bring his children into the mix makes me wonder if maybe he is telling the truth about her, and she simply put on a good show for my investigator. Otherwise, what kind of person would do that?

I pause for a moment as I consider my next inquiry. I need to be delicate, but it's something that has been bothering me. "Let's discuss the disturbance at your house last fall."

"That wasn't a disturbance," Greenwood asserts quickly. Too quickly.

"The police that showed up at your house begged to differ."

"It was a misunderstanding," he says, his voice suddenly eerily calm. His eyes trained on mine. "There was no report filed."

"Right. I couldn't find one, just the record that the 911 call was made," I say. Chase had sweet-talked his spy down at the station into confirming it existed. I make a notation to ask Detective Sully to see if he could pull the recording. He's still failed to return my calls and texts from yesterday. He's never taken that long to get back to me in the ten years I've known him.

"Lynn was drunk, as usual, and went nuts. She was going crazy on me, on the boys. When I tried to calm her down, she said I was trying to kill her and called the police. When they showed up and saw how belligerent she was, they wanted to take her in, especially when she tried to push one of them, but she fell before she made contact. But I convinced them to let her stay with me and sleep it off."

"And how did you do that?"

He smirks. "I'm very persuasive when I want to be."

"Meaning?"

Greenwood breaks into a grin. "Let's move on, Lila. There's nothing there. I was a husband, trying to protect his wife, even if she didn't deserve it. What can I say? I'm a good guy."

I return his smile and nod but have to swallow the bile in the back of my throat. This is going to be the longest two hours of my life.

I sit and stare out my window long after he leaves, his potent cologne still lingering, reminding me of the way I felt while he was here—like I was missing something. I have a hard time believing his not pressing charges was out of the goodness of his heart. There must have been something in it for him. More than saving face with his snobby Pacific Palisades neighbors. But what?

I'm so absorbed in my thoughts that I don't hear Sam enter my office, his deep voice startling me. I literally jump out of my seat, the memory of the attack from last night coming back in full force. I'm okay in the busy moments—Greenwood had been an effective distraction; I'll give him that. When I'm working I can almost forget the way it felt when the assailant pulled my hair back and grabbed me by the neck. But whenever I stop, the fear I felt then comes slithering back.

Sam puts his hands up. "Sorry. I come in peace."

I bring my hand to my chest and breathe deeply until I feel my heart rate slow again. "You scared me."

"Chase isn't at his desk. I knocked, and when you didn't answer, I assumed you weren't in here. I was coming in to leave you a note," Sam explains, his eyes soft. Possibly apologetic. "I heard about what happened last night. I wanted to make sure you were okay."

"I didn't think you cared anymore," I say. "You made that pretty clear yesterday in your office."

"Come on, Lila." He closes the door to my office. "It's not that simple, and you know it."

"Really? It seems pretty simple to me. I break up with you; you destroy my career."

"Come on now. I know you can handle whatever is thrown your way. Take it as a compliment." Sam laughs nervously and shoves his hands in his pockets. I've seen him do it before in court and later dubbed it his "aw shucks" move when he needs to win the jury over. They never fail to eat it up.

But me, I know better.

He walks to my side of the desk and touches the lump on my forehead. I flinch and can't quite decide if it's because of the pain or his proximity. Maybe both. "Let me help you," he says, his face so close I can smell the spearmint gum he's chewing. "It doesn't have to be like this."

I close my eyes and lean my head on his shoulder, the mental and physical exhaustion from the night before finally hitting me. I won't deny that it feels amazing to lay my cheek against the soft wool of his suit jacket, to have his arms encircle me tightly. I feel safe.

"I miss you," he whispers into my hair. And that makes it much harder. Because I miss him too. But that doesn't change the fact that we can't be together.

I lift my head and push him away gently. "I can't, Sam."

His eyes grow hard. "It makes no sense, Lila. Six months it's all good, and now it's not. What's changed?"

I search his face. Has Carrie told him about the baby? How could that not change things for him? For all of us? "Me. I've changed. I can't do this to Carrie. Not anymore," I confess. The pregnancy has snapped me out of whatever trance I've been in—shattered any illusion or justification that what we were doing isn't wrong on every single level.

Sam's expression is tight. "That's never stopped you before."

I bristle. "Maybe I want to be better."

"Not possible, Bennett." Sam shakes his head. "You are who you are. You take what you want, no matter the consequences. Since when do you care who gets hurt?"

I walk over and open my door. "Bye, Sam."

He stands eye-to-eye with me. "You're making a huge mistake."

"Maybe. But it's mine to make."

He turns on his heel and walks down the hallway without looking back. He's made his choice. And I've made mine.

Hopefully we'll both survive them.

Chase finally reappears a few minutes later with a green juice and a Locomoco bowl from Gwench Juice Bar, so I decide to forgive him for not screening Sam from barging in earlier. "It was terrible," I say as I recount the conversation with Sam, and Chase hands me two Advils. "He hates me more now," I add and think of the way Sam's mouth clenched on his last words to me. You don't cross a man like him and get away with it unscathed.

"Hold on," I say to myself as a thought comes to me, and I walk back to my desk, grabbing the notes from my meeting with Greenwood.

"What?" Chase asks.

I play back the conversation with Greenwood in my head. "When Greenwood was here, he insisted that he made that disturbance go away because he'd been trying to protect Lynn."

"Right," Chase says, confused.

"But that incident was what, less than six months ago? Why would he be willing to protect her then and destroy her now?"

Chase nods slowly. "It would have made more sense for him to make sure the incident was documented. It would really help solidify the allegations against her."

"Right. So what if he hid it for a different reason?"

"Like what?"

"I don't know. But we need to find out before we go any further." Sam's face flashes in my head again. His anger toward me. "Because men like that, they have a way of making the world play in their favor."

I grab my phone and text Detective Sully. We need to talk, ASAP. Stop ignoring me!

I send off the text and wonder why I haven't heard from him, as he always gets back to me right away. I hope someone inside the force hasn't swayed him against me. This latest win surely hasn't sat well with the department. But no, he was loyal to me. Wasn't he? I notice three missed calls from Carrie and several texts from Ethan, all asking how I'm doing and begging me to call. "I need to make a few calls," I tell Chase. "Can you connect with Joe and see if he found anything out on Franklin yet?"

"Sure thing," he says and shuts my door on the way out. I take a deep breath and text Ethan that I'm fine, just busy, and not to worry. Then I dial Carrie.

"Hey, there." I try to sound peppy when she answers, not wanting to worry her.

"Oh my God, Lila! I've been freaking out all day because you haven't called me back. I was so afraid something bad happened to you again. I had to call Ethan to make sure you were okay. He said you went to work. Why would you go in today?"

"I'm sorry I haven't called you back," I say, the sting of Sam's words coming back at the sound of Carrie's voice. "I had some things that couldn't be rescheduled. And anyway, I'm fine."

"You don't have to do that with me, you know."

"What?" I ask. "What am I doing?"

"Acting like what happened is nothing. Like this is another day at work. You were brutally attacked last night. You could have died!" She lowers her voice and says, "It's okay to admit that. It's okay to be scared."

I don't know if it's what she says or the way her voice gentles, but I start to cry, tears I didn't know I'd been holding inside escaping from my eyes and down my cheeks, sliding off my chin and onto Steve Greenwood's file. Which only makes me cry harder. She's right. I don't want to admit how close I came to being kidnapped or killed. The scariest part is that I have no idea what the attacker intended to do to me. His only words to me indicated that whatever it was, he was going to take great pleasure in it. And he's still out there. Is he watching? The back of my neck tingles at the thought.

Carrie politely waits for me to stop crying. "Feel better?" she asks after I blow my nose loudly.

"I do." Admitting the fear has taken away a little bit of its power.

When I've caught my breath, Carrie peppers me with more questions about the attack. For every single detail I didn't disclose previously. How exactly did he grab me? What did he say? Did he seem familiar at all? I answer all her questions but have to admit I'm relieved when Chase ducks his head in my doorway and gives me our signal for *get off the phone, I need to tell you something important.*

I sign off with Carrie, offering her lunch the next day when she says she has to see me in person to make sure I'm really okay.

"What's up?" I ask Chase.

"Two things."

"Is this a good news, bad news situation?"

"No, this is more like a bad news, really bad news thing. Which one do you want first?"

I rub my eyes. I have no doubt I look like hell at this point. "Surprise me."

"This arrived for you via messenger. It's from Stephanie."

"What is it?"

Chase shakes his head. "I think you should open it."

I pull out a stack of papers from a manila envelope and scan the top sheet. It's a wrongful-death civil lawsuit that Stephanie has filed against Jeremiah. "Oh my God—she's not letting this go."

"That's not the worst of it."

"The fact that she is trying to pull an OJ on Jeremiah isn't the worst of it?"

"There's more. A smaller envelope. It must still be inside."

I reach in and pull it out. On the outside is a note written to me:

Lila, I don't know how you live with yourself after helping a murderer go free. Did you help him hide evidence? Is that how you two got away with it? Inside is a present from me. Consider it a reminder of what you've done. Of who you are.

I open the envelope and pull out a picture. I gasp.

I look up. "It's his wife. It's Vivian." She's smiling, looking at something just off camera.

"I know," Chase says, giving me a sad smile.

"I thought I was done with her. With this case."

"I'm sorry."

"Please tell me this is the *really* bad news."

Chase pauses. "It's not. I also spoke with Joe. Franklin is missing."

My head starts to spin. "What do you mean, he's missing?"

"He's completely off the grid. No credit card, cell phone, or social media activity for at least two weeks."

I struggle to catch my breath. Did he go into hiding a few weeks ago, biding his time until he found the right window to assault me? But that couldn't have been Franklin last night—the man I'd tussled with had been buff. Strong. Had Franklin recruited help?

"Maybe it's a coincidence," Chase offers weakly, as if he's read my mind.

"Or maybe it's not," I say and reach up to touch the tender skin on my face, pushing it hard. It stings horribly at first, but eventually the pain becomes a part of me.

CHAPTER NINETEEN

WEDNESDAY
CAPTURED

Dear Janelle,

It's been a long time. Too long, really. I'm reaching out now to apologize for a mistake I made a long time ago. It's something I've thought about often, wondering if it could have caused a ripple effect on your life. On mine. Because I'm beginning to realize that at the end of the day, we are just a sum of the choices we make. And I've made a lot of bad ones.

I set the pen down and touch the wound on my arm, now wrapped in a bandage Q reluctantly removed from his backpack once blood had dripped on the letter, smearing the ink. *I can't have you bleeding out all over this*, he hissed, then handed me a fresh piece of paper, where I began my mea culpa once again. I asked him for some privacy, insisting the words would be more natural if he weren't hovering over me while I wrote them, but he refused. Although he turned his back to me.

But I knew the camera was still watching.

As I hold the pen above the paper, my hand is shaking, from both fear of what I'm about to admit and the reality of why I'm admitting it. The irony that Q is holding me captive, yet my character is being called into question, does not escape me. But it makes one thing very clear: This is not a random abduction. This is not about sex. Or a big payday.

This is about justice.

I look up at the camera. Whoever is behind that blinking red light wants me to pay for my sins. And it's very possible I deserve to do just that.

I rest my hand on the paper and try to think of how to give Q what he wants without exposing myself. This information will ruin my reputation at the firm. Although considering the predicament I'm in, does it matter? Will I live to see the consequences of my confession? I swallow a sob as I realize the answer is no. There's no reason for Q to keep me alive after he gets everything he wants. So if I'm going to die, Janelle deserves to know the truth. And I'm in desperate need of absolution.

You were a good friend to me. Remember when I came down with strep the night before my biggest final in my criminal procedure class, and you stayed up with me all night, making sure I was prepared? I've never forgotten the way you gave me a cold towel for the back of my neck, how you risked your own health to help mine. Do you remember what you said when I thanked you? "You would have done the same for me, Lila." I simply nodded.

Here's my first confession—I wouldn't have. I probably would have thrown some Advil at you and run away to the library to study. I would have lamented your bad luck, but it wouldn't have crossed my mind that I should help you. That was always the difference between you and me. I pretended to be good, but you were actually good. Almost like there was no way either of us could avoid our destiny—you, the savior, me, the destroyer. And it's not only you. I've developed a very nasty habit of hurting the people closest to me—saving my worst venom for the most loyal. I've had some alone time to wonder why. Why I build things up and then destroy them with my bare hands.

It would be so easy to blame this on my dad—I'd told you he passed away when I was twelve, but I left out that he'd been unfaithful to my mom while he was alive. Or maybe I could pin it on my mom for confessing the secret to me after he died, a few months before I met you in torts class. Because the truth is it did crack something open inside me. It changed the way I viewed love. Loyalty. It changed the way I viewed myself. If I was in court defending myself right now, I'd argue it was the basis for every bad decision I've made since. I'd ask for leniency.

But both those defenses are bullshit. No matter what happened to me, it still did not give me the right to betray others the way I have. It does not excuse what I did to you.

Tears stain the page as I write. Excavating a deep truth hurts. But I take a breath and keep going before I lose my nerve.

You're probably shaking your head right now. Wondering why I'm being so hard on myself. I can hear you saying, "Nobody's perfect!" in your throaty voice. You would want me to feel better. But I don't deserve any sympathy from you.

I'm sure you recall Professor Callahan, our ethics professor. Remember how he'd let his eyes linger a little too long on his female students while he lectured? How he had a reputation for flirting during his office hours? We'd laughed and wondered which coed would be his next conquest.

I guess I was the lucky one. I slept with him the day before he chose the recipient of the internship at Douglas, Shirby, and Jones, the law firm that gave me the start to what has been an amazing career. I've told myself over and over that my desire to win the internship wasn't the reason I slept with him, that the timing was simply a coincidence. But that is one of the many lies I've told myself.

When I was at his apartment, I saw his internship choice on a paper on his desk. It had your name on it. But the next day he called mine instead. I swear to you, Janelle, I never asked him to give it to me. To take it from you. But there is no denying that the intention was there. That I stole something that wasn't mine.

I know it hurt you when I pulled away soon after that, and I'm sorry. You didn't know it at the time, but I was doing you the biggest favor of your life. You are, quite simply, too good for me.

I've heard you've become a very successful prosecutor, and I'm happy for you. I will say this—the internship I hijacked that led to my high-profile job— it has a price. Sometimes the ambiguity of my client's guilt or innocence weighs me down so hard I can barely breathe. It has broken me down piece by piece, until there is almost nothing left. And for that reason, there is a small part of me that hopes I saved you from such a fate. That my selfishness propelled you on the noble path for which you are meant.

I can't change the past, but I can make one promise: I'll never betray myself or anyone else that way ever again. I hope you can forgive me.

Lila Bennett

I fold the letter in half, not wanting to see the words, to relive my confession. I meant every single word, and it was shocking how much the truth hurt to write. I'm crying now and don't look up when I hear Q's heavy footsteps walking toward me. The paper crunches slightly when he picks it up. Silence invades the room for several minutes. I assume he's reading my words, but I refuse to look up. To give him the pleasure of seeing that I give a shit what he thinks.

I feel his foot nudge me. "You really mean this? Or is this more of your fake bullshit you do with all the people in your life?" His words are soft. Questioning. Skeptical of my capability to be introspective. But curious that I might not be as evil as he'd so clearly been told.

"Yes," I whisper, forcing myself to look at him finally. "She deserved better."

His shadowed eyes search mine. More silence.

"You bet your ass she did!" he eventually spouts, but his words sound a tiny bit hollow. Almost as if he doesn't like this side of me. He doesn't want me to care. To be remorseful. Human. He wants me to fight. It will make it easier for him to hate me. Hurt me. To kill me.

He leans down and recuffs my hands tightly. "I'm off to deliver this letter. Hope your hand isn't cramping. I have a strong feeling you've got many more of these to get off your chest."

"Right," I affirm and turn away from him. My confession to Janelle has sucked the fight out of me.

Maybe I'm ready to die.

CHAPTER TWENTY

When I finally get home, it's 10:15 p.m. I flip the dead bolt and the second lock on the doorknob and lean against the door, feeling as if I've lived two full days in one, my head and heart playing tug-of-war about Jeremiah's case all day. My head continually justified the acquittal. *You were doing your job! There wasn't any hard evidence!* My heart shouted back immediately, *But still. That feeling you had. Could you have missed something?* Those conflicting thoughts battled it out inside me as I pored through the wrongful-death civil lawsuit Stephanie filed but finally agreed on one thing: regardless of Jeremiah's guilt or innocence, karma has finally come knocking on my door.

I couldn't push the thought aside as I'd stared at the photo of Vivian that Stephanie had included in the envelope. I studied Vivian's wide smile, her oval chocolate eyes, her slightly crooked nose. *Did he kill you?* I whispered. Stephanie and her sister were only sixteen months apart in age and best friends. She testified in court that Vivian had told her that Jeremiah was controlling as well as abusive, verbally and physically. But she had no proof—had never witnessed it herself. It was hard to believe this woman in the picture was the same one in the crime scene photos. But still, I could not seem to put the photo back in the envelope. Instead, I got Jeremiah's case file out and started to read through it. Chase popped his head in once or twice, arching his eyebrow at me. I waved him off, deep into the police report that was filed the night Vivian was killed. Had I overlooked something? But when I finished reading through it, I came to the same conclusion: there wasn't enough evidence to support a guilty verdict. My head reminded me I simply did my job as a defense attorney; I gave my client what was promised by the US Constitution—representation. But my heart still layered doubt into every thought. What if Jeremiah lost his temper and killed his wife, then staged the scene to look like a burglary? Hid the murder weapon? It was all possible, but not provable. At least not in a criminal court.

And then Jeremiah called. He'd been served the lawsuit, and he was livid—freaking out over the fact that the standard of proof is lower in a civil case: the jury must decide that there is at least a 50.1 percent probability that Jeremiah is responsible. And the jurors wouldn't have to come to a unanimous decision—only nine of the twelve would need to believe Jeremiah is guilty, whereas in his criminal case, the jurors had to unanimously believe that he is guilty beyond a reasonable doubt. Jeremiah would be forced to testify if he were called to the stand. When I defended him criminally, I strongly advised him not to testify, and he agreed that it was better to have the lack of evidence speak for itself. I was concerned that Jeremiah would come across too unemotional on the stand. It's always a risk to do that, and I've had one time in my career where it backfired miserably. To this day, I wonder what would have happened if I had made a different choice. But I hadn't felt like we'd had another option in this case, and this time it had worked out.

"So they lose in court and now are trying to backdoor some sort of guilty verdict, in an attempt to ruin my life? This will bankrupt me if I lose. Not to mention my career as a surgeon will be over. My reputation. I already have backlash at the hospital, people not wanting me to operate on them," he bellowed.

"There is still no evidence. With the lower threshold, I still don't think they have enough to find you liable in a civil case."

"They found OJ guilty!"

"Are you comparing yourself to OJ?" I asked, careful to keep my voice light, bothered slightly that he saw himself in the same light.

"Of course not!" He sighed into the phone. "But in OJ's case, the Goldman and Brown families got a second chance for the verdict they wanted. And they *won*. And now Stephanie's getting a second shot too. What if she somehow wins?"

I wanted to tell him they'd far from won—the people they loved had been brutally murdered. A $50 million settlement was never going to bring them back. But before I could say anything to that effect, he started spouting again.

"I was acquitted, dammit. Why isn't that enough? She clearly wants to shame me. That's all this is! A smear campaign!"

I rubbed my throbbing temples as he yelled so loudly into the phone I had to hold it away from my ear. Jeremiah had never shown any anger during the trial. In fact, he had displayed very little emotion at all. At the time I had chalked it up to his personality. But now I wondered if he'd ever gotten this angry at Vivian. Had she ever had to hold the phone away while he screamed? Even with all our issues, I tried to recall a time Ethan had ever raised his voice to me like this, but I couldn't. I waited quietly for Jeremiah's rage to run its course until the only sound was his rapid breathing. We sat like that for a few moments before he spoke again, his voice hoarse, asking if I'd be representing him again.

I told him another call was coming in, and I had to take it. That I'd give him an answer by Friday. I know how it will look if I quit on him now. Will people think I no longer believe he's innocent? I don't want to condemn him. But what if I did agree to be his lawyer? How could I face Stephanie in court each day? And if I have to look at the case again—in the detail it would require—what will I find? I didn't discover anything today, but that doesn't mean it isn't there. Not to mention what Stephanie's lawyers might uncover the second time around.

My house is completely dark save for the soft glow of the lamp in the entry. I reach down to remove my heels and rub my throbbing feet. Out of nowhere I feel a burning sensation in my ankles, and the pain slithers up my legs. I sit down on the pine bench we picked up at a flea market last summer and grimace, the heat burning my calves. But suddenly the pain disappears almost as fast as it came. What caused it, I wonder? I start to grab for my phone so I can google it when I think I hear a sound. I freeze, holding my breath, waiting. But I don't hear anything else. I wait a few more beats and still nothing. So I get up and head down the pitch-black hallway to the kitchen, stumbling slightly on a trash bag Ethan must have forgotten to take to the curb. I feel for the light on the wall of the hallway, and my finger hovers over the switch. A slice of moonlight coming in from a window in the living room reveals a shadowy figure at the end of the hall. My heart starts jackhammering in my chest.

My assailant is back.

How did he get inside? The front door was locked when I came in, I'm sure of it. My heart thrusting against my rib cage, I tiptoe back toward the entryway and grab the first thing I see—my shoe—and hold it up with the spiked heel facing the intruder. I press my back up against the wall, hoping he didn't see me. Suddenly the light flips on, and I scream reflexively. It takes me a moment before I realize it's Ethan.

"You scared me," I say, trying to catch my breath.

"I live here, don't I?"

"Of course," I say, caught off guard by his tone. "The house was so dark, and I thought . . ." I stop midsentence when I see Ethan's pinched expression. Then I notice he's fully dressed and wearing his shoes, something we never do in the house.

He folds his arms across his chest and stares at me for several seconds.

"Did I do something? Did I wake you?" I ask, wondering why he isn't giving me a pass for being jumpy—especially after what happened to me last night.

"Nope—don't usually sleep in my shoes."

"Okay, then, what's wrong?" I ask, dropping my heel next to its mate on the floor.

He leans against the wall and closes his eyes for a moment. When he opens them he gives me a hard look, as if trying to see through me. Finally he speaks, slowly, as if he's not sure I will understand him if he doesn't. "I'm going to ask you something. And I'm only going to ask once. I need you to be honest with me."

"Okay," I say, my heart starting to race again.

He knows. I shake my head slightly. *Deny. Deny. Deny. He can't have any proof, only suspicions. I can talk my way out of this.*

"Lila, please do not lie to me."

"I won't. I would never," I say, trying to keep my voice steady.

He cocks his head at me. He thinks I've already lied.

"What's going on?" I ask. It could be something else. Maybe he found the credit card bill for the $500 pair of shoes Chase talked me into buying last month. God, please let it be that.

"Are you having an affair with Sam?"

"What?" I say, widening my eyes to show my shock.

"You heard me."

I weigh my options. I could tell him everything right now, but then I'd lose him. I know he will never stay with me if he knows the truth. And if he has a suspicious text message or an email, there's nothing I can't spin. Sam is my boss. We work together a lot. We see each other outside of the office—for work. We are also friends. He's my best friend's husband. I study Ethan's face. He's angrier than I've ever seen him. Not Jeremiah angry, but really, really pissed off. But there's no way he could know for sure.

"Answer me, Lila."

"No," I say.

He frowns, his face falling. He walks out of the room and comes back with the same beat-up roller bag he's had since I met him—gray with brown pleather seams. He opens the front door and starts to walk out but then turns around. My stomach flips—he's not going to leave. Right? We're going to talk this out? He'll give me a chance to explain?

"Oh, I almost forgot to give you these . . ." He bends down and unzips the outer pocket of the suitcase. He slides out a navy-blue envelope with white trim and tosses it on the table. "I really wish you hadn't lied to me. Maybe we would have had a chance if you'd told the truth. If you know what that is anymore," he says, then holds my gaze for several beats.

My voice is caught somewhere in my throat as I watch him leave me. I have wondered several times over the last six months what this moment might look like. Fear inching in during the times Sam and I were careless, paranoia that someone saw something, that Ethan would discover us. But it always felt a bit out of reach, as if I were in a dream-like state, unable to imagine what it would actually feel like to have it happen. I could never have understood the searing pain that would rip me apart as Ethan walked away. How powerless it would feel.

He sails through the door and slams it so hard, our wedding picture hanging on the wall shakes and almost falls. I steady it and walk slowly to the envelope. I touch the outside lightly, afraid of what the inside holds. Scared of how my life will change the instant I open it. I shake my head slightly. I let my guard down. And I've lost my husband as a result.

My gut tells me what's inside. But still, I have to look. Slowly I pull out the contents: two eight-by-ten photographs of Sam and me. They are both from two nights ago when I broke up with him—he has his hand tipped under my chin and is kissing me, his eyes shut, mine open wide. It's from the parking garage—that same night. Right before I pushed him away and reminded him of the cameras above, of the people who could walk out and catch us. It is unmistakably us. Unmistakably Sam kissing me. And it does not appear that I'm trying to stop him. Even though I did. I think of the irony—that Ethan had me followed the same night I broke things off with Sam. If only it had been one day later. If only Ethan understood that it had been our last kiss. That I had chosen him, albeit a little too late.

I fling the door open and call after him. "Wait, Ethan."

He's about a half block down but turns, and I feel a burst of hope that he is going to come back, talk this through.

I run to the bottom of the stairs and onto the sidewalk. "Did you know, before the pictures?" I ask. "Because your new book, about the cheating wife . . ." I let my voice trail off.

Ethan lets out a shrill laugh, and a man jogging by looks over. "I thought about that." He runs his hand through his hair. "Fuck, maybe part of me knew. Always knew that you were capable of this. Knew that our marriage was on the brink. Knew that you didn't have the patience to ride it out. So maybe my subconscious was trying to tell me something— trying to tell me to get my head out of the sand."

"Ethan—"

Ethan holds up his hand. "Stop. There's nothing more to say," he says and turns down the sidewalk, away from me and our life together.

I fall to my knees and start to cry, the pictures scattering to the ground. A woman walking her apricot poodle stops when she sees me and asks me if I'm okay. "Yes, I'm fine, sorry," I say as I stare at the photos until they blur.

But I'm not okay. It's just another lie.

CHAPTER
TWENTY-ONE

"I have a present for you," Q says when he returns later. It hasn't been long. Maybe an hour? He nudges me much harder in the side than before. "Get up."

I flinch when his sneaker makes contact with my rib cage and try to touch my chest, but the cuffs pull hard on the raw skin of my wrists. "Can't you take these off?" I ask, still in the fetal position but holding my hands out in front of me. "It's not like without them I'll be able to escape." I eye the heavy door.

"Nope," he says simply.

"I need to use the restroom again," I say, my cheek still pressed against the floor.

"Oh well. You need a bath too, but you ain't going to get that either." Q smirks.

I push myself up so I'm leaning on my right forearm, then roll into a seated position. It takes an embarrassingly long amount of time.

Q watches me, his tough-guy stance in full effect—his shoulders are pressed back, his hands balled into fists at his sides. His mission is clear—to make me pay. But who set him on this path?

Stephanie? Sam? Janelle? Franklin?

Carrie? That possibility pains me to think.

Adam from work? I haven't considered him before, but he and I have always been rivals. And this would be something I could see him doing. I always thought he seemed like a man who would do anything to further himself. As the minutes clipped by, sometimes lightning fast and at other times painstakingly slow, everyone has begun to look like a suspect.

My bladder burns, and I glance at the bucket. "Then can you turn around so I can go," I say matter-of-factly. "Please," I add.

To my surprise, his shoulders relax, and his eyes don't look as hard. "I'll take you down the hall," he says, then pulls me up, and we walk toward the door. My legs are wobbly from the absence of movement, my head light from lack of food and water.

"Make it quick," he says when we reach the bathroom.

As I sit on the dirty toilet seat, I try to come up with a plan. Can I use my cuffs to knock him out? It's doubtful. I might hurt him a little, but he'd immediately retaliate. And what would *that* look like? Maybe I could knee him in the groin? But with my ankles bound, I'm not sure I could. And if by some miracle I did succeed in getting away from him, how long before the person watching through the camera noticed? Before Q got up and followed me? Could I get to his knife? His gun? I hit a brick wall with every idea. I know the only way I'd have a fraction of a chance is if I could get him to remove the cuffs and the ankle bindings. But the odds would still be stacked against me.

When I come out of the bathroom no closer to a plan, he's squinting at something on his phone. He types quickly, and I try to see who he is writing to, but he pulls it away before I can. "Knock it off." He gives me a shove, and I stumble forward. "That's for sticking your nose where it doesn't belong."

"Sorry," I grumble.

"You should be." Then he lowers his voice almost to a whisper. "Listen, don't do shit like that, you hear me? Don't make this harder than it has to be." He stares at me, and I'm so close, I can see the spatters of gold in his eyes.

Is he sending me a message? If he is, I have only one shot to say something impactful—to make him doubt the person behind that camera.

I lean in and drop my voice to a whisper. "But you would be the one to have to kill me, right?"

"Right." I think I see something flicker in his eyes.

"So why *you*?"

"Because."

"But you'll be the one who goes to prison."

"If I'm caught."

"*When.*"

"What makes you so sure?" His voice lacks its normal confidence.

"Are you already in the system, Q?"

He shrugs. "What's it to you?"

"Your prints are everywhere. You've worn a mask, but not gloves. They'll track you down if you have priors."

"What makes you think they'll find this place at all?"

"They will. Because here's what the person you're working with has failed to realize. Whether the LAPD actually cares if I'm found or not doesn't matter. What's important is they've held a press conference. The public knows about the case. The LAPD will take so much shit if they don't solve it."

Q looks as if he hasn't considered this.

"Listen, you can still get out of this. I don't know who you are. Let me go, and I promise I won't tell anyone where I was. I'll say I can't remember anything."

"What do you think this is right now?" He shakes his head. "That suddenly we're besties? Because I told you not to be stupid?"

"No—but I don't think you're a killer."

"You don't know shit about me. About the things I'm willing to do," he says, but there's something in his voice. I've clearly hit a nerve.

"Okay," I say, shrugging. "I guess I was wrong—I got the impression you were trying to protect me."

"Well, I wasn't." He pushes me into the room and locks the door behind us. The sound of the latch instantly makes a pit form in my stomach. But I also feel hopeful. Because, despite what he said, Q showed me a part of himself. I don't think he's convinced that killing me is the solution. So if I can work on him, use that sliver of doubt that's inside him to my advantage, maybe, just maybe, I can get out of here.

"Like I said earlier, I have a present for you."

"You shouldn't have," I say sarcastically.

He takes off his backpack and unzips it. I watch as he pulls out a blue envelope with white trim. As I stare at it, I get a sense of déjà vu. As if I've seen it before. But why? At work, we only use manila or white. Never blue. As he unfastens the brackets on the back, there's something about *this* envelope that's sparking a memory. He reaches inside. I sense that it's something that will tie me to Sam.

But how could I possibly know that?

He thrusts a piece of paper in front of my face. I have to pull my head back to see it clearly.

It's a photograph of Sam tipping my chin and kissing me in the parking garage at work.

"You took this?"

He nods. "Right before I followed you to the restaurant."

"You were watching us?"

He nods. "Had been for a while. You really should use your blinker more, by the way. It's not safe to just turn like that."

"What do you plan to do with this?"

"Oh, Lila. Haven't you figured that out yet?" He turns the picture around and looks at it. "You really do have a thing for Sam. It's so clear." He shows it to me again, points it at my face. "I think it's his power that attracts you."

That's true. But how does Q know it? How much time do you have to spend observing someone to see beyond their actions and into the motivation behind them?

"How long have you been watching me?" I ask.

Q laughs. "Does it matter?" He waves the pictures like a fan. "You've got bigger problems than my stalking timeline to deal with."

I feel dizzy. It takes me a moment before I can speak.

"What do you mean?" I ask.

"I sent them. The pictures."

"To whom?" I ask, but I know. I see Ethan walking to the mailbox and turning the key. Unsuspecting that his life is about to change in one instant. Carrie. Sifting through the stack of mail in her kitchen. Stopping when she sees one she doesn't recognize. Opening it, her marriage, her life, everything imploding in that moment.

"You're a smart girl. I'm sure you know the two people who received a copy," Q says. "So why don't you tell me the names of the lucky recipients of this photograph, Lila."

"Does it matter at this point?" I say, my voice low. First Janelle and my reputation. Now this. My marriage and my closest friendship, destroyed. If escape is possible, I'll have nothing left once I'm free. Maybe that has been the plan all along.

"It does matter." Q steps closer. "Say their names."

"Ethan," I say, lowering my gaze.

"Ah yes. The soon-to-be ex-husband! I have to admit, he puts up with a lot of shit from you. But he won't stand for this."

I nod. He's right. This will shatter Ethan's fragile ego. He always told me loyalty is the most important gift one person can give another. I guess a part of me always thought his love for me was indestructible, that the fact that I've muddled through the highs and lows of his moods made me infallible. How arrogant I've been.

"And?" Q prompts.

"Carrie," I mutter. "Sam's wife."

"And don't forget she's also your *best friend*! Although I'm thinking she'll now be your ex-best friend." He points to the photo. "Because this shit breaks all kinds of girl code." He leans close to my face, and I can smell the spearmint gum he's chewing. "Do you fuck over every single person who cares about you?"

I open my mouth to speak, but he places a finger over my lips. "Don't answer that. It was rhetorical." Q walks to the door and looks back one more time. "Consider life as you knew it to be over."

For the first time, I know he's not talking about killing me.

CHAPTER TWENTY-TWO

I tighten my grasp around the bottle of the Prisoner as I raise it to my lips. I skipped the formality of a glass after Ethan stormed out, screwing off the cork and sinking onto our worn caramel leather couch, the one we bought on a whim six years ago shortly after getting married. We couldn't keep our hands off each other that day, the sales associate at the store trying not to stare as we kissed on the sofa.

I close my eyes now and remember the way it had felt to lie between the sheets with Ethan, moving my hands toward his bare chest instinctively when I woke. I try to recall the desire I felt. It burned hot within me for how long? When did I start to turn away instead of reaching for him? Time is interesting that way. How did it slip through my fingers without me noticing? And now here I am, forced to face the present—the reality that it's been years since I desired Ethan in a *real* way. The passion I once felt for him fell away slowly at first, and then it disappeared, almost as if it had never been there. And yes, I could blame my relationship with Sam. It certainly hasn't helped to have someone else occupying my thoughts and often my dreams as I lay next to Ethan, my conscience betraying him even when my body wasn't.

It's true that I most likely gave up on our marriage well before Sam and I connected in my office that night. Or why else had I let him kiss me? If there hadn't been a crack in the foundation of my marriage to Ethan, would Sam have been able to find an opening to slip into? As I sit here in the dark, swigging a fifty-dollar bottle of wine, sunk so deep into the cushions of a couch I never really liked, I can no longer hide from the facts: the walls of my marriage have fallen down, and I simply watched it happen.

Ethan loves this couch. I don't. But we were new, in that phase where something as innocuous as a sofa doesn't matter—before you're giving each other hard looks over inconsequential purchases the other made, simply because you weren't consulted. Back then, I had been thinking something more like white chenille. Something stark yet comfortable. He shook his head hard as I slid my hand along the soft fabric, envisioning the crisp and simple life we'd have with that couch. Especially since it most likely wasn't going to involve kids, so we didn't have to worry about them staining the fabric. Although when I said that to Ethan, he raised his eyebrow as if we hadn't yet decided, as if to say, *You never know.* And because you never do know anything with absolute certainty, I didn't fight that hard for it.

"No way on white!" Ethan said loudly, but there was laughter behind his words.

"Come on," I said, walking over and leaning my hips into his. "Think of all the things we could do on it," I whispered into his ear, biting it slightly.

He pulled me in tightly, and I could feel his arousal. "Stop playing dirty to get what you want," he whispered back before pushing me away from him slightly so he could see my face.

"What?" I asked, feigning innocence. "I'm building a case for this glorious white seven-foot chenille couch!"

"You know exactly what you're doing," he said playfully and walked toward a caramel leather couch, the cushions rounded and puffy. "What about this one?" He set his hand on it. "Think of the naps we could take on this!"

"So now we're napping on the couch? What are we, fifty?" I teased, and an older couple looked over at us and smiled. At the time, I assumed they found us charming. Now, as I ponder the memory, I think they may have thought us naive, assuming our playfulness would get us through the tough times—the real shit. Ethan's skyrocketing success and then the ensuing anxiety and depression as the pressure to replicate it tore him down. I was unable to help him feel better, which in turn made me feel like a failure, then angry, then eventually indifferent. Why didn't the drive up the coast to the restaurant where we'd first said "I love you" help snap him out of his funk? Why hadn't showing him our wedding album reminded him that he could feel happy? Why wouldn't he attend the doctor's appointments I made for him, so he could get diagnosed and get help? His depression won time and time again. I was powerless, which was the very worst feeling for me, someone who had always been in control. Eventually I turned away from him. But had I tried hard enough?

"I've always wanted one like this," Ethan continued. "I want to be comfortable."

I should have seen the red flags that day. Because a couch can say a lot about you. I wanted something that looked smart and beautiful, that you had to be careful of, something that you couldn't be lazy and sit on forever. Ethan wanted a sofa he could sink into for hours, maybe days. Something boring, but sturdy and reliable.

In the end, I let Ethan choose our couch. And not because he insisted, but because I knew it would make him happy. Back then I thought that was enough—giving him a win once in a while. I naively thought that was how to make a marriage work. But I understand now I didn't know anything at all.

~

I pull myself out of the deep cushions when the doorbell rings and feel my way through the dark to the door. I'm not ready to turn on the lights yet. To see that Ethan is really gone.

I peek through the peephole, and my pulse slows down when I see Chase holding two bags. After Ethan stormed out, I broke down and asked Chase to come stay with me tonight. I hated to be weak, but my head was still spinning from my attack twenty-fours ago. I didn't think I could stand to be alone in the house. But it meant I had to tell him why I was alone in the first place.

Carrie texted me seconds after Ethan had driven away, asking if I was doing okay and if I was still up for lunch tomorrow. I let out a sigh. It was almost as if she sensed I needed her. The only problem? I couldn't tell her. She would insist on understanding *why* Ethan left. And I'd have to lie—again. So I texted back and said I was doing great and sent the smiley face emoji wearing sunglasses to reiterate the point. She confirmed for lunch, and I reluctantly agreed, deciding that I would keep the conversation to her pregnancy and her hot trainer at Blast Zone. Before we inevitably ended up talking about me.

I open the door, and Chase holds up the two brown paper bags. "I drove all the way to La Cienega in traffic to get you the black cod from Nobu," he says dramatically. "And full disclosure—I got us extra rice. And not the shitty brown kind. We're doing white tonight. Carbs always make you feel better."

I smile wanly and take one of the bags out of his hand. "You are my hero, you know that?" I say, hugging him with my free arm. "Thank you," I whisper and feel a tear fall from my cheek to his shoulder, his kindness breaking my earlier resolve.

"You won't be thanking me when that white rice bloats you," he says, stepping into the dark foyer. "Jesus, Lila, can we turn on a light? I get that you are going through something, but you were attacked only one day ago, and I think sitting by yourself in a pitch-black house is not the best option."

I laugh weakly and flip on the lights, squinting as my eyes adjust. "Come on," I say, leading Chase to the kitchen.

"Hey, before I forget, Detective Sully called back. Said he has some information for you."

"Great," I say, my earlier voice mails to him feeling like another life ago. "I'll call him in the morning." I begin to grab two plates, but Chase stops me, instead holding out the take-out carton and a pair of chopsticks, which he rips from their paper casing.

"We're not stopping until we are a full-on cliché, girl! And I've got four pints of Talenti caramel cookie crunch gelato to prove it."

"Fantastic," I say quietly and walk back out to the couch, embarrassed to see Chase eye the half-drunk bottle of wine with no glass in sight.

"I see you started the clichés without me."

"Let me get some glasses," I say.

"No, I'll grab a beer—if you have one?"

I nod. "In the fridge."

"You can continue on drinking from the bottle like a savage," he says over his shoulder as he walks to the refrigerator.

We settle in cross-legged on the couch and eat in silence for a few minutes. Finally, Chase asks, "So you want to talk about it? Your text was vague."

My text SOS begged him to come over and said that it was important, but that was it. Texting the actual words *Ethan has left me* would make them real.

"Ethan knows about Sam," I say, and Chase sets down his chopsticks, his eyes growing wide. I take a deep breath before I say my next words. "He left."

"Holy shitballs," he says and laughs. "Sorry," he adds quickly, his hand flying over his mouth.

"No, it's okay. I need some levity. I need you. Because right now I can't shake the feeling that life as I know it might be over," I confess, saying out loud the words that have been echoing in my mind for the last two hours. Since Ethan left me. Since I fell to the floor in a pool of tears, staring at evidence of me betraying my husband. I fill Chase in on what happened and hand him the blue envelope. "He gave me this on his way out the door."

Chase pulls the pictures out and taps his finger on one. "The parking garage?"

I nod. "Ironically, right before I broke up with Sam."

"Who would do this?" Chase asks.

"I have no idea. Maybe Ethan suspected and had me followed." I tell him about how Ethan told me his next novel is about a cheating wife.

"That can't be a coincidence." Chase frowns, then takes a swig of his Heineken.

"I don't know. He showed no malice toward me when he told me about his book idea. And he's a guy who wears his emotions on his sleeve. I can't believe he'd be capable of pretending everything was okay."

"I think you're letting your emotions cloud your judgment. Because Lila the attorney would never believe that those two things aren't connected," he said, then gasped.

"What?" I ask, sitting up.

"The attack. Do you think . . ."

"No," I say firmly, the bump on my head throbbing as I say it.

"Lila . . ."

"No. Ethan would never," I say, my voice rising slightly.

"Even if he knew?" Chase points at the photos.

My mind flashes back to the attack, the fear I'd felt as a hard knot in my chest. "Even if he knew," I confirm. But a part of me weighs it for another moment, remembering the look on my husband's face when he told me I had one chance to tell him the truth.

Chase cocks his head. "You know better than anyone that love, loss, and betrayal can make people do the very worst things. Things no one believes they're capable of doing."

I glance at the image of Sam kissing me in the garage. Chase is right. Maybe Ethan and I don't know each other at all.

CHAPTER TWENTY-THREE

WEDNESDAY

CAPTURED

Q and his fucking iPad are back.

As he enters the room, he saunters, bringing a smugness with him that I am certain of, even though I can't see his face. It's the way he moves his body, the slicing of his arms through the air, how he holds the tablet as if it's the most important thing in the world. The force of his legs charging forward. His shoulder blades pulled down his back. I've taught myself to read his body language and to study his only two exposed parts—his eyes and mouth. His lips are a pale pink that, when parted, reveal a row of white teeth—bright like fresh-fallen snow. I'd bet anything he gets them whitened—Crest White Strips at the very least. His smile is mostly straight, but today I've noticed something new about his mouth. As he taunts me with the iPad, waving it in front of my face, I spy an errant tooth. I'm not sure how I haven't seen it before, but there it is, sitting a little too far to the left, angled slightly away from the others. He catches me seeing it and breaks into a large grin. As if he's proud of it, believing that it gives him character. If the mask were off, I have no doubt he'd smile more freely—not the least bit self-conscious. But possibly one thing he hasn't considered is that it's also an identifying factor—one I file away. One that *if* I get out of here, *if* somehow I manage to escape, could be a way for the police to track him down.

If he's in the system. If snaggleteeth aren't common. If, if, if.

Q also brought a chair with him today. He pulls it over, the legs making a sharp sound against the floor. He balances the tablet carefully on the seat.

"What are we watching this time?" I ask, feeling a mixture of fear and curiosity. Knowing whatever he's about to show me will be bad. But still, I have to know. I can't *not* know at this point. Because every little thing, no matter how terrible, is a clue. A hint at the reason for all of this. I adjust my body and smell myself—the musty odor of sweat floating up toward my nostrils when I move my arms. The result of not showering for days, but also from my fear, my blouse soaked, then dried, then soaked through again. My bandage from the cut he gave me is dirty and needs to be changed.

"Well, this one's a real tearjerker—and I'm not talking about the latest Oscar-nominated movie. This is a true story." He squats down. "You see, there's this woman. She basically does anything she wants. Takes anything she wants. Doesn't care who she hurts. Sound like anyone you might know?"

I stare at him but say nothing.

"So, anyway, one day someone decides they've had it with this woman who takes, takes, takes. I mean, you can only push a person so far, you know?" He leans in so close that I can see the gum he's chewing rapidly. "And so that individual, who the selfish person had wildly underestimated, takes her down, one brick at a time, until there is nothing left."

A bead of sweat forms above my lip, and I begin to tremble. "So how does it end?" I ask.

"Don't be so impatient, Lila! You'll have to wait and see what happens. I wouldn't want to ruin it for you." He smiles widely, and the snaggletooth appears, mocking me. "You're going to need these." He hands me a wad of tissues.

He rises up and walks over to his backpack and pulls out a six-pack of beer, popping off the top of the can expertly and taking a long swig. I nod up at the camera. "Your boss lets you drink on the job?"

"I do what I want," he says. "Nobody owns me." He shakes his head, but I don't miss his quick glance back up at the red blinking light.

I give him a long look.

"Don't look at me like that, Lila Bennett," he says. "You don't know shit. That's how you ended up here in the first place."

I stare at the Budweiser can as Q brings it to his lips once more. I haven't drunk Budweiser since it was all I could afford in college, but right now I want to taste it more than anything in the world. I've barely had what would amount to an eight-ounce glass of water today, and the slivers of baguette he's been feeding me are barely sustaining me. "I know that I'd love one of those beers," I say somewhat pathetically, my mouth watering at the prospect of feeling the cold liquid slide down my dry throat. The way it would begin to loosen my limbs and my mind. I'm no longer as interested in staying sharp, each and every hour feeling bleaker, my future fading away like a summer sunset. This seems to be the plan—to break my spirit. To make me crave my own demise. I'm not there quite yet—right now the one thing I am craving is the aluminum can full of alcohol in Q's beefy hands.

To my surprise, he seems to consider my request, glancing from my crumpled form to his can, then to the remaining five beers, and then back to me. "Why not." He shrugs, grabbing one, opening it, and setting it on the floor next to me. "You're going to need a drink after I show you this," he adds, pointing at the iPad.

"Thank you." I pick up the can awkwardly and lift it to my chapped lips, some of it spilling down my neck as I take my first gulp.

"Slow down there, slugger," Q says. "You need to make it last."

But I can't. I continue to chug it, channeling my former beer-bong-drinking self from undergrad. I feel it traveling from my throat to my chest to my abdomen and then settling, making my body warm for the first time since Q climbed into my back seat and upheaved everything I've ever known. "One more?" I give him my best pouty face, the one I have been known to use when I want Ethan to rub my feet or Chase to go back to Starbucks a second time.

Q glares at me, but then his body visibly softens, and I can detect amusement in his eyes. "I told you to make the *one* last." He adjusts the mask.

"I bet it's hot under that thing." I say the words I've been too scared to utter. But the glorious buzz from the beer begins to tingle inside my body, the lack of food and water no doubt intensifying it, my mind spinning just enough to give me the courage. I want to know who he is—whether I live or die, I need to see his face.

"Doesn't matter how it feels," he says, tugging at it again. "I have to wear it."

"Do you?" I ask, my neck and shoulders relaxing, my tongue loosening. "Because if you're going to kill me, then who cares if I can identify you?"

"That's not your concern," he snaps.

"Fine, I was trying to help."

"Help me?" He laughs. "You've never helped anyone but yourself in your life."

"How do you know?"

"Trust me, I know."

"Well, you should ask yourself if the person you've been told I am is the person you've met in this room. I've made mistakes, sure, but those errors in judgment don't have to define me. I'm somebody's daughter, wife . . ."

"That's enough small talk," Q says, putting up his hand. "I don't need anyone to tell me. I know exactly who you are." He balls his other one into a fist.

"Okay," I say softly and try to stay perfectly still until he calms down. We sit in silence for a moment. He takes another drink of his beer, and I scrape up the courage to speak once more. "So, Q. I'm probably going to die here anyway. Either from you . . ." I pause, looking up at the camera, deciding whomever put it there wanted me to have a reminder that he or she was there. "Or your boss . . ." I let the word sit in the air between us. Does he like being someone's bitch? He doesn't strike me as the type. He balls his hand into another fist, and I decide I've found my crack in the foundation. The place I'll slip in and do what I do best. Manipulate. "Or from starvation. Can I at least have one more beer before I do? Consider it a last act of mercy." I smile at him, longing suddenly for a toothbrush, wondering if I'll ever participate in the mundane act of brushing my teeth again.

Q finishes off his own beer and grabs another, eyeing me carefully, then glancing up at the camera. "How did you ever convince anyone to marry you, anyway? You're a pain in the ass."

I shrug. "Maybe I am," I concur, thinking about Ethan. The way he must have felt when he opened those pictures of me and Sam. Doing a double take. Scrutinizing them. Trying to make them *not* be of me. But then the reality would have set in. He'd sink to the couch and study them. Would he cry or punch something? Or neither? It would depend a lot on his state of mind. If it was a good day or bad one. If he'd taken his medication. If he'd been productive when he'd sat in front of the computer. But there's also the chance that Q didn't send them. That it was an empty threat, the possible exposure to him and whomever he was working with not worth the risk of humiliating me or whatever he was trying to do. But if Q went through with it, had them delivered to our doorstep—it makes my insides burn. I hate that I might never get the chance to explain to the man I married why I strayed. To at least tell him I'm sorry.

Ironically, I spent so many of our years together trying to help Ethan. To pull him out of his dark holes, to guide him back toward the positives, to get him back on track. To be the man I fell in love with, the author who wrote an insightful and compelling story that captivated the country. I always promised him that I would be patient. Loyal. And for many years I was. I bit my tongue when he lashed out. I pulled the blanket over him when he fell asleep on the couch yet again, his laptop never removed from the desk, a half-empty bottle of wine on the coffee table in front of him. But after time, and this isn't an excuse, I started feeling like it didn't matter what I did. I couldn't help him if he didn't want to help himself.

And now he's probably spiraling down into depression once more. What I find most interesting? I've always known I loved Ethan. Sure, I haven't been the best wife. I get that. But in this dirty room, buzzed off the beer my captor gave me, I'd gladly give my life if it meant Ethan would no longer be depressed. If he could be happy. Being here, facing my own mortality is difficult. But knowing I'm crushing Ethan? That idea alone makes me want to die.

Maybe it's easier to say that because I am most likely going to die soon anyway. "I tried. Marriage is hard," I finally offer weakly to Q. Because it is true. I did. And marriage is harder than anything I've done—law school, passing the bar, defending questionable clients. Those situations all have books you can study, classes you can take. Marriage? There's no guidebook. Only learning on the job.

I look over at him. "Are you married?"

He looks down, then back up at me. Something flashes in his eyes. Pain? Regret? Anger? It is hard to say. "Marriage is for saps."

"Doesn't mean you didn't try it anyway," I retort, the beer making me ballsy.

Q snorts. "Stop it. We aren't going to bond over bad relationships. This isn't a fucking Lifetime movie."

"So it was bad, then?" I push. "Did she cheat on you? Is that why you want to punish me? You hate women?"

His eyes flare up again. "Shut your mouth." He reaches over and grabs another beer, giving it to me. "Here. Will you stop talking if I give you another?"

I nod. I would do pretty much anything for one more beer.

"Good. And don't think I'm doing you any favors. Like I said, you're going to need it after watching this." He unlocks the iPad and presses Play.

Ethan's face fills the screen, and I gasp involuntarily, the reminder of the life I had jolting me. It feels like months rather than mere days since I've seen him. Since I've touched the stubble-lined jaw I see now. My breath quickens as he begins to speak, the camera drawn in tight to his profile. He's definitely been crying. Not sleeping. He looks terrible.

I take a sip of my new beer. Ethan is sitting in a plump green chair on a set, being interviewed by a talk show host I recognize from the *People* magazines that Chase steals from the waiting room. What's her name? Alice? Anna? Audra? Yes. That's it. Audra O'Conner. I feel hopeful. She is a huge national celebrity, which means my case must be getting major media attention. I look over at Q. Does that worry him?

Audra is talking about the search. She mentions that the FBI is now involved. The reward is $250,000 for information that leads to my safe return. I wonder who's putting up the money. My mom and Ethan don't have that much cash. My mom could only afford it if she took a mortgage out on her place. Ethan and I do have that kind of money, but it's not liquid. He'd have to sell our home or cash out our stocks or my 401k. There's some in savings but nowhere near that amount. Would the firm have fronted it? Sam?

I feel a surge of hope. This is all good news so far. When do the promised tears come? Maybe he thought seeing Ethan would make me sad. And it does. But I'm not going to cry over it. Especially not when I think it's what Q wants. I peek over at him. "Keep watching," he says without looking at me.

Audra asks Ethan about the day I disappeared. He describes our last morning together, and I begin to cry again. Then he mentions the texts I sent from the parking garage. How I said I was getting gas.

"Did that bother you? That she often worked long hours?"

"Lila has always been driven," Ethan says, but there is an edge to his words. "She knows what she wants, and she goes out and gets it."

"Do you think that drive led to her disappearance?" Audra asks.

"It's possible," Ethan answers, but he doesn't sound like himself. He is almost robotic.

She asks him a few more questions about the cases I recently worked on, specifically Jeremiah's. I wonder if they've vetted Stephanie yet. Of course they would've, right?

She asks about Franklin but doesn't actually say his name. She refers to it as the recent *stalking incident*. She's fishing, and Ethan stonewalls her like a pro, only saying that the police and FBI aren't ruling anything out. I find myself studying every syllable he utters. Yes, there is something there. Sadness, yes. But something more. He's pissed. He's trying to mask it. And if I didn't know him as I do, I might have missed it. But it's there.

The pictures. I prayed Q was bluffing. But seeing Ethan now, the way his lip is curling up to the right, the resentment as he describes my long hours, probably thinking I'd been making out with Sam in my office the whole time, there is no doubt that he's seen them.

Which means Carrie probably has as well.

"You sent him the pictures," I say to Q.

He reaches over and pauses the video. "You aren't a very good listener. I already told you I did." He points toward the screen. "And I've never met the hubs before, but he looks pretty pissed to me. I wonder how Carrie is taking it?" He runs his hand over his chin, adjusting the mask. "What happens if no one cares anymore if you come back? Do you think they'll stop looking for you?" He laughs to himself.

I turn away from the screen. "I don't want to see any more." My earlier buzz has now paved the way for exhaustion. "I'm done."

Q grabs me by the shoulder and pulls me up roughly. "What in the world made you think you're in charge, Princess?" he hisses into my ear. "You're going to sit right here and watch. It's about to get really good, and I don't want you to miss it."

"How would you describe your marriage?" Audra is asking now.

"Good," he says. Then he adds, "Like any marriage, we have our problems."

"Does that include your struggle with depression?"

I snap my head back, shocked to hear the words out loud. He's never told anyone that I know of, and I certainly haven't. It's been our private struggle, or so I thought. I can see the surprise in his eyes too and then the embarrassment. It's subtle. Only I would notice, but it's there. I know it's his biggest nightmare to have his struggles outed this way. My chest aches for him, and I blame myself. He was doing this all for me, and now he's paying yet another price. When will his sacrifice end?

Ethan balks. "I don't see what that has to do with anything."

Audra brushes blonde hair out of her face and gives him a hard look. "Your wife went missing under suspicious circumstances. Everything is relevant." She glances at the green index cards on her lap. "Is it true your wife was having an affair with a coworker?"

The color drains from Ethan's face.

My blood goes cold in response. I look at Q, who shakes his head at me.

A deep anger starts to work its way out of me. How dare this woman confront Ethan.

"What makes you say that?" Ethan looks stricken, and my heart begins to break. He's still trying to cover for me. But why?

"Is it true?" Audra asks. *Bitch.*

Ethan glances back at something off camera. He nods almost imperceptibly. But I notice, and so does Audra. I taste the bile in the back of my throat and swallow it.

"Okay, then," Audra says, shuffling her index cards. "We also received a letter right before we went on air that appears to be written by Lila. I'm hoping you can confirm it's her handwriting . . ."

My stomach plummets. *Please, no.*

Ethan says nothing, clearly confused. "A letter? From Lila? To whom? And how?"

Audra ignores his questions. "Is this your wife's handwriting?" She holds the letter out to him. He tries to grab it, but she pulls it away before he can.

I wonder what letter she has. For a second I consider she may have found one of my old diaries. At this point, anything seems possible.

"It looks a hell of a lot like it. But I can't be sure," Ethan says.

"May I read it to you?" she asks.

I take a deep breath, wondering what's coming next, what words I have written that she finds so interesting.

"I think you're going to read it regardless," Ethan snipes. Q smiles and tilts his chin upward. He looks satisfied. Suddenly I know what letter she has. It's the one I wrote to Janelle.

"Why?" I say to Q, who simply points to the iPad.

Audra clears her throat dramatically and slides on a pair of tortoise-shell reading glasses. And I wonder why Ethan agreed to be interviewed. Did he think it would help in the effort to find me? Or did he have an ulterior motive? To show he's *not* aligned with me anymore?

I'm not surprised when Audra utters the words *Dear Janelle*, but the enormity of what's happening still hits me hard. As she reads the heartfelt words I wrote the day before, I stare hard at Ethan's face. I told him years ago about Janelle, but I still wait for his eyes to soften at the sincerity of my confession, especially now that I've gone missing. But there is nothing—he remains still.

There is silence for a few seconds after Audra finishes. "Did you know about this?" she finally asks.

"I knew about the situation," he answers.

And now so does the world. It's an idea that makes me both deeply embarrassed and quite liberated. It's out. Everyone knows. I can't hide from it or behind it anymore.

"When did Lila write this?" she presses. "She seems incredibly distraught. Questioning her career. Could she have . . . Could this be a suicide note?"

"No," Ethan cuts her off. "She wouldn't hurt herself. And I've never seen that letter. Where did you get that? Why haven't you given it to the police?"

I begin to panic. If they start to think I took my own life or that I ran off, they might stop looking. They need leads and suspects to chase.

"As I mentioned, it was delivered literally minutes before air. We called the proper authorities and plan on turning it over to them immediately." Audra smiles.

"Immediately after you confront me with it on national TV!" Ethan retorts.

I feel a surge of pride as Audra blushes.

"It doesn't sound like Lila at all," Ethan stammers. "She didn't write it."

His words sting, but I know why he's saying them. The old Lila would have never written that letter. She may not have been capable of the introspection. And she certainly was never sincerely contrite about something. The old Lila was terrified those things would make her weak.

She had been dead wrong. Pun intended.

Audra tries to look sympathetic. "Is it possible you may not have known her as well as you thought?"

Ethan's eyes are steely. "I think that's something I have to consider at this point. But there is one thing I know for sure. Lila would have never killed herself. Not over *that*."

I exhale hard. *Thank you, Ethan.*

"Fair enough." Audra shakes her head. "But I have to say, Ethan, with all of this information coming to light, an affair, a tryst with her professor, these things would surely make you angry. I have to ask: Did you have anything to do with your wife's disappearance? You say you were at home when she went missing, but it's never been corroborated."

Ethan stands up and rips his mic off. "I'm done here," he says before storming off the set.

The video goes black a moment later, but I continue to stare at the screen, perplexed as to why that was the one question he wouldn't answer.

CHAPTER TWENTY-FOUR

THURSDAY
FREE

I step out of my car in front of Watermarke Tower and start to hand my key to the valet but quickly pull it back. I study him—his wiry mustache, his comb-over that's failing to do its job, his black eyes. He gives me a funny look as I contemplate parking on the street instead or in my office parking structure, which is only a few blocks away. That was my plan, but I've been moving slowly today after last night's imbibing. A sharp pain jags through my belly, and I lean against my car, the man asking me in a high-pitched voice if I'm all right. I nod, but I hate this feeling—that I can no longer trust the most innocuous of things. That I have to keep looking over my shoulder in broad daylight. I'm off-balance, and I feel as if I could teeter one way or the other in the slightest of breezes. Finally I stand up straight, hand him the fob, and walk down the street toward the restaurant before I can change my mind. As I'm approaching the entrance, there's a homeless man sleeping to the right of the doors. I pull out a five-dollar bill and tuck it under his arm.

"There you are!" Carrie throws her arms around me the second I cross over the rug with *Faith & Flower* embroidered on it. "It's so good to see you."

"You too," I manage to say, exhaling deeply as I take her in. Did she also receive the pictures? Does she have them in her white patent leather purse, prepared to throw them at me once we're seated? No. Carrie wouldn't handle it that way. She'd do it in private, where she could say everything she wanted to say. And I want her to have that chance—to rip me down to the core if that's what she needs.

She smiles at me, her cheeks glowing against her sunflower-yellow dress. She seems genuinely joyful to see me, which almost feels worse. How long will I be able to live here, between the gaping lies and crevices of truth of my own life? And how can I ever be the friend Carrie deserves?

We follow the hostess to a leather booth on the wall. After we're seated, a server, a lithe young woman dressed all in black save for a paisley bow tie, swiftly approaches and fills the green goblets in front of us. Carrie orders a club soda for herself and a chardonnay for me. I put my hand up to decline, but she shakes her head. "Don't take this the wrong way," she says, leaning in, "but you look like hell—you need this drink. I would join you if I could."

She's right—I do look and feel like hell, my head still pounding from the wine I chugged straight from the bottle last night. Chase and I opened a second one somewhere around midnight, laughing that we'd feel it in the morning. And I do. My mouth is still dry no matter how many glasses of water I drink, my heart still aching no matter how many times I tell myself Ethan is coming back.

"So how's work?" Carrie asks, her lips slightly parted, her bright eyes locked on mine. Her hair is pulled up into a purposely messy bun. I run a hand through my own hair, which I always wear exactly the same way, blown straight with bangs that fall just above my eyebrows, and wonder why I don't ever try anything different.

I sigh.

"That good, huh?" She exhales. "Does Sam need to put in a word to get you more money? You know he'd do anything for you."

I flush at her words and swallow hard before answering. "The money's not the problem," I say, thinking about my healthy bank account. I work so much that I don't have time to spend what I make. It sits there untouched. Ethan's not a big spender either. I wish suddenly that I'd made the time to take a vacation with him. Would that have helped us connect? Made him happier? Me more satisfied? It's hard to say. Still, I wish I had at least tried.

"Then what is?"

I glance at the menu. Do I want the baby kale Caesar or the cod sandwich? Or both? I avoid making eye contact and continue to analyze my lunch options. Because the answer I can't give her is: *Ethan left me.* The words sit there, ready to be spoken. Any other person would have blurted them to her best friend by now, unable to hold such a terrible thing inside. But of course, I can't tell Carrie. I can't have her soft eyes dig in on the details of why Ethan would suddenly pick up his shit and leave.

Last night Chase asked me if I regretted being with Sam or just getting caught. His tone was light, but his eyes held mine tight as he waited for my reply. And the answer isn't as easy as one would assume. Of course I hadn't *wanted* Ethan to find out. To leave. And I suppose, ultimately, I wished that I'd never felt the *need* to be with Sam in the first place. But it's not as simple as that—I've made choices that layer upon other choices, and now I've found myself somewhere I never thought I'd be. I feel as if I am standing at the bottom of the deepest hole, desperate to climb out. But how? I need to scrape my way back to flat ground. I didn't set out to be a bad friend, a bad wife, but that's who I've become.

I decide to spare her my own ugly truth. Instead, I tell her the other pressing matter on my mind.

"I have this client, and I don't trust him—"

"So what's new?" Carrie laughs, then stops when she notices I'm not smiling. "Sorry, go on."

"Obviously I can't elaborate. But I'm worried the wrong person is going to get hurt." I pause, thinking about Sam's threat. I take in Carrie's long lashes framing her clear eyes. Does she have any idea how ruthless her husband can be? Then I shake the thought away. I knew, and I didn't let it get in the way of my feelings for him. In fact, it may have been the singular thing that drew me in. I've never thought this before, but I begin to ponder whether Carrie and I are more alike than I've ever thought. We've been involved with the same man. Was it for the same reasons? Does he make her feel powerful too? I take a sip of my wine, suddenly grateful for the relaxing effect of the alcohol. "I want to be sure I'm on the right side of things."

"Wow, this is a new Lila!" Carrie beams. "Wanting to see how the other side lives!"

"How does empathy look on me?" I grin sheepishly and feel a flash of hope that I might be able to redeem myself one deed at a time. If I do the right thing with Greenwood's case, will it make it easier when it's time to do the same with Carrie?

Carrie's smile disappears, and she folds her hands in her lap. "Seriously, Lila, I'm proud of you."

I roll my eyes. "I'm closing in on forty. Not six."

"I don't mean to be patronizing, but I'm happy to hear you talk like this. Sometimes I think Sam doesn't consider his clients or the people he's defending them against, only the win."

I flash back to a moment with Sam two weeks ago. He'd just gotten an investment banker client acquitted on embezzlement charges for which he was most certainly guilty. "*Another W!*" Sam said, pumping his fist. "We'll celebrate properly later," he whispered into my ear before exiting my office.

"It's true, we do get caught up in winning. We're all fiercely competitive. And there's pressure to succeed, of course, but sometimes—"

"That comes at a cost." Carrie finishes my sentence.

I nod slowly, filled with shame at the accuracy of her words. "It does. I guess I'm beginning to wonder if it's worth the price of admission." I look away after I say this, unable to meet her eyes, the truth hanging on a thread in the air between us.

You could tell her right now, my good girl voice says. *It's better if it comes from you.*

I shake my head slightly. *No, not now. She's so happy.*

The server walks up a moment later and asks if we'd like another round. I nod toward my empty glass, and we both order. The fried cod sandwich for me. The young kale and pear salad for her. Even when it comes to eating, she makes better choices.

"How are *you* feeling?" I ask her.

Carrie looks down at her abdomen. "Great! No morning sickness. Plenty of energy."

"You look gorgeous."

"Oh, please." She swats at the air.

"How did Sam react when you told him?" I ask, trying to sound nonchalant. But it's been on my mind since the second I sat down. Since the moment she told me she's pregnant, if I'm being completely honest. I don't want to be back together with Sam, but this baby is a symbol of so many things. Of us. Of them. Of the future.

Carrie takes a sip of her club soda, and I think I see a flicker of sadness cross her face. "I'm waiting until my next ultrasound appointment. I want to be sure everything is okay."

"Why? Is there a reason it might not be?" My heart lurches at the thought. Carrie has been loyal, kind. She should get her healthy baby.

She shakes her head. "No, but I'm thirty-eight. And I've done too much googling."

I start to tell her that's a mistake, but she keeps talking. "I know, I shouldn't be. But I couldn't help myself. So I'm being cautiously optimistic until my next appointment, and then I plan to tell him." She smiles, and I wonder if she has any idea what Sam is capable of. Of how brutal he can be when he feels someone has betrayed him. Will becoming a father spark a change in him or make him worse?

"I'm sure he'll be ecstatic," I say, my chest tightening. I don't want children, let alone children with Sam. But there's something about the finality of it. Sam and I are done. Ethan and I might be done. Things will never be the same again, for any of us.

"So, I don't know how to say this . . ." Carrie looks down at her napkin, then back up at me.

My pulse quickens. *Does she know about the affair? If she confronts me, what will I say?*

"I ran into Ethan this morning . . ."

My stomach falls hard to the floor. I stare at her, unable to speak, waiting. Is this the moment I lose her? I've already lost Sam and Ethan and now Carrie? I understand I deserve it. But that doesn't make it hurt any less.

"Why didn't you tell me, Lila?" Her eyes fill with tears, making them shimmer more.

Oh God. What do I say? I try to find the words. But all that comes out is, "I'm sorry." I start to cry. All of the lies, the deceit, the betrayal seeping out. I'm surprised when a huge wave of relief washes over me. Maybe I need her to know so we can all begin to heal.

And then I feel her hand over mine. I look up, shocked. *She's consoling me?*

"There was a time when I would have been your first call."

She's not talking about the affair. Ethan must have told her he left. But not *why* he left.

I search her face for signs that she's upset about more than me not telling her. That Ethan also told her about Sam and me. But clearly he didn't. Because he's honorable. I feel a pit in my stomach. He protected me, even when I betrayed him in the most primal way.

"I know, I'm sorry I didn't call you last night. I'm guess I'm feeling pretty humiliated," I say. And it's true; I am. "I was going to tell you today. After a few of these," I add, pointing at my almost empty wineglass. Her shoulders relax slightly.

"For the record, he looks awful," she says. "I asked him what happened, why he left . . ." She hesitates as if she doesn't want to tell me the rest.

"And? What did he say?" I picture him tossing the dark-blue envelope in my direction, the disgusted look on his face that no amount of wine will wipe away from my memory.

"He told me I should talk to you. That it was your story to tell."

"Me?" I say, pondering whether he was trying to protect me by not divulging what happened or point her in my direction so I'll confess—take the opportunity to wipe the slate clean. Whether his intention was protective or aggressive, one thing is certain—the truth is going to come out eventually. I've hurt Carrie in so many countless ways the past several months, but I can't look her in the eye, in her perky yellow dress and messy bun, with her pregnancy belly that isn't quite a bump yet, and destroy her life.

Not yet. Not today.

"I figured he thought you'd want to tell me what happened. Or maybe he didn't want to talk about it."

"Possibly."

"I didn't know you two were having problems. It seems all so . . . I don't know. Shocking? Sudden?" Carrie tips her head to the side.

"It is," I say weakly, thinking that finding out his wife was cheating on him must have been very shocking for Ethan.

"Okay. So now I'm asking. What happened?" Carrie wrinkles her brow.

I take a long drink of my second glass of wine, its sweetness surprising me. This time it tastes more like a riesling than a chardonnay. Or maybe it's gone bad. I'd normally send it back, but not today. Today I drink it, despite its sickly sweetness, because I need it. I debate what to do—if I tell her, it will be only to relieve my guilt. Because how could it help her to know? But she's pregnant. Maybe she deserves the information because it will influence whether she'll stay married to a man who would have a six-month affair with her best friend. Who would systematically attempt to destroy someone who betrayed him. But if I tell her, there's no coming back from this.

I decide I can't hurt her—not more than I already have, even if she doesn't know it. Yes, not telling her also selfishly helps me. There seem to be no good choices left on the table—hurt Carrie now, but she knows the truth about her best friend (who is trying for once to do the right thing) and her husband (who may not be who she thinks he is), or spare her, knowing I will break her heart at some point.

"We had a fight about work. It had been coming for a while now. And I didn't say anything because I was hoping we'd figure it out," I say.

Carrie presses her lips into a fine line. I wonder if he did tell her. And if she's testing me. "Really?" she questions. "But he's always been so supportive."

"He's had it with my hours. I was a little late for Mongolian beef and *The Good Wife* the other night. I was tardy picking him up for my mom's. It's been one time too many, and I don't think he feels like a priority. And you know what? He hasn't been. He's right. He deserves better. So he left. And I let him." The lies don't slide off my tongue the way they did a week before. Now I can feel the price I'm paying as I speak them.

Carrie stares at me incredulously. "Lila, these are solvable issues! Come home from work earlier. Eat the damn Mongolian beef and binge-watch bad TV shows, for goodness' sake!"

I laugh—a bitter sound that I don't recognize.

Carrie narrows her eyes. "Why does it sound like you've already given up? That you've already decided he's not coming back?"

"I haven't. But it's not up to me—he's the one who left."

"Hmm," she says. "But you could change."

"Maybe I can't," I say softly and feel tears tickle the back of my eyes. I think that's one of my biggest fears. That if I could convince Ethan to return, I'm not sure I can ever be the person he deserves. It's possible I'm not built like that.

"You sound like you don't want to try," Carrie challenges.

"It's more complicated than Chinese food and Hulu," I say, sounding much more resolved than I intend. I take another drink of my wine. It's starting to taste better, or maybe I've lowered my standard of what I deserve. "I think I'm not in the right place to talk about it right now. Will you give me a few days to work through it?"

Carrie starts to say something, then stops herself and takes a drink. "Of course." She leans in. "I'm sorry I pushed—"

"You were being a good friend," I interrupt. I can't have her apologizing *to me.*

"I would crumble if Sam left me. Especially now," she says, placing her hand on her stomach.

Her words override my guilty heart and make me somewhat thankful I spared her my confession. She needs Sam. And if Ethan didn't blurt our affair to her today in the heat of leaving, then maybe he never will. I think about the navy envelope with the white trim again. The pictures. Realizing Ethan never told me *how* he came into possession of the photos. Did he suspect my affair all along and hire a private investigator to follow me? Or was he blindsided by my indiscretion when someone sent them to him? That dark thought pops up again—could it have been the same person who tried to attack me? The photos ending up in Ethan's hands isn't random. It was targeted.

"Can I ask one more thing?" Carrie says, and I nod. "Do you really think he doesn't want to hear from you? Doesn't want an explanation? That he's for sure not coming back?"

Chase and I had volleyed these same questions last night. Other couples have come back from infidelity, some becoming much stronger than before, the shock of cheating making each partner reevaluate the relationship. I had already felt the pull back to Ethan before he uncovered the truth. The timing is bittersweet, I suppose. I finally chose him, let myself settle into something in my life that was right, chose the man who loves the good girl inside me, only to lose it all anyway. "I don't know," I finally say, happy to be saying something completely truthful.

"I think if you're willing to change, he'll come around," Carrie offers, her tone slightly sharp. She thinks I'm the problem (totally true, but not for the reason she thinks) and that it's a quick fix (clearly not, but she doesn't know that either). I haven't missed Carrie's and Ethan's shared glances when the four of us have gone out to dinner and Sam and I end up in a discussion about our work. I think both of us have always felt more at home at the office than at our actual houses—and not because of our affair. We're wired the same way. Or at least we used to be. Maybe I let the race to win change me. Maybe there is still hope for me that I can be better. That I can become a person worthy of the people closest to me.

Our food arrives, and we dive in. My cell phone buzzes, and I see Detective Sully's name on the screen, and I'm thankful for the distraction. "Sorry, I have to take this," I say and move outside to the front patio.

"Sully!" I exclaim. "I was beginning to wonder if I was ever going to hear from you!"

"I know, I'm sorry." He pauses, and I can hear sirens in the background. "The wife took me on a fishing vacation up north and made me turn the phone off. She said I'm addicted to it!"

I smile as I imagine her confiscating his phone as if it were evidence. I've met her several times over the years and quickly noted she was the one person who Sully let tell him what to do.

"So I got the information you wanted."

"And?" I say, squeezing my fingernails into my palm.

"You did *not* hear this from me," he says sharply. "You understand?"

"Yes. Of course. I will keep you out of this."

"I did some digging. Tracked down one of the officers on the scene at the Greenwood home the night of the dispute. The officer will not go on the record, but I helped him out of a jam when he was rookie, and I was able to convince him to hand over his notes. Notes that were never made into an official report, and it always bothered him. So you were right—your man Greenwood did something to ensure a police report was never filed. It turns out *he* was the drunk and belligerent one, not her."

My heart leaps. This is it. The smoking gun we've been looking for. "I'm going to need a copy of those notes."

"I've already messengered them over to your office. But it's not traceable back to me. Or the officers on the scene. Let's keep it that way."

"Good—I don't want you or anyone else involved."

"Well, it's a little late for that." He lets out a short laugh.

"For what it's worth, thank you," I say.

"You're welcome."

"Wait, one more question."

"Yeah?"

"Who did Greenwood get to bury it?"

He sighs. "Does it matter?"

"Just between us."

"It looks like it came from the top."

"As in . . ."

"Don't say his name, but yes, *him*."

I hang up and mull the information over. The chief of police made sure the officers' notes never made it to an official police report? But why? The knot in my stomach continues to grow to the point that it's now aching. I feel more trapped inside this case than before. Because if the chief has a tie to it and I don't win—or worse, if I find a way to abandon it—what will that mean for me?

I know one thing for sure: it will be far worse than simply a ruined career.

CHAPTER TWENTY-FIVE

Thursday
Captured

I wake up to the frozen image of the bright lights shining down on the empty beige chair where Ethan was sitting, his abandoned mic pack left behind. I curled into a ball earlier, trying to forget what I had seen, and my exhaustion must have overtaken me.

Where had Ethan headed when he stormed off the television set? And to whom? Was it the person he had glanced at off camera during his interview? I try to tell myself that he ripped off his mic when asked if he'd been involved in my disappearance because it was a ludicrous question. Right?

But what if Ethan had known about Sam? What if he had planned my abduction with the same patience and accuracy that he plotted his books? Made sure every needle was threaded, every detail accounted for. It makes sense. He knows me better than anyone. He knows about Janelle. My dad. And he could have discovered my affair with Sam. I've seen people do worse with far less motive. My hands begin to shake as I come to the sickening conclusion that it's possible I haven't been the only one with secrets to hide. Not the only one with the capacity for betrayal.

I try to suck in some air, but it feels impossible to breathe. Looking around my concrete cell, my gaze lands on Q, who is studying me.

"Morning, Princess," he says.

I look away and beg my muddled mind to think. Could it be possible Ethan is behind all of this? That he found out about my affair with Sam and hired Q to take me? But Ethan is my husband. He wouldn't hurt me.

Would he?

I scroll back to his behavior before I disappeared. Was there anything off? Not that I can remember, but then again I was busy with Jeremiah's case and still caught up in my relationship with Sam, not understanding that my life had become a house of cards, that one wrong move—in this case, our last kiss in the garage captured on camera—could bring it all crashing down. But Ethan could have already known. He could have been the one to hire Q to take the pictures and then to capture me. Did he laugh when he received my text saying I was celebrating with colleagues? Thinking, *That will be your last lie, Lila*? Shake his head as I sealed my own fate?

I always carefully guarded my notebook, the one where I made the tally marks every time I saw Sam. There are no other identifying factors. No names. Just slashes to mark the passing of time of our affair—six months of them. But it's possible he knew. That he could have bided his time, planning how to get back at me. The thought would have made me laugh out loud a week ago. Ethan? The guy could barely watch a violent TV show. He made me turn off *Game of Thrones* a few months ago after one of the characters got decapitated, declaring he didn't have the stomach for it. But being in this concrete prison, having my former life systematically torn apart, has made me realize there's someone in my life who is very, very angry with me. Who feels incredibly wronged by me.

And it could be my husband.

In my career I've discovered those are always the worst cases—the ones stemming from rage. When people murder for practical purposes, it's usually fairly clean—a bullet to the heart, one quick hammer hit to the back of the head. They want to get the job done so they get what they want—money, usually, in one form or another. But when the assailant has personal motives, it's a whole different ball game. That's when we see fifty stab wounds to the chest, people set on fire, acid thrown on faces. They don't only want them dead; they want to inflict incredible pain, hoping it will alleviate their own.

Jeremiah's case, at first glance, had seemed the opposite. His wife, Vivian, had been bludgeoned with something—according to the autopsy report, it had been a blow to the head, one direct hit. It hadn't seemed personal. Things were stolen. In the crime scene photos, the house appeared to be burglarized. There was forced entry. Statistically speaking, an easy win and another feather to tuck into my cap. But still, after I signed on, something had always gnawed at me. It was an instinct. Something that tickled the back of my conscience. But you learn very quickly as a lawyer that instincts don't have a place in the courtroom. Without evidence, there is no way to prove beyond a reasonable doubt that someone is guilty. The prosecution simply didn't have the evidence it needed. And now Jeremiah is free.

This situation I find myself in now feels like it's all about me. Whoever is behind this wants suffering and lots of it. The scariest part? I realize now it has to be someone much closer to me than Stephanie or Franklin, someone who is aware that ruining my career, making me face my mistakes that I am so good at burying, and driving away the people I love most is the worst torture they could inflict.

Personal. For sure. Could it be Ethan?

"Makes you think, doesn't it?" Q infiltrates my thoughts. I move my head up and down in response, my mind racing.

Ethan has been frustrated with my work hours and how I handle—or rather don't handle—some of the baggage that comes along with it, but never with my work. He often seems proud of me. I've always thought it's because he values that we're so different—that he secretly loves that harshness that lives inside me, respects my determination to win in the same way I value his quiet and gentle nature. His patience. We cherish the qualities most in the other that we're lacking, or at least that's what I told Carrie one night this past summer after sharing an ice-cold bottle of rosé on her deck overlooking the Pacific Ocean. She confided that she felt the same way about Sam—that there was a part of her that respected how he went for what he wanted, not minding it meant taking huge risks. Hurting people sometimes. At that point I was one month into my affair with him, and I had felt my cheeks color, knowing I was one of those risks.

But what if Ethan pulled back the curtain and saw what my desire to win really equates to? That it spills over into wanting forbidden things, looking the other way when I shouldn't? He knew about Janelle, but it hadn't seemed to faze him when I told him the story years ago. He'd mentioned a creative writing teacher he'd fantasized about and that he wished he had the balls to have done something about it. He'd also assured me that I couldn't have known Callahan would pick me over her for the internship. And although that was technically true, I could have made the situation right once I knew. But Ethan let me off the hook. Found a way to make me right when I was clearly wrong.

What if my affair with Sam changed everything for him? Caused him to want to teach me an overall lesson in morality, in the creepiest of ways?

Almost sounds like the plot of a movie. A blockbuster.

"Is that all it took to get you to shut up? Play a video of your husband getting ambushed on national TV?" Q says, his deep voice interrupting my thoughts.

"I guess so," I say, glaring at Q, who is hovering over me. "You think you've got me all figured out, don't you?" I snap.

"Don't take it out on me that he looked guilty as hell." Q laughs and points to the camera. "You wondering if it's him up there, watching? Maybe you should wave hello."

My cheeks start to burn, and sweat tingles my scalp. I'm suddenly so hot. The walls of the room seem to be closing in on me. I've always been slightly claustrophobic—in elevators, small cars. And while this room is not tiny, it feels so now. I swallow, fearing another panic attack is coming. I have to get out of here. "I need to use the bathroom," I say, my voice catching. I can feel the sweat rolling down my back.

Q surveys me but doesn't respond.

"All those beers," I add when he tilts his head as if he doesn't believe me. I don't want to mention how light-headed I am, how my heart is beating too fast. He'll get off on that, make me stay in here.

"All right," he finally says, surprising me. He pulls me up. My feet have fallen asleep—again—and I stumble slightly when he lets go. They tingle as I walk, hurting as they wake up. I will the circulation back with each step.

He unlocks the door, and I walk out first; then I hear him closing it. I lean against the wall and suck in all the air I can. I squeeze my eyes shut and try to swallow back the sobs. But it's impossible—the tears come pouring out before I can stop them. I force myself not to make a sound.

"What's the holdup?" Q asks from behind me.

I shake my head because I can't talk. I start walking again, hoping he won't notice I'm crying. If I show him my vulnerability, I will be giving him exactly what he wants.

"Hey," he says, grabbing my elbow. He walks in front of me, and I drop my head. "Look up," he demands.

Slowly I raise my eyes, the tears still falling. I brace myself for one of his snide remarks, for his lighthearted *I told you so* laugh. But it doesn't come.

"You'd better get moving—we only have five minutes before I have to get you back in the room." He says this softly, as if he's talking to a child.

"Okay," I say, somewhat stunned at his reaction to my tears. I thought he'd be elated, slap his knee. Isn't this what he wanted? He gave me tissues. Suddenly it hits me—this isn't his game. There are no cameras here in the hallway that I've seen. Is it possible he's been playing for the one in the room? Could he actually have a heart inside his chest?

I squat over the toilet, and as I'm peeing, I hear Q. He's arguing with someone. I quickly finish and move over to the door, straining to listen.

"I've done everything you've said. Everything we had discussed. No, that's not true. I slashed her, for fuck's sake."

It has to be his boss he's speaking to. I swallow. Is he hearing Ethan's voice right now? Is he angrier after that interview—wanting me to suffer more to help appease the rage that is now bubbling over in him like the water in a simmering pot? I press my ear closer to the door but don't hear anything for a moment. Then Q starts up again.

"It was a few beers—who cares? Figured it would loosen her up—get her to talk more after the interview . . . I know, she didn't. I don't know why! What? I thought we weren't going to do that yet."

I stand up straighter. Are they talking about killing me? Because that's the only thing left. And I'm pretty damn sure that it isn't going to be a quick bullet to the head.

"Fine. Okay. Yes! I understand. You've made yourself very clear. I have to go."

A banging on the door makes me scream out.

"What the hell, Lila? I'm knocking to make sure you're done."

"You scared me."

"It's time to go back in," he says.

I open the door slowly and don't make eye contact. I don't want him to know I've overheard. That I am now quite sure my husband or whoever has me in here has ordered me dead.

Because there's nothing else to take from me except my life.

CHAPTER TWENTY-SIX

THURSDAY
FREE

I wave to Carrie one last time, taking in the young valet whose gaze lingers on her lithe body as she climbs into her Mercedes SUV, blushing slightly when she turns around and catches his eye. "Keep me posted!" she calls out to me.

I nod obediently.

The same valet walks toward me and asks for my ticket. "I think I'm going to walk back to my office," I answer. When he glances down at my three-inch stilettos, I add, "I probably shouldn't. But it's not far. A few blocks. I'll pick up my car later. I just need some air, you know? To figure everything out," I say, noticing his eyes are glazed over. Clearly I'm talking to myself at this point, but I don't care.

"Whatever you like, ma'am," he replies politely, already moving in the opposite direction. I'm obviously not having the same effect on him as Carrie did. Maybe he could see the contrast between us that went beyond her shiny blonde hair and my jet-black locks. That her lightness and my darkness went far beyond hair color.

I head down Ninth, leaning my face toward the sun. It's one of those days—breezy with the perfect amount of heat. The tall buildings block the sun, but then it will pop out again exactly when I need it most. I breathe in deeply in an attempt to clear my mind, to get my bearings. *Ethan. The pictures. Greenwood and the report that was never filed.* A large black SUV blares its horn, and I jump, almost losing my balance. I know I shouldn't be walking by myself after everything that's happened, but I'm desperate for clarity. The next moves I make need to be the right ones.

I pull my phone out and dial my mom. She picks up on the first ring. "How are you feeling? Have you been taking it easy?" she asks. No hello. She doesn't know Ethan left last night. She's referring to the attack on me near her house earlier this week. That feels so long ago now.

"I'm okay, Mom," I say evenly.

"Any dizziness? Trouble sleeping?"

Yes, but not for the reason you think.

"No, everything's good. I feel fine," I say and step off the curb to cross Hope Street, cursing under my breath when I feel my toes pinch inside yet another pair of uncomfortable but *oh so fashionable* shoes I let Chase talk me into.

"Then what aren't you telling me? You sound off. And why is it so loud?"

"I'm walking back to the office from lunch. It's street noise."

She draws a sharp breath. "Lila! Why are you walking by yourself after what happened?"

"I'm in the middle of downtown LA. There are a million people around. It's safe. And I'm only a block or so from work. I've walked this route more times than I can count. Plus, I'm on the phone with you. You can call the police if something happens," I say and laugh awkwardly. I can understand why she's upset—I should have gotten my car out of the valet and driven. But there's something about pulling into my parking structure that's been giving me pause each day. I can't put my finger on it, but it feels like it's no longer safe. That the key card we all need to enter isn't enough to protect me. I remember the car that I thought was following me. Was it? Or was I simply being paranoid?

"Have the police found out anything about Franklin? Could he have been behind your attack?" My mom's voice sounds jittery. I know I can't blow her off.

"Not yet," I say. "But they're looking into it, and I also have my own private investigator on it as well," I add and hear her exhale.

"Listen, Mom," I say, changing the subject. "There's something else . . ." I pause and decide whether I really want to do this—tell her before I've had a chance to talk to him.

"What is it?" she asks.

I sigh. "It's Ethan. We're having some problems."

"Everyone has problems. Want me to get some counseling referrals? My friend Diana—remember her? The one with that cute dog, the one that looks like the one they use in those Target ads? What are those called again?"

"Bull terriers," I say flatly.

"Yes, that's right. Anyway, her son was having all kinds of issues with his wife, and they went to a therapist in Culver City, and they renewed their vows last month! Let me get you her number," she says, and I can hear her rummaging around her kitchen, probably looking for a pen so she can add saving my marriage to her hearty to-do list.

"I don't think he'll go with me," I say. "At least right now."

"Well, tell him—"

"Mom. He left me. Last night."

"What do you mean he left you?"

"He packed his shit and walked out the door," I say, my voice rising. A young woman in a striped maxidress strolling with a woman who appears to be her grandmother shoots me a dirty look. *Sorry*, I mouth to her and pick up my pace.

"Why would he do that? He seemed fine the other night." She lowers her voice. "Is he depressed again?"

"No. I mean, I don't know. It's too complicated to get into right now," I say vaguely. I don't know why I called her. I'm not ready to admit why he's gone. I guess I wanted to hear her voice. Have her tell me everything will be okay, even if it won't. With each passing hour I don't hear from Ethan, it becomes more real, more likely that he won't call.

"You need to uncomplicate it! No one said marriage is easy."

"I've never acted as if it were easy! Believe me, I understand how hard it can be."

"You have such a difficult time showing your heart," she muses. "You think being strong is the only way to survive. You never know when to ask for help. You never have."

"Mom—"

"And it didn't help, me telling you about your dad . . ."

"This isn't about that," I interject quickly.

"Isn't it, though?" Her voice is soft, and I feel my eyes begin to burn. "Call Ethan, Lila. Call your husband, and tell him you're sorry for whatever happened. That you need him. Don't let what I did to you define who you are. Or your dad's actions. You are your own person. Please."

"How can I unknow what I know? How can I separate myself from your and dad's missteps? They are part of the fabric of who I am. Aren't they?"

"They are, but they don't have to be. You can make your own choices that aren't reactive to what we've done. You can apologize."

"Why do you assume it's me who needs to apologize?" I ask, my voice rising. "That I'm the one who screwed up? That I'm the only one capable of hurting people?" Her assumption angers me. But only because I realize she's spot on.

"Lila—" she starts.

"I have to go. I'll call you later. Bye, Mom," I say briskly, tears stinging my eyes. I stop walking and stare at the sun glinting off the windows of the Bank of America building. She's right, of course. That's probably the real reason I called her. To be told that I'm the one who must make amends. Which of course I knew. But it doesn't make it any easier to hear.

~

I brush a finger under my eyes and straighten my dress (black, of course) as the elevator whisks me to my floor. I stride off the lift, ignoring the pain in my feet from the walk back.

As I approach Chase's desk, I take him in. He looks sharp in skinny ankle-length black pants, a fitted gray blazer, a blue-and-white-checkered button-down, and black slip-on loafers. A look not many men could pull off. "I know," he says, pretending to pick a piece of lint off his jacket. "I've outdone myself today."

"You really have," I say, leaning down and pulling my shoes off and sinking into the plush gray carpeting. I notice a folded *LA Times* on his desk. My stomach drops as I read the headline—a vigil being held by the family of Tom Wellner, a man killed in a controversial case ten years ago this month.

It was that case. My very first one that went to trial, to be exact. The one I can't let go of.

It's the second time it's come up this week. I stare at the newsprint until it blurs as I recall representing Ed Cooper. Ed's wife had supposedly been having an affair with Tom, their neighbor. When Ed went over to confront him, a gun went off. But it hadn't been Ed's gun, and there had been clear signs of struggle. Ed claimed that Tom had pulled the gun on him, and he'd attempted to disarm him, the gun going off in the process. The DA claimed Ed had shot Tom in cold blood. The jury agreed, and he was sentenced to thirty years in maximum-security prison. I had promised the family a zealous appeal, but Ed was shanked and killed behind bars before I got the chance. It kept me up many nights for years as I went over the case in my head, dissecting what I could have done differently. How I could have kept him out of prison and essentially kept him alive.

I pick up the paper and begin to read the article, feeling nauseated after only a few words. I start to ask Chase if he's seen it, but he interrupts me.

"You"—he gives me a once-over—"are one hot mess."

"It's that obvious?" I swat my camel-colored suede pump in his direction, and he grabs it. Honestly, I'm grateful for the distraction.

"Let me guess. You walked back from Faith & Flower in these?" he asks, looking at the shoe.

"How did you know?" I ask. "Did you see me limping?"

"No," he says, pointing the pump at me. "You scuffed this." He shakes the shoe. "Footwear like this is not for walking several city blocks! It is meant to be cherished!"

"Sorry," I offer. "I needed some air. But for the record, they are *not* comfortable."

"Girl! These aren't Easy Spirits! What were you thinking?"

"What are they supposed to be used for, then?"

"Looking fabulous!" He rolls his eyes. "You're never going to get it. Fashion first!" Chase holds his hand out. "Give me the other one. Let me see if I can fix them up."

"Thank you," I say as I walk toward my office with the newspaper under my arm.

It's been a decade, but I still remember clearly the faces of Ed's kids in a picture that ended up in the paper alongside an article about him being murdered in prison. They were outside their home, their mom hugging both of them, her back to the camera, but their faces, their eyes wide open and staring straight into the lens. Two boys. Twelve and fourteen. I wonder what became of them? Their mom had written me letters, blaming me. I feel the old pain and regret slide up inside me. I failed that day. And that family, those boys, paid the price for my mistakes.

"Also, the notes from Sully came in. They're next to your computer," Chase calls out, breaking my train of thought.

I whip back around. "And?"

He sets his mouth in a straight line. "I'll let you see for yourself."

I make a beeline for my desk, throwing my bag down in the chair and picking up the photocopy of the handwritten notes. The careful block script tells a much different story than Greenwood did.

According to what I'm reading, the officers showed up on site to find Mrs. Greenwood hiding in the closet with her two children. The children were untouched, but she had a large bruise on her arm and one on her neck that she insisted were from her husband, who she claimed had been drinking and who fled the premises before the police arrived. The neighbors corroborated her story. She refused any medical treatment but did seem interested in getting a restraining order. The officer left a patrol car in front of the house in case Greenwood returned that evening and went back to the precinct to file the report. When Greenwood did finally arrive back home, he was taken into the station for questioning.

But the report was never filed. And according to Sully, the chief of police had intervened. But why? Were they golf buddies? Was Greenwood a large donor to the LAPD? Or had he paid him off personally? I'd heard things here and there about the chief, that he was a schmoozer who occasionally valued politics over the law, but nothing like this. This was borderline obstruction of justice.

I call out to Chase, asking him to come into my office. "This changes everything," I say when he walks in.

"It sure does. What are you going to do?"

"I can't ignore it," I say, chewing on a cuticle, mulling over my options. I feel like I'm in a speedboat racing over choppy waves—exhilarated and terrified all at the same time. I have a choice to make. A crossroads, if you will. But this time there's no doubt in my heart. No push and pull between the two Lilas that live inside me. Right now I hear only a singular voice, calling on me to be the person I should have always been. "Can you set up a meeting with the wife and her attorney? His number is in the file."

"Lila, the preliminary trial is tomorrow. You could get—"

I wave my hand at him. "Tell them it's urgent, and see if they'll meet me somewhere off the path—discreet. Today. I don't want anyone to see us. Also, will you take me to grab my car?"

"You can't go by yourself."

"I'll be fine—" I start to say but relent. "Will you follow me there?"

"That works," Chase says, eyeing me skeptically. "But are you sure you want to do this after everything that's happened? You've barely had a moment to absorb any of it."

"It's better this way," I answer, resolute.

"There's no turning back once you do this." He stares at me intently. "You will be throwing away everything you've accomplished up to this point. Is that what you want?" His question sounds more like a dare.

I dare you to do the right thing and possibly end your career in the process. I dare you to put someone else first. To do what's right, even if it isn't easy.

It's a dare I'm ready to take. I'm done letting my terrible choices define me. I've listened to the bad Lila for so long—let her steer me into ditch after ditch. It's time to let the good Lila take the wheel.

I look down at the notes on my desk. "There's no turning back anyway. No matter what happens, I know I'll have done what's right for Lynn Greenwood and her kids." I lean my hand on the desk and take a deep breath. "I never told you this, it was a long time ago, but I had a case early on in my career that went horribly wrong. I've never stopped thinking about whether the choices I made ruined the lives of the children involved." I make the connection out loud that has been sitting on the edge of my consciousness. "I can't explain it, but I need to do this for *those* kids. Like the universe won't right itself until I make amends." I laugh awkwardly. "That sounds a little bit crazy, doesn't it?"

"Yeah. A little." Chase takes a step back, as if my confession has knocked him off-balance. And I can't say I blame him. The Lila he's always known never gave two shits about the universe and what it wanted. But this week has me wondering if there are much bigger forces at play—energies that try their best to gently lead us in the right direction and, if we don't listen, will blow up your life to get your attention.

I'm listening finally. I'm going to throw my career under the bus for the greater good—to help Greenwood's family. There is no way my career will survive handing over crucial evidence to opposing counsel. Greenwood will no doubt report me to the state bar, and it is indefensible. As I stare at Chase's perplexed expression, it's obvious he doesn't know what to do with this Lila.

"It's okay," I say as I reach out to steady Chase, who now looks peaked. "You won't be tainted by this. I'll make sure your job is safe. That everyone understands you had nothing to do with any of it."

Chase nods but says nothing, and I feel bad. I haven't really thought through how all this will affect him. His livelihood. He is well respected at this firm and so young. I can't have this hurt his chances at moving up the ladder. I can't have Sam and the others see him as an extension of me.

"Everything will be okay, I promise," I say, my voice strong. I have no idea what the next twenty-four hours will bring. But one thing is for sure—it's the first lie I've felt good about telling in a long time.

Two hours later, Chase is uncharacteristically reticent as he waits outside in his car (I don't want him to be culpable for what I'm about to do), no doubt swallowing my confession and pondering what it means for his own future. I feel exhilarated as I walk in and slide into a battered booth in a run-down diner near LAX as Lynn Greenwood and her attorney eye me with curiosity. I take her in—she's much prettier than her pictures. There's a softness to her that they don't convey, her honey-colored hair and porcelain skin dovetailing perfectly with her caramel eyes. Those eyes stare at me expectantly now.

"Thank you for meeting me. I know this isn't conventional—"

"We shouldn't be here," her attorney, Mark, interrupts. He has a round face and tiny eyes, his balding head reminding me of a dull pencil. "But Mrs. Greenwood insisted, despite my protests." He pulls out his phone. "I'd like to record this, so that we keep everyone honest about what's really going on here."

I don't blame him—I could easily have ulterior motives, such as entrapment, that I'd use to tank their case once I leave here. I nod. "That's fine."

He pauses, clearly surprised I agreed. We lock eyes, both of us knowing that if I let him record this conversation, I'm basically signing the death warrant for my legal career. Just meeting with them to intentionally undermine my own client, even if I choose not to give them the police notes, would be enough to get me disbarred. He presses a button on his screen, and I begin to speak again.

"Mrs. Greenwood—"

"You can call me Lynn," she says and fiddles with a strand of pearls around her neck. I notice her phone sitting on the table in front of her, its case personalized with pictures of two little boys I assume are her sons.

"Okay, Lynn," I say and smile, hoping to reassure her that this meeting will help her. "Can you walk me through what happened the night the police came to your house?"

Lynn's voice is hesitant, and she glances at her attorney, who nods. "Steve was in a rage."

"Why?"

"There was something going on at one of the dealerships. They didn't make their numbers for the third month in a row. He thought maybe he'd have to fire the general manager. He came home drunk. Angry. I was putting the kids to bed upstairs. I had left the kitchen a mess. We'd made slime after dinner." She smiles slightly at the memory.

"Slime?" I ask.

"Oh, it's this stuff we make with starch that the kids love, but God, what a disaster it is to clean up—it's all gooey. But it makes them so happy, so we do it."

I imagine Lynn Greenwood patiently helping her children divide up the ingredients and blending them together, getting her fingers dirty as she helps them knead the sticky substance.

She continues. "Anyway, Steve flipped out about it. Was screaming. Ran up the stairs, grabbed my arm, and pulled me down the stairs. Clasped my neck and pushed me up against the fridge, only stopping when the kids came down, crying and begging him to let me go." She chokes on her last few words and wipes her eye quickly. "Sorry," she says.

I reach out my hand to hers. "It's okay. Is that the only time he's been like that?" I ask gently.

"No," she says, and I see her lip begin to shake slightly. "It's not. But it was the first time he'd done anything in front of the kids. That's why I called the police. It's one thing if he does it to me behind closed doors."

"That's still not okay," I say, mortified.

Lynn shakes her head. "I know that. But I had always told myself maybe I deserved it for making the mistake of marrying the bastard. But seeing the kids' faces that night made me realize it can never happen again. When the police came, I was relieved. I texted Steve and told him I was divorcing him. And not to come back."

"And the police? Did they help you?" I ask.

"She thought they would," Mark interjects. "But then they buried the whole damn thing. Fucking criminal! He files for divorce the next day like it never happened. And flips the narrative—alleging that she's a pill-popping drunk. A bad mom. She doesn't drink! And without the police report from that night, it's impossible to prove otherwise. It's simply his word against hers. And then he fires his normal attorney and retains the most expensive firm with the most ruthless attorneys." He holds my gaze until I have to look away.

Lynn begins to cry softly. I reach into my tote and pull out a tissue. "I don't know what to do," she says. "I feel under attack. Like no one believes me."

I feel a deep anger rise up in my chest as I think back on the terrible accusations Greenwood made against her. "I believe you," I say and reach back into my bag, feeling the copies of the officer's notes beneath my fingertips. Knowing that if I pull them out, if I hand them over, it will be the final nail in the coffin of my career. But I can't escape the notion of what is right. Right and wrong used to feel like gray areas to me, the two forces often overlapping just enough to make choosing one slightly out of reach. Now the notion of what is right feels visceral, as if I could palm it with my hand.

I think back to the times I've ignored what was right. Janelle. Sam. Ethan. Carrie. I've made the wrong choice each and every time. I've chosen my self-preservation over justice. And it has worked for me for a long time. I've been able to outrun the consequences of my actions. But I'm finished running. It's time for me to face the truth and let the cards fall where they may.

"Here," I say, removing the papers and sliding them across the table.

Mark grabs the documents and scans them quickly. "You have the notes from the scene?"

"I do."

"Why are you giving these to us?"

"It's the right thing to do," I say as I begin to slide out of the booth. I was unsure of what this moment might feel like. Would I be frightened? Angry? Feel ill at what consequences I might face? But I feel not one ounce of any of those things. There is only one sentiment racing through my veins: triumph. Almost as if I've released myself from some sort of prison and I'm finally free to be the person I should be. The person I know I can be.

"Wait, where are you going?" the attorney asks.

"I've already been here too long. Those notes should be enough to get Greenwood to drop his suit and for Lynn to get custody of the kids," I say, pulling my sweater on.

"But we can't use this in court," Mark says.

I can't help but smile. It's so refreshing. A lawyer who follows the rules. "As you know, the preliminary hearing is tomorrow. Show this to him right before, and tell him you'll have no choice but to release these notes to the *LA Times* if he doesn't give Lynn what she wants. I'm sure the newspaper would be very interested to know why that report was never filed."

"And then what happens to you?" Lynn finally speaks. "Can they trace this back to you?"

"Maybe. I guess we'll see."

"But won't you lose your job if they do?"

"I'm on my way out anyway," I say and turn on my heel, walking out with a genuine smile on my face for the first time all day.

I stride out of the diner and over to Chase's Audi A4. He rolls down the window. "How did it go?"

"Really well."

"Details?" he prods, glancing toward the restaurant.

"Let's just say justice will be served up fresh to the devil Muppet."

"Wow," he says, shaking his head. "I can't believe you went through with it."

"Me either," I say and laugh, but he doesn't join me. I feel a stab of sadness thinking of how my choices affect him. He has to start over now too, whether he wants to or not.

"I'm sorry," I say to him.

"For what?" he asks.

"For everything," I reply, because it feels the right thing to say in that moment.

"Thank you for saying that," he says, his voice cracking slightly, his eyes hidden behind his dark sunglasses.

I stand by his car window for a moment without speaking, the silence breaking when a car horn blares out from across the street, breaking the spell.

"Any news on Franklin?" I ask, looking around as if he might appear in the parking lot.

Chase shakes his head. "Still haven't found him. But, Lila," Chase says, "they will."

"Thanks." I wave as he throws his car in reverse and pulls away, wishing I felt more comfort in his words.

The drive back to the office is long, the snarled traffic on the 110 North at a standstill. I roll down the windows and breathe in the smoggy air. I've pretty much tanked my career. Then why do I feel so good? Is this what it feels like to do the right thing, regardless of consequence? Every other victory in my life feels pale in comparison. Lynn Greenwood is a good woman. A good mom. And now she has a chance to live the life she deserves, free of her dirtbag husband.

Is that what Ethan deserves too? To be free of me? My mom's words bounce around in my mind. She reminded me that my refusal to be vulnerable often shapes my decisions—that there is this primal part of me that will do anything to protect itself. When I couldn't fix Ethan and his depression, I felt lost, and I turned to Sam because he made me feel powerful. I slept with Professor Callahan to ensure that my future stayed bright, not caring if it meant Janelle's dimmed. I ignored the fire alarms going off in my brain when it came to Jeremiah—that he could be guilty. Always protecting myself over others.

That stops now.

I feel an urgent need to hear Ethan's voice. To tell him that every road to save myself leads back to him—to our marriage. My heart pounds, and I grab my phone and dial his number, the ringing echoing off the windows of my car. To my surprise, he answers.

"Hello," he says, as if I could be anyone, and maybe I am at this point. His voice is gravelly. He sounds tired.

"Hi," I say. "Can we talk?"

Silence. Then, "What is there to say?"

"A lot," I answer. "You deserve answers."

Ethan exhales. "I don't think I'm ready for those answers yet, Lila. I don't think I'm strong enough to hear why you've been cheating on me for God knows how long with Sam." I can hear his sharp breath. "I don't want to know. It will make it worse."

"Tell me what you need from me, Ethan. I'll do anything. I'm so sorry." My voice breaks a bit. "How can I fix this?"

"I'm not sure this is something you can fix. And to be honest, I can't believe I didn't see it coming."

"What do you mean?"

"What I mean is that you've been screwing people over your whole life to get ahead. And silly me, I thought somehow I was exempt from it all, like I was the one person to whom you were loyal. But I was wrong. So fucking wrong . . ." His voice trails off.

The knot in my chest begins to throb. "I'm sorry, Ethan."

"Your sorrys don't change one damn thing."

"I know that," I say and chew on my lower lip. "But what if I could change? What if I've already changed? I can't go back in time and undo what I've done. All I can do is promise you the future."

"You always say people can't change."

Damn it. It's true. I do always say that. But I realize now that's because I didn't think I was capable of change. Now I understand that I am. I tell Ethan as much, and he laughs bitterly.

"You're only willing to change because you were caught."

"No," I challenge. "I had already told Sam it was over. You can ask him!"

"I'm not going to ask him, Lila!" Ethan's voice bellows through the speakers in my car. "But maybe I should ask Carrie?"

"If that's what you think you need to do," I say evenly, but my chest feels like it's going to explode. I would do anything for Carrie not to find out. To not have to hurt another person. "Ethan," I begin again, "I know you won't believe me, but I'm trying to change. To be better. And not only because of those pictures. It started before that. And it's not just about you. I mean, yes, you are the most important thing to me, but I'm making other amends as well."

"Like what?" he asks.

"I can't say quite yet," I answer, knowing I can't tell him about the Greenwood case. I need to make sure things work out for Lynn first. And there will be more. I am going to tell Jeremiah he'll have to find another lawyer to defend his civil case. But I also need to hold that back for now.

He balks. "Why should I believe you?"

"You don't need to. I'll prove it to you. Give me one day. I will show you that I can be a better person. That I can be someone worthy of your love."

"One day," he repeats and then we sit in silence, the only sound the hum of my car on the highway.

"Please, Ethan. Think about it," I plead. "I was wrong—I thought being vulnerable with you made me weak. But I realize now—the vulnerability you afford me is the very thing that might save us." I am met with a silence that scares me. What if I'm too late?

"Prove to me you can change. I mean really change. Not something bullshit. And then maybe we can talk," he finally says, and then the phone goes dead.

"You bet your ass I can change," I mutter under my breath as I exit the 110 Freeway, feeling as tall and strong as the skyscrapers that surround me. "Just watch me."

CHAPTER TWENTY-SEVEN

THURSDAY
CAPTURED

I can feel my resilience oozing from every limb, my dirty legs numb from lack of circulation. My inner strength leaks from my bandaged arm, the dried blood a reminder of what's to come. I thought my life was worth fighting for. But the one person I naively thought would never hurt me wants me to suffer. To die. What does that say about me? That my own husband wants to torture me?

I understand now. The cast of characters who hate me is way too long. The list of things I've done wrong longer. Why am I fighting for myself when there's no one fighting for me? Is this how my disgruntled clients have felt? Failed? Helpless? Like they had no one in their corner? Like their lives didn't matter? Was I meant to walk in their shoes—to understand their resentment and pain? Were they truly my pawns? I wanted them to win, but if they didn't, on to the next. Should I have tried harder? Should my appeals have been more vigilant? Why did I think I was invincible? Untouchable?

Maybe it will be better for everyone if I'm gone.

CHAPTER
TWENTY-EIGHT

THURSDAY
FREE

I push the button for my window, and it opens, a rush of cool air hitting my cheeks. As I exit James M. Wood Street, I let the magnitude of what's happening settle on me—my shoulders slumping under the weight. I've given the respondents in our divorce case the ammunition to stop Greenwood in his tracks. I've helped *them* sink *us*. Ethan's words cut through my thoughts: *I don't think you can fix this*. But I can. I must.

I turn left on Francisco and stare up at the deep-maroon TCW Tower, my gaze landing on the windows of my corner office, and something that Professor Callahan used to say strikes me. He preached that most lawyers study law to help the poor, the helpless, the wronged, only to be lured by the dollar signs later. I can recall shaking my head smugly, thinking that I understood myself so much better than my peers. That I had no illusions about my career path—I intended to make money. Of course, I'd help innocent people along the way too. But even as a twenty-two-year-old law student, I knew myself. That I would be addicted to the challenge, the chase, and the paycheck.

What I had been too naive to realize was that in exchange for all those things, I'd have to give up part of my soul.

And as respected as I've become at the firm, I've always understood that I am replaceable. That there is always another shark circling the waters, willing to do the things I won't do anymore. Someone with bigger balls than mine. With a smaller conscience.

The conversation I'm about to have with Sam is going to be hard. And not only because I'm quitting the firm, a decision that didn't come lightly but one that's been on the horizon for a long time. It's been an itch just out of reach. It taunted me and bothered me, but I pushed it aside until now. And I can't completely explain it, but this week I finally reached back and got it and scratched the hell out of it. It's finally time—I'm quitting the career we've shared and enjoyed. We're like two lions who lick their lips after demolishing their prey—getting off on the kill, barely letting it digest before we go on the hunt yet again. We let this wild animal instinct be the glue that cemented our bond, telling ourselves that our spouses could never understand us the way we understood each other. We told ourselves that this was *their* flaw to own. But we were so wrong. It was ours. It was always ours.

Ethan had been right when he'd implied I didn't know where my honesty ended and the deceit began. I've been painting my life in grays for too long, stretching truths until they snapped, twisting lies to fit into whatever reality I'd created, telling myself that deception was the only way to win.

I stare at the stream of cars headed west, on their way toward the freeway or to their homes near the beach. Leaving the hustle and bustle of downtown Los Angeles and heading to their families.

As I wait to turn right into the parking garage, I lock eyes with a woman in the other lane. She's laughing and talking on her Bluetooth. Is she chatting with her husband about what to pick up for dinner tonight? Filling him in on her day because it can't wait until she gets home? It seems so long ago that Ethan waited for me with Mongolian beef and Hulu queued up to *The Good Wife*. Has it only been a few days? So much has changed since then. *I* have changed. But I don't know if my personal evolutions will be enough to make Ethan want to forgive me. For Carrie to not end our friendship once she discovers the truth.

A blaring horn makes me jump a little in my seat. I look in my rearview mirror and see a middle finger being waved at me. I'd stopped driving and failed to start again, letting three car lengths of space accrue. I ignore the bird being flashed at me and decide I'm not going to play into this road rage. I'm going to refuse to be an active participant and allow the person to rant. There have been many times in the past I would have engaged, hidden behind my big heap of metal, feeling powerful. Why did I do that?

That answer is simple: my ego.

It has become clear that I need to check my ego, my pride, the chip on my shoulder—all of it—at the door when I tell Sam I'm walking away from the career that I took years building. Ironically only taking a matter of days to tear down.

I pull up to the entrance to the garage beneath my building and swipe my key card in front of the censor. As the gate starts to lift, I look over my shoulder, check my mirrors, a habit I've now developed that I'm not sure I'll ever completely shake. No one is behind me. I pull in slowly and stop on the other side of the gate and wait for it to close. The garage is well lit, and because it's not underground, some light does stream in, even at night. I drive around to my level and notice the lights have been fixed where I usually park. But still, the familiar jolts of adrenaline are rushing through me now. The feeling that an assailant could be waiting crouched in the shadows the lights can't illuminate. The police have not proven the attack was planned, but I'm certain it was. My gut is screaming that the man in the mask meant to take *me*.

My phone rings as I'm parking. Janelle's name pops up on the screen. I debate letting it go to voice mail. But instead I take a breath and tap the green button to accept the call. "Hello?" I answer and lean back in my seat, prepared at this point for anything.

"We need to meet," Janelle says, her speech rushed.

"Okay, I'm busy tomorrow, but would Saturday work?" I ask, pulling down the rearview mirror and studying my face. My eyes are bloodshot, the circles beneath them dark. I flip it back up, not wanting to look at myself for another minute.

"No. Tonight."

"Everything okay?"

"No, Lila, it's not. Not by a long shot."

I feel a jolt of adrenaline shoot through me, my pulse quickening not only in fear of what she will say to me but also because I can't avoid her any longer.

"What's up?" I ask, trying to sound casual.

"I don't think we should talk about it over the phone."

I stare at the door leading into the building and sigh. I know I need to say yes to her request. I think back to what Carrie said a few days ago—that I need to face this in order to move forward. And I know she's right. I'll have to email Sam and tell him I want to meet early tomorrow morning and hope he can. I need to notify him that I'm resigning *before* the preliminary hearing. That way I can make that my last task, and he can begin to figure out a game plan. I back out of the space. "Let's meet at the Intercontinental on Figueroa. I can be there in less than ten minutes."

After we hang up, I try to figure out why it's so urgent to Janelle that we meet. When she called the other day, it sounded like she simply wanted to touch base because she was moving down to LA. But now? Something about the edge in her voice makes me wonder if it's more than that. Could there be some way she's found out what happened with the internship? My mind wanders to Ethan. He is furious with me right now. Would he have told her? I shake my head at the thought. He didn't tell Carrie about the affair, so it's unlikely he'd track down someone from college and tell her about something I did fifteen years ago. Still, a tightness forms in my stomach that I can't get rid of. Because I know that if she doesn't already know, I have to tell her. There is no more room in my life for anything but the truth.

As I walk into the hotel, my phone buzzes with a text from Joe Dennis, the investigator.

Found Franklin. He's been at his aunt's house in Florida for the last few weeks. Can't be your guy. He's also still quite scrawny—definitely hasn't seen the inside of a gym in a long time.

Perpendicular feelings consume me. Relief he's not stalking me. But there is also fear—because Franklin had always seemed somewhat harmless. Almost predictable. And if it wasn't him, who could it be?

When I walk through the doors of the hotel, I spot Janelle sitting at the bar in the lobby, her back to me. Her hair is still long and a muted red, slightly darker and less fiery than it used to be. Her figure lithe. She turns as if she senses me, and my lips creep up into a broad smile, despite my nervousness. I made myself forget all the great times we had together after what I did. But those memories now break through the surface.

She simply nods at the stool next to her, her red-painted lips tight.

"Hi," I say tentatively.

"Thanks for meeting me tonight," she says, the conciliatory words not matching the tone of her voice. As if she's reading a script.

"Of course." I sit.

The bartender greets me.

"Whatever she's having." I point to the dark-colored liquid in her highball. Some sort of whiskey, I'm assuming.

"She's always wanted what I've wanted," she says more to herself than anyone else, her eyes narrow as she plays with the straw in her drink.

"What is this about, Janelle?" I ask. But there's not a doubt in my mind now. She knows.

"I think you know," she says, reading my mind. Then she turns to me, her chocolate eyes hard.

I wait. Sam's words ring in my ears. Never give anything away. Make them talk first. But no, that's not who I want to be anymore. I want to start over. Be honest. Be accountable.

"I do," I say. "And I'm sorry. If I could go back and change things, I would." The words come quickly and painlessly. I feel relief. It's getting easier and easier to tell the truth.

Janelle's eyebrows rise slightly, but she says nothing. She's surprised I'm not denying it. "I was sent an anonymous email," she finally offers.

"When?"

"Yesterday. That's why I wanted to meet."

Was it Ethan? He decides to confront me about the affair with pictures; then he contacts someone I screwed over in college?

"I tried to trace it," she says. "Had the tech guy in the DA's office work on it. But it was a dead Gmail account. I was thinking you might know who sent it," she says, laughing softly. "It seems from what I've heard since I got to town that you've made a lot of enemies."

"I have," I say as the bartender sets my drink in front of me. I take a long sip and let the whiskey burn my throat.

"What you did. Was it worth it?" she asks, not unkindly, and I understand. She's asking me whether I've made the most of what I took from her. And in many ways I have—I've lived up to be the kind of person who would steal a once-in-a-lifetime opportunity from a friend.

"I'd always thought that it was, until recently. I mean, I felt terrible at the time," I add, when her eyes widen. "But I told myself that I couldn't change it, that it would have done more harm than good to out Callahan, to reveal myself and our affair." I circle my finger around the rim of my glass as I choose my next words. "But now I wonder if it was the very first of my many, many failures as a human being."

Janelle studies me for several beats before speaking. "Well, I'm not here to tell you that you ruined my life because I didn't get the internship."

"Thank God," I mutter under my breath.

"But that doesn't make it okay, Lila."

"I know that. I'm sorry."

"I think the worst part was that you stopped speaking to me. For years I racked my brains wondering what I did wrong," she says. "It made me question everything, because I had thought we were real friends."

"We were," I say reflexively but stop myself. "No, you were."

"What are you saying?" A shadow crosses her face. "That you were never my friend?"

"No!" I shake my head. "I loved our friendship," I say, grasping for the way to best describe what I'm feeling. I remember Janelle taking notes for me in class when I got the flu. I recall the many times she skipped dates with her boyfriend to hang out with me. Or when I didn't go home for Thanksgiving that first year because the news of my dad's philandering was like a vise grip around my heart, so Janelle took me to her parents' place in San Francisco. She was so dependable that I took her for granted. Like a foundation that you think will never give out until it's shaken so hard that it does. "You saw me for who I was and liked me anyway." And it's true. She had celebrated my sharp edges. Until they cut her.

"Yeah, you were a tough one," Janelle quips, and we laugh awkwardly. "But, Lila, you have a heart in there—a big one. Don't think I didn't see how hard it was for you—not connecting with many people. I never understood why you pretended to be the Tin Man."

We fall into silence as I search for my response. "Because it was easier. Or so I thought."

Janelle arches an eyebrow, and it transports me back to our shared apartment that we rented second year. She'd look at me that way when

I'd leave my dishes piled high in the sink. I'm about to tell her as much when she starts talking.

"You know there were guys who wanted to date you. People who wanted to be your friend. But you rebuffed them, gave off that vibe of yours. You were so guarded . . ." She trails off.

"I know. I think the stuff with my dad really screwed me up in a way I couldn't see for a long time." *Until this week.*

Janelle nods.

"I couldn't face you after what I did," I finally say. "I knew it was so wrong but didn't know how to fix it."

Janelle frowns. "Yes, you did. But you didn't want to."

She's right. I could have corrected the wrong with one phone call. But once I had the opportunity in my hands, I knew there was no way I would let it go. "True," I concede. "But I don't want to be that person anymore."

"Because you got caught?" she asks, holding my gaze, her accusation similar to Ethan's.

"Maybe that was the reason initially, but it's much more than that. I want to be better. I know I can be."

"I know you can too, Lila." She smiles at me and touches my arm.

"I'm tired of covering up lies with more lies."

"They add up, don't they?"

"More than you know," I answer. "Janelle, I want to make this right with you. What will it take? For what it's worth, I'm quitting that job tomorrow."

"Wow," she says. "And what are you going to do?"

"I have no idea. Maybe I'll sell Rodan and Fields," I deadpan, and we both laugh.

"Or sell those leggings on Facebook." She rolls her eyes.

"Hey, I bought several pairs! They really are smooth as butter!" I smile, my heart aching as I think of all the years with her that I lost.

Janelle shakes her head. "What's done is done. And you know what they say, everything happens for a reason."

"You really believe that?"

"I do," she says. "If I'd taken that internship, I never would have met John, my husband. I never would have had my kids." She grabs her phone and pulls up a picture of a young boy and a girl jumping on a trampoline. "Chris is eight and Calista is nine," she says, beaming.

"They're beautiful," I say as I stare at their matching dark-blond hair, surprised when I feel tears in my eyes. Janelle got the life she deserved. Maybe Chase was right. Because here karma is, once again making sure the universe is just.

"I'm okay, Lila," Janelle says, her voice kind. "You always had much more ambition than I did anyway."

I nod, knowing what she's really saying—*I'm so relieved I didn't turn out like you.*

"Are you happy?" Janelle asks.

I wasn't expecting the question, and it hits me strangely. I sip my drink, trying to decide what the answer is. The old Lila would have immediately said yes. But this Lila, she is going to be honest. "No. But I'm getting there," I say. "I have a lot of work to do."

"The Lila I knew was never afraid of a little hard work." She grins. "Are you? Happy?"

"I am, but the prosecuting job I took is draining me already. Much more intense here than up north. The pay is crap, which I expected. But what I didn't consider was how that would factor into the crazy cost of living and the private school I had to put my kids in because the public one was, well . . ."

I nod, having heard the stories.

She continues. "We already closed on our house in Pasadena, so I can't back out now. We'll have to find a way to make it work."

An idea strikes me. A way I can attempt to right my wrong with Janelle. "Well, I can give you the inside track on a spot at a prestigious firm right here in downtown LA that specializes in criminal defense and pays much better."

"So, let me get this straight—you hate your job, feel like it made you a terrible person, and now you want me to take it?" She grimaces. "And to think I thought you wanted to make things right!"

"The firm didn't make me who I am. I did," I say. For every fork in the road, I chose the wrong path. I know that Janelle will not. Where I would always push the envelope, she preferred to follow rules. Drove the speed limit always—even when she was late for something, which was often. Never accepting notes from an upperclassman who'd already taken a course she was in. Not willing to keep extra change that was given to her by mistake. "They could use someone like you to balance out all the assholes."

"Okay, let me think about it," she says. "I'm definitely intrigued."

"Good. But there are two things you'll have to be okay with."

"What?"

"The fridge is always stocked with sugar and carbs. Which can be a good thing or a bad thing, depending on how you look at it."

"Okay, I can handle that. What's the second?"

"Most of the clients are probably guilty."

"Aren't they all?" Janelle tilts her head back and laughs, and I join in.

CHAPTER TWENTY-NINE

THURSDAY
CAPTURED

Q nudges me awake. Although I wasn't asleep, I'd been floating in between the darkness of my reality and the lightness of my dreams.

"Sit up," I hear Q demand.

I don't move. I don't open my eyes. I am through playing his games. I don't think I'm scared to die anymore.

He shakes my shoulder. "Lila." The pitch of his voice doesn't rise, but with my eyes squeezed shut, I'm able to detect the small shake in his speech. Wondering if I'm dead. If he's pushed me too far. His warm fingers grasp my wrist, and I hear him exhale as he detects my weak pulse. "Come on." He nudges me once more, gentler this time. I can feel him close to my face. "I brought some food and water for you," he whispers and pulls me upright.

I force my heavy eyelids open as he cuts the bindings on my ankles. He sets a sub sandwich on the ground next to me with a small bottle of water. I look at it blankly. I don't want to eat. Drink. I want to be done.

Q grabs the hoagie and brings it to my lips. "Eat," he commands. I shake my head. "Dammit," he swears under his breath. "I'm not a fucking babysitter," he adds, glancing over his right shoulder at the camera. "Lila," he says, sharper this time. "You need food."

"Why?" I mutter, my voice sounding foreign. "You're going to kill me anyway. I overheard your conversation earlier. Can't we get it over with?"

He doesn't take my bait. Instead, he pulls something out of his pocket. I stare hard, blinking several times. It's a cell phone. "I'm going to let you make a call."

I shoot a look at the camera. The red light is still blinking, watching. "You're letting me go?" I ask tentatively.

Q laughs loudly, his eyes shining from behind the mask. "No, Princess. You're misunderstanding. You aren't going anywhere. But you still have some work to do." He cups the phone with his large hand. "We're going to ring Stephanie."

It takes my mind a second to register what he has said. "Vivian's sister?" Is she the one behind all this, as I had originally suspected? "She wants to talk to me?" I ask.

"I doubt it. She hates your guts," Q says and removes a piece of tattered paper from his pocket, punching the numbers into the phone. "But you're going to let her know that you're sorry you defended Jeremiah and got him off. You're going to apologize, because you knew the entire time that he was guilty."

"No."

"What did you say to me?" Q pulls a gun out of the waistband of his red track pants.

I stare at the barrel, but my breath remains steady. I'm ready for it all to end. Although the competitive side of me thought I would've lasted more than, what, four days? I look away from the pistol. "I'm done being your puppet. Do what you need to do." I brace myself for whatever is coming next. The sound of my breath is amplified in my ears. My heart is racing. Is this how my story ends?

Q moves to the ground in one motion. "This isn't a choice, Lila," he says, and I'm not sure if he's talking about dying or making the phone call or both. Either way, I hear desperation in his tone. It's slight, but it's wedged in there, between the syllables. I feel his hot breath on my ear. "Please get up and make the call," he whispers quickly. Then he pulls back and yells, "You'd better get your ass up!" in a much harsher tone.

I drag myself to a sitting position and study him. Behind the mask I can see his eyes are soft. His eyebrows are covered, but I sense they are drawn together, that his expression is one of concern. I don't feel his contempt for me any longer. Something has changed. Or maybe I'm imagining it, a desperate figment of my imagination in the interest of my own self-preservation.

"Okay. I'll do it," I say quickly. If I'm going to die, I'd love the chance to apologize to Stephanie too, to absolve myself of one more sin. But I also feel a small spark of hope ignite within me. My call to Stephanie could let the world know I'm still alive. To look for *me*, not my dead body. I begin to think of ways I could use this call to save myself. I don't know where I am. Who has me. If Ethan is behind it all. Do I tell her as much as I can before Q grabs the phone? And how will Q punish me if I do? What will his boss direct him to do? Will I lose the sliver of sympathy he seems to have developed for me? "I'm not sure what you want me to say to her. I never found any evidence he was guilty."

Q holds the phone to his chest. "But you know he was. You didn't put him on the stand. Isn't that your move when you think someone is guilty?"

"What?" I ask. I've said that exact thing to someone before. I close my eyes and force my mind to dig through the darkness. Was it Ethan? Sam? Carrie? "No. There are a ton of reasons you keep someone off."

"Doesn't matter," Q says briskly. "Listen to me—all you're gonna do is apologize and tell her *why* you are sorry. Nothing more. *If* you try to say anything else, I will shoot you before you can tell her anything that will help. And I have to warn you, it won't be through the head or heart.

I'm thinking knee? Foot maybe? So expect pain." He says the words, but they don't hold the intensity they once did. It's as if he's reading a script.

Before I can think about it more, he presses a button, then holds the phone out. It's black and nondescript, not the one I saw him speaking on earlier. Probably a burner. The police won't be able to trace it—and that's *if* Stephanie reports to the authorities that she talked to me. A dart of fear penetrates me. What if she doesn't tell them or anyone else? Does her hate for me run that deep? It's possible she might take pleasure in my situation. Her sister's dead. Maybe she wants me dead too? The phone begins to ring. He has it on speaker. My chest feels like it might explode when I hear Stephanie's airy voice say hello.

"Stephanie?" I say, my eyes darting around the room. Looking for what? A clue that's suddenly going to appear, indicating where I am? My surroundings are still the same concrete walls. The heavy metal door is still locked. Q is still wearing a mask. The camera light continues to blink.

"This is she," Stephanie says, snapping me back to our call. It sounds as if she's in the middle of something. I can hear water running, dishes clanking.

"This is Lila Bennett." I say the words slowly. Talking to someone on the outside—even Stephanie—is as close to freedom as I'm probably ever going to get. I wish I knew what to say—a message I could somehow send—that would help me without getting me shot.

The water turns off. "Lila? Is this some kind of sick joke?"

"I wish," I say. "It's really me. Lila Bennett." I say my name again to make sure she understands. "I've called to apologize," I continue.

"Then this can't be Lila Bennett. She would never apologize." Stephanie laughs lightly.

"It's me. It really is," I say desperately, looking at Q, who nods at me to keep talking.

"Nice try. Lila Bennett is missing. No one has heard from her in days. The police were here yesterday asking if I knew anything about it."

So the police *are* investigating.

"I'll prove it. You confronted me on the courthouse steps after the trial."

"Anyone could have seen that."

I look at Q, who mouths the words, *Say I'm sorry.* I put my pointer finger up, asking for another minute.

I try again. "You told me karma was a bitch and you had no doubt I'd get mine," I say, the words still crystal clear. I've rolled them over and over in my mind so many times while here, wondering if she was right. That karma finally found me.

Stephanie gasps. "Lila? Oh my God. Where are you?"

The concern in her voice shocks me.

The word *kidnapped* sits on my tongue, poised for takeoff. But Q still has the barrel of the gun pointed toward me. I don't want him to pull the trigger. Can I take the risk that he won't?

Q is frozen in place, watching me intently. I think of the risk he and his boss are taking by letting me make this call in the first place. It makes no sense. Why? Is it that vital to them that I right my wrongs? No matter their motivation, it's clear I don't have much time left before I die, and it's now important to me as well.

"I've called about Jeremiah. I could never prove that he killed Vivian, but I felt all along in my heart that he did. I'm sorry I represented him. I'm sorry I helped get him off for the murder of your sister. I'm so very sorry." And the truth is, I am. As I apologize, I feel that knot in my throat come loose. I sniff hard to hold the avalanche of tears back, but it's useless.

"Lila, what is going on? Tell me," Stephanie pleads. "Maybe I can help."

My heart leaps at her kindness. "You can't. Please accept my apology," I beg, and not just because my life may depend on it. I also crave her forgiveness in the rawest of ways. If I really am to die soon, it would bring me peace to have received it.

"I do." She sighs. "I know you were doing your job. That you're not the one who killed her. And I'll never move on with my life if I can't come to terms with that, or at least that's what my mom keeps telling me. To forgive." Her voice breaks a little.

"My mom offers similar advice," I muse through my tears, thinking of her. Wondering where she is. Has she slept? Is she camped out in the chief's office asking him what new information he has about my disappearance?

"Lila, quickly, tell me where you are. Who you're with." Stephanie's voice is barely a whisper, as if she can intuit someone is listening. "I want to—"

Q pushes me hard in the small of my back and rips the phone away. "That's enough. This is not a coffee date!" He seethes quietly.

"It's possible it's Ethan, my husband—please, I'm being held—" I yell out as Q hangs up the phone. I'm not sure how much of that she heard, if anything. I'm not sure she'd do anything with the information anyway. But I had one chance to let someone know, to possibly make it out of here alive, and I had to take it.

Q moves closer to me, his finger hovering over the trigger of the gun.

"It *is* Ethan, isn't it?" I accuse, thinking of the many conversations we've had about Jeremiah. My uneasiness with the case. It all makes sense now. "Ethan!" I yell up to the camera. "I know why you did this. And I'm sorry. So sorry. Sorrier than you'll ever know!" I begin to sob again, loud and messy, my stomach muscles tensing with each burst of emotion. How did I get here—convinced my husband did this to me? My exhaustion, hunger, and fear all join into a huge force, and I feel myself melting into the dirty concrete. Literally hitting rock bottom.

Q's other phone rings, and he pulls it back out, looking at the screen. "Yeah," he answers and is silent for a moment before ending the call and observing me for several seconds. Finally he speaks in a reserved tone. "He wants you to know you did this to yourself."

And then my heart leaps from my chest as I hear the deafening crack of the bullet rocketing out of his gun.

CHAPTER THIRTY

FRIDAY
FREE

I jolt upright in bed, breathing hard. My hand instinctively reaches to the left side of the mattress where Ethan's head used to poke out from under our silk sheets. But I'm alone to process the nightmare I woke from.

I was in a concrete room. Dirty and disheveled. Bleeding. Hopeless. It was so real—I could feel my breath begin to grow more shallow with each intake of air. Two dark shadows stood over me. The last thing I could remember before I tore myself awake was the blinking red light of a camera.

The feeling of dread follows me into the shower. It refuses to peel off as I scrub my skin with my loofah until it's as red as the blinking light that haunts me. It feels like there's not enough hot water in the world to rinse it off. I exit the shower and wrap myself in my lavender robe, the one Ethan gifted me for my thirtieth birthday. It's thick and cozy, but it makes me sweat if I wear it after March. But Ethan had insisted that there would be days that I'd crave the comfort of it.

Today is one of those days.

I have important tasks to handle, and I can't afford to be distracted by an errant nightmare. First up is Jeremiah, then Sam, then the Greenwood preliminary hearing. A trifecta to end my old life, needed in order to plant the seeds for my next one. I'm terrified, of course. But there's a buzz of excitement as well, like a baby taking her very first steps. Unsure and wobbly at first, trying in vain to find her balance before she realizes how easy it really is. Then confidence. And finally, joy.

My phone buzzes with a text from Chase, asking me what time I'll be in. Be there in an hour, I text back and set my phone down, staring into the mirror. "You've got this, Lila."

~

I nod at Chase as I walk past his desk fifty-two minutes later. I'm never late, though I'm usually right under the wire. But not today. Today I need every spare minute I can get. "We need to talk," I say, and he follows me in, shutting the door behind him. I sit at my desk and fill him in on my meeting with Janelle, and I say that I'm not taking Jeremiah's case. And then I tell him the hardest part of all. Because I will miss working with him.

"Quitting?" He laughs. "You've never quit anything in your damn life. Where are the cameras?" He looks around.

I see that blinking red light again and shake it away. When I don't so much as crack a smile, he runs his hand over his smooth hair. "Oh. You're serious."

"Yep," I say, getting up from the chair behind my desk and sitting next to him instead. "This is real."

"This feels like a major knee-jerk reaction to the attack earlier this week. Ethan leaving you," he says, turning his chair so it faces me, his forehead wrinkled with concern. "It's been an insane couple of days. Maybe you should think this through more."

"I have, trust me." I offer him a sad smile. "I think it's been a long time coming."

"But, Lila Bennett, this is who you are. The one who makes the tough calls. Does what needs to be done," he says, and I know he doesn't mean it the way it sounds. That being a conscience-challenged attorney is my identity. But the words still strike me hard and reaffirm my decision.

"I don't want to be that Lila Bennett anymore."

"But who am I going to shoe shop for now?" He smiles awkwardly and shifts in his seat.

"I'm quitting, not moving to another country!" I laugh. "We're always going to be friends. But depending on where I end up next, there's a chance I won't be able to afford four-hundred-dollar pairs of shoes anymore. You might have to start shopping for my footwear at DSW."

He gasps, then puts the back of his hand against his forehead. But it seems forced. "Never." He smiles. "I'm going to stay here, though," he adds. "I hope you understand."

"Of course," I say. "You have an incredible future ahead of you. You'll do it the right way. And if the person I'm recommending takes this job, the two of you will be a force."

Chase leans in. "I still can't believe you're leaving."

"I can't stay here. I've changed too much."

Chase eyeballs me. "I'm happy for you, but do you think it will stick? It's only been a few days. How do you know you won't sink back into who you used to be?"

I think a moment before answering. "Only time will tell. But I have no interest in being that person. I can only have faith in that."

"I've never been a big believer in faith. I've always thought actions speak louder."

I smile. "Well, maybe I'll have to prove myself on both counts."

"Maybe you will," he says quietly. "Have you considered that whoever sent Ethan those pictures and Janelle that email might want you to quit this job? That you're playing right into their hands?"

I take a deep breath, not sure I can find the words. "At some point I have to stop running from myself, from all the half truths and missteps and selfishness. Is there someone out there who clearly wants me to atone for the things I've done? Yes. And have they gone about it the very worst way? Definitely." I think about how this person has dismantled my life brick by brick, how they've expertly exhumed every single skeleton from my past. "But that doesn't change the fact that I need to own my mistakes."

"Never thought I'd see the day. Lila Bennett, deconstructed." Chase smiles. "But I'm proud of you that you're so committed to being good." He nods at me, looks down for a moment, then back up. "And don't tell anyone, but I'm going to miss that bad girl in you too. If she really is going on hiatus?" He winks.

I smile back at him. "She is going on a *very* long vacation with a one-way ticket!"

"Somewhere exotic, I hope. Jamaica?"

"Farther. I'm thinking Indonesia. Bali!"

"Oh, tell her to bring me back a handmade rattan messenger bag."

I smile at him sadly. I will miss him and his wicked sense of humor.

I think about all of the people who would celebrate *that* Lila being shipped off to some remote island and reluctantly come to terms with the fact that whoever is uprooting my life has to be someone I care for deeply. A person to whom I've entrusted the darkest parts of myself.

Ethan or Sam. And as much as I hate to admit it, Carrie. I tried to convince myself that there's no way that she could be capable. But I've certainly given her the right motivation. Did she snap? Is this her twisted way of making me pay? My mind begins to race at the possibility, but I shake the thoughts away. Tomorrow I will unravel that mystery. I have more important tasks at hand.

"I still don't completely get it. But if you insist on blowing up your entire life, I guess I'll have to watch from the cheap seats as you detonate it," Chase concedes.

I stand up, lean over, and wrap my arms around him. "Thank you," I whisper.

"You're welcome," he says before looking down at my shoes. "I'm glad you wore the cherry-red Manolos today. If you're going down swinging, at least you'll look fabulous."

~

I'm not sure how long I've been staring out the window of my office at the streets of downtown Los Angeles when Chase buzzes and lets me know I need to take off or I'll be late to my next meeting.

"Got it," I say and stand up, grabbing my bag and straightening my jacket, pulling on my pencil skirt that has always been a bit too snug and cuts into my waist. I make a note to get rid of it.

"I love that you're dumping him in public." Chase smirks as I pass him.

"That way he can't make a scene," I say with a smile. I had Chase call Jeremiah and move our meeting to Hotel Indigo, the contemporary boutique hotel across the street, hoping it will sting less if he's sitting in one of their plush lime velvet booths, staring at the wall of fedoras that hang from the ceiling.

I jaywalk across Francisco Street and push my way through the heavy glass doors, spotting Jeremiah typing on his phone in a booth behind the bar.

I greet him and slide in on the opposite side, facing him. "Thanks for meeting me here."

The bartender walks up and sets a bloody mary in front of him, then shoots me a questioning glance. "Nothing for me," I say and shake my head.

"You sure?" Jeremiah asks, carefully lifting the glass to his lips. "They make them good here."

"I'm sure, thanks," I say, running my hand through my hair and sitting up a little straighter.

"Suit yourself, then." He pulls out a thick notepad, notes scrawled in blue ink covering the page. "I've already begun to put some thoughts on paper. I think this lawsuit is total bullshit. We need to go after Vivian this time. Attack her char—"

I cut him off. "You want to attack the character of your late wife?" I stare at him incredulously, noticing how beady his eyes are. The way his chin juts out like a knife. I never paid attention to those details before. His charm camouflaging his flaws.

"I think we should revisit the affair." He glances at his notepad. "She recently had lunch with that old college boyfriend."

"An affair was never proven. And the police cleared him. His alibi was airtight," I say calmly. "He was at the movies with his wife. The kid taking tickets confirmed it."

"That pimple-faced teenager could have been wrong. He was probably texting when they walked in. And his wife could have been covering for him."

I start to interrupt him again, and he puts his hand up. "Hear me out. Maybe Vivian broke things off with him, and he got upset. Followed her home from Pilates. Hit her with the lamp."

I snap to attention. "The lamp?" I repeat the words, and his eyes bulge, his face turning red.

The murder weapon was never known during the trial. The police and coroner agreed that Vivian was bludgeoned with an object. But that object was never determined or found. The lead investigator on the case had speculated it could have been a number of things: a fire poker, a paperweight, a lamp. But nothing was found in Jeremiah's home. He also couldn't account for anything that was missing other than some valuables.

The lack of a murder weapon was the main reason Jeremiah wasn't convicted. I feel like I've been sucker punched in the stomach, and it takes a second to catch my breath.

Jeremiah quickly recovers. "I just mean the murder weapon, whatever it was. Wasn't it your guy that said it could have been a lamp?"

"He speculated that it *could have been* that or a number of other things," I say, my stomach churning as I connect the dots. "But the police couldn't prove that any of the objects that could have killed her had ever been in your house. As you might recall, my defense was that the intruder used something he'd had with him. But a lamp? Why would an intruder bring a lamp into your house, Jeremiah?"

Jeremiah's face turns red again. "I don't know. If they ever find him, they should ask him." He holds my gaze for a beat too long, and I can see that his hands are shaking slightly. His next words are a non sequitur. "Let's talk about what your strategy is."

I stare at him, all the pieces falling into place. My gut screamed at me from the minute I took this case. *He's guilty*, it tried to tell me. Yet I looked and didn't see any red flags, so I'd told myself it was okay. That I was on the right side of it all. But I knew all along. "I'm sorry, but I won't be able to represent you." I pull a sticky note out of my bag and begin to write. "I can refer you to one of the other attorneys at our firm who specialize in—"

"What do you mean, you can't represent me?" Jeremiah asks, his voice barreling through the room. A woman in a red dress at the bar glances over. We make eye contact, and she looks away, taking a drink of her white wine.

"I think you did it," I blurt, and the words hang in the air between us.

His head snaps back at my assertion, and then he sneers. "Do you really care if I did it, Lila? Why do you think I chose you? Because guilty or not, you battle till the end. You love the fight. You're like a boxer in the ring." He knocks back the last of his drink. "This is going to be a fight, and I need the toughest there is. I need Tyson. For you to bite an ear off if necessary. And you would."

I grimace at the idea that he thinks of me that way. But then again, when he met me, that's who I probably was. I hold out the sticky note. "Sam will find someone better for you. Better yet, you can hire *him*. There's no better Tyson, trust me."

Jeremiah grabs the note and crumples it in his hand. "You're going to regret this. I'll make sure it's the end of your career here, bailing on me like this."

"I never agreed to represent you for the civil part in the first place. So I'm not bailing. I already got you off for murder. You're welcome." I pick up my tote and start to leave.

He grabs my elbow. "You can't do this," he says, snarling.

I shake my hand hard to try to break away from him. The woman notices us again, and I nod to let her know I'm okay. I'm sure she thinks this is a lovers' spat. How many times had he and Vivian been through this? She didn't do what he wanted, and he got physical. A surge of nausea rips through me as I fully realize my part in helping a killer go free. In the knowledge that there was not a damn thing any of us could do to change it.

"Let go of me," I say through my teeth.

Jeremiah releases my hand. His jaw is clenched, and I'm staring at the man I'm now sure killed his wife. "One piece of advice. You can't run from your secrets forever. Eventually they'll catch up to you with a vengeance. Trust me," I say before turning around and walking quickly toward the exit, refusing to look back.

∽

Chase knocks softly on my office door a few minutes after I return from Hotel Indigo. "Come in," I call.

"He's down in Sam's office," he confesses gingerly. He's still a little off from our earlier conversation. Still digesting all the change. "He's going nuts."

"I figured as much." I hit the Print button and pull the warm paper out. "I need you to do one more thing for me." I hand him the sheet, and he scans it quickly.

"Lila." He shakes his head. "You can't send this. Telling Vivian's family about your privileged conversation with Jeremiah."

"He did it, Chase. I always knew. And damn it, I ignored it to take the easy win." I think about all the other times I've looked the other way because it was simpler to do so. "Now they have a chance to prove it."

"If what you did with Greenwood's wife doesn't get you disbarred, this certainly will." Chase gives me a strange look. Almost as if he's never seen me before. "It feels like you want them to punish you."

"Maybe I do," I say. Then I add quickly, "Send it anonymously. Contact that guy we used for the Santos case. The one with the beard who always smells like weed."

"Fine." Chase slips the paper into a manila envelope. "I hope you know what you're doing." His tone is low, and his face is slack. He knows once he sends this there is no turning back.

I grin for the first time all morning. "Don't worry. I do."

CHAPTER THIRTY-ONE

FRIDAY
CAPTURED

I throw my hands up in front of my face instinctively when I hear the crack of the bullet, bracing myself for it to penetrate my skull. Time suspends, and I can feel each rapid heartbeat knock my chest, the blood pump in my ears. I see Ethan's lopsided grin when he proposed, his hand shaking as he held out the ring. I've read stories about people who marry sociopaths. Hell, I've defended them. But I thought I was more intuitive than that. I thought I knew my slightly nerdy, bookish, introverted, moody but lovable husband. The man who's watching me on the camera right now, waiting for the bullet to end me. I cower on the floor and brace myself for the impact. For the life I thought I knew to be over. And that's okay. Because the agony in the fact that I've driven Ethan to do this is the most painful part of all.

But I'm still breathing. There is no pain. Only silence after the deafening pop. I tear my head around and stare at the wall behind me. There is a divot in the concrete where the bullet ricocheted off it.

He missed?

My gaze makes its way to Q. He's still pointing the pistol at me. But it's moving ever so slightly. *Up and down. Up and down.* Is he shaking? Did he mean to bypass me? Or did he simply miss his mark in the heat of the moment?

"Q?" I say his name, but my mouth is so dry it comes out as more of a whisper.

"Shut up!" Q says through gritted teeth. He starts to pace, the gun still aimed in my direction.

His cell phone rings, but he ignores it. It must be Ethan demanding to know why there's a bullet in the wall instead of in my body. After all, I've informed Stephanie that he's involved. If she tells the police, that could be it. But this Ethan, the one I had no idea existed, has hired a masked man to abduct, demoralize, harm, and ultimately kill his wife, so he will not let this all be for nothing. He'll want to get away before they get to him. And he'll also want Q to dispose of me. But maybe he made a mistake and left a clue that will lead the police to me in time. Although it seems as though I have very little of that left.

"Q?" I try again. I need to break through, get him to listen. To talk. Anything.

"I told you to shut up. I need to think. This isn't what I thought it would be."

"What does that mean?"

"Just shut up!" he says and runs his hand over his mask.

I say nothing and take a long breath in. I'm still here. I'm still alive. And there's a chance he's *not* going to kill me. At least that's what I want to believe as I glance at the hole in the wall again. Q's phone beeps several times. He pulls it out and looks at it, then shoves it back into his pocket. I try to work out what's going on between him and Ethan. Is Q no longer on board with the plan—whatever that plan was? Is there a disagreement about payment? Q wants more? I would.

I'd want a fuckload if I was doing someone's dirty work for him. The only problem is we don't have that kind of money. I do well, but not *that* well. Not take-my-wife-hostage-and-kill-her-for-me well. Do they have a history, Ethan and Q? Does Ethan have something on Q? Maybe I'll never know.

Ethan told Q I had brought this on myself. Those words still haunt me. It's the *this* part of his statement that bothers me the most. That he believes I deserve *this* because I had an affair. Because I defended Jeremiah too well. Because I did something stupid in law school. Only the affair directly affected him. And while it was terrible, was it *this* terrible?

Something nags at the corners of my mind, willing for me to let it take shape. Words I heard Q say earlier that I've heard before. *I only keep a client off the stand when they're guilty* . . . I'd said it flippantly to someone once. I remember thinking I shouldn't have uttered it out loud, and I certainly hadn't meant it. I had been making the point that sometimes there are too many holes in a story to survive a good cross-examination. But to whom had I been speaking? I squeeze my eyes tight and beg my tired mind to recover the entire thought.

"Q, please, talk to me. I need to know. Is it really Ethan who's behind this? I know you said it was, but did you mean it?" I'm surprised that my voice is cracking. That tears are springing from my eyes. Because I still love Ethan. My heart hasn't caught up with what my mind knows. Or thinks it knows.

He stops walking, the gun still trained on me. One pull of the trigger, and that's it. I'm done.

"Q?" I try again. "Please . . ."

"I told you to shut up!" He hunches his shoulders and punches the wall. "Fuck," he says, shaking his hand.

"You're hurt," I say, watching the blood from his knuckles run down his arm.

"No shit."

His phone rings again. He looks at it and huffs, then puts it away again.

"What's going on?" I jiggle my leg because it's fallen asleep. My pencil skirt is now ripped almost all the way up to my waist. My blouse is stained with sweat. My bare legs have taken on a grayish tone from dirt and dust.

"I didn't disagree with you when you said it was Ethan."

"I know, but you also didn't directly say it was . . ." I don't finish my thought. I wait, hoping he'll fill the silence.

"You calling me a liar?"

I shake my head. "It seems odd that you'd want me to know he was responsible for my abduction *before* I made the call to Stephanie."

Then it hits me. They knew I'd tell her. They *wanted* me to tell her. I shake my head at my stupidity. I was so desperate to speak to someone who could help me that I ignored the absurdity of them letting me make the call in the first place. This isn't an episode of *Bosch*. These are real-life kidnappers who would never want anyone to hear my voice again unless it benefitted them somehow. And I walked straight into their trap, thinking I was helping myself when I was only hurting Ethan. Yet again. What does that say about me? That I was so quick to assume that Ethan would make the kind of terrible choices I have? Clearly I've learned nothing. He isn't anything like me, which is one of the many reasons he'll be better off without me.

"Damn it," I say.

"I see you've figured it out," he answers. "You did exactly what we wanted you to do. I actually thought you were smarter than that. But my partner knew different."

"That I'm not smart?" I look up at the camera.

"No—that you'd be so focused on the possibility the phone call could help you, you wouldn't notice the trap. That you'd be so arrogant as to think you could outsmart us."

Who gets me like that? My mom is the only person who knows me better than I know myself, and there is no way she has anything to do with this. And if it's not Ethan, then who?

Suddenly I remember who I spoke the line to.

I whip my head around to stare at Q's unique eye color—how could I have missed it? But, God, he was just a kid back then. No older than thirteen. I remember him as sweet and quiet. Seemed to really look up to his older brother. The brother that I realize now infiltrated my life so easily. He has a new name, his hair is dyed blond. But I have no doubt it is he who is behind this now, the pieces of this complex puzzle finally clicking into place. My chest heaves as my mind races through our history together. The laughter I realize was fake, the loyalty I felt from him an elaborate ruse so that he could gain my trust. If you had asked me a million times who had kidnapped me, his name would have never escaped my mouth.

I force myself upright and shuffle toward the camera.

"What are you doing?" Q asks, his voice shaking slightly. "I still have this gun pointed at you."

"I'm aware," I say, working hard to keep the terror out of my voice.

"Now you're telling me what to do?" He purses his lips.

"I am," I answer slowly, then face the camera, hoping I'm not miscalculating. That what I'm about to say won't backfire on me. "Because I know who you are. I know who's been watching." As I speak the words, I hope I'm wrong.

"You're bluffing," Q says, but I hear something in his voice. Relief?

I turn my back toward the camera and look at him. I whisper so the microphone won't pick it up. "You can let me go. You don't have to do your boss's bidding anymore."

"No, I can't. It doesn't work like that. I can't just walk away."

I stare at him for a moment, wondering what's going through his mind. Wondering why he was cast as the heavy.

"It could work like that. You could take control of this. You have more power than you think." I speak quickly.

He shakes his head. "Not gonna happen. There's a lot you don't understand," he says loudly. But his eyes are soft from behind the holes in his mask. Is he sending me a message? I decide to leave it there. Not to push him anymore.

I turn back toward the camera and take a deep breath. Ironically, this is the one time in my life I've never wanted to be more wrong.

"I know who you are. Come on out. It's time we speak face-to-face."

CHAPTER THIRTY-TWO

FRIDAY
FREE

I'm still on a high as I walk down the hall toward the elevator bank. Sam is on the floor above, and as I push number twenty-three, I take note of my balanced breath, my steady heartbeat, my clear head. For the first time in as long as I can remember, I have clarity. Is this what it means to do the *right* thing? The doors open, and I step inside next to a dark-haired woman in a black power suit who is barking orders into her headset while simultaneously pecking on her phone. *I told you to get me that brief. Opening arguments are tomorrow.* She glances up as if noticing me for the first time, and when our eyes meet, I get the strangest sensation. As if I'm watching myself. As if I'm seeing what my life would be like if I stayed here at Douglas, Shirby, and Jones. I smile at her knowingly, and she nods, then returns to her call, her voice shrill. I tune her out until all I can hear is the Muzak. It's the song "Easy." Possibly a preface to what's coming? Well, if it is, sing me home, Lionel!

I step out onto the plush deep-blue carpeting and walk toward Sam's office. Thanks to Chase's intel, I know two things: Jeremiah has exited the building, and Sam is on the rampage and looking for me. No doubt wondering why I won't take the case—why I would turn down hundreds of thousands of dollars for the firm without so much as consulting him. As I approach his door, my heart starts to rattle, and I feel my confidence slipping away with each step. The little voice inside me, the one that guides most of my questionable choices, my inner bad girl who always encourages me to have that third glass of wine, to eat that second sleeve of Girl Scout cookies, to *sleep with Sam*, is screaming, *What are you doing? I already think you're a fool for breaking things off with Sam, but now you're leaving the firm too?*

I stop walking. "Stop! You are not influencing me anymore!" I say to my inner voice.

I look up and see Adam coming toward me.

"Sorry. Prepping for trial," I lie.

"Whatever," he says unconvincingly as he continues past me.

"Wait!" I say, and Adam turns slowly.

"Look, I don't feel like getting yelled at right now if it's all the same to you." Adam starts to walk away again.

"Adam," I say. "I'm sorry."

He stops walking and swivels around. "Did Lila Bennett just apologize?"

"She did."

He steps closer. "For what it's worth, I didn't know the details. And I'm sorry I triggered an old wound. It wasn't my intention."

"I know."

"And the case . . . I dumped it. The guy had four prior DUIs, and this time he killed a teenager."

I shake my head.

"Truce?" He holds out his hand.

"Truce," I say and shake it.

I take a deep breath and walk into Sam's office, with the understanding that nothing will ever be the same again once I do. Hoping things will go as smoothly as they did with Adam, but I already know better.

He leans back in his chair when he sees me. "There she is." He raises his eyebrows, causing the lines on his forehead to deepen.

"Here I am," I say and stand up a little straighter even though my heels are pinching my toes.

"We need to talk. Jeremiah just left. He said—"

"Let me stop you right there," I say with more force than I intend.

He starts to speak, but I cut him off. "Sorry, I didn't mean to be so curt." I walk over and sit in the chair across from him. He starts to get up to come around the desk and sit next to me as he's always done in the past. "It's okay," I say. "You're fine right there."

"Lila?" He frowns, trying to assess what's going on with me.

"Sam, please, I need to say something, and it isn't going to be easy."

"You already ended things," he quips.

"It's not about us."

"It's always about us." That smile. The one that stretches from ear to ear and hides his eyes. The one that used to make my stomach flip. The one that could make me agree to anything. *Have one more drink. Kiss me. Stay the night.* But right now, in this moment, the smile only conjures images of Carrie, a tiny life growing inside her. Of Ethan, my husband, who is trying to do better in his life.

"Maybe it has been. But not today," I say, looking down, avoiding my kryptonite. Finally, my eyes make their way back up to him. "I'm not representing Jeremiah. Or Greenwood, for that matter. Because—"

"I told you, Greenwood is not optional. You are not getting off that case. Stop whining about it, and get the job done!"

I swallow my frustration. Fight the urge to storm out. To simply send him an email with my resignation. But I have to do this. In person. Not for him. For me.

"I'm done, Sam. I'm leaving this firm. Consider this my resignation. I'll handle the preliminary trial for Greenwood this afternoon, since it's too late to change counsel. But after that, I'm out."

"You're what?" He stands up. His tie is loosened around his neck, and his pants are wrinkled. "Is this some kind of joke?"

"No, it's not a joke. I'm serious. I need you to hear me on this. I'm done. I'm finished with all of this. The chase. The hunt. The thrill." As I say it, I'm not sure if I'm talking about the job or him or both. And I'm not sure he is either.

"That's what makes you tick, Lila. It's who you are."

"No, Sam, it's who I *was*." And with that, I walk around the desk and give him a hug, his body stiff against my embrace because he's processing. I put my arms around him because in a really strange way, he's helped me get here, to the person I was meant to be. And for that I'm thankful. As he starts to relax and tighten his grip around me, I pull back and look at him.

"Can you do one thing for me? I'm in the appeals process for that drug possession case, and it's looking good for a win. Can you give it to someone good, please? I really want to do right by the client."

He starts to say something, but I rush out of the room before he can. I am pressing the elevator button hard when I hear him coming after me.

"Lila, wait . . ."

The doors slide open, and I step inside. I press the button several times so the doors will close. They've almost met in the middle when he comes into view. The look of understanding on his face is clear. And then the doors close, and he's gone. I know he won't follow me down. I know he's finally letting me go.

∾

I'm starting to sweat in my car and finally hit the ignition button, cranking up the air until I begin to feel relief. I rode down in a trance from

Sam's floor. I don't recall walking to my vehicle, letting myself inside, or slipping into the seat I sit in now. So many thoughts layered upon more thoughts. I'm gripping the steering wheel, my knuckles white. I take a deep breath and start the car, heading toward Santa Monica. To Carrie and Sam's house. As I exit the freeway, I pull over quickly at a gas station. I reach into my bag and pull out the spiral notebook. One by one, I tear out the pages with the tally marks, rip them into tiny pieces, and let them float downward into a trash can.

~

I pull up in front of their white craftsman thirty minutes later. Its blue shutters and red front door always reminded me more of a home you'd see in Martha's Vineyard than along the Pacific coast. But it suits Carrie. She has timeless style, much like this home, with its ruby-red roses blooming and daffodils standing tall, almost as if they are proud to be displayed so elegantly. I walk slowly up to her front door and ring the bell. After a few moments, it swings open.

"Lila?" Carrie says, tucking a blonde strand of hair behind her ear and cinching the belt on her robe. She frowns slightly. "Is everything okay?"

"Sorry, I should have called . . ."

"No, I'm glad you're here," she says, smiling widely. "I was about to take my coffee to the backyard. It's a beautiful day. Join me."

I hesitate, Carrie's warm greeting reminding me yet again that I don't deserve her; I've never deserved her. I follow her into the kitchen. All white, save for the black knobs on the cupboards. She reaches into one of them and grabs a mug and fills it with coffee. I take a sip; it's strong.

"Milk?" she asks.

I shake my head. "Not today. How are you feeling?" I inadvertently glance at my Apple Watch. It's not like Carrie to be disheveled this late in the morning.

"I'm okay," she says. But she looks pale, and her hands are shaking slightly. "What about you? I don't think I've ever seen you in my neighborhood before six p.m.! Sam either, for that matter!" She gives me a look, and my heart drops.

Does she know?

"Both of you, two peas in a pod. Such workaholics!" she continues, and I try to catch my breath again. I drove here on pure adrenaline, deciding that when I arrived I'd know whether or not I should tell her about Sam and me. But now that I'm standing in her kitchen, staring at her in her pale-pink robe and fuzzy gray slippers, I don't think I can. I remember how I felt when my mom told me about my dad. How afterward all I wished for was to not know. If I tell Carrie, she can never go back to the blissful unknowing.

"I'm okay. There's just a lot going on," I say and take another drink of my coffee and look around the kitchen. Not so much as a spatula out of place. Her pile of mail is stacked neatly, the bigger envelopes on the bottom cushioning the smaller ones on top. My eye is drawn to a large navy-blue one with white trim, and I do a double take. I could swear it's identical to the one Ethan tossed on the table before he stormed out of our house. The one that had the pictures inside. I step closer to try to see it better and then look over at Carrie, who's watching me, a small smile on her lips.

"Let's go outside," she says, grabbing her mug. Could it be possible that she has a copy of the pictures too? That she knows? Is that why she's still in her bathrobe? My heart starts to hammer.

We step into her backyard, and the view of the ocean is breathtaking. Every time I see it, it's as if I'm taking it in for the first time.

"I'm lucky," she says, then pauses. "To have this."

"You are," I say, thinking of Ethan. Of what I've now lost. I had never stopped and thought about my good luck in finding him—of what life might look like without him. "How do you do it?" I ask her. "Remember to feel lucky? I always feel like I'm looking to the next great thing. Never stopping to see what's right there, you know?" I squint and reach for my sunglasses in my pocket. "I don't want to be like that anymore," I say, and after the words are out I feel like I'm standing naked in front of her. Suddenly hiding behind absolutely nothing. The feeling is both uncomfortable and empowering.

Carrie assesses me for a moment as if she believes me. If Carrie believes I can change, that gives me so much hope. "Life can change in an instant, Lila. One decision. One wrong turn. One missed opportunity. That's all it takes. And everything you had could be gone. So cherish it while you still can." She gives me a knowing look.

I wonder again if she knows about Sam. If she *should* know about him. My mind spins as I try to decide how she could possibly be better off knowing. She has a baby coming, a marriage to which she's always been devoted. Why should I rip that from her? A lifetime she could spend with Sam and their future son or daughter shouldn't be stripped away because of six months of stupidity. But then again, doesn't she deserve to know that her husband has broken their vows? That he doesn't seem to love and respect her the way he should? But is it my job to tell? I'm the adulteress but also the best friend—which person should speak to her?

She begins talking again. "Do you ever think what your life would be like if you didn't work at Douglas, Shirby, and Jones?" she asks, settling into a chair, patting the one next to her in a gesture for me to sit.

I let out an uncomfortable laugh, scanning Carrie's face for a reaction. But she simply waits for me to answer. "Sure. I wouldn't have met Ethan. We were set up by Patrick, the equities guy at the firm." I sit next to her.

"You also wouldn't have met me." She smiles playfully.

"Right. And that would have been a travesty!"

We both laugh lightly at my joke. But my insides are tightening. It would have been awful if I'd never met Carrie. She brought light into an otherwise dark place inside me. But somehow, I was able to separate my work self—the one who represented bad people, the one who had the affair—from my other self, the one who loved Carrie and would do anything for her, the one who made sure her mother would never struggle again.

"You also wouldn't know Sam. You two are tight," Carrie says, her lips slightly parted as she stares at me.

We hold each other's gaze for a few moments, and it's so quiet I feel like I can hear the blood pumping in my ears. I swallow, trying to determine what she means by this. But her face gives nothing away. Finally, I nod. "Everything important to me originated one way or another from my job there. The positive and . . ." I pause, the good Lila pressuring me to say it. Finally I do. "And the negative."

"I know. And isn't it so weird to think you weren't meant to have it? I mean, I wonder where you'd be now if you hadn't taken it?" She gives me a knowing smile. And I can't ignore the irony of her keeping a secret about my indiscretion all these years.

I take a deep breath. "It's impossible to know, I suppose."

"Would you go back and change anything if you could?" She raises her eyebrows over her coffee mug.

I sit very still before answering, trying to decipher whether there's any hidden meaning in her words. "I can't change the past—the only thing I have control of is my future."

"Hmm," she says, sipping her coffee and staring out at the ocean.

"Which is actually what brought me here today. My future."

"Oh?" She turns, her eyes wide.

"I quit today."

"Your job? At the firm?" Carrie inches forward in her chair.

"Yes."

"Why?" She leans in, as if wanting to absorb my answer as fully as possible.

"A million reasons. But mostly because I want my future choices to be better than my past, and I don't think I can do that if I stay."

"Wow." Carrie sets her mug down. "Just wow," she says again.

"What?"

Carrie takes a deep breath, and I wonder if she's weighing whether she should say what's really on her mind. "I don't know. I guess I never thought you'd leave Sam. I mean the firm." She shakes her head. "I thought I knew you so well."

"What does that mean?" I ask, and it comes out sharper than I intend.

Carrie looks hurt.

"I'm sorry, I didn't mean—" I start, but Carrie cuts me off.

"No, I'm sorry. I wasn't trying to take away from your news. I was sure you were a lifer. Despite what I said, your mom said, you seemed so devoted to your job."

"I was, but things have changed."

"What exactly?" Carrie's eyes are soft, and she turns quickly as if she's seen something out of the corner of her eye.

This is the moment I could tell her. Lay the truth on the table. Explain why Ethan really left. Tell her I'm not only leaving the firm because I no longer like the job. Tell her all of it.

She takes another sip of her coffee, and I follow her gaze. She's staring at a hummingbird floating beyond a nearby tree. And it is then that both voices inside me say in unison, *Don't tell her; don't break her heart.*

I nod in response and wonder if Carrie noticed. But she's still watching the bird. If Carrie and Sam are meant to work out, they will. I will let it play out for them however it should and hope whatever the outcome, it's what's best for Carrie and the baby.

"Do you see it? The hummingbird?" Carrie asks.

"I do."

"Sorry I got distracted. He's so beautiful. So tell me, what changed?"

"My heart's not in it anymore," I say, and Carrie smiles as if she understands.

"Does Sam know?"

"I told him about an hour ago. I have to go to a preliminary hearing this afternoon and handle a couple things, and that will be it."

"Congrats," she says, but there's a sadness in her tone, reminding me of when I congratulated her on the baby. The words sounded hollow to me then just as hers do now. I wait for her to ask me how he took the news, but she doesn't. I wonder why.

"Thanks. And . . . Carrie?"

"Yeah?"

"Thank you for always reminding me I was better than that place. Than that job." I give her a hug, and she tenses but then relaxes into my grip. "Wow, two signs of physical affection in one week!" She laughs awkwardly.

"I should go. I need to get to the hearing."

"Okay." She smiles, the color returning to her cheeks. "I'll walk you out."

We're almost to the door when she stops next to the pile of mail. Next to the envelope. She glances at it. And for a moment I think she's going to pick it up, throw it at me the way Ethan did. But she doesn't. If she's already read it, then she knows and has been waiting this whole time for me to do the right thing and tell her. But if she hasn't opened it yet, she could likely be alone when she does. Suddenly the thought of her finding out while by herself in this sterile kitchen slams me hard. I change my mind. I'm going to tell her.

"Carrie—"

"I lost the baby," she says. "Miscarriage."

"Oh, Carrie . . . I'm so sorry . . ." I say, and my eyes fill with tears.

"No, it's okay. My body made the right choice. My body knew better." She doesn't cry, but her upper lip trembles, and her shoulders shake. She's trying so hard to keep it together.

"Do you want to talk about it?" I ask, unsure of what to say if her answer is yes. But I will be the friend I should have been all along and listen to her as long as she wants to talk.

She doesn't answer for a moment. Then she opens her mouth but closes it again. Finally she speaks. "Sam didn't know. I hadn't told him because I wanted to wait until the next appointment. My mom had three before me. Did I ever tell you that?"

I shake my head, but she keeps talking.

"I worry I caused it. That my fear brought it on."

"This isn't your fault," I say. "You are such a good person; you aren't responsible. Like you said, your body was telling you what should happen. That's all."

She starts to bawl then and throws her arms around me. I hold her while she trembles against my shoulder. Her tears soak through my shirt. How can I tell her about Sam now when she's already grieving this loss? I don't know what to do. It seems callous to tell her in this moment, but if I don't, she will find out when she looks at those pictures.

"Are you going to tell Sam?"

"No," she says sharply and pulls away from me.

"Why not?" I ask, my heart hammering against my ribs as I watch her face change.

"He's not a good husband, but you already know that, don't you?"

"Carrie . . ."

"Let me guess. You were about to tell me."

"I was."

"You've been here an hour. You had so many chances. I led you down several paths."

"I was afraid to hurt you."

"Don't you think it's too late for that?"

I nod, the tears falling faster than I can wipe them away. "I've made so many mistakes. But what I've done to you is the very worst. And I know you won't believe me, but I am so very sorry."

Something flashes in her eyes. "Lila, you don't get it, do you?"

I don't respond, waiting for her to continue.

"You can't wipe it all away with a sorry."

"I know that," I say.

"Nothing will undo what you've done."

"I know that too."

"You didn't ruin my marriage. The truth is, Sam has never been that great a husband. And I kept thinking I could change him. So I wasn't surprised by *his* behavior when I saw the photos of you kissing. I was shocked that *you* were involved. That *you* would betray me this way. You broke my heart. And it will take me a long time to put it back together again. But I will. It's you that will have to live with what you've done to me. And I guess that will have to be your penance."

CHAPTER THIRTY-THREE

FRIDAY
CAPTURED

Q snaps his head back and forth, his jaw tight. Looking at me. The camera. Then back at me again.

"Chase, or should I say Derrick?" I call out, my voice shaking slightly, remembering him and his brother, Quincy, as teenagers. "It took me a while, but I finally remembered." I stare up at the blinking light and think back to the two teenage boys who sat next to their mom at the trial every day. Whose eyes I could barely meet when their dad was sentenced to thirty years in prison.

"I'm so sorry for what happened to your dad. But I did what I thought was right!" I look from Q to the camera and back again, crying in earnest now, the tears falling faster than I can wipe them.

Q—Quincy, I know now—is walking back and forth in front of me, seemingly lost in thought. He keeps wiping at his forehead, which must be sweating under his mask.

"Q, how long have you two planned this?" I calculate back—Chase has worked for me for two years. I flash to his interview—the way he already seemed to anticipate my needs. At the time I chalked it up to being earnest. But now I realize he'd already been studying me— his agenda already set. "I had no clue who you were. What you were capable of. That much is clear."

I turn away toward the wall. The room is silent for several minutes, except for the sound of Q's pacing. I lie there, my cheek flush against the concrete floor, rewinding and then fast-forwarding my time with Chase. He's never shown an ounce of his festering rage, always seemingly on my side—looking out for my best interests. How had he done that—acted like nothing was wrong, all while planning his revenge? I've made a living determining what demons live inside people. And I was drawn to Chase because he seemed to have none of the internal complications that my clients and colleagues struggled with. It feels unfathomable that he could be responsible for what I've been through the past week. His dad's case was one of my biggest failures. There is a part of me that understands his anger. His need for revenge.

The door creaks open a few minutes later, and I hear Q's large feet loom, along with the smaller shuffle of someone else's feet.

Chase.

I pull myself up and am face-to-face with my friend, kidnapper, and torturer.

"Derrick," I say, his name rolling off my tongue awkwardly. To me, he is still Chase.

"Hello, Lila," Chase says, touching his chest, blocking Q from view. "I used to be Derrick, but you already know that. I'm so glad you finally figured everything out. I've been dying to chat with you about everything!" He squats down to face me. "We have so much to catch up on," he says and smiles wickedly. "All your dirty little secrets are out now, aren't they?" He moves slightly, and now I can see Q. "Go ahead and remove her cuffs and bindings, so we can have a proper conversation," Chase demands, and suddenly I can see him as the fourteen-year-old boy in that courtroom, looking stoic as he sat next to his mom. His features are more pronounced now, his nose larger, his eyes darker, but it's clearly him. How had I not seen the resemblance before?

Q's shoulders slump slightly, and he wrings his hands. His normal demeanor has all but vanished. "You sure, bro?" he asks, his tone much less confident than before. Deferential. Is he *scared* of his older brother?

"Yes, I'm sure. And take your mask off, you chickenshit!" Chase chides. "Don't worry, she'll never be able to tell anyone who we are." He shoots me a look, and I stop breathing for a moment.

Slowly, Q reaches up and pulls the black ski mask over his head, revealing sandy-blond hair, chiseled cheeks, and an angular nose, similar to his brother's. His eyes, separated from the holes in the mask, now appear soft. I cannot believe this is the same man who's held me captive. I can't believe he's the same boy who sobbed on his mom's shoulder in that courtroom.

Q stands there as if afraid to move until Chase tells him he can.

I search Chase's face for the guy who had once driven to *the freaking valley* to pick me up when I got a flat tire and didn't have my AAA card on me or my wallet—having forgotten it at the office. Ethan was out of town. It took a special person to drive through the crowded and miserable Sepulveda Pass after four o'clock when he didn't have to. For his boss. When had that been? Eighteen months ago, maybe? Had things already been in motion back then?

"Why are you still standing there? Cut her loose," Chase says in a voice I have never heard. I do a double take. How can he be the same man who helped me pick out my mom's birthday present?

Q obediently cuts the bonds away from my ankles and unlocks the cuffs around my wrists, refusing to make eye contact with me. I watch him, his movements seeming so much less frightening now that I can see his face.

"Hand me the knife," Chase commands, and Q gives it to him.

Besides the few and far between trips to the disgusting bathroom down the hall, it's the first time I've been completely free since I was kidnapped, and as the blood begins circulating in my limbs again, I glance at the door.

"Don't think about it, Lila. I've got the knife right here." He turns to Q. "You can go now. Wait outside," he says dismissively.

"But I don't think—" Q looks over at me, and I plead with my eyes. *Please help me.* But he looks away quickly.

"We've already discussed this, little brother. *I* do the thinking," Chase says, his voice hard. "You told me you could handle this."

"I can."

"Then. Wait. Out. Side."

I will Q to look over at me. But he doesn't. I shiver. Is this it? The moment when I die? When the universe balances by ridding itself of me?

Q gives his brother a long look before turning to leave. "Fine," he says and storms off.

Chase starts to say something but stops and shakes his head. Once the door is closed, he picks an imaginary piece of lint off his perfectly pressed pale-blue shirt. "He's always been the soft one, ever since we were kids." He sighs. "Never wanting to make the tough choices."

"What's the tough choice here? Killing me?" I say this last part with much more bravado than I feel. Inside, I'm stung with fear.

"Oh. That's not a tough choice at all." Chase smiles, and I can't believe I never saw the real him. That I was fooled by his act. That I let him infiltrate my life so intensely. That I made it so easy for him to destroy me. Considering the things I've done, I probably deserve his disloyalty. But it still hurts to know none of it had been real.

We sit in silence for a moment. I wonder if I can muster the strength to grab the knife. To knock him down. To break free.

"I'm sorry for what happened to your dad. I always have been."

"You never responded to my mom's letters!"

"I know I didn't. I should have. I wasn't sure what to say. She was blaming me."

"She had a right to do that."

"I did my best on your father's case. I thought we were going to win."

Chase laughs. "You fucked up his case, Lila. He begged you to let him take the stand—to tell his side of the story. And you thought you knew better. One year out of law school. Never tried a case in court. But you were willing to roll the dice with his life." He leans in close. "Even back then you were so fucking arrogant. And nothing has changed."

I let his words sink in. He's saying everything I berated myself for after his dad, Ed, was sent to prison. And then after I found out he'd been killed. I lived with guilt about that one for a very long time. Every time his wife sent me a letter blaming me, I relived it. But how am I supposed to convince Chase of that now? He'd never believe me.

"Derrick, I'm sorry."

He shakes his head hard. "Don't call me that. I'm not Derrick anymore. And I don't believe for a second that *you* feel bad. You just don't want me to kill you."

That's true. I don't. But how can I make him understand I only wanted the best for him and his family?

"I've been good to you," I plead. "Doesn't that mean anything?"

"You've been good to me because I was helping you. Was on your side. Helping do your dirty work. But were you good to Janelle? Ethan? Carrie?"

When I hear all their names strung together like that, I feel ashamed and regretful and so remorseful. "How did you know about Janelle?"

"You told me."

"I did? When?" I shuffle through my memories, trying to grasp that one.

"About a year ago. You'd lost that drug possession case. You were wasted."

"The single mom who got fifteen years," I interject, remembering the devastation I felt when the court handed her sentence down. She'd been drug running for her boyfriend, who only got two years. I'm still in the appeal process and actually started to make some headway recently. "But I don't remember us having that conversation."

"I plied you with margaritas. And then I asked you what the worst thing was you'd ever done."

I shake my head. I remember drinking the first two margaritas. Then flash forward to throwing up in the early hours of the next morning. "Did you drug me?"

Chase smiles. "Maybe."

My head begins to spin, and I try to hold on to my senses. Get my bearings back. "That case is a perfect example of how you can do all the right things and still not get the verdict you're looking for. Juries are human and completely unpredictable."

"That's what I was so desperate to find out when I came to work for you. Were you an amazing person who made one mistake? But you weren't. You were exactly the selfish bitch I thought you'd be."

I cringe. What if I had been different? If he'd taken the job and discovered I was a good person who had simply screwed up on a case? But instead, I proved his point—over and over again. I think about what to say. I'm not a horrible human being, and I am good at my job. "You're right. I've made mistakes in my personal life. I am not a good wife. Or a great friend, for that matter. But I'm an excellent attorney. And you need to know I thought I was doing right by your dad. I thought not taking the stand was the best chance we had for acquittal."

"He didn't deserve what happened to him! He never should have been in that prison with those lunatics! He never had a chance!" Chase shouts. "But this?" He holds his arms up. "This you deserve."

I think back to when I received the news Ed had been stabbed seven times with a shiv in the yard. How I went to the bathroom and threw up, heartbroken over whatever role I had played in putting him in harm's way. Because ironically, I believed in my gut Ed was innocent. That what happened in his neighbor's house that night had all been a terrible accident. "Maybe I do," I say carefully. "But you aren't this person. Don't do this. There is still time to make the right choice. Don't condemn yourself to a lifetime of regret. Trust me."

"Oh, honey, that's what you don't get. I'm not going to regret this at all."

I bite my tongue. I can't take his bait. He wants me to rage. He wants a fight. But I can't give him that. He has conned me for years. Taken advantage of the secrets I've told him. Chosen to exploit my life in his sick and twisted way. He seeks revenge. And to punish him, I won't give him the battle he wants. We sit in silence for a while, both of us waiting for the other to speak.

"I lost my dad when I was young too," I finally say. "Drunk driver. A careless teen—you know that."

"It's not the same."

"Isn't it, though? One bad choice led to tragedy. At least in the case with your dad, I thought I was doing the right thing. I was trying to help."

"You thought he was guilty."

"I didn't. I swear. But I didn't think him being cross-examined about how angry he was that his wife—your mom—was having an affair was going to help him. If anything, it would have made him *look* guilty."

He flinches slightly when I reference his mother. When I'd hired him, he'd told me he was an only child and that his parents lived in Boston. Retired schoolteachers. Asked for vacation days to go visit them once or twice a year.

"They needed to hear his side of the story!" Chase yells, the knife shaking in his hand. "You've said you don't put the ones you think are guilty on the stand!"

The memory slams into me hard, and I shake my head. "That was a bad joke. I shouldn't have said that."

"It's why you didn't put Jeremiah on."

I pause. He's right. I thought Jeremiah was guilty, so I didn't let him testify. But it's not the reason I always kept clients off the stand. As I watch Chase now, his face pale, his pupils dilated, I realize he doesn't want my reasoning. He wants his dad back. And I can't give him that. But I can relate to that feeling.

"You're right about Jeremiah. And in hindsight, maybe I should have let your dad testify. Because now we'll never know if things could have been different. I'm sorry you grew up without a father, Chase. I truly am."

His eyes flash. "Does it really matter at this point?" He laughs as he plays with the knife, twisting it by the handle. "At first I was going to kill you. Run you over with a car, something quick and easy. But then I realized that would do nothing—you would *learn* nothing. Because it's not only me and my brother you hurt. You breeze through life and leave all these people in your wake—me, Ethan, Janelle, Carrie, and God knows who else."

Again, hearing all their names one after the other hits me hard. My mistakes with all of them bringing me to where I am right now. I watch Chase roll his shoulders back and crack his neck. Just like his brother did. He's planned this for so long. I try to catch my breath. So many fake smiles, insincere hugs, years of counterfeit conversation. He bided his time so he could make me pay in the very worst way—not only with my life, but with life as I know it. The very worst part?

I deserved it.

"You don't have to do this," I say, my voice bordering on a whimper. "You've already taken everything away—Ethan, Carrie, my reputation. Why not force me to live with that?"

"It's not enough," he says, gripping the knife tightly.

I tense. "This may not mean anything to you at this point, but I wish I could change things. I don't want to be the person I was. Whether or not you believe it, I'm ready to take responsibility. To be the person I should have been."

In an ironic twist of events, by kidnapping me and holding me hostage, my delusional and homicidal assistant actually forced me to see my missteps. To *want* to change.

Chase looks at me hard. "I wish I could believe that. But there've been too many lies. Too many times you could have made the right choice and didn't. I've been waiting for two years for you to change. For you to do the right thing. And *now* you're ready, because I took you and put you in this concrete box and destroyed everything you love, the same way you did to me."

"No, that's not it. It's because you forced me to look at myself in a way I wouldn't. In a way I couldn't." I realize I mean it with every fiber inside me. And not just because he's going to kill me.

"Stop! You aren't going to lawyer your way out of this." His mouth forms a hard line as he speaks. The anger he holds for me changes the shape of his face, making it seem more sharp and angular.

"It's not too late, Chase. For any of us. We can all make it out of this intact," I say, my voice soft. Desperate.

He looks at me. "God, for someone so smart, you can be so dense sometimes! Only one of us is making it out of here alive," he says and raises the knife to my neck.

CHAPTER THIRTY-FOUR

FRIDAY
FREE

"Ethan?" I call out as I push through the front door of our house, still reeling from my conversation with Carrie. From the knowledge that she was done with me. That there was no forgiveness, no grace to be had. I didn't blame her and wasn't surprised. But still, the finality of it stung like salt in a cut. I smell the aroma of the Colombian roast coffee he loves. The beans I had shipped in for his birthday last month. When I walk into the kitchen, seeing him in his favorite faded gray T-shirt and jeans, his feet bare, his hair still messy from sleeping, nearly breaks me in half. If someone didn't know better, it would look like any other morning, Ethan making coffee and me getting ready to run out the door to a preliminary hearing. But Ethan hasn't occupied our bed in two nights and has only agreed to meet me after I'd begged him over text and voice mail. And now I think he may have only come to get a cup of that coffee.

He smiles sheepishly. "It's just not the same at the place down the street."

"For what I paid to have it shipped here, it shouldn't be," I quip, and I can see him hold back his laughter. Not ready to laugh at my jokes yet.

We stand there. The only sound the percolation of the Ninja coffeemaker I bought several years ago to celebrate selling his first book. Back when I was supportive of my husband's career, when I believed in him and his ability to finish manuscripts. After he told me he had a book idea, rented an office space, and started actively writing, I'm still not sure I gave him the credit he deserved. I was still holding him accountable for all the time he'd spent lost and flailing. But maybe if I'd worked harder to help him see his way out of the fog. If I'd tried to understand his writer's block. If I hadn't written it off as laziness. Maybe he would have regained his confidence sooner. I'm taking in every line of Ethan's face, the extra stubble hugging his chin, looking for signs he misses me. "Where have you been sleeping?"

"Does it matter?" He frowns.

"I guess not. But you look tired." I hesitate, trying to find the words to tell him that I want to make things right again, that I need to acknowledge my part in breaking us down, to atone for my sins. To tell him how much I miss him. "Come home," I blurt, instantly regretting the request as soon as it leaves my mouth. Before I can rectify it, Ethan starts talking.

"I'm tired because I can't sleep, not because of where I'm sleeping," he says. "Or have you forgotten that you blew up our lives earlier this week? Oh, wait. Maybe you'd like *me* to forget you did that. That's why you wanted to meet, right? To put me in the jury box? Convince me what you did wasn't wrong?"

I take a breath before speaking. How do you explain to someone that you hurt, someone whose trust you took and stomped on, that you'll never do it again? How do you *show* someone that you can change if you've been the same way for as long as he's known you? I don't know how to make Ethan truly understand how profound my metamorphosis will be. All I know is that something inside me has shifted—that I will never be that person again. "Ethan," I start as he pours the rich coffee into his favorite mug, one that I brought back from New York City last year with the city's skyline painted on it. "There are no words that can make what I did go away."

"Finally, we agree on something," he says as he adds cream into his mug and stirs it slowly, taking me in. "This isn't a courtroom. You can't litigate your way around what you did."

I realize suddenly that I may never get him back. I want so desperately to be different. I already *feel* so changed in so many ways, but it may be too late. I might have to accept that part of my path is to lose my husband. But as I look at him now, I want to fight. For him. For us. For me. So I tell him the thing that I know will make him happy.

"I quit my job."

He stops stirring. "What?"

"I quit. I'm done."

"Done with them or done being a lawyer?"

I shrug. "I'm not sure. I guess I'll figure that out."

"Why? Because of me? Sam?"

I tilt my head. "Not really. I mean, yes, I guess it's all related," I backtrack when his eyes widen. "I've done a lot of terrible things. And it feels like the only way to start over is to get rid of everything that made me that person. And yes, of course I want you to be a part of my new life. In fact, I would sacrifice almost anything for that to happen. But if I'm being totally honest—"

"Do you know how to do that?" Ethan interjects, and I look at my feet.

"That's a fair thing to say," I acquiesce. Because he has a point—the truth and I have a very complicated past. "But what I'm trying to say is that leaving my job is really to save myself."

Ethan nods. "From what?"

"I think from my own fate," I say instinctively, and goosebumps travel up my arm. I had been trying to put my finger on the feeling I'd been carrying around with me all week—the way certain things felt familiar when they shouldn't, the way my choices had begun to feel as if their consequences were life or death—as if my *fate* depended on them.

"Your fate?" Ethan repeats. "That's a little deep for you, isn't it?"

I reach over and grab his hand, and he flinches slightly. "I can't explain what has happened this week. To you. To me. To us. But I am profoundly changed. And if you give me one more chance, I'll spend the rest of my life proving that to you." I swallow back the knot in my throat. "Please?" The look he gives me when I beg him is a cross between disappointment and pity. And I'm hit with a reality I hadn't seen before. Or maybe one I hadn't wanted to see. I need to ask forgiveness and know that I might not get it. That he may not think I deserve it. I have to let Ethan go and be okay if he doesn't come back.

Ethan holds my gaze for several seconds, which feel like minutes. "You really believe you can change, don't you?"

"I do," I say. "But you don't have to stick around to see it. As much as I love you and want to work this out, I understand if you need to move on with your life without me." My chest burns after I say it, the idea that I've lost him forever sending waves of sadness through me.

We sit in silence for a long while, my heart breaking over and over again.

"Let me think about it," Ethan says, and I can't tell what he's thinking. I can only hope he does what's best for *him*. What he believes is right. I pray that path leads him back to me, but I know I'll have to be okay if it doesn't.

～

I'm stuck in midday traffic on the 101 Freeway on my way to the preliminary hearing when my mom calls. I have one more errand to run, one more bomb to detonate on whatever remains of my old life before I can return home to my new one, hopefully with Ethan.

"Hey, Mom," I say. "What's up?"

"How are you?" she asks, then continues before I can answer. "I've been worried sick about you since we spoke last. You have too much stress, Lila. Your job, Ethan. Whoever attacked you. You need to take a break."

"That sounds really good," I say.

She's silent for a moment. That's not how I usually respond to her demands.

"You want to go somewhere, Mom? Take a spa weekend out in Palm Springs? I have at least ten gift certificates I need to use at the Kimpton out there."

"Lila? Are you all right?"

"I'm finally agreeing with you, and you are questioning my sanity?" I laugh. "I'm going to have a little more free time on my hands. And I'd like to spend it with you."

"What's going on?"

I glance at the clock. "I don't have time to explain in detail now. I'm on my way somewhere very important. Can we meet for dinner? I'll tell you everything then."

"Okay, honey. But you are sure everything's okay?"

"It is. For the first time in a long time. I'm finally going to be a daughter you can be proud of."

I hear her sigh. "There has never been one moment of your life I haven't been proud of you. You've always been your own person, and I admire that. No one tells you what to do. You've always put too much pressure on yourself. Thinking you have to take care of me." She pauses. "Not that I don't appreciate it. I just worry—"

I choke up slightly. "I wanted to take care of you, Mom. I never wanted you to struggle again. You deserve to be happy."

"But so do you. And I don't want you to trade your happiness for mine. I'm perfectly fine. I have everything I could ever want."

"Mom, I haven't been the best human. In fact, I might have been a terrible person." This may sound strange, but it feels really good to say it out loud to someone I love.

"Stop. No one is all good or all bad. And life isn't black and white. You of all people should understand that. We do our best."

"But what if I haven't? Done my best?" I whisper.

"Then go fix it," she says simply. "That's all we can do when we make mistakes. Try to make them right."

"What if it's taken me a *really* long time to do that?"

"Still counts!" she exclaims, and we both laugh.

"I love you, Mom," I say. "Thank you."

"For what?"

"For being you."

"I love you too, Lila. I'll see you later."

We hang up as traffic lets up, opening a path that I'm now sure that I'm meant to take. I hope my mom is right, that it's never too late to right your wrongs.

CHAPTER THIRTY-FIVE

FRIDAY
CAPTURED

I try to stop the shaking, but I can't. My entire body wants to collapse under the waves of fear rolling through me. There's something about Chase holding the knife that scares the hell out of me. More than Q. Because Chase has much more conviction. His desire for my destruction literally oozes out of him.

"You're trembling," Chase says, a wry smile forming. "I thought nothing scared you, Lila Bennett."

"What makes you think that?"

"*You*. You make me think that. The way you prance into court like you own the place. How you defend murderers the same way you would Mother Teresa. I've been watching, fascinated. Studied you, really."

"You did have a front-row seat," I say. "That's why you of all people should know we have to make hard choices every day."

"Was fucking your best friend's husband complicated?" Chase whispers as he leans in with the knife. "Please explain to me that difficult choice."

"I broke up with Sam that night. Before you took me."

"Liar."

"It's true! If you'd only given me a few more days, you would have seen that I was ready to make some major changes in my life."

Chase rolls his eyes. "Very convenient, Lila. You had plenty of time to change."

He's right, of course. But how could I explain the visceral change that occurred that night? That I knew it was a turning point? I swallow as I back up until I feel the concrete.

"Sit down. And, Lila? Don't try anything stupid. Let's not make this harder than it has to be."

I slide to the floor with a small thud.

"You poor thing, been wearing that for . . ." He stops before he tells me how long I've been in here. He likes that I don't know. "You are for sure a 'fashion don't' at this point. A great pair of shoes couldn't help this ensemble."

"Why now?" I ask him.

"The Jeremiah case. I knew Stephanie's rage would make her the perfect scapegoat for your disappearance. And if not her, I figured Ethan would make a close second. Or sweet Carrie. She could have raged after she found out about the affair. But I also like the fact this all coincides with the ten-year anniversary of my dad's case. Poetic, don't you think?"

"Jesus, Chase. This seems . . ." I search for the words as I stare at his perfectly arched eyebrows, his crooked smile. I've always prided myself on knowing people, my gut all I needed to separate the good from the bad. But I never suspected Chase was anything but my friend. "It seems pretty insane." I think about the few times we've grabbed a drink after a hard-earned victory. One of the things I liked best about Chase had been his loyalty to me. How wrong I was. My mind quickly shuffles through all the stories he had shared about his past—college roommates, bad breakups. Was any of it true?

"Does it sound insane?" He shrugs. "Sometimes things might appear crazy to others, but they aren't. Our lives were destroyed by my dad's death. My mom blamed herself, so she packed us all up, and we hid in this Podunk town in Michigan for years while she drank herself to death."

I hang my head. "I didn't know she had passed. I'm sorry." For a moment, I forget that Chase has kidnapped me. That he wants to kill me. All I feel is sadness for my part in a ruined life. For a son who prematurely lost his father and then his mother.

"She couldn't forgive herself. If she hadn't had the affair, none of this would have happened."

"And you? Did you forgive her?" I ask softly.

Chase laughs. "What do you think?"

"What about your brother?" I nod toward the door. "Does he feel the same way?"

"Doesn't matter what Quincy thinks."

"He seems less invested than you," I challenge.

"Oh, don't you worry about him. He and I learned a long time ago that we have to stick together. I practically raised him after my father was killed and my mom became a zombie. He does what I tell him to do. He can be soft." He glances at my arm. "Although he did some good work here. With you."

I ignore this, my eye flitting to the knife. "What's your end game here? You really think you'll get away with this?"

"By the time we're finished, no one will ever know any of us were here. That's one thing I've learned from working with you these past two years. All the stupid mistakes criminals make. Trust me, there'll be no trace of you, me, or my brother. No body to find. No fingerprints to uncover. No DNA to run. It will be like none of us ever existed in this space."

I feel something inside me snap, and I'm on my feet, lunging toward him. I knock him to the ground, and the knife flies out of his hand. I don't know where the energy comes from, but I channel every ounce of it toward him, adrenaline firing through my blood. I pin him to the ground with my knees and grab the knife. I stand over him and start to back away.

His eyes are wide, and he looks stunned, as if he never imagined this possibility—that *I* would overpower *him*. "Lila, what the hell do you think you are doing? You know you won't hurt me."

He starts to move.

"Stay down," I say in a voice that doesn't sound like mine.

I back away from him slowly, my hand so wet from sweat, I'm afraid I'll drop the knife. I inch backward toward the door.

"Quincy!" he screams.

"Shut up. Shut up."

"Or what?" he challenges.

"I'll use this if I have to," I say, but when I look at him, he's still Chase. The one who picked out my shoes, who brought me my favorite coffee. Who worked so tirelessly. It's hard to believe none of that was real, that he put on an act for years. He's so broken. The loss of his father changing him into this. I think of how my own loss changed who I was. Made me hard. There is a part of me that understands his anger. Empathizes with it intensely. Can I actually hurt him?

"Q!"

Suddenly he's upright and coming toward me.

Adrenaline answers my query, and I kick him hard in the groin. He stumbles backward, losing his balance and falling over. I stare for a moment as he writhes in pain.

This is your chance, Lila. Go!

I put my hand on the door and pull it open, not sure what I'm going to do when I see Q. He has a gun. He's also stronger. I hurt his brother. I'll have to just try—try anything to get away, because this is my only shot. My heart is pounding as I pull on the door hard and start running as fast as I can. I have no idea where I'm going. And then

I see a figure at the end of the hall. I know it's Q, but I keep going. If he's going to stop me, he'll have to do it while I'm running at full speed with a knife.

"Lila, come back here. Quincy, where the fuck are you? Stop her!" Chase's voice echoes through the hall. I can hear him behind me. His shoes banging against the concrete. "Q!"

I'm breathing hard; when I try to inhale, I gasp. The air is there somewhere, but I can't get to it. My lungs are burning, and then Q comes into focus. I keep running. His masked face comes into view. His large looming body. But I keep racing. Chase is behind me, screaming my name, then Quincy's name. And then I'm right next to Q; our eyes meet.

And he doesn't try to stop me. Doesn't move a muscle. He lets me pass.

I keep running as hard as I can. I push through a door and see a stairwell. I fly down it. My feet getting cut on God knows what. I run down four flights of stairs, through another door, down a hallway, and find a door that looks like it leads outside. A hint of sunlight streaming through a boarded window. I pull on it. It's locked. I turn down another hall, find another door. It's locked too. I turn and run back the way I came and see a door I missed. I can still hear Chase screaming. Feet in the stairwell. I put my hand on the knob and turn it. It opens. The sun is sharp against my eyes, and I wince slightly but keep running, my lungs depleted. I crane my neck back at the building I was in. It's blue with boarded windows. I see a street sign. I'm at the corner of Town and Fourth. I run down Fourth.

I get my bearings as I'm thrusting my legs forward, my feet now cut and bleeding as they hit the sidewalk. I'm on Skid Row. I look up and can see the skyscrapers that define downtown Los Angeles. I was so close to everyone who was looking for me. Who could help me. Which I'm sure was Chase's plan—his final fuck-you. Holding me captive less than a mile from police headquarters.

I haul my body past camping tents that homeless people are living in. So many tents of every color. Some shiny and erect, many sad and sloping. Many connected as if they'd incorporated their own little villages. Shopping carts blocking the doorways as protection. People are staring at me, a madwoman running with a knife, but they remain neutral, neither moving in my direction or away from me. They've seen it all down here. My skirt is barely on, hanging low on my hips. I scream for help, but no sound will come out of my mouth, my throat raw and dry. Then I see a building. Something written on the side. I race toward it, praying. The words come into focus. The Los Angeles Mission. I dare to look over my shoulder for a moment, and Q and Chase aren't following me. I push through the glass doors of the mission. I made it. I'm free. A man walks up to me. I drop the knife and hold my hands up in surrender.

"My name is Lila Bennett, and I've escaped my kidnappers. Please help me."

CHAPTER THIRTY-SIX

FREE

The parking karma gods clearly aren't having an issue with me, and I find an amazing space on Temple Street. I pay the meter and hurry down to Spring. I catch sight of the *Los Angeles Times* building, hoping that Lynn and her attorney followed through on our plan and confronted Greenwood with the evidence I provided them. That the threat of exposure will make him back off. That when I arrive at the courthouse, Greenwood will sheepishly tell me he's withdrawing his suit against his wife. That she can have the kids, the house, the money to which she's entitled. He'll pretend it's because he's decided to be reasonable, and I'll nod and smile in agreement, neither of us acknowledging the things we did to get to this point. I cross my fingers that this is where it will end, because if the chief of police discovers that notes have been leaked from something he tried to cover up, he will go on the warpath to find out who was behind it. I've already planned to take the heat and say that I hired someone to find the notes for me any way possible—even if that meant breaking in and stealing them. Sully did the right thing by handing them over, and there is no way I'd expose him.

I push myself into a half run, half walk, as fast as my pencil skirt will let me move, and adjust my bag on my shoulder. The preliminary hearing is less than fifteen minutes from beginning. And I know this particular judge; she won't start a second after eleven. I cannot be late. I had hoped to get here sooner but am relieved at what I accomplished this morning. There is only one item on my mental to-do list left to check off, and then my new life can begin. I'm already picturing myself at dinner with my mom tonight, her raising her glass of cabernet and toasting me for finally quitting, us making plans to travel somewhere relaxing together. Then returning home and calling Ethan to tell him I went through with it. Praying he offers to come over. But at the very least that he confirms it makes him happy to hear.

"Lila!" I hear my name and squint to see where the male voice is coming from. Traffic is heavy on Spring, and a bus releases its exhaust as the person says my name again. I keep moving forward, and this time when I hear "Lila," there's no question whose voice it is: Greenwood's. He's in a shadowed area in front of the courthouse, but his looming silhouette is still obvious. His arms are flailing in the air as he walks toward me and away from the building. Behind him is Lynn Greenwood and her attorney, Mark. So there's my answer. He knows. And judging by his demeanor, their meeting hadn't gone as I hoped it might.

"Where have you been?" he screams, his face a deep shade of red.

"I'm here now," I say, out of breath. I glance at my watch. It's ten to eleven.

"You're late!" he bellows.

"What is it that couldn't wait until I got inside?" I glance behind him at Lynn and her lawyer, standing shoulder to shoulder, Mark barely an inch taller than Lynn. Both of them are at least a head shorter than Greenwood, whose anger makes him seem taller than his six-foot-five frame. Mark nods at me quickly, confirming that they told him what we'd talked about.

"They're blackmailing me!"

"With what?" I ask, widening my eyes for effect as two lawyers sail past us into a waiting car. I move closer to Greenwood so we're not overheard.

"They're accusing me of crazy things. I bet they concocted this scheme because they're sleeping together!" Spittle comes out of his mouth as he rants, and I step back quickly. "Said they'll go to the *Times* with what they are saying I've done," he huffs.

"Is what they said true?" I ask, trying to keep my face impassive, glancing at Lynn, who looks pale.

"What the hell does that matter?" Greenwood hisses.

"I'm trying to assess what's going on here." I straighten my back slightly and suck down all the words I want to call him.

He turns swiftly on his heel and points at his wife. "All you need to know is that she's a lying bitch!"

"I am not," she says, tugging on the bottom of her black jacket, then looking up at him, her eyes full of tears. "You know what the truth is and that we can prove it. So drop your suit against me and let me have the boys and the money I'm entitled to, and then you can go on with your sad little life." Her bottom lip quivers slightly. She's probably never stood up to him before.

I move around to the other side of Greenwood, and now I'm positioned in between him and his wife. His face reddens more. "What did you say to me?" he yells at her. "*You* do not talk to *me* like that."

"I forgot that's your area," Lynn mutters, her voice trembling. Then, after a beat, she sucks in a deep breath, brushing at her eyes to stop the tears. "What's next, are you going to hit me? Because it wouldn't be the first time. Do we want to talk about that too?"

Her attorney puts his hand on her arm and whispers something in her ear.

"What are you doing?" Greenwood moves in Mark's direction, and Mark's face loses some of its color. "Giving her more bullshit advice?"

He clears his throat. "Mr. Greenwood, court is set to begin. We need to know what you plan to do. We cannot be late. Judge Mattheson will not hold our time. She is a stickler for punctuality." He looks at me, and I check my watch again. We have four minutes.

"I'm not going in there," Greenwood says and puffs out his chest.

"If you and your lawyer don't show up, the judge will rule in our favor."

"You're not going in there either," Greenwood barks. "We are going to settle this right here, right now. I'd already decided there would be no woman in a robe telling me how my life turns out."

Mark gives him a quizzical look, then shakes his head. "Come on, Lynn, let's go."

As if it's happening in slow motion, I see Greenwood reach inside his suit coat pocket, and the sun glints off the handle of a pistol. I scream Lynn's name, and she turns, her eyes wide in recognition of what's about to happen. I move toward Greenwood slowly. "Stop. You don't have to do this," I yell, but he only laughs.

"Get out of the way, Bennett. This isn't about you."

"Don't do this!" I scream again. But he holds the gun out anyway and moves his finger closer to the trigger. I pounce, pushing Lynn out of the way as I hear the crack of the revolver firing, and I instantly experience a sense of déjà vu. But from where? I've never been near a gun firing in my life. I fall backward as the bullet pierces me, the pain in my chest excruciating. I hit the ground with a thud, the concerned faces above me fading in and out. Lynn and her attorney hover over me, pleading with me to hang on. They tell me over and over that it's going to be okay, almost like a mantra. But I already know it's not going to be—they're only trying to make themselves feel better. My lips quiver, but I can't speak—the life I knew is draining out quickly.

I'm so tired.

Lynn is begging me to keep my eyes open, but I can't. It's too hard. I summon an image of Ethan. Will he forgive me in death? I pray he does. My earlier conversation with my mom flashes through my head—I'm so thankful that my last words were *I love you*. As I draw a final breath, I think of Chase and my very first case—Ed, the man who was convicted of the murder of the man his wife was sleeping with. I see Chase's eyes, and then I see a boy named Derrick sitting stoically in court next to his tearful brother, Quincy, and his sobbing mother, and I feel the dots connect, and I finally understand that Chase had been the one intent on destroying me—my impending death bringing me an intense clarity I had lacked in life.

Then it all fades to black.

CHAPTER THIRTY-SEVEN

FRIDAY
CAPTURED

I barely feel the weight of the heavy blanket the tall, barrel-chested man places gently on my shaking shoulders. I think he said his name is Bill as he led me away from the prying eyes of those watching me from the rec room of the Los Angeles Mission into a back office, but I'm not sure. "The police are on their way," he says now, his eyes soft as he slides his wire-framed glasses up his nose. He must see the fear still etched on my face from what I've been through, because he adds, "Don't worry, we've locked the doors until they arrive. You're safe now. They've been scouring the city for you all week. I almost couldn't believe my eyes when you came through the door. I recognize you from the news."

His declaration of my safety slows the adrenaline that's been shooting through my veins since it gave me the power to hit Chase and run from captivity. I can now feel the warm throbbing of my bloody feet, the aching in my back and legs, my body's desire to curl up and sleep as that veil of adrenaline lifts and reality sets in. I glance at a tattered copy of the *LA Times* sitting on the desk. It's Friday. I've been missing for five days. Five days that have felt like a year.

I was supposed to die. But I lived. I'm free.

Q *let* me go. There's no other explanation. He could have stopped me. Cut me. Shot me. But he stood frozen, his eyes as green as I've ever seen them. I'm sure in the coming months the many theories as to why he let me run past him will be explored—that he finally realized he wasn't capable of taking another life, or maybe he was tired of doing Chase's bidding. I'd like to think he came to the conclusion that it wasn't another person's job to punish us for our mistakes. We have to do that for ourselves. I choose to believe *that* theory—that there was a silent understanding between us as I flew past him in the hallway.

Although I escaped and am sitting here on a stiff wooden chair in the mission's tiny office, the warm Diet Coke Bill placed in front of me sitting untouched, there is a hard ache in my chest. Because, although I survived my concrete prison, the person who lived inside me, the Lila who was capable of driving Chase to devise an elaborate revenge plan to torture me and ultimately kill me, is gone. And I'm feeling her loss. Because she drove who I was my entire life. And had it not been for Chase, would she still be here? Did it take something that cruel, that harsh, that unthinkable to drive her out of me? I won't say that I'm happy to have gone through it. God, no! Because that would be crazy, wouldn't it? But I'm not unhappy either. Maybe we leave it right there.

Then I notice a headline on the front page of the *LA Times*. **Man's alleged attempted murder of his wife thwarted by his lawyer at courthouse.** My heart beats faster as I scan the article. Steve Greenwood tried to kill his wife. His lawyer saw that he had a gun and was starting to point it at his wife, and she knocked it out of his hand. The gun went flying, and security was able to detain Greenwood as he attempted to grab the pistol that had landed several feet away. I think back to the night I'd been taken—I'd met with Greenwood just prior. He'd swaggered into my office like he couldn't lose. I wonder what had happened to take him from the man I met to someone who would try to murder his wife. Would things have turned out differently if I hadn't gone with Sam that night? If I'd gone home to curl up on the couch with Ethan? If I'd been free and able to represent Steve, would he have made different decisions? The thought brings hard, wet tears flying off my cheeks and onto the newspaper, blurring the print until I can't make out the words any longer.

Maybe all we are is the sum of our choices, each one leading us down a different path, each with its own unique outcome. The notion that each decision holds that much power is overwhelming, and I squeeze my eyes shut to shake the thought away.

The sirens are growing louder. Coming closer. The police will want my story. They will interrogate me about the ins and the outs of my captivity. They will take their notes and write up their reports and do their best to bring Chase and Q to justice. They may pity me for what I endured. But what they'll never comprehend is that the experience has made me shed the worst part of myself, like a snake outgrowing its skin. I will never be that person again.

I may have lived. But that Lila Bennett, she is dead. Two parts of me, now one.

Today is the first day of the rest of *this* life. And *this* Lila plans to listen to the good voice inside her, the one who reminds her to be the best version of herself. That she is her father's daughter, but she's not her father. I know that sometimes the bad voice will creep in, because I'm still human after all, but when she does, I will tell her I'm not interested. Now that I understand every decision counts, I intend to make better ones.

ACKNOWLEDGMENTS

The process of writing books is different for everyone, we're sure. In our case, we've found it can be like a pendulum. Swing too far one way, and it can break you. But sway the other direction, and it can also put you back together. As we wrote in the acknowledgments for *Girls' Night Out*, that book fractured us. As coauthors. As friends. But Lila Bennett? She mended us. She brought us back from what we thought was our last collaboration and breathed new life into our partnership. She reminded us of our love for the written word. So, thank you, Lila. You reminded us why we are stronger together. Why the ups *and the downs* are necessary. You very well may have saved us from ourselves.

And now on to the real-life people we can't live without. We'll start with all our wonderful supporters at Lake Union: Danielle Marshall, for always believing in us; Dennelle Catlett, for your amazing multitasking wonderfulness; Alicia Clancy, for your wonderful editorial insight; and Gabe Dumpit, for everything in between. We tell each other often how lucky we are to be a part of the Amazon Publishing family, and that's because of each and every one of you.

And of course, Tiffany Yates Martin. As we type this, we await your editing notes on this novel. We know they will be smart, laser-focused, and fierce as hell—just like you. (And while we have you, should we have put that em dash there?)

And we wouldn't be anywhere without Elisabeth Weed and the Book Group. Thank you for all you do to further our career and, more importantly, for texting in emoji-speak occasionally. You get us—you *really, really* get us. Hallie, we appreciate you putting up with us!

Kathleen Carter. Have we mentioned what a joy it is to work with you? (Actually, we're pretty sure we have, several times, after too many martinis on the *GNO* book tour!) But seriously, thank you for your unwavering professionalism and integrity as our publicist—two qualities we consider to be invaluable.

Ellen Goldsmith-Vein with the Gotham Group—thank you for taking us on! And for liking our Instagram posts!

To all the book bloggers and bookstagrammers who work tirelessly to promote novels, "thank you" doesn't even begin to cover it. You are each a force of nature with a mission: to encourage people to read, something so desperately needed in our world. Please know that we see and appreciate all your tireless work.

Andrea Katz! Thank you for your valued—and brutal—honesty. We love you.

To our author friends: thanks for all the hilarious group chats and invaluable advice. They are a lifesaver, and we feel honored to know all of you.

To our readers: it's really simple—we wouldn't be here without you. Thank you for every word you have read.

To Riley: we dedicated this book to you because of your wonderful idea of revisiting the *Sliding Doors* concept—a movie we *made* you watch! We were creatively depleted, and you stepped in and saved the day. We hate to break this to you, girl, but you are a writer! Embrace it!

To our families: we know we can drive you all a little nuts with all the texting, emailing, and talking we do with each other. Thank you for understanding why this needs to go on. (And not only because we have to discuss a marketing idea that can't wait or text-fight about a timeline for accomplishing something book related. Sometimes it's necessary to have an hour-long chat about how hot John Krasinski is in *Jack Ryan*.) So thank you for humoring us and all our craziness. We appreciate your sincere and unwavering love and support of what we do. On that note, Mike and Matt, have we told you we've narrowed down the exotic location for our next book?

ABOUT THE AUTHORS

Photo © 2017 Debbie Friedrich photography

Liz Fenton and Lisa Steinke have been best friends for over thirty years and survived high school and college together. They've coauthored five novels, including *Girls' Night Out* and the Amazon Charts bestseller *The Good Widow*. In their former lives, Fenton worked in the pharmaceutical industry, and Steinke was a talk show producer. They both reside with their families and several rescue dogs in San Diego, California. Find them at www.lizandlisa.com and on Instagram @lisaandliz.